D0173822

With her roots firmly planted in the South, #1 *New York Times* bestselling author **Sherryl Woods** has written many of her more than one hundred books in that distinctive setting, whether it's her home state of Virginia, her adopted state, Florida, or her much-adored South Carolina. Now she's added North Carolina's Outer Banks to her list of favorite spots. And she remains partial to small towns, wherever they may be.

Sherryl divides her time between her childhood summer home overlooking the Potomac River in Colonial Beach, Virginia, and her oceanfront home with its lighthouse view in Key Biscayne, Florida. "Wherever I am, if there's no water in sight, I get a little antsy," she says.

Sherryl loves to hear from readers. You can visit her on her website at sherrylwoods.com, link to her Facebook fan page from there or contact her directly at Sherryl703@gmail.com.

Patricia Davids has led a storied life, so it is no wonder she enjoys writing books. She has been in turn a Kansas farmer's daughter, a nurse, a pen pal to a lonely sailor, a navy wife, a mother, a neonatal transport nurse, a champion archer, a horse trainer, a grandmother times two, a widow, a world traveler and finally an award-winning, bestselling author. Pat now lives on the Kansas farm where she grew up. She loves to hear from readers. You can contact her through her website at patriciadavids.com or follow her on Facebook at Author Patricia Davids.

#1 *New York Times* **Bestselling Author**

SHERRYL WOODS

EDGE OF FOREVER

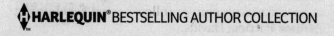

HHARLEQUIN® BESTSELLING AUTHOR COLLECTION

ISBN-13: 978-1-335-92934-1

Edge of Forever & Military Daddy

Copyright © 2019 by Harlequin Books S.A.

The publisher acknowledges the copyright holders of the individual works as follows:

Edge of Forever
Copyright © 1988 by Sherryl Woods

Military Daddy
Copyright © 2008 by Patricia MacDonald

Recycling programs for this product may not exist in your area.

This edition published by arrangement with Harlequin Books S.A.

For questions and comments about the quality of this book, please contact us at CustomerService@Harlequin.com.

www.Harlequin.com

Printed in U.S.A.

CONTENTS

EDGE OF FOREVER   7
Sherryl Woods

MILITARY DADDY   235
Patricia Davids

Also by Sherryl Woods

Chesapeake Shores

LILAC LANE
WILLOW BROOK ROAD
DOGWOOD HILL
THE CHRISTMAS BOUQUET
A SEASIDE CHRISTMAS
THE SUMMER GARDEN
AN O'BRIEN FAMILY CHRISTMAS
BEACH LANE
MOONLIGHT COVE
DRIFTWOOD COTTAGE
A CHESAPEAKE SHORES CHRISTMAS
HARBOR LIGHTS
FLOWERS ON MAIN
THE INN AT EAGLE POINT

The Sweet Magnolias

SWAN POINT
WHERE AZALEAS BLOOM
CATCHING FIREFLIES
MIDNIGHT PROMISES
HONEYSUCKLE SUMMER
SWEET TEA AT SUNRISE
HOME IN CAROLINA
WELCOME TO SERENITY
FEELS LIKE FAMILY
A SLICE OF HEAVEN
STEALING HOME

For a complete list of all titles by Sherryl Woods,
visit sherrylwoods.com.

EDGE OF FOREVER

Sherryl Woods

Chapter 1

The lilac bush seemed as if it was about to swallow up the front steps. Its untamed boughs drooping heavily with fragile, dew-laden lavender blossoms, it filled the cool Saturday morning air with a glorious, sweet scent.

Dana Brantley, a lethal-looking pair of hedge clippers in her gloved hands, regarded the overgrown branches with dismay. Somewhere behind that bush was a small screened-in porch. With some strategic pruning, she could sit on that porch and watch storm clouds play tag down the Potomac River. She could watch silvery streaks of dawn shimmer on the smooth water. Those possibilities had been among the primary attractions of the house when she'd first seen it a few weeks earlier. Goodness knows, the place hadn't had many other obvious assets.

True, that enticing screened-in porch sagged; its

weathered wooden planks had already been worn down by hundreds of sandy, bare feet. The yard was overgrown with weeds that reached as high as the few remaining upright boards in the picket fence. The cottage's dulled yellow paint was peeling, and the shutters tilted precariously. The air inside the four cluttered rooms was musty from years of disuse. The stove was an unreliable relic from another era, the refrigerator door hung loosely on one rusty hinge and the plumbing sputtered and groaned like an aging malcontent.

Despite all that, Dana had loved it on sight, with the same unreasoning affection that made one choose the sad-eyed runt in a litter of playful puppies. She especially liked the creaking wicker furniture with cushions covered in a fading flower print, the brass bed, even with its lumpy mattress, and the high-backed rocking chair on the front porch. After years of glass and chrome sterility, they were comfortable-looking in a delightfully shabby, well-used sort of way.

The real estate agent had apologized profusely for the condition of the place, had even suggested that they move on to other, more modern alternatives, but Dana had been too absorbed by the endless possibilities to heed the woman's urgings. Not only was the price right for her meager savings, but this was an abandoned house that could be slowly, lovingly restored and filled with light and sound. It would be a symbol of the life she was trying to put back together in a style far removed from that of her previous twenty-nine years. She knew it was a ridiculously sentimental attitude and she'd forced herself to act sensibly by making an absurdly low, very businesslike offer. To her amazement and deep-down delight it had been accepted with alacrity.

Dana turned now, cast a lingering look at the white-capped waves on the gray-green river and lifted the hedge clippers. She took a determined step toward the lilac bush, then made the mistake of inhaling deeply. She closed her eyes and sighed blissfully, then shrugged in resignation. She couldn't do it. She could not cut back one single branch. The pruning would simply have to wait until later, after the blooms faded.

In the meantime, she'd continue using the back door. At least she could get onto the porch from inside the house and her view wasn't entirely blocked. If she pulled the rocker to the far corner, she might be able to see a tiny sliver of the water and a glimpse of the Maryland shore on the opposite side. She'd probably catch a better breeze on the corner anyway, she thought optimistically. It was just one of the many small pleasures she had since leaving Manhattan and settling in Virginia.

River Glen was a quiet, sleepy town of seven thousand nestled along the Potomac. She'd visited a lot of places during her search for a job, but this one had drawn her in some indefinable way. With its endless stretches of green lawns and its mix of unpretentious, pastel-painted summer cottages, impressive old brick Colonial homes and modern ranch-style architecture, it was the antithesis of New York's intimidating mass of skyscrapers. It had a pace that soothed rather than grated and an atmosphere of unrelenting calm and continuity. The town, as much as the job offer, had convinced her this was exactly what she needed.

Four weeks earlier Dana had moved into her ramshackle cottage and the next day she'd started her job as River Glen's first librarian in five years. All in all, it had been a satisfying month with no regrets and no time for lingering memories.

Already she'd painted the cottage a sparkling white, scrubbed the layers of grime from the windows, matched wits with the stove and the plumbing and replaced the mattress. When she tired of being confined to the house, she had cut the overgrown lawn, weeded the flower gardens and discovered beds of tulips and daffodils ready to burst forth with blossoms. She'd even put in a small tomato patch in the backyard.

To her surprise, after a lifetime surrounded by concrete, she found that the scent of newly turned earth, even the feel of the rich dirt clinging damply to her skin, had acted like a balm. Now, more than ever, she was glad she'd chosen springtime to settle here. All these growing things reminded her in a very graphic way of new beginnings.

"Better be careful," a low, distinctly sexy voice, laced with humor, warned from out of nowhere, startling Dana just as she reached out to pluck a lilac from the bush. She hadn't heard footsteps. She certainly hadn't heard a car drive up. On guard, she whirled around, the clippers held out protectively in front of her, and discovered a blue pickup at the edge of the lawn, its owner grinning at her from behind the wheel.

"I heard that lilac bush ate the last owner," he added very seriously.

Her brown eyes narrowed watchfully. She instinctively backed up a step, then another as the stranger climbed out of his truck and started toward her with long, easy strides.

Dana had met a number of townspeople since her arrival, but not this man. She would have remembered the overpowering masculinity of the rugged, tanned face with its stubborn, square jaw and the laugh lines that spread like delicate webs from the corners of his eyes. She would have remembered the trembling nervousness he set off inside her.

"Who are you?" she asked, trying to hide her uneasiness but clinging defensively to the hedge clippers nonetheless. It was one thing to know the adage that in a small town there were no strangers, but quite another to be confronted unexpectedly with a virile, powerful specimen like this in your own front yard. She figured the hedge clippers made them an almost even match, which was both a reassuring and a daunting thought.

The man, tall and whipcord lean, paused halfway up the walk and shoved his hands into the pockets of his jeans. If he was taken aback by her unfriendliness, there was no sign of it on his face. His smile never wavered and his voice lowered to an even more soothing timbre, as if to prove he was no threat to her.

"Nicholas… Nick Verone." When that drew no response, he added, "Tony's father."

Dana drew in a sharp breath. The name, of course, had registered at once. It was plastered on the side of just about every construction trailer in the county. It was also the signature on her paycheck. She was a town employee. Nicholas Verone was the elected treasurer, a man reputed to have political aspirations on a far grander scale, perhaps the state legislature, perhaps even Washington.

He was admired for his integrity, respected for his success and, since the death of his wife three years earlier, targeted by every matchmaker in town. She'd been hearing about him since her first day on the job. Down at town hall, the kindly clerk, a gleam in her periwinkle-blue eyes, had taken one good look at Dana and begun scheming to arrange a meeting. To Betsy Markham's very evident maternal frustration, Dana had repeatedly declined.

The connection to Tony, however, was what mattered this morning. Turning her wary frown into a faint tentative smile of welcome, she saw the resemblance now, the same hazel eyes that were bright and inquisitive and filled with warmth and humor, the same unruly brown hair that no brush would ever tame. While at ten years old Tony was an impish charmer, his father had a quiet, far more dangerous allure. The sigh of relief she'd felt on learning his identity caught somewhere in her throat and set off a different reaction entirely.

Ingrained caution and natural curiosity warred, making her tone abrupt as she asked, "What are you doing here?"

Nick Verone still didn't seem the least bit offended by her inhospitable attitude. In fact, he seemed amused by it. "Tony mentioned your roof was leaking. I had some time today and I thought maybe I could check it out for you."

Dana grimaced. She was going to have to remember to watch her tongue around Tony. She'd been alert to Betsy Markham's straightforward matchmaking tactics, but she'd never once suspected that Tony might decide to get in on the conspiracy to find his father a mate. Then again, maybe Tony had only been trying to repay her for helping him with his history lesson on the Civil War. At her urging, he'd finally decided not to try to persuade the teacher that the South had actually won.

"Well, we should have," he'd grumbled, his jaw set

every bit as stubbornly as she imagined his father's could be. In the end, though, Tony had stuck to the facts and returned proudly a week later to show her the B minus on his test paper, the highest history grade he'd ever received.

At the moment, though, with Nick Verone waiting patiently in front of her, it hardly seemed to matter what Tony's motivation had been. She had to send the man on his way. His presence was making her palms sweat.

"Thanks, anyway," she said, giving him a smile she hoped seemed suitably appreciative. "But I've already made arrangements for a contractor to come by next week."

Instead of daunting him, her announcement drew a scowl. "I hope you didn't call Billy Watson."

Dana swallowed guiltily and said with a touch of defiance, "What if I did?"

"He'll charge you an arm and a leg and he won't get the job done."

"Haven't you heard that it's bad business to knock the competition?"

"Billy's not my competition. For that matter, calling him a contractor is a stretch of the imagination. He's a scoundrel out to make a quick buck so he can finance his next binge. Everybody around here knows that and I can't imagine anyone recommending him. Why did you call him in the first place?"

She'd called Billy Watson because he was the only *other* contractor—or handyman, for that matter— she'd been able to find when water had started dripping through her roof in five different places during the first of April's pounding spring showers. All of Betsy's unsolicited praise for Nick Verone had set off warning bells inside her head. She'd known intuitively that asking him to take a look at her roof would be asking for trouble. His presence now and its impact on her heartbeat were proof enough that she'd been right. To any woman determinedly seeking solitude, this aggressive, incredibly sexy man was a threat.

She stared into Nick's eyes, noted the expectant gleam and decided that wasn't an explanation she should offer. He was the kind of man who'd make entirely too much out of such a candid response.

"You're a very busy man, Mr. Verone," she said instead. "I assumed Billy Watson could get here sooner."

Nick's grin widened, dipping slightly on the left side to make it beguilingly crooked. A less determined woman might fall for that smile, but Dana tried very hard to ignore it.

"I'm here now," he pointed out, rocking back and forth on the balls of his feet, his fingers still jammed into the pockets of his jeans in a way that called attention to their fit across his flat stomach and lean hips.

"Mr. Watson promised to be here Monday morning first thing. That's plenty soon enough."

"And if it rains between now and then?"

"I'll put out the pots and pans again."

Nick only barely resisted the urge to chuckle. He'd heard the dismissal in Dana's New York–accented voice and read the wariness in her eyes. It was the look a lot of people had when first confronted with small-town friendliness after a lifetime in big cities. They assumed every neighborly act would come with a price tag. It took time to convince them otherwise. Oddly enough, he found that in Dana's case he wanted to see to her enlightenment personally. There was something about this slender, overly cautious woman that touched a re-sponsive chord deep inside him.

Besides, he loved River Glen. He'd grown up here and he'd witnessed—in fact, he'd been a part of—its slow evolution from a slightly shabby summer resort past its prime into a year-round community with a fu-ture. The more people like Dana Brantley who settled here, the faster changes would come.

He'd read her résumé and knew that one year ago, at age twenty-eight, she'd gone back to school to fin-ish her master's degree in library science. He was still a little puzzled why a native New Yorker would want to come to a quiet place like River Glen, but he was glad of it. She'd bring new ideas, maybe some big-city ways. He didn't want his town to lose its charm, but he wanted it to be progressive, rather than becoming mired down in the sea of complacency that had destroyed other communities and made their young people move on in search of more excitement.

He figured it was up to people in his position to see that Dana felt welcome. Small towns had a way of being friendly and clannish at the same time. Sometimes it took a while for superficial warmth to become genu-ine acceptance.

He gazed directly into Dana's eyes and shook his head. "Sorry, ma'am, it just wouldn't be right. I can't let you do that." He saw to it that his southern drawl increased perceptibly.

"Do what?" A puzzled frown tugged at her lips.

"Stay up all night, running from room to room with those pots and pans. What if you slipped and fell? I'd feel responsible."

The remark earned him a reluctant chuckle and he

watched in awe at the transformation. Dana smiled provocatively, banishing the tiny, surprisingly stern lines in her lovely, heart-shaped face. She pulled off her work gloves and brushed back a curling strand of mink-brown hair that had escaped from her shoulder-length ponytail. Every movie cliché about staid librarians suddenly whipping off their glasses and letting down their hair rushed through Nick's mind and warmed his blood. Under all that starch and caution, under the streak of dirt that emphasized the curve of her cheek, Dana Brantley was a fragile, beautiful woman. The realization took his breath away. All Tony's talk hadn't done the new librarian justice.

"I swear to you that I won't sue you if I trip over a pot in the middle of a storm," she said. Her smile grew and, for the first time since his arrival, seemed sincere. Finally, she completely put aside the hedge clippers she'd been absentmindedly brandishing at him.

"I'll even put it in writing," she offered.

"Nope," he said determinedly. "That's not good enough. There's Tony to consider, too."

"What does he have to do with it?"

"Don't think I don't know that you're the one behind his history grade. I can't have him failing again just because the librarian is laid up with a twisted ankle or worse."

"Tony is a bright boy. All he needs is a little guidance." She regarded him pointedly. "And someone to remind him that when it comes to history, facts are facts. Like it or not, the Yankees did win the Civil War."

Nick hid a smile. "Yes, well, with Robert E. Lee having been born just down the road, some of us do like to cling to our illusions about that particular war. But for a battle here and there, things might have been different."

"But they weren't. However, if you're determined to ignore historical reality, perhaps you should stick to helping Tony with his math or maybe his English and encourage him to read his history textbooks. In the long run, he'll have a better time of it in school."

Nick accepted the criticism gracefully, but there was a twinkle in his eyes. "I'll keep that in mind," he said, careful not to chuckle. "Now about your roof..."

"Mr. Verone—"

"Nick."

"That roof has been up there for years. It may have a few leaks, but it's in no danger of caving in. Surely it can wait until Monday. I appreciate your offering to help, but I did make a deal with Mr. Watson."

Nick was already moving toward his truck. "He won't show up," he muttered over his shoulder.

"What's that?"

"I said he won't show up, not unless he's out of liquor." He pulled an extension ladder from the back of the pickup and returned purposefully up the walk, past an increasingly indignant Dana.

"Mr. Verone," Dana snapped in frustration as Nick marched around to the side of the house. She had to run to keep up with him, leaving her out of breath but just as furious. The familiar, unpleasant feeling of losing control of a situation swept over her. "Mr. Verone, I do not want you on my roof."

It seemed rather a wasted comment since he was already more than halfway up the ladder. *Damn,* she thought. *The man is impossible.* "Don't you ever listen?" she grumbled.

He climbed the rest of the way, then leaned down and winked at her. "Nope. Give me my toolbox, would you?"

She was tempted to throw it at him, but she handed it up very politely, then sat down on the back step muttering curses. She picked a blade of grass and chewed on it absentmindedly. With Nick Verone on her roof and a knot forming in her stomach, she was beginning to regret that she'd ever helped Tony Verone with his history project. In fact, she was beginning to wonder if coming to River Glen was going to be the peaceful escape she'd hoped it would be. Sensations best forgotten were sweeping over her this morning.

While she tried to put her feelings in perspective, Nick shouted at her from some spot on the roof she couldn't see.

"Do you have a garden hose?"

"Of course."

"How about getting it and squirting some water up here?"

Dana wanted to refuse but realized that being difficult probably wouldn't get Nick out of her life any faster. He'd just climb down and find the hose himself. He seemed like a very resourceful man. She stomped off after the hose and turned it on.

"Aim it a little higher," he instructed a few minutes later. "Over here."

Dana scowled up at him and fought the temptation to move the spray about three feet to the right and douse the outrageous, arrogant man. Maybe then he would go away, even if only to get into some dry clothes, but at least he'd leave her in peace for a while. She still wasn't exactly sure how he'd talked her into letting him stay on the roof, much less gotten her to help him with his inspection. For a total stranger he took an awful lot for granted. He certainly didn't know how to take no for an answer. And she was tired of fighting, tired of confrontations and still, despite the past year of relative calm, terrified of anger. A raised voice made her hands tremble and her head pound with seemingly irrational anxiety.

So, if it made him happy, Nick Verone could inspect her roof, fix her leaks, and then, with any luck, he'd disappear and she'd be alone again. Blissfully alone with her books and her herb tea and her flowers, like some maiden aunt in an English novel.

Suddenly a tanned face appeared at the edge of the roof. "I hate to tell you this, but you ought to replace the whole thing. It's probably been up here thirty years without a single repair. I can patch it for you, but with one good storm, you'll just have more leaks."

Dana sighed. "Somehow I knew you were going to say that."

"Didn't you have the roof inspected before you bought the place?"

"Not exactly."

He grinned at her. "What does that mean?"

"It means we all agreed it was probably in terrible condition and knocked another couple of thousand dollars off the price of the house." She shot him a challenging glance. "I thought it was a good deal."

"I see." His eyes twinkled in that superior I-should-have-known male way and her hackles rose. If he said one word about being penny-wise and pound-foolish, she'd snatch the ladder away and leave him stranded.

Perhaps he sensed her intention, because he scrambled for the ladder and made his way down. When he reached the ground, he faced her, hands on hips, one foot propped on the ladder's lower rung in a pose that emphasized his masculinity.

"How about a deal?" he suggested.

Dana was shaking her head before the words were out of his mouth. "I don't think so."

"You haven't even heard the offer yet."

"I appreciate your interest and your time, Mr. Verone…"

"Nick."

She scowled at him. "But as I told you, I do have another contractor coming."

"Billy Watson will tell you the same thing, assuming he doesn't poke his clumsy feet through some of the weak spots and sue you first."

"Don't you think you're exaggerating slightly?"

"Not by much," he insisted ominously. Then he smiled again, one of those crooked, impish smiles that were so like Tony's when he knew he'd written something really terrific and was awaiting praise. Like father, like son—unfortunately, in this case.

"Why don't we go inside and have something cold to drink and discuss this?" Nick suggested, taking over again in a way that set Dana's teeth on edge. Her patience and self-control were deteriorating rapidly.

He was already heading around the side of the house before she even had a chance to say no. Once more, she was left to scamper along behind him or be left cursing to herself. At the back door she hesitated, not at all sure she wanted to be alone with this stranger and out of sight of the neighbors.

He's Tony's father, for heaven's sakes.

With that thought in mind, she stepped into the kitchen, but she lingered near the door. Nick hadn't waited for an invitation. He'd already opened the refrigerator and was scanning the contents with unabashed interest. He pulled out a pitcher of iced tea and poured two glasses without so much as a glance in her direction. To his credit, though, he didn't mention the fact that the door was missing a hinge. She'd ordered it on Thursday.

Nick studied Dana over the rim of his glass and tried to make sense of her skittishness. She was no youngster, though she had the trim, lithe figure of one. The weariness around her eyes was what gave her age away, not the long, slender legs shown off by her paint-splattered shorts or the luxuriant tumble of rich brown hair hanging down her back. Allowing for gaps in her résumé, she was no more than twenty-nine, maybe thirty, about five years younger than he was. Yet in some ways she looked as though she'd seen the troubles of a woman twice that age. There was something about her eyes, something sad and lost and vulnerable. Still, he didn't doubt for an instant that she had a core of steel. He'd felt the chill when her voice turned cold, when those intriguing brown eyes of hers glinted with anger. He'd pushed her this morning and she'd bent, but she hadn't broken. She was still fighting mad. Right now, she was watching him with an uneasy alertness, like a doe standing at the edge of a clearing and sensing danger.

"Now about that deal," he said when he'd taken a long swallow of the sweetened tea.

"Mr. Verone, please."

"Nick," he automatically corrected again. "Now what I have in mind is charging you just for the roofing materials. I'll handle the work in my spare time, if you'll continue to help Tony out with his homework."

Dana sighed, plainly exasperated with him. "I'm more than willing to help Tony anytime he asks for help. That's part of my job as librarian."

"Is it part of your job to stay overtime? I've seen the lights burning in there past closing more than once. We don't pay for the extra hours."

"I'm not asking you to. I enjoy what I do. I'm not interested in punching a time clock. If staying late will give someone extra time to get the books they want or to finish a school project, it gives me satisfaction."

"Okay, so helping Tony is part of your job. Then we'll just consider this my way of welcoming you to town."

"I can't let you do that," she insisted, her annoyance showing again.

"Why not? Don't tell me you're from that old-fashioned school that says women can't accept gifts from men unless they're engaged."

"I don't think fixing my roof is in the same league as accepting a fur coat or jewelry."

"Then I rest my case."

"But I will feel obligated to you and I don't like obligations."

"You won't owe me a thing. It's an even trade."

Dana groaned. "Is there any way I can win this argument?"

"None that I can think of," he admitted cheerfully.

"Okay, fine. Fix the roof," she said, but she didn't sound pleased about it. She sounded like a woman who'd been cornered. For some reason, Nick felt like a heel instead of a good neighbor, though he couldn't find any logical explanation for her behavior or his uncomfortable reaction.

Changing tactics, he finally asked, "How come I haven't seen much of you around town?"

"I've been pretty busy getting settled in. This place was a mess and I had the library to organize."

He tilted his chair back on two legs and glanced around approvingly. "You've done a lot here. I remember the way it was. I used to play here as a boy when old Miss Francis was alive. It didn't look much better then. We thought it was haunted."

He was rewarded with another grin from Dana. "I haven't encountered any ghosts so f r. . 'ey're here, they certainly haven't done much of .he cleaning. The library wasn't any improvement. It took me the better part of a week just to sweep away the cobwebs and organize the shelves properly. There are still boxes of donated books in the back I haven't had a chance to look at yet."

"Then it's time you took a break. There's bingo tonight at the fire station. Why don't you come with Tony and me?"

He watched as the wall around her went right back up, brick by brick. "I don't think so."

"Can't you spell?" he teased.

Her eyes flashed dangerous sparks. "Of course."

"How about counting? Any good at that?"

"Yes."

"Then what's the problem?"

The problem, Dana thought, was not bingo. It was Nicholas Verone. He represented more than a mere complication, more than a man who wanted to fix her roof and share a glass of tea now and then. He was the type of man she'd sworn to avoid for the rest of her life. Powerful. Domineering. Charming. And from the glint in his devilish eyes to the strength in his work-roughened hands he was thoroughly, unquestionably male. Just looking at those hands, imagining their strength, set off a violent trembling inside her.

"Thank you for asking," she said stiffly, "but I really have too much to do. Maybe another time."

To her astonishment, Nick's eyes sparked with satisfaction. "Next week, then," he said as he rinsed his glass and set it in the dish drainer. He didn't once meet her startled gaze.

"But—" The protest might as well never have been uttered for all the good it did. He didn't even allow her to finish it.

"We'll pick you up at six and we'll go out for barbecue first," he added confidently as he walked to the door, then bestowed a dazzling smile on her. "Gracie's has the best you've ever tasted this side of Texas. Guaranteed."

The screen door shut behind him with an emphatic bang.

Dana watched him go and fought the confusing, contradictory feelings he'd roused in her. If there was one thing she knew all too well, it was that there were no guarantees in life, especially when it came to men like Nick Verone.

Chapter 2

After a perfectly infuriating Monday morning spent waiting futilely for Billy Watson, Dana opened the library at noon. She'd found Betsy Markham already pacing on the front steps. Instead of heading for the fiction shelves to look over her favorite mysteries, Betsy followed Dana straight to her cluttered desk, where she was trying to update the chaotic card file so she could eventually get it all on the computer. The last librarian, a retired cashier from the old five-and-ten-cent store, obviously hadn't put much stock in the need for alphabetical order or modern equipment. When a new book came in, she apparently just popped the card in the back of whichever drawer seemed to have room.

"So," Betsy said, pulling up a chair and propping her plump elbows on the corner of the desk. "Tell me everything."

Dana glanced up from the card file and stared at her blankly. "About what?"

"You and Nick Verone, of course." She wagged a finger. "You're a sly little thing, Dana Brantley. Here I've been trying to introduce you to the man for weeks and you kept turning me down. The next thing I know the two of you are thick as thieves and being talked about all over town."

Thick brown brows rose over startled eyes. "We're what?"

"Yes, indeed," Betsy said, nodding so hard that not even the thick coating of hair spray could contain the bounce of her upswept gray hair.

Betsy's eyes flashed conspiratorially and she lowered her voice, though there wasn't another soul in the place. "Word is that he was at your house very early Saturday morning and stayed for quite a while. One version has it he was there till practically lunchtime. Inside the house!"

When she noticed the horrified expression on Dana's face, she added, "Though what difference that makes, I for one can't see. It's not as if you'd be doing anything in broad daylight."

Dana was torn between indignation and astonishment. "He didn't stop by for some sort of secret assignation, for heaven's sakes. He came to look at my roof."

Betsy appeared taken aback. "But I thought you'd called Billy Watson to do that, even though I tried to make it perfectly clear to you that Billy's a bit of a ne'er-do-well."

"I had called him, and don't get me started on that. The man never showed up this morning. He said he'd be there by eight. I waited until 11:30." Dana wasn't sure what incensed her more: Billy Watson's failure to appear or having to admit that Nick Verone was right.

"Then I still don't understand what Nick has to do with your roof."

"Mr. Verone apparently heard about the leaks from Tony and stopped by on his own. He wasn't invited." Darn! Why was she explaining herself to Betsy Markham and, no doubt, half the town by sunset? Nick's visit had been entirely innocent. On top of that, it was no one's business.

Except in River Glen.

She'd have to start remembering that this wasn't New York, where all sorts of mayhem could take place right under your neighbors' noses without a sign of acknowledgment. Here folks obviously took their gossip seriously. She decided that Crime Watch organizers could take lessons from the citizens of this town. Very little got by them. Perhaps she should be grateful they hadn't prayed for her soul in the Baptist church on Sunday or put an announcement in the weekly paper.

Betsy was staring at her, disappointment etched all over her round face. "You mean there's nothing personal going on between the two of you?"

Dana thought about the invitation to bingo. That was friendly, not personal, but she doubted Betsy and the others would see it that way. She might as well bring it up now, rather than wait for Saturday night, when half the town was bound to see her with Nick and Tony and the rest would hear about it before church the next day. "Not exactly," she said finally.

Betsy's blue eyes brightened. "I knew it," she gloated. "I just knew the two of you would hit it off. When are you seeing him again?"

"Saturday," Dana admitted reluctantly, then threw in what she suspected would be a wasted disclaimer, "but it's not really a date."

Betsy regarded her skeptically, just as Dana had known she would. Dana forged on anyway. "He and Tony and I are going out to eat at some place called Gracie's and then to bingo."

She thought that certainly ought to seem innocuous enough. Betsy reacted, though, as if Dana had uttered a blasphemy. She was incredulous.

"Barbecue and bingo? Land sakes, girl, Nick Verone's nigh on to the richest man in these parts. He ought to be taking you to someplace fancy in Richmond at the very least."

"I think the idea is for me to get to know more people around here. I don't think he's trying to woo me with gourmet food and candlelight."

"Then he's a fool."

Dana doubted if many people called Nick Verone a fool to his face. But Betsy had taken a proprietary interest in Dana's social life. She might do it out of some misguided sense of duty.

"Don't you say one single word to him, Betsy Markham," she warned. "Barbecue and bingo are fine. I'm not looking for a man in my life—rich or poor. To tell the truth, I'd rather stay home and read a good book."

"You read books all day long. You're young. You ought to be out enjoying yourself, living life, not just reading about it in some novel."

"I do enjoy myself."

Betsy sniffed indignantly. "I declare, I don't know what's wrong with young people today. When my Harry and I were courting, you can bet we didn't spend Saturday night at the fire station with a bunch of nosy neighbors looking on. It's bad enough we do that now. Back then, why, we'd be parked out along the beach someplace, watching the moon come up and making plans."

She picked up a flyer from Dana's desk and fanned herself absentmindedly. There was a faint smile on her lips. "Oh, my, yes. That was quite a time. You young folks don't care a thing about romance. Everybody's too busy trying to get ahead."

Dana restrained the urge to grin. Being River Glen's librarian was hardly a sign of raging ambition, but if thinking it kept Betsy from interfering in her personal life, she'd do everything she could to promote the notion.

Dana reached over and patted the woman's hand. "Thanks for caring about me, Betsy, but I'm doing just fine. I love it here. All I want in my life right now is a little peace and quiet. Romance can wait."

Betsy sighed dramatically. "Okay, honey, if that's what you want, but don't put up too much of a fight. Nick Verone's the best catch around these parts. You'd be crazy to let him get away."

Dana spent the rest of the afternoon thinking about Betsy's admonition. She also spent entirely too much time thinking about Nick Verone. Even if her mind hadn't betrayed her by dredging up provocative images, there was Tony to remind her.

He bounded into the library right after school, wearing a huge grin. "Hey, Ms. Brantley, I hear you and me and Dad are going out on Saturday."

Dana winced as several other kids turned to listen.

"Your dad invited me to come along to bingo. Are you sure you don't mind?"

"Mind? Heck, no. You're the greatest. All the kids think so. Right, guys?" There were enthusiastic nods from the trio gathered behind him. Tony studied her with an expression that was entirely too wise for a ten-year-old and lowered his voice to what he obviously considered to be a discreet whisper. It echoed through every nook and cranny in the library.

"Say, do you want me to get lost on Saturday night?" He blushed furiously as his friends moved in closer so they wouldn't miss a word. "I mean so you and Dad can be alone and all. I could spend the night over at Bobby's. His mom wouldn't mind." Bobby nodded enthusiastically.

If Dana had been the type, she might have blushed right along with Tony. Instead, she said with heartfelt conviction, "I most certainly do not want you to get lost. Your father planned for all of us to spend the evening together and that's just the way I want it."

"But I know about grown-ups and stuff. I don't want to get in the way. I think it'd be great, if you and Dad—"

"Tony!"

"Well, you know."

"What I know," she said briskly, "is that you guys have an English assignment due this week. Have you picked out your books yet?"

All of them except Tony said yes and drifted off. Tony's round hazel eyes stared at her hopefully. "I thought maybe you'd help me."

Dana sighed. She knew now where Tony had gotten his manipulative skills. He was every bit as persuasive as his daddy. She pulled *Robinson Crusoe, Huckleberry Finn* and *Treasure Island* from the shelves. "Take a look at these."

She left him skimming through the books and went to help several other students who'd come in with assignments. The rest of the afternoon and evening flew by. At nine o'clock, when she was ready to lock up for the day, she discovered that Tony was in a back corner still hunched over *Treasure Island.*

"Tony, you should have been home hours ago," she said in dismay. "Your father must be worried sick."

He barely glanced up at her. "I called him and told him where I was. He said it was okay."

"When did you call him?"

"After school."

Dana groaned. "Do you have any idea how late it is now?"

He shook his head. "Nope. I got to reading this. It's pretty good."

"Then why don't you check it out and take it home with you?"

He regarded her sheepishly. "I'd rather read it here with you."

An unexpected warm feeling stole into her heart. She could understand how Tony felt. He'd probably gone home all too often to an empty house. He'd clearly been starved for mothering since his own mother had died, despite the attentions of a maternal grandmother he mentioned frequently and affectionately. Whatever women there were in Nick Verone's life, they weren't meeting Tony's needs. A disturbing glimmer of satisfaction rippled through her at that thought, and she mentally stomped it right back into oblivion, where it belonged. The Verones' lifestyle was none of her concern.

Knowing that and acting on it, however, were two very different things. Subconsciously she'd felt herself slipping into a nurturing role with Tony from the day they'd met. Despite his boundless energy, there had been something a little lost and lonely about him. He reminded her of the way she'd felt for far too long, and instinctively she'd wanted to banish the sad expression from his eyes.

For Dana, Tony had filled an aching emptiness that increasingly seemed to haunt her now that she knew it was never likely to go away. From the time she'd been a little girl, her room cluttered with dolls in every shape and size, she'd wanted children of her own. She'd had a golden life in which all her dreams seemed to be granted, and she'd expected that to be the easiest wish of all to fulfill.

When she and Sam had married, they'd had their lives planned out: a year together to settle in, then a baby and two years after that another one. But too many things had changed in that first year, and ironically, she'd been the one to postpone getting pregnant, even though the decision had torn her apart.

Now her marriage was over and she wasn't counting on another one. She didn't even want one. And it was getting late. She was nearing the age when a woman began to realize it was now or never for a baby. She'd forced herself to accept the fact that for her it would be never, but there were still days when she longed for that child to hold in her empty arms. Tony, so hungry for attention, had seemed to be a godsend, but she knew now that her instinctive nurturing had to stop. It wasn't healthy for Tony and it assuredly wasn't wise for her—not with Nick beginning to hint around that it might be a package deal.

"Get your stuff together," she said abruptly to Tony. "I'll drive you home."

Hurt sprang up in his eyes at her sharp tone.

"I can walk," he protested with the automatic cockiness of a young boy anxious to prove himself grown up. Then his eyes lit up. "But if you drive me home," he said slyly, "maybe you can come in and have some ice cream with dad and me."

"Ice cream is not a proper dinner," Dana replied automatically, and then could have bitten her outspoken tongue.

"Yeah, but Dad's a pretty lousy cook. We go to Gracie's a lot. When we don't go there, we usually eat some yucky frozen dinners. I'd rather have ice cream."

Dana felt a stirring of something that felt disturbingly like sympathy as she pictured Nick and Tony existing on tasteless dinners that came in little metal trays. If these images kept up, she was going to have to buy army boots to stomp them out. The Verones' diet was of absolutely no concern to her. Tony looked sturdy enough and Nick was certainly not suffering from a lack of vitamins. She'd seen his muscle tone for herself, when he'd been stretching around up on her roof.

"So, how about it?" Tony said, interrupting her before she got lost in those intriguing images again. "Will you come in for ice cream?"

"Not tonight." Not in this lifetime, if she had a grain of sense in her head. She tried to ignore the disappointment that shadowed Tony's face as he gave her directions to his house.

It took less than ten minutes to drive across town to an area where the homes were separated by wide sweeps of lawn shaded by ancient oak trees tipped with new green leaves. The Verones' two-story white frame house, with its black shutters, wraparound porch and upstairs widow's walk, stood atop a low rise and faced out to sea. The place appeared to have been built in fits and starts, with additions jutting out haphazardly, yet looking very much a part of the whole. Lights blinked in the downstairs windows and an old-fashioned lamppost lit the driveway that wound along the side of the house. More than three times as large as Dana's two-bedroom cottage, the place still had a warm, cozily inviting appeal.

She was still absorbing that satisfying first impression when the side door opened and Nick appeared. Tony threw open the car door and jumped out. "Hey, Dad, Ms. Brantley brought me home. I asked her to come in for ice cream, but she won't. You try."

Dana wondered if she could disappear under the dashboard. Before she could attempt that feat, Nick was beside the car, an all-too-beguiling grin on his face. He leaned down and poked his head in the window. His hair was still damp from a recent shower and he smelled of soap. Dana tried not to sigh. She avoided his gaze altogether.

"How about it, Ms. Brantley?" he said quietly, drawing her attention. "Will I have any better luck than Tony?"

She caught the challenge glinting in his hazel eyes

and looked away. "It's late. I really should be getting home and Tony ought to have some dinner."

"You both ought to have dinner," Nick corrected. "I'll bet you haven't eaten, either."

"I'll grab something at home. Thanks, anyway."

She risked glancing up. Nick tried for a woebegone expression and failed miserably. The man would look self-confident trying to hold back an avalanche single-handedly. "You wouldn't sentence Tony to another one of my disastrous meals, would you?"

Despite her best intentions, Dana found herself returning his mischievous grin. "Surely you're not suggesting that I stay for dinner and that I fix it."

His eyes widened innocently. On Tony it would have been the look of an angel. On Nick it was pure seduction. "Of course not," he denied. "I'll just pop another TV dinner in the oven. We have plenty."

Suddenly she knew the battle was over before it had even begun. If Nick had been by himself, she would have refused; her defenses would have held. He would have been eating some prepackaged dinner, while she went home to canned vegetable soup and a grilled cheese sandwich. The idea of being alone with him made her heart race in a disconcerting way that would have made it easy to say no, even when the alternative wasn't especially appealing.

But with Tony around, she began to waver. He needed a nourishing meal. And while a ten-year-old, especially one who already had matchmaking skills, was hardly a qualified chaperon, he was better than nothing. She wouldn't have to be there more than an hour or so. How much could happen between them in a single hour?

"Do you have any real food in there?" she asked at last.

"Frozen dinners are real food."

"I was thinking more along the lines of chicken or beef or fish. This town has a river full of perch and crabs. Surely you occasionally go out and catch some of them."

"Of course I do. Then we eat them. I think there might be some chicken in the freezer, though."

"And vegetables?"

"Sure." Then as an afterthought, he added, "Frozen."

Dana shook her head. "Men!"

Telling herself it might be nice to have a friend in town, then telling herself she was an idiot for thinking that's all it would be with a man like Nick, she reluctantly turned off the ignition and climbed out of the car. "Guide me to your refrigerator. We'll consider this payment for your first day's labor on my roof."

"So Billy didn't show up?" he said, jamming his hands in his pockets.

She scowled at him. "No."

"I told—"

"Don't you dare finish that sentence."

"Right," he said agreeably, but his grin was very smug as he turned away to lead her up the driveway.

If she'd thought for one minute that she'd be able to relax in Nick's presence, she was wrong. Her nerves were stretched taut simply by walking beside him to the house. He didn't put a hand on her, not even a casual touch at her elbow to guide her. But every inch of her was vibrantly aware of him just the same and every inch screamed that this attempt at casual friendship was a mistake. At the threshold, she had to fight against a momentary panic, a desire to turn and flee, but then Tony was calling out to her and curiosity won out over fear. She told herself she simply wanted to see if this graceful old house was as charming on the inside as it was outside.

In some ways the house itself had surprised her. She would have expected a builder to want something modern, something that would make a statement about his professional capabilities. Instead, Nick had chosen tradition and history. It raised him a notch in her estimation.

They went through the kitchen, which was as modern and large as anyone could possibly want. She regarded it enviously and thought of her own cantankerous appliances. A built-in breakfast nook was surrounded by panes of beveled glass and situated to catch the morning sun. This room was made for more than cooking and eating. It was a place for sharing the day's events, for making plans and shaping dreams, for watching the change of seasons. It was exactly the sort of kitchen she would have designed if she and Sam had ever gotten around to building a house.

Enough of that, she told herself sharply. She dropped her purse on the gleaming countertop and headed straight for the refrigerator. Nick stepped in front of her so quickly she almost stumbled straight into his arms. She pulled back abruptly to avoid the contact.

"Hey, don't you want the grand tour first?" Nick said. "I really didn't invite you in just to feed us. Relax for a while and let me show you around."

Once more, with her heart thumping crazily in her chest, Dana prayed for a quick return of her common sense. She knew she was feeling pressure where there was none, but suddenly she didn't want to see the rest of

the house. She didn't want to find that the living room
was as perfect as the one she'd dreamed about for years
or that the bedrooms were bright and airy like something straight out of a decorating magazine. She didn't
want to be here at all. Nick was too overwhelming, too
charming, and there was an appreciative spark in his
eyes that terrified her more with every instant she spent
in his company.

She took a deep, slow breath and reminded herself
that leaving now was impossible without seeming both
foolish and ungracious. She took another calming breath
and tried to remind herself that she was in control, that
nothing would happen unless she wanted it to, certainly
not with Tony in the house. Unfortunately, Tony seemed
to have vanished the minute they came through the
door. If only he'd join them, she might feel more at ease.

"Let me see what treasures are locked in your freezer
first," she finally said. "Then while dinner cooks, you
can show me around."

It was a logical suggestion, one that didn't hint of
her absurd nervousness, and Nick gave in easily. "How
about a drink, then?"

Once again, Dana felt a familiar knot form in her
stomach. "Nothing for me, thanks." Her voice was tight.

"Not even iced tea or a soda?"

Illogical relief, exaggerated far beyond the offer's
significance, washed over her. "Iced tea would be great."

They reached the refrigerator at the same instant and
Dana was trapped between Nick and the door. The in-
timate, yet innocent press of his solid, very male body
against hers set off a wild trembling. His heat and that
alluring scent of soap and man surrounded her. The
surge of her blood roared in her ears. She clenched her

fists and fought to remain absolutely still, to not let the unwarranted panic show in her eyes. Nick allowed the contact to last no more than a few seconds, though it seemed an eternity. Then he stepped aside with an easy grin.

"Sorry," he said.

Dana shrugged. "No problem."

But there was a problem. Nick had seen it in Dana's eyes, though she'd looked away to avoid his penetrating gaze. He'd felt the shiver that rippled through her, noted her startled gasp and the way she protectively lifted her arms before she dropped them back to her sides with conscious deliberation. He was experienced enough to know that this was not the reaction of a woman who desired a man but who was startled by the unexpectedness of the feeling. Dana had actually seemed afraid of him, just as she had on Saturday, when she'd been brandishing those hedge clippers. The possibility that he frightened her astonished and worried him. He was not used to being considered a threat, not to his employees, not to his son and certainly not to a woman.

He'd been raised to treat everyone with respect and dignity, but women were in a class by themselves. His mother, God rest her, had been a gentle soul with a core of iron and more love and compassion than any human being he'd ever met. She'd expected to be treated like a lady by both her husband and her sons and thought there was no reason other women shouldn't deserve the same.

"Women aren't playthings," she'd told Nick sternly the first time she'd caught him kissing a girl down by the river. He'd been fourteen at the time and very much interested in experimentation. Nancy Ann had the reputation of being more than willing. He never knew for sure if his mother had heard the gossip about Nancy Ann, but she'd looked him straight in the eye at the dinner table that night and said, "I don't care who they are or how experienced they claim to be, you show them the same respect you'd expect for yourself. Nobody deserves to be used."

Though his brothers had grinned, he'd squirmed uncomfortably under her disapproving gaze. He'd never once forgotten that lesson, not even in the past three years since Ginny had died and more than a few women had indicated their willingness to share his bed and his life. Dana's nervous response bothered him all the more, because he knew it was so thoroughly unjustified.

But *she* didn't know that, he reminded himself. Experience had apparently taught her another lesson about men, a bitter, lasting lesson. He felt an unreasoning surge of anger against the person who had hurt her.

Dana was already poking around in the freezer as if the incident had never taken place. Since she'd apparently decided to let the matter rest, he figured he should, as well. For now. In time, his actions would teach her she had nothing to fear from him.

Delighted to have such attractive company for a change, he leaned back against the counter, crossed his legs at the ankles and watched her as she picked up packages, wrinkled her nose and tossed them back. Finally she emerged triumphant, her cheeks flushed from the chilly air in the freezer.

"I'm almost afraid to ask, but do you have any idea how long this chicken has been in there?"

Nick reached out, took the package and brushed at the frost. "Looks to me like it's dated February something."

"Of what year?"

"It's frozen. Does it matter?"

"Probably not to the chicken, but it could make a difference in whether we survive this meal."

"We can always go back to the frozen dinners. I bought most of them last week." He paused thoughtfully. "Except for those Salisbury steak things. They've probably been there longer. Tony said if I ever made him eat another one he'd report me to his grandmother for feeding him sawdust."

The comment earned a full-blown, dazzling smile and Nick felt as though he'd been granted an award. Whatever nervousness Dana had been feeling seemed to be disappearing now that she had familiar tasks to do. She moved around the kitchen efficiently, asking for pans and utensils as she needed them. In less than half an hour, there were delicious aromas wafting from the stove.

"What are you making?"

"Coq au vin. Now," she said, "if you'll point out the dishes and silverware, I'll set the table."

"No, you won't. That's Tony's job. We'll take our tour now and send him in."

Nick anxiously watched the play of expressions on Dana's face as he led her through the downstairs of the house. For a man who'd never given a hang what anyone thought, he desperately wanted her approval. The realization surprised him. He held his breath until she exclaimed over the gleaming wide-plank wooden floors, the antiques that he and Ginny had chosen with such care, the huge fireplace that was cold now but had warmed many a winter night. The beveled mirror in a huge oak cabinet caught the sparkle in Dana's huge brown eyes as she ran her fingers lovingly over the intricate carving.

As they wandered, Missy, a haughty Siamese cat that belonged to no one but deigned to live with Nick, regarded them cautiously from her perch on the windowsill. Finally, she stood up and stretched lazily. To Nick's astonishment, the cat then jumped down and rubbed her head on Dana's ankle. Dana knelt down and scratched the cat under her chin, setting off a loud purring.

"That's amazing," Nick said. "Missy is not fond of people. She loved Ginny, but she barely tolerates me and Tony. Usually she ignores strangers."

"Perhaps she's just very selective," Dana retorted with a lift of one brow. "A wise woman is always discriminating."

"Is there a message in there for me?"

"Possibly." There was a surprising twinkle in her eyes when she said it.

"You wouldn't be trying to warn me away, would you?" he inquired lightly. "Because if you are, let me tell you something: I don't give up easily on the things I value."

Dana swallowed nervously, but it was the only hint she gave of her nervousness. She met his gaze steadily as she gracefully stood up after giving Missy a final pat.

Tension filled the air with an unending silence that strummed across Nick's nerves. Flames curled inside and sent heat surging through him. Desire swept over him with a power that was virtually irresistible. For the first time in years he recalled the intensity of unfulfilled passion, the need that could drive all other thoughts from your mind. He gazed at Dana and felt that aching need. Dana, so determinedly prim and proper in her severely tailored brown skirt and plain beige silk blouse, was every inch a classy lady, but she stirred a restless, wild yearning inside him.

It was Dana who broke the nerve-racking silence.

"You can't lose what you don't have," she said very, very quietly before moving on to the next room. Left off balance by the comment, Nick stayed behind for several minutes trying to gather his wits and calm his racing pulse.

By the time they found Tony, it was time to serve dinner. There was no time for a complete tour of the bedrooms. It was probably just as well, Nick told himself. The sight of Dana standing anywhere near his bed might have driven him to madness.

What caused this odd, insistent pull he felt toward her? Certainly it was more than her luxuriant hair and wide eyes, more than her long-limbed grace. Was it the vulnerability that lurked beneath the surface? Or was it as elusive as the sense that, for whatever reason, she was forbidden, out of reach? He'd been with her twice now, but he knew little more about her than the facts she'd put on her résumé. She talked, even joked, but revealed nothing. He wanted much more. He wanted to know what went on in her head, what made her laugh and why she cried. He wanted to discover everything there was to know about Dana Brantley.

Most infuriating of all to a man of his methodical, cautious ways, he didn't know why.

During dinner, Tony chattered away, basking in Dana's quiet attention, and Nick tried to puzzle out the attraction. Soon, though, the talk and laughter drew him in and he left the answers for another day.

Saturday. Only five days and he would have another

chance to discover the mysterious allure she held for him. Five days that, in his sudden impatience, yawned before him like an eternity.

Chapter 3

Dana spent the rest of the week thinking up excuses to get her out of Saturday night's date. None was as irrefutable—or as factual—as simply telling Nick quite firmly: *I don't want to go.* Unfortunately, each time she looked into Tony's excited eyes, she couldn't get those harsh words past her lips.

She searched for a word to describe the tumult she'd felt after her visit to Nick's place. Disquieting. That was it. Nick had been a gentleman, the perfect host. On the surface their conversational banter had been light, but there had been sensual undercurrents so swift that at times she had felt she'd be caught up and swept away. Nick's brand of gentle attentiveness spun a dangerous web that could hold the most unwilling woman captive until the seduction was complete.

Yet he'd never touched her, except for that one electrifying instant when she'd been accidentally trapped between him and the refrigerator. She'd anticipated something more when he walked her to her car, and her heart had thundered in her chest. But he'd simply held open the car door, then closed it gently behind her. Only his lazy, lingering gaze had seared her and made her blood run hot.

That heated examination was enough to get the message across with provocative clarity. Nick had more in mind for the two of them. He was only biding his time. The thought scared the daylights out of her. She'd been so sure she had built an impenetrable wall around her emotions, but in Nick's presence that wall was tumbling down. She didn't know quite how she'd ever build it up again.

On Friday she sat on her front porch rocking until long past midnight. Usually listening to the silence and counting the stars scattered across the velvet blanket of darkness soothed her. Every night since she'd come to River Glen, the flower-scented breeze had caressed her so gently that her muscles relaxed and she felt tension ease away. But tonight there was no magic. Cars filled with rowdy teenagers split the silence and clouds covered the stars. The humid night air was as still as death and, in her distraught, churning state of mind, just as ominous.

As a result, she was as nervous and tense when she went in to bed as she had been when she'd first settled into the rocker seeking comfort and an escape from her troubling thoughts. She tried reading, but the words swam before her exhausted eyes. When she turned out the light, she lay in the darkness, staring at the ceiling, first counting sheep, then going over the titles of her favorite books, then counting sheep again.

Although she waged an intense battle to keep the prospect of tomorrow's date out of her mind, it was always there, lurking about the fringes of her thoughts.

It's only one evening, she reminded herself. *Tony will be there. So will half the town, for that matter.*

But even one evening in the company of a man with a surprising power to unnerve her was too much. It loomed before her as an endless ordeal to be gotten through, even though it would drain whatever supreme courage she could still muster from her worn-down defenses. Nick was constantly at the center of her thoughts, and in these thoughts his casual touches branded her in a way that awed and frightened her at the same time.

In reality, he was doing nothing but flirting with her. But how long would it be before those touches became intense, demanding? How long before the pressure would start and the torment would curl inside her like a vicious serpent waiting to strike?

Finally exhaustion claimed her and she fell into a restless, uneasy slumber. Considering her state of mind, it wasn't surprising that she awoke in the middle of the night screaming, her throat hoarse, her whole body trembling and covered with sweat. She sat up in bed shaking, clutching the covers around her, staring blindly into the darkness for the threat that had seemed so real, so familiar. At last, still shivering but convinced it had been only a dream, she reached for the light by her bed to banish the last of the shadows. Her hand was shaking and tears streamed down her face unchecked.

Oh, God, please, when will it end? When will I be free of the memories?

Tonight was the first time in months the nightmare had returned. In her relief, she had even deluded herself that her bad dreams were a thing of the past, that they'd been left behind in a Manhattan skyscraper. She should have known that horror didn't die so easily. Perhaps it was simply because for the first time in months, she had failed to leave a night-light burning, something to keep away the ghosts that haunted her. She vowed never to make that mistake again.

It was hours before she slept again and noon before she woke. Six hours before Nick and Tony were due. Six hours to be gotten through with nerves stretched taut, her mind restless. More than once she reached for the phone to call Nick and cancel, but each time she hung it back up, labeling herself a coward.

It was her first date since Sam, and first times were always the hardest. After tonight, she hoped the jitters would go away, although with Nick Verone, it was quite possible—likely, in fact—that they'd only become worse.

"I can't do it," she muttered at last. "I can't go, if I'm going to jump like a frightened, inexperienced schoolgirl every time the man gets within an inch of me."

This time when she picked up the phone, her hand was steady, her determination intact. The resonant sound of Nick's voice seemed to set off distantly remembered echoes along her spine, but she managed to sound calm and relatively sure of herself when she greeted him.

"Nick, there's a problem." She hesitated, then hurried on. "I really don't think I'll be able to go with you tonight after all."

"Why?"

"I'm not feeling very well." That, at least, was no lie, but she discovered she was holding her breath as she awaited his reply.

"I'm sorry," he said, and she could hear the genuine regret, the stirring of compassion. He didn't for a single instant suspect her of lying. "Is it the flu? Do you need something from the pharmacy? I could run by the grocery store and pick up some soup or something if you need it."

His unquestioning concern immediately filled her with shame. She swallowed the guilty lump in her throat. "No, it's not the flu," she admitted, closing her eyes so she wouldn't have to look at herself in the mirror over the phone table. "I just had a bad night last night. I didn't get much sleep."

"Is that all?" Nick's relief was evident. "Then take a quick nap. It's only five o'clock now. I'll give you an extra half hour. We won't pick you up until six-thirty. We'll still have plenty of time."

"No, really." She rushed through the words. "I won't be very good company. I appreciate your asking. Maybe another time."

"Now you listen to me," he said, his voice dropping to its sexiest pitch, sliding over her persuasively. "This won't be a late night. I promise. Getting out will probably make you feel better. You'll forget whatever was on your mind, meet some new people, and tonight you'll catch up on your sleep."

Dana could almost envision him nodding his head decisively as he added, "No doubt about it. This is exactly what you need. I'm not taking no for an answer."

"But, Nick—"

"No buts. You're coming with us. If you're not ready

when we get there, we'll wait. And what about Tony?" he continued. "You don't want to disappoint him, do you?"

Dana felt the pressure build, but oddly she was almost relieved that Nick wasn't listening to her ridiculous excuses. She had blown this single date out of proportion. Nick was right about her getting out and meeting new people. Maybe it would be the best thing for her to do. Besides, he wasn't about to let up now that he had her on the ropes. She sighed and conceded defeat. "You really don't care what kind of sneaky, rotten tactics you use, do you?"

Nick merely chuckled at her grumbling. "Well, he would be disappointed, wouldn't he? That's the unvarnished truth. I was just trying to point that out to you before you made a dreadful mistake that would make you feel guilty for the rest of your life."

"Precisely. You knew it would work, unless I was on my deathbed, right?"

She could practically visualize Nick's satisfied grin. "It was worth a shot," he agreed. "Did it work?"

"It worked. Make it six-thirty. The idea of a nap sounds wonderful."

"See you then," he said cheerfully. "Sleep well."

"Sleep well," she mimicked when she'd replaced the receiver. Blast the man! The only way she'd sleep now would be to get this evening over with. So instead of lying down, she went to the tomato garden and furiously uprooted every weed she could spot. If she was going to have a temper tantrum, it might as well serve a useful purpose. The tantrum felt good, even if it was misdirected. She could just imagine what the townsfolk would say if she pulled the hairs from Nick Verone's overconfident head just as enthusiastically.

An hour later, after a soothing bubble bath, she dressed with unusual care, wanting to find exactly the right look for her first social appearance in River Glen. The fact that she was making it on the arm of the town's most eligible bachelor should have given her self-confidence. Instead, it made her quake.

Barbecue and bingo hardly called for a silk dress, but jeans were much too casual. She finally settled for a pale blue sleeveless cotton dress that bared the slightly golden tan of her arms but not much else. Its full skirt swirled about her legs. She wore low-heeled sandals, though she had a feeling three-inch heels might improve her confidence. Then she thought of all the times she'd dressed regally in New York and realized the clothes had made no difference at all.

This time she heard Nick's car drive up before she saw him. She'd been pacing from room to room, refusing to sit out on the porch, where it might seem she was waiting for him. Nick called through the screen door in back, rather than knocking, and the sound of his low drawl sent a shiver down her spine. Did she feel dread? Anticipation? Did she even know anymore?

When she came to the door his gaze swept over her appreciatively, then returned to linger on her face. A slow smile lit his rugged features, making him even more handsome.

"Yet another personality," he muttered cryptically.

Dana gave him a puzzled glance. "What does that mean?"

"Last Saturday you could have been a farmer, all covered with dirt and sweat."

She wrinkled her nose. "Sounds attractive. I'm surprised you asked me out."

A teasing glint appeared in his tawny eyes. "I knew you'd clean up good. Monday proved it. You could have been working on Wall Street instead of our library in that outfit. The only thing missing was the briefcase."

"And now?"

"I'm not sure. I only wish we were going square dancing, so that skirt could fly up and—"

"Never mind," she interrupted quickly. "I get the idea."

"I hope so," he said so softly it raised goose bumps on her arms. Unfortunately, her reaction was all too visible and Nick was rogue enough to take pleasure in it. He shot a very confident grin her way.

It was going to be a very long evening.

Despite his compliments and light flirting, Nick had noticed something else when Dana greeted him, something he politely didn't mention. The woman was exhausted. That story she'd spun on the phone to try to get out of their date hadn't been as manufactured as it had sounded. Underneath the skillful makeup, her complexion was ashen and there were deep, dark smudges under her eyes. Something was clearly troubling her, but he doubted if she'd bring it up and he had a feeling she wouldn't appreciate it if he did.

At Gracie's, where the tablecloths were plastic and the saltshakers were clogged because of the humidity, huge fans whirred overhead to stir the unseasonably sultry air. As they entered, every head in the place turned curiously to study the three of them with unabashed interest. Dana flinched imperceptibly under the scrutiny, but Nick caught her discomfort and they hurried straight to a table, rather than lingering to exchange greetings. He told himself there would be time enough for introductions at the fire station.

"So, what's it gonna be, Nick?" Carla Redding asked, stepping up to the table and leaning down just enough to display her ample cleavage.

Nick grinned at her and never once let his gaze wander lower than her round, rosy-cheeked face. "Are you trying to hustle us out of here in a hurry tonight, so you can pick up more tips? We haven't even seen the menu."

Carla straightened up and tugged a pencil out from behind her ear. "Menu hasn't changed in ten years, as you know perfectly well, since you eat here at least twice a week."

"But we have a newcomer with us tonight. This is Dana Brantley, the new librarian. Dana, meet Carla Redding. She owns this place."

"But I thought this was Gracie's," she said, as Nick chuckled at Dana's obvious confusion.

Carla grinned. "It was Gracie's when I bought it ten years ago. Saw no need to change it. Just mixes people up. You need to see a menu, honey?"

"Nick claims you have the best barbecue around, so I suppose I ought to have that."

"Good choice," Nick said. "We'll have four barbecue sandwiches." He glanced at Tony, who seemed to be growing at the rate of an inch a day lately. "Nope. Better make that five. Some coleslaw, french fries and how about some apple pie? Did you do any baking today?"

"I've got one hidden in the back just for you," she said with a wink as she ruffled Tony's hair. Nick glanced over to check Dana's reaction to Carla's deter-

minedly provocative display of affection. He and Carla
had gone through school together. There was nothing
between them—not now, not ever. But from the look
on Dana's face, he doubted she'd believe it.

As soon as Carla had gone back to the kitchen, Dana
commented, "Interesting woman."

"She and Dad are old friends," Tony offered innocently.

"I'll bet."

Nick chuckled. "Her husband's a friend of mine, too.
Jack has the size and temperament of a tanker. Carla
just loves to flirt outrageously with all her male customers. She says it keeps Jack on his toes."

She grinned back. "I don't doubt it for a minute. She's
very convincing."

Nick feigned astonishment and leaned over to whisper in her ear, "Don't tell me you were jealous?"

"Of course not," she denied heatedly.

But from that moment on, to Nick's dismay the evening went from bad to worse. Rather than the natural, somewhat aggrieved banter he'd come to expect,
Dana was making an effort to be polite and pleasant.
Her laughter was strained and all too often her attention seemed to wander to a place where Nick couldn't
follow. Only with Tony was she completely at ease. A
lesser man's ego might have been shattered, but Dana's
behavior merely perplexed Nick.

Even in the small, friendly crowd at bingo, Dana
seemed alienated and nervous, as though torn between
wanting to make a good impression and a desire to retreat. Somehow he knew she suffered from more than
shyness, but he couldn't imagine what the problem was.

When he could stand the awkwardness no longer, he

suggested they take a walk. Dana glanced up from her bingo card in surprise. They were in the middle of a game and she had four of five spaces for a diagonal win.

"Now?" she said.

"Sure. I need some air." He saw her gaze go immediately to Tony, so he said, "You'll be okay here for a few minutes, won't you, son?"

"Sure, Dad. I'll play your cards for you." He looked as though he could hardly wait to get a shot at Dana's.

With obvious reluctance Dana got to her feet and followed him outside. There was the clean scent of rain in the air. Thunder rumbled ominously in the distance.

"Seems like there's a storm brewing," he said, as they strolled side by side until the sounds from the fire station became a distant murmur.

"It is April, after all," she replied.

The inconsequential conversation suddenly grated across his nerves. Nick was a direct man. Too direct for politics, some said. He had a feeling that's what they'd be saying if they could see him now, but he couldn't keep his thoughts to himself another second.

"What's troubling you, Dana? You've been jumpy as a cat on a hot tin roof all night."

"Sorry."

He felt an unfamiliar urge to shake her until the truth rattled loose. In fact, he reached for her shoulders but restrained himself at the last instant, stunned by what he'd been about to do. No woman had ever driven him to such conflicting feelings of helplessness and rage before. "Dammit, I don't want you to apologize. I want to help. Did I do something to upset you?"

Astonishment registered in her brown eyes before she could conceal it. "Why would you think that?"

"I don't know. Maybe it's just the way you went all silent after I teased you about being jealous back at Gracie's. You haven't said more than two words at a time since then except to Tony."

"Jealousy is a very negative emotion," she responded slowly, her expression distant again. "It's not something I like to joke about."

"I take it you've had some experience."

She nodded, but it was clear no personal confidences would be forthcoming. She had that closed look in her eyes, and it tore at him to see anyone hurting and seemingly so alone. The depth of his protectiveness startled him. It hinted of the sweet and abiding passion he'd felt only once before, with Ginny, whom he'd known all his life and who had hidden a gentle heart behind a determinedly tough tomboy facade. She'd accepted his protection only at the end, when cancer had riddled her body with pain.

Somehow he knew that Dana would be just as unwilling to permit him to take up her battles. Despite her vulnerability she had a resilience that he admired. He had been intrigued by her even before they'd met, because of her kindness to Tony. It had been uncalculated giving, unlike so many attempts he'd seen by single women to reach him through his son. Tony had sung her praises for days before Nick decided to meet her for himself. Her leaky roof had been no more than an excuse at first. Now he wondered if it might be the only link she would permit.

Suddenly Nick realized that Dana was shivering. He hadn't noticed that the wind had picked up and that the air had cooled considerably as the storm blew in. He also hadn't realized just how far they'd walked while he tried to sort out his thoughts.

"You're cold," he said. "Let's go back."

"Would you mind terribly if we just got Tony and left?"

Nick sighed. "I hope it's not because I've stuck my foot in my mouth again."

"No. It's just that it's getting late and I really am tired."

Nick studied her face closely. He wanted to trace the shadows under her eyes, run his fingers along the delicate curve of her jaw, but he held back from that as cautiously as he'd kept himself from that more violent urge.

"Fine," he said eventually. "I'll get Tony."

The storm began with a lashing fury as he walked Dana back to the car. Nick took her hand and they broke into a run, hurrying to the relative safety of a darkened doorway. Both of them were soaked through, and as they huddled side by side, Nick's gaze fell on the way Dana's dress clung to her breasts. The peaks had hardened in the chilly air and jutted against the damp fabric. Tension coiled inside him. Dana shivered again and before he had a chance to consider what he was doing, he drew her into his arms.

She went absolutely rigid in his embrace. "Nick." His name came out as a choked entreaty.

"Shh. It's okay," he murmured, wondering how anything that felt so right to him could possibly scare her so. And he didn't doubt that she was afraid. He felt it in her frozen stance, saw the startled nervousness that had leaped into her eyes at his touch. "I just want to keep you warm until we can make a break for the car."

"I-I'll b-b-be fine."

"Your teeth are chattering."

"N-n-no, they're n-not," she said, defiant to the end. She struggled against him.

"Dana." This time his voice was thick with emotion and an unspoken plea.

Her gaze shot up and clashed with his. Then she held herself perfectly still, and he felt her slowly begin to relax in his arms.

The rain pounded down harder than ever, creating a gray, wet sheet that secluded them from the rest of the world. Nick could have stayed like that forever. Holding Dana in his arms felt exactly as he'd imagined it would. Her body fit his perfectly, the soft contours molding themselves to the hard planes of his own overheated flesh. He felt the sharp stirring in his loins again and wondered if he could fight it by concentrating on the distant sounds of laughter and shouts of victory drifting from the fire station down the block.

"Nick?" Her tentative voice whispered down his spine like the fingers of an expert masseuse.

"Yes."

"I have to get home." The words held an odd urgency. At his puzzled expression, she added, "The roof."

"The roof," he repeated blankly, still lost in the sensations that were rippling through him.

"I put the pots and pans away. The whole place will be flooded if this keeps up."

"Right. The roof." Reluctantly, he released her. He looked into the velvet brown of her eyes and saw that miraculously the panic had fled, but he wasn't sure how to describe the complexity of the emotion that had replaced it. Surprise, dismay, acceptance. Any of those or maybe all of them. Relief and hope flooded through him.

"You wait here. I'll go back for Tony and the car."

"I'm already drenched. I can come with you."

With her words, his eyes were drawn back to the swell of her breast, unmistakably detailed by her clinging dress. He held out his hand, and after an instant's hesitation, she took it.

"Let's run for it," he said, and they took off, her long-legged strides keeping up with his intentionally shortened paces. Rain pelted them with the force of hailstones, but they splashed through the puddles with all the abandon of a couple of kids. For the first time all night Dana seemed totally at ease.

When they reached the car, she moaned softly. "Your upholstery."

"Will survive," he said. "Now get in there. I think I have a blanket in the trunk. I'll get it for you."

He found an old sandy beach blanket and shook it out before draping it around her shaking shoulders.

"Is that better?"

"Much, thanks." She smiled up at him with the first unguarded expression he'd seen on her face all night. It had been worth the wait and he was tempted to stay and bask in its warmth.

Instead, he nodded. "Good. I'll be back in a minute with Tony."

He walked into the fire station and scanned the room for his son. Water ran down his face in rivulets and squished from his shoes. Puddles formed where he stood.

Betsy Markham sashayed up and gave him a sweet, innocent smile. "Been for a walk?"

"Something like that."

"And here I always thought you have sense enough

to come in out of the rain, Nicholas. Must be a pretty girl involved."

"Could be, Betsy."

Suddenly her expression turned serious and she wagged a finger under his nose. "You see to it that gal doesn't get pneumonia, Nick Verone, or I'll have your hide."

A chuckle rumbled up through his chest. He grabbed Betsy by the shoulders and planted a kiss on her cheek. She smelled of talcum powder and lily of the valley, just as his mother always had. His hands left wet marks on her shoulders, but she gave him a wink as she went back to her place beside her husband. Nick watched as the intent expression on Harry's face changed to delight when he looked up and saw Betsy. He saw Harry's arm slip affectionately around her waist for a quick squeeze before his attention went back to the game.

"Hey, Dad, what happened to you?" Tony regarded his father with astonishment. "You're dripping all over everything."

"In case you haven't noticed, it's raining outside. Dana and I got caught in it. We've got to get her home."

"Aw, Dad, come on. It's early. Why don't I wait here? You can come back for me." He cast an all-too-knowing look up at his father. "You and Ms. Brantley probably want to be alone, anyway, right? I mean, that's how you got wet in the first place, trying to be alone with her."

Nick managed a stern expression, though he was fighting laughter. Ignoring Tony's incredibly accurate assessment of his desires with regard to Dana, he said firmly, "You'll come with us now."

Tony knew that no-nonsense tone of voice. He shrugged and headed for the door without another protest. Nick stared after his son and wondered what perversity of his own nature had made him insist that Tony come with him.

"It's for the best," he muttered under his breath and he knew it was true. He wanted Dana Brantley, and without Tony along he might very well ruin things by showing her that. Whatever trust had just been born was still too fragile to be tested by any aggressive moves.

The rain let up as they drove to Dana's place. When he pulled up in front and shut off the engine, she turned to him. "You don't have to walk me in."

"Yes, I do. You could have a foot of water inside."

"I can take care of it."

"I'm sure you can, but why should you, when Tony and I can help?" He was out of the car before she could utter another protest. "Son, you wait here a minute until I check things out. If we need you, I'll yell."

"Right, Dad," Tony said agreeably, though there was a smirk on his face.

Dana was already up the walk and around the side of the house. He caught up with her as she tried to put the key in the door. It was pitch-dark and her hands were shaking. She kept missing the lock. Nick nudged her aside. "Let me."

"I forgot to leave the light on."

"No problem." The door swung open. He reached in and flipped on the kitchen and outdoor lights. "Let's check the damage."

There were pools of water on the floor in at least half a dozen places. "Where's your mop?"

"I'll do it," she insisted obstinately, a scowl on her face. "It's not that bad."

He planted his feet more firmly and glowered down

at her. "You are without a doubt the stubbornest woman I have ever met."

Dana glared back at him. "And you're the stubbornest man I've ever met, so where does that leave us?"

"With a wet floor, unless you'll get the mop."

She whirled around and stomped away, returning with the sponge mop and a bucket. He grinned at her. "Thank you."

She perched on the edge of a chair and watched him work, a puzzled expression in her eyes. "I've been perfectly rotten to you all night and you're still hanging around. I don't understand it. Are you afflicted with some sort of damsel-in-distress syndrome?"

"Not that I know of."

"Then it must be a straightforward, macho mentality."

"Maybe I'm just a nice guy. You don't have to be macho to wield a mop."

"Exactly my point. I could have done this."

"Do you have some sort of independence syndrome?" he countered.

"As a matter of fact, I do," she said so softly that his head snapped up and he stared at her. Suddenly he realized that whatever was wrong went far beyond who mopped the floor.

"What happened to you that makes you want to close out people who care about you?"

She appeared disconcerted by the directness of the question. "That's none of your business."

"It is if I'm going to get to know you better."

"Like I said, it's none of your business." She got up and walked back into the kitchen, leaving Nick to mop alone and mull over the conversation. He'd just been granted an important clue to Dana's personality. Now he had only to figure out what it meant.

When he finished, he found Dana sitting at the kitchen table, her chin propped in her hand. She was staring out the door, a faraway expression in her eyes. Nick wanted to pull up a chair right then and finish their talk, but with Tony in the car, he couldn't. He'd already left him out there alone too long.

"I'll come over tomorrow and work on the roof," he announced quietly. Dana looked up at him, and for an instant, a challenge flared in her eyes. Then it died. She nodded, and for some reason Nick considered her acquiescence a major victory. He had the strangest sensation that she'd been unconsciously testing him all evening and that without knowing exactly how, he'd passed.

She stood up and walked him to the door, standing on the top step so that her eyes were even with his.

"Thank you," she said in a low whisper, pitched to match the night's quiet serenity now that the storm had gone.

"Did you have a good time, really?"

"Of course. It was my first chance to meet so many people. I enjoyed it."

The words were polite, the tone flat. Nick pressed a finger to her lips, wanting to silence the lies. He smiled. "Then maybe next time you'll look a little happier."

Dana flushed in embarrassment. "I'm sorry. I didn't realize…" She sighed. "I didn't mean to be rude."

"No, I'm the one who's sorry. I shouldn't have made such a big deal of it. Maybe sometime you'll tell me what really went wrong tonight."

"Nick—"

"Shh." He rubbed his finger across the soft flesh of her lips. "Don't deny it. Please."

Her eyes brimmed with tears, and she swiped at them with the same angry motion as a child who shows weakness when he craves bravery. She would have turned away to hide the raw emotion in her eyes, but Nick caught her chin and held her face steady before him.

"You're so beautiful, Dana Brantley. Inside and out. How could any woman as lovely as you have so much to be sad about?"

He caught a tiny flicker of something in her eyes—surprise, perhaps, that he'd guessed at the sadness that hid under her cool demeanor and quiet laughter. She licked her lips nervously and he couldn't take his eyes from the ripe moistness.

But when he leaned forward to kiss her, his heart pounding and his pulse racing, she pulled away, turning her face aside. Intuitively he knew it wasn't a coy reaction. There had been a real panic in her eyes. Again. He felt a hurt, one he imagined was every bit as great as hers, building up inside. God, he'd give anything to make things better for her, to make those smiles come more frequently, to hear the laughter without the restraint.

But Nick hadn't made a success of himself in business without knowing when to back away, when to let a deal simmer until the other person was just as hungry for a resolution. In time Dana would acknowledge that her hunger for him ran just as deep, was just as powerful as his was for her.

He brushed away a lone tear as it glistened on her cheek. "Good night, pretty lady. I'll see you in the morning."

He had nearly turned the corner of the house before he heard her faint response carried by the breeze.

"Goodbye, Nick."

There was a finality in her voice that sent a shiver down his spine. It also fueled his determination. This would not be an ending for them. It was just the beginning.

Chapter 4

"Don't you like my dad?" Tony asked Dana with all the disconcerting candor of an irrepressible ten-year-old. She came very close to choking on the glazed doughnut they'd just shared as they sat on her back step.

At least he'd waited until they were alone to start his cross-examination. Nick was on the roof, stripping off the old shingles. It was Sunday morning, and Tony and Nick had been on her doorstep practically at dawn, a bag of fresh doughnuts and a huge, intimidating toolbox in hand. Her eyes had met Nick's, then darted away as an unexpected thrill had coursed through her. She tried to recapture that sensation, so she could assess it rationally, but Tony was staring at her, waiting for her answer.

"He's very nice," Dana equivocated. Tony looked disappointed by the lukewarm praise.

Damn it all, the man was more than nice, she acknowledged to herself, even though she absolutely refused to acknowledge it aloud. Last night she had been rude and withdrawn without fully understanding why, but Nick had shown only compassion in return. She had sensed his struggle to understand behavior that must have seemed decidedly odd to him.

No doubt most women were eager for an involvement with one of the most powerful, eligible men in River Glen. At some other time in her life, she might have been one of them, but now that was impossible. She had nothing but trouble to bring to a relationship. And she knew as well as anyone that involvement always began with something as sweet and innocent as a kiss.

She'd given marriage a chance. Sam Brantley had been handsome, charming and brilliant—a real catch, as Betsy would say. There had been a classic explosion of chemistry the night they met, followed by a storybook courtship, then a lavish wedding and an idyllic honeymoon.

Dana had been twenty-three, only months away from receiving her master's degree, but she had given up school willingly to help Sam meet the social obligations of a young lawyer on the rise in a prestigious New York firm. They were the perfect couple, living in the best East Side condo, spending much of their spare time with the right friends at gala events for the most socially acceptable charities.

It had been slightly less than a year before the reality set in, before the pressures of keeping up began to take their toll. By their first anniversary, their marriage was already in trouble. It took much longer to end it.

She closed her eyes against the rest of the memories, the months of torment that had turned into years. It was over now. The past couldn't hurt her anymore unless she allowed it. And she wouldn't. She had put it behind her with a vow it would stay locked away forever.

"Are you okay?" Tony's brow was furrowed by a worried frown. "You look all funny."

"I'm just fine," she said as cheerfully as she could manage.

Tony looked doubtful but then plunged on with determination. "Then explain about my dad. If you think he's nice, how come you didn't kiss him last night? I know he wanted you to."

Dana was torn between indignation and laughter. "Tony Verone, were you spying on us?"

"I wasn't spying," he denied, his cheeks reddening with embarrassment. "Not the way you mean. Dad was gone a long time. I got tired of waiting in the car by myself. I decided to come check on him. That's all. That's not really spying."

"Your father would tan your hide if he knew what you'd done."

"No, he wouldn't," Tony said with absolute confidence. "He never spanks me. He says people should be able to talk out their differences, even kids and parents."

It sounded as though he were quoting an oft-repeated conversation. The significance of Nick's philosophy of discipline registered in a corner of Dana's mind and she stored it away. She regarded Tony closely. "In that case, you'd be getting quite a lecture, wouldn't you?"

Tony met her gaze with a defiant challenge in his eyes, then hung his head guiltily. "Probably."

"Then I've made my point."

"Yeah. I guess."

"Now that that's settled, why don't you go inside and do your book report?"

"Okay," he said a little too agreeably, getting up from the step and heading inside. He opened the screen door, then gazed back at her inquisitively. "You're not really mad, are you?"

Dana smiled. "No, I'm not really mad."

Tony nodded in satisfaction. "So, are you going to kiss him next time?"

"Tony!"

"Yes, ma'am," he said politely, but there was an impertinent glint in his eyes that reminded her very much of his father.

Dana had to turn her face away to hide her smile until Tony had gone into the house. The kid was something else. Would she kiss his father next time? What a question!

Well, will you? a voice inside her head nagged.

"No, dammit," she said aloud, then glanced around quickly to make sure that no one had caught her talking to herself.

"Who are you talking to down there?" a voice inquired from above her head.

"I was just asking if you wanted something to drink," she improvised hurriedly.

"Oh, is *that* what you said?" Nick's voice was filled with amusement.

Maybe she should have a talk with him about eavesdropping. Then again, maybe there had been all too much talk around here this morning as it was.

She stepped out into the yard, then shielded her eyes from the sun as she scowled up at the roof. "Well, do you want something or not?"

He came to the edge, moving gingerly around the weak spots. Dana gazed at him and her breath caught in her throat. He'd stripped off his shirt as he worked and his tanned, well-muscled shoulders were glistening with sweat. Dark hairs swirled in a damp mass on his broad chest and narrowed provocatively down to the waistband of his jeans.

"I'd love some lemonade," he said.

"I don't think I have any," she murmured in a distracted tone, fighting the surprisingly strong urge to climb straight up to the roof so she could run her fingers over his bare flesh. She hadn't felt this powerful, aching need to touch and be touched in a very long time.

"I thought everybody had lemonade."

"What?" she said blankly, forcing her eyes back to his. That was a mistake, too, because there was a very knowing gleam in their hazel depths.

"I said I thought everybody had lemonade," he repeated tolerantly.

Dana clenched her fists, now fighting a desire not just to touch but to strangle the man. "Not me. Your choices are juice, iced tea, diet soda or water."

"But I have a yen for..." His eyes roamed over her boldly before he added with slow deliberation, "Lemonade."

"Nick," she snapped impatiently.

He chuckled at her obvious discomfort, apparently enjoying the heightened color in her cheeks. "Send Tony to the store. He can run up there and back in fifteen minutes."

"He's inside, doing his homework. If you can't live without lemonade, I'll go."

"Tony!" he called as though she'd never spoken.

The back door crashed open all too quickly and Dana got the oddest sensation that Tony had been waiting just inside. His refusal to meet her gaze as he stepped out to look up at his father virtually confirmed it.

"What do you need, Dad?"

"How about running to the store for me?" Nick climbed down the ladder, dug in his pocket and gave Tony some money and a list of provisions long enough to stock a refrigerator for a month.

When he'd gone, Dana glowered at Nick. "Why did you do that? I could have gone."

"But then we wouldn't have had a few minutes alone." He stepped toward her. Dana held her ground, but her pulse began to race.

"A few minutes? It'll take him the better part of an hour to get all those things. Are you planning to feed an entire army?"

"Just us. I'm very hungry," he retorted, drawing the words out to an insinuating suggestiveness. "And I want to know, just as much as Tony does, why you didn't kiss me."

Dana swallowed nervously. "I don't kiss men I don't know well." She sounded extraordinarily self-righteous and absurdly Victorian, even to her own ears.

"Whose fault is it we don't know each other better? I'm trying to change that." He took another step toward her. This time she backed up instinctively.

"Why did you do that?" he asked, and she could see he was more curious than angry.

"Do what?"

"Move away from me." A frown knit his brow. "Do I frighten you?"

"Of course not."

"Liar," he accused gently. "I do, don't I?"

"Don't be absurd."

He stood perfectly still, like a hunter waiting for his prey to be disarmed and drawn into his range. "Then let me kiss you, Dana."

His voice was a quiet plea that set off a violent trembling inside her. He wooed her with that voice.

"Dana, I'm not going to hurt you. Not ever."

There was so much tenderness in his voice. It touched a place deep inside her and filled her with unexpected warmth. Her eyes widened in anticipation, but he didn't move.

Finally, he sighed. "Someday, I hope you'll believe me."

His hand trembling, he brushed his knuckles gently along her cheek, then started back up the ladder. After he'd turned away, her hand went to her cheek and stayed there. With unwilling fascination, she watched the bunching of his muscles as Nick reached over his head to pull himself onto the roof. She heard the hammering begin again, and then, finally, she went inside, her knees as weak as if she'd just escaped from some terrible danger.

And she had. Nick Verone was getting to her. She could deny it all she liked. She could hold him at arm's length, but she knew perfectly well what was happening between them, and for the first time she began to sense the inevitability of it. She almost regretted not letting Nick kiss her now, not getting the agony of anticipation over with.

His backing off, however, both puzzled and pleased her. She had no doubt that Nick desired her. She'd seen the rise of heat in his eyes. But his willingness to wait told her quite a lot about his character and his patience. If they were ever to have a chance, he needed to have both.

To Dana it was soon apparent that Nick had more character than patience. Oblivious to her determination to avoid a relationship—or simply choosing to ignore her wishes, which was more likely—Nick Verone persisted in his pursuit throughout the following week. She had to give him credit. He was subtle and wily and he wasn't one bit above using Tony as his intermediary. He'd sensed that Tony was her weakness, that she would no more see the boy hurt than he would. It was Tony, as often as not, who suggested a drive in the country after the library doors were closed for the day. Or the fishing after Nick had spent an hour or two working on the roof. Or the twilight picnics on the beach.

With Tony along, she began to relax. By the end of the week she found that she was enjoying herself, smiling more frequently, laughing more freely, no longer frightened by shadows. She was actually disappointed when neither of them suggested an outing for the weekend.

On Saturday morning, feeling thoroughly disgruntled and furious because she felt that way, she pulled on her dirt-streaked gardening shorts and tied her sleeveless shirt just under her breasts. As soon as she'd finished her coffee, she went outside to tackle the thick tangle of weeds in the bed of tiger lilies. Sitting on the still damp grass, she yanked and grumbled.

"So, you don't have plans for the weekend. Big deal. You're the one who doesn't want to get involved."

The bright tiger lilies trembled in the stiff breeze

coming off the river, but whatever opinion they might have had, they kept to themselves.

"Not talking, huh? That's okay. I can keep myself company." Had it been only a week ago that she'd craved being alone? Had it taken so little time for Nick to overcome her caution and become a welcome part of her life? "You made a humdinger of a mistake last time, Dana Brantley. Don't do it again."

"Talking to yourself again?" Nick inquired softly.

Dana's head snapped around so quickly she almost got whiplash. "Where do you have your car's engine tuned? Your mechanic must be a genius. I didn't even hear you drive up."

"No car," he said, pointing to the very obvious bike he was holding upright by its handlebars. His gaze traveled slowly over her, lingering on the expanse of golden skin between her blouse and shorts. "Nice outfit."

"You commented on it before. I believe you referred to it as my farmer look."

"I take it back. You're prettier than any farmer I ever saw, though I know a couple of farmers' wives who'd give you a run for your money."

"I'll just bet you do."

Nick pulled the bike onto the grass and laid it on its side, then headed for the house. Dana stared after him in exasperation. He was doing it again, just dropping in and taking over as though he belonged. One of these days they were going to have a very noisy confrontation about his behavior.

"Where are you going?" she inquired testily.

"To get some coffee. You have some made, don't you?"

"Of course, but…"

He was out of sight before she could finish her protest. "Back in a minute," he called over his shoulder.

Sparks flashed in her eyes, but just as she was about to stand up and go storming in the house after him, he shouted out, "Hey, do you want any?"

"Nice of you to ask," she grumbled under her breath. She peered in the direction of the kitchen and called back, "No."

She yanked a few more weeds out of the ground and tossed them aside with more force than was necessary. A colorful variety of names for the man now in her kitchen paraded through her mind. "Why don't you speak up and tell him he's driving you crazy?" she muttered aloud.

But she knew she wouldn't. She couldn't face the potential explosiveness of angry threats, the tension that made your heart pound, even the mild stomach-churning sensation of seeing control slip away.

"How long are you planning to be at that?" Nick suddenly inquired, hunkering down beside her.

Dana jumped a good three inches off the ground. "Dammit, Nick. Stop sneaking up on me."

"Sorry." He didn't look one bit sorry. "What's on your agenda for the day?"

"I don't have an agenda." She paused thoughtfully. "Do you know this is practically the first time in my life I can say that? First it was ballet lessons, then gymnastics, then piano. By the time I got to high school, it was cheerleading, half a dozen clubs and tennis lessons. College was more of the same and my marriage was a merry-go-round of luncheons and dinner parties and bridge. I don't think I ever had ten unscheduled minutes until I moved here."

"Good, then you can come with me."

Dana regarded him warily. "Where?"

"I thought we might go for a long bike ride."

"Don't you have things to do?"

"Nothing that appeals to me more than spending the day with you."

"Where's Tony?"

"He's at a friend's." He draped his arm casually over her shoulders and squeezed. "It's just you and me, kid."

The phrase reverberated through her head and set off warning signals, but that was nothing compared to the skyrockets set off by his touch. She started to look at Nick but realized he was much too close and turned away. She'd have been staring straight at his lips and she had a feeling she wouldn't be able to hide her fascination with them. Ever since she'd avoided his kiss after bingo and again on Sunday, she'd been wondering what his lips would have felt like, imagined them brushing lightly across her mouth or kissing the sensitive spot on her neck, just below her ear.

"I don't have a bike."

"No problem. You can borrow Tony's."

"I haven't ridden in years."

"It's something you never forget."

"But my legs are in terrible condition." Nick's dubious expression as his eyes traveled the length of said legs almost made her laugh, but she rushed on. "I wouldn't make it around the block."

"We'll only ride until you get tired."

"If we ride until I can't go any farther, how will we get back?"

"Hopefully you'll have the good sense to complain

in front of some nice, air-conditioned restaurant so we can have lunch while you recuperate."

"We may need to have dinner and breakfast before that happens."

"I can live with that," he said with a dangerously wicked sparkle in his eyes. "Just be sure to collapse in front of an inn."

Dana laughed, suddenly feeling a carefree, what-the-hell sensation ripple pleasantly through her. It had been a long time since she'd done anything on the spur of the moment. "I give up. You have an answer for everything, don't you?"

"I am a very determined man," he replied so solemnly that her heart raced. She avoided his clear-eyed, direct gaze as she got to her feet.

"Let me take these weeds to the garbage and change. Then I'll be all set."

"I'll take the weeds. You go and get dressed."

A half hour later, after a wobbly start on Dana's part, they were on the road. Once she got the hang of riding again, it felt terrific. The spring sun was warm on her shoulders, the breeze cool on her face.

"This is wonderful," she called out to Nick, who was riding ahead of her past a huge brown field that was dotted with corn seedlings. He dropped back to ride beside her.

"Aren't you glad I didn't pay any attention to your excuses again?"

"Very."

"Can I ask you something?"

"Of course."

"Why do you need the excuses in the first place? Do you really want me to back off?"

Dana's heart thudded slowly in her chest. She met Nick's curious gaze and her pedaling faltered. She caught herself just before the bike went out of control. Staring straight ahead, she finally said, "It probably would be for the best."

"Best for whom? Not for me. I've enjoyed being with you the past few days. It's been a long time since I felt this way."

"What way?"

He seemed to be searching for words. The ones he found were eloquent. "As though my life was filled with possibilities again. When Ginny died, I didn't think I'd ever care for another woman. We'd had a lifetime together and that was important to me. We'd played together, tended to each other's cuts and bruises, gone to school together. We'd grown up together. There were no secrets, no surprises. We were blessed with love and understanding and we were blessed with Tony."

Dana heard the sorrow behind Nick's words, but she also heard the joy. For the first time in her life she was struck by an envy so sharp it rocked her. She wanted to share somehow in that enviable life Nick had led.

"Tell me about Ginny," she said, a catch in her voice.

Nick studied her closely. "Are you sure you want to hear about her?"

"Absolutely. I want to know what she was like, what you loved about her."

He nodded. "Okay, but let's get to a stopping place first."

A few hundred feet farther down the road, he pulled into the gravel parking lot in front of a small country store and gas station.

"I'll get us some soft drinks and a couple of sandwiches, okay?"

"Fine."

Dana propped her bike against the weathered side of the store and stared around her at the recently planted fields that were just beginning to turn green. She felt the same sense of peace and continuity she'd experienced when she'd discovered River Glen. She wanted to draw that feeling inside, to capture it and put her heart at rest. The air was heavy with the rich scent of the fields, the sun was hot on her skin, and she felt more contented than she had in years.

When Nick came out a few minutes later, she realized he was becoming a part of her contentment. There were no jarring notes with Nick, only an easygoing calm that fit well with the surroundings. If only that calm were real, she might dare to hope again.

"There's a place up ahead where we can sit under the trees for a while," he said, and led the way.

When they were settled on the cool grass, he opened the bag and handed her a drink, then held out the sandwiches. "Ham and cheese or tuna?"

"Ham and cheese," she said instantly.

Nick made a face. "I should have known."

"Is that what you wanted? Take it. I like tuna just as well."

"No you don't or you would have asked for it. Take the ham and cheese."

"We'll split them." She was proud of her ingenuity until she caught the expression in Nick's eyes. "What?"

"Why do you do that? Why do you go to such lengths to avoid an argument?"

Dana stared down at the ground. "I wasn't aware

that's what I was doing. I just thought it would be nicer if we shared."

He shook his head. "It's more than that. There have been times in the past week when I know you've been furious with me...." He waved aside her instinctive denial. "No. It's true. But you've never once done more than snap a little. Sometimes I want to do outrageous things, just to see how you'll react."

"I don't see much point in arguing."

"Not even when you have a valid difference of opinion?"

"It depends on how important it is. If it's something that doesn't matter, like the sandwiches, it's easier to give in."

"And that's all it is?"

"What else could it be?" she said, retreating behind her shuttered expression again.

Nick felt like pounding the earth or snatching the damn tuna sandwich out of her hands. He wanted, just once, to see her reach her limits and say exactly what she thought, instead of tiptoeing around anything that wasn't pleasant.

It was Dana who broke the silence. "Do you realize how absurd we sound? We're sitting here fighting because I don't like to argue."

"I don't want to fight with you, Dana. I just want to be sure you're not afraid to say what you mean with me. You're entitled to your opinion, even when we disagree. That's what makes life interesting. If we agreed on every single thing, we'd be bored to tears in no time."

"You may be sorry you said that."

"Oh?"

"Once I get started, I might give you a very rough time."

"I'll survive."

Dana nodded. "Okay, Mr. Verone, from now on, you'll only hear the unvarnished truth from me. Now, you were going to tell me about Ginny."

"So I was."

Nick leaned back against the tree and let his mind drift back over the years of his marriage, over the entire lifetime he'd shared with Ginny. With three years of perspective, he could finally recall the good times, rather than dwell on those last painful months.

"She was someone very special," he said at last. A faint smile lit his face. "I remember once when we were maybe six or seven. My mom had bought strawberries to make strawberry shortcake for a big family dinner. Ginny was crazy about strawberries and she saw them sitting on the kitchen table and she couldn't resist. She climbed up on a chair and started eating. I kept begging her to get down, but she wouldn't. She just sat there with bright red juice all over her face and hands, stuffing them in.

"Then my mom came in. Oh, boy, was there hell to pay. Ginny just listened to her, then said, bold as you please, 'Nick dared me to.'"

Dana grinned. "I suppose you're the one who got punished."

"I spent the rest of the day in my room." He chuckled. "But it wasn't so bad. Ginny climbed a tree right outside the window and talked to me till suppertime."

"Did you always know you wanted to marry her?"

Nick grew thoughtful. "I think I did. I know there was never anyone else. I never met another woman who had her spirit, who reached out and grabbed the day and held on to it until she'd lived every single moment. Yet, for all that fire, she was also very gentle and caring."

He glanced up and met Dana's eyes, caught the tears shimmering in them. "In so many ways, you remind me of her."

Dana was shaking her head. "No, you're wrong. I'm not like that at all."

"I think you are. I see it in everything you do."

"But I don't take risks. You said it yourself. I just drift along, trying to keep things on an even keel."

He regarded her perceptively. "But I don't think you were always like that."

Dana closed her eyes as if to ward off some pain inflicted by his words. He reached over and touched her cheek, his callused thumb following the line of her jaw.

"Dana," he said softly.

Her eyes opened and a tear slid along her cheek.

"That is the woman I see when I look at you."

"You're wrong," she protested. "I wish I were like that, but I'm not."

"Then use my eyes as your mirror," he said gently. "See yourself as I do."

He knelt on the ground beside her, and this time when he lowered his head to kiss her she didn't pull away. Her lips trembled beneath his, then parted on a sigh. She tasted of sunshine and tears, a blend as intoxicating as champagne. He felt her restraint in the rigid way she held her body, in the stiffness of her shoulders, but her mouth was his, and for now, it was enough.

Chapter 5

Over the next few days, Nick thought about very little besides that kiss. It had brought him an incredible depth of satisfaction. He recalled in heart-stopping detail the velvet touch of Dana's lips against his, the moist fire of her tongue, the sweetness of her breath. The memory of each second stirred a joy and longing in him that went far beyond the physical implications of a single kiss.

Each time he replayed the scene in his mind it sent fire raging through his blood. He felt like an adolescent. His body responded to provocative images as easily as it had to the reality. Far more important, however, that kiss had told him that Dana was beginning to trust him. He was wise enough to see that earning Dana's trust in full would be no easy task.

As anxious as any lover—and astonished by the sudden return of the special and rare tug of deep emotion—

he could hardly wait to see her when he returned from a four-day business trip. It was Thursday, one of the two nights the library stayed open until nine. He saw the lights burning in the windows when he drove into town. With Tony safely with Ginny's parents there was no reason he couldn't stop. No one expected him until tomorrow, but he'd been too impatient to see Dana to stay away another night.

He found her putting books back on the shelves. She didn't see him as he stood at the end of the aisle, watching as she lifted her arms and stood on tiptoe to reach the top shelf. Her hair had been swept up on top of her head in a knot, but curling tendrils had escaped and curved along her cheeks and down the nape of her neck. The little makeup she normally wore had worn away, leaving her lips a natural pink and her cheeks flushed from the effort of lifting the piles of returned books and carrying them back to the shelves. The stretching motion pulled her blouse taut over her breasts and he yearned to cup their fullness in his hands. His body throbbed with a need so swift and forceful he had to turn away to catch his breath.

"Nick!"

Taken by surprise, her voice was as excited as a child's on Christmas morning, and he turned to see that her brown eyes glowed with unexpected warmth. In an instant, though, she had tempered the display of honest emotion and he almost sighed aloud with disappointment.

"How was your trip?"

Endless, he wanted to say but instead said only, "Fine. Productive."

"Did you get the contract?"

"I won't know for sure until the final papers are in my hand, but it looks that way."

"Congratulations!" She reached out tentatively and touched his arm. "I'm proud of you."

Then, as if the impulsive gesture troubled her, she hurried back toward the desk and began sorting through another stack of books. Nick watched her for several minutes, wondering at the swift return of her nervousness. Finally he followed her and pulled up a chair, turning its back to her and straddling it, his arms propped across the back.

"So, what have you been doing while I've been gone?"

"I've done some more work on the house." Her eyes lit up with enthusiasm. "I found the perfect wallpaper for the bedroom and I'm going to tackle that project next, as soon as I can figure out how to hang the stuff. I'm terrified of getting tangled up in a sheet of paper and winding up glued up like some mummy."

"Want some help?"

Dana promptly looked chagrined. "Nick, I wasn't hinting. You spend all day working on houses. Why should you work on mine in your free time?"

"Because it makes me happy," he said simply. He studied her closely, then promised quietly, "There are no strings attached."

His words, a recognition of what he perceived as her greatest fear, hung in the silence before she finally said, "I know that. You're not the kind of man who'd attach them."

"I'm glad you're finally able to see that."

Dana hesitated as she seemed to be searching for

words. "Nick, my attitude toward you…well, it wasn't… it isn't personal."

"Meaning?"

"Just that."

"And you don't want to explain?"

She shook her head. "I'm sorry. I really am, but I can't."

He nodded, frustration sweeping through him until he reminded himself that they were making progress. Dana had as much as admitted that trust was growing between them. If he was any judge of her character, he would have to say that the admission had been a giant step for her.

"Shall we talk about your wallpaper instead?" he suggested, adopting a lighter tone. "We could work on it tonight."

She looked tempted but protested anyway. "You're just back from your trip. You must want to get home and see Tony."

"He's not expecting me back until morning and he loves staying with his grandparents. They spoil him, and he'll be furious if I turn up a day early. Now, come on. You can fix me a spectacular dinner while I hang that wallpaper."

Dana still seemed hesitant. Finally, as though she'd waged a mental battle and was satisfied at the outcome, she smiled. "If you'll settle for something slightly less than spectacular, you've got a deal."

"You've seen my refrigerator. You know I have very low standards. Anything you do would have to be an improvement. Now let's get out of here. I'm starved."

As soon as they arrived at her house, Dana threw potatoes in the oven to bake, tossed a salad and cooked steaks on the grill while Nick measured the wallpaper. He liked listening to the cheerful sounds from the kitchen as he worked. It reminded him of happier times in his past, of coming home to the smell of baking bread and to Ginny, waiting in the kitchen with a smile on her face, anxious to hear about his day. After being without those things for three years, he appreciated all the more Dana's ability to fill a house with welcoming sounds and scents.

He also approved of the simple wallpaper design Dana had chosen. Muted shades of palest mauve and gray intermingled with white in tiny variegated stripes that were both tasteful and easy on the eye. It wasn't frilly and feminine, although that would have suited her, too. It was sophisticated and classy, with just a touch of innocence. As he cut the strips, he chuckled at reading so much into a selection of wallpaper.

Dana already had a bedspread in similar tones on the brass bed, and matching curtains had billowed in the spring breeze. Nick pulled the furniture away from the walls and had taken down the curtains in readiness for hanging the first strip of paper. As he shifted the bed to the center of the room, he was struck by a powerful sense of intimacy. He felt as close to Dana as if they'd been in that bed together, clinging to each other in the heat of passion.

He could imagine lying there after a night with her in his arms, propped on one elbow, watching as Dana pulled a brush through her long hair. He envisioned all the thousand little things a husband learns about his wife by watching her dress in the morning. His gaze lingered on the pillow as if he could see the indentation from her head, before he finally blinked away the image just in time to hear her call his name from the kitchen.

"Well," she said when they were settled at the table, "are you regretting your impulsive offer?"

"Not a bit. I like to hang wallpaper. When Ginny was alive—" He stopped himself in midsentence. "Sorry. I shouldn't do that."

"Do what?" She seemed genuinely mystified.

"I shouldn't keep bringing up my wife."

"Don't be absurd. She was an important part of your life for a very long time. It's natural that you should want to talk about her."

"It doesn't bother you?"

There was a subtle shift in her mood, a hint of caution in her tone. "No. At least, not the way you mean."

He regarded her curiously, surprised to find her expression almost wistful. "I don't understand."

"I just mean that I wish everyone had a marriage as happy as yours was."

He recalled her comment once before about the social whirl her marriage had entailed and wondered again at the edge in her voice.

"How long were you married, Dana?"

"Five years."

The response was to the point. He sensed she had no desire to elaborate, but he asked anyway, "Do you want to talk about it?"

"No." The response was quick and very firm. "I'd rather leave the past where it belongs."

She retreated again to that place Nick couldn't follow, a place that separated them by both time and distance as effectively as if they still lived in separate worlds. She stared into space and placed her fork back on her plate. Nervously, she drummed her fingers on the table. When he couldn't bear witnessing her unacknowledged pain any longer, Nick put a hand over hers and rubbed his thumb across her knuckles.

"Sometimes that's not possible," he said softly.

Her gaze lifted to meet his, the mournful expression in her eyes painful to see. "It has to be," she said, an unmistakable edge of desperation etched on her face.

Then, as if she'd found some new source of inner strength, she pulled herself together and even managed a faltering smile. "Enough of all that. Surely we can find other things to talk about. Are you finished with your steak?"

"Dana..."

"No, Nick. Let it go." The words were part plea, part command. Her demeanor brightened with a determination that awed him a little, even as it worried him.

"I have strawberry shortcake for dessert," she tempted.

He gave in. "When did you have time to fix that?"

"Today. It was no trouble. I had the strawberries and it was easy enough to do the rest. I seemed to remember you like it."

"I love it."

"Would you like to eat on the porch? I think it's warm enough tonight."

"Sounds perfect."

Nick brought out a chair, and Dana settled into her creaking rocking chair. They sat for a long time in companionable silence, letting the night's calm steal over them as they ate.

"Would you like some more?" Dana asked when he'd finished.

"No, please. Another bite and I'll never get off this chair and back to your wallpaper."

"You don't have to do that."

"The matter is settled," he insisted, getting up. "Now come and help me." He held out his hand and pulled her to her feet. She stood gazing up at him, her wide brown eyes searching his face. She tried to withdraw her hand from his, but he held on tightly.

"Dana."

She waited, the only visible sign of her emotions the darkening of her eyes into nearly black pools of pure enchantment. He tried to interpret her expression, but anxiety made him wary of the message he thought he saw. Was it, in fact, a yearning desire or the now familiar trepidation? Never had he felt such uncertainty, such self-doubt. Would the kiss he wanted so badly be welcomed or would it drive her away?

Few things in life came without risks and fewer were more valued than emotional commitment between a man and a woman. True, his feelings for Dana were still too new to be called commitment, yet they tortured him for fulfillment. He stared into her upturned face and slowly, with great care not to frighten her, he lowered his mouth to hers.

It was like touching a match to dry timber. There was an explosion of light and heat. His arms slid around her and this time she accepted the intimacy of the embrace as willingly as she did the kiss. Her hands fluttered hesitantly in the air for no longer than a heartbeat, then settled on his shoulders as a sigh shuddered through her.

The flames burned brighter as memory became reality. His lips caressed her cheeks, sought the strong pulse in her neck and lingered where her perfumed scent rose to greet him. She was soft as silk beneath his plundering mouth, and though she was unresisting he sensed the hesitancy of a new bride. It was the only thing that kept him sane. If he were to let himself go, if he were to give in to the recklessness of his feelings, he knew he might very well lose her forever.

When he released her at last, his breathing was ragged, his pulse racing.

"I think I'd better go, after all. I'll come by the library tomorrow and pick up your keys. I can do the wallpaper while you're at work."

"What about your work?" She was suddenly stiff and distant again. He read regret in her eyes and wondered whether she regretted the kiss or regretted what might have been.

"This should only take a couple of hours and I'm not expected in the office until afternoon."

"Are you sure I'm not imposing?"

He grinned at the worried set to her lips. "You could never impose on me. I want to do this for you."

She nodded then, apparently satisfied, and offered no further protest.

With a second, much quicker kiss on the cheek, Nick left before he could change his mind, before temptation made him break his unspoken vow to move slowly with Dana, to set a pace that would coax her eventually into his arms.

Dana came home late on Friday, putting off her return to avoid another meeting with Nick in such a private setting. He'd come by the library early, as he'd promised, and even with people around, she'd felt the flaring of impatient desire. It was a sensation she had sworn to resist, but it was getting more and more difficult to do. Her traitorous body craved Nick's touch despite the warnings of her mind.

Now, as she walked through the cottage, it was almost as though she could sense Nick's presence, as though his male scent lingered in the air and his strength surrounded her. In recent days she'd come to trust that strength, rather than fear it, yet old habits were hard to break. Now that she was home, she almost wished that she'd arrived earlier so she could have thanked Nick in person for his efforts.

She found that her room was exactly as she'd envisioned it. The wallpaper was hung, the furniture back in place. Nick had even painted the woodwork. On the nightstand beside the bed, he had left a vase of white and lavender lilacs. The sweet fragrance filled the room. Dana picked them up and buried her face in the fragile blooms, filled with emotions she'd never expected to feel again.

When she put the vase back, she discovered a note.

Dana,
Hope you like the room. Tony and I will be by for you in the morning about eight-thirty. Bring your bathing suit. We're going to the beach.
Until then,
Nick

Her first reaction was annoyance. Once again he was making plans without consulting her, backing her into a corner. Then she reread the note and found that, despite herself, she was smiling, her heart beating a little faster.

What woman could stay angry at a man who left flowers in a room he had prepared for her with such care?

That night she slept well for the first time in ages. The next morning she had barely turned over to peer at the clock when the impatient pounding started on the back door.

"Rise and shine, sleepyhead."

"Nick?" Her voice came out in a sleepy croak. She tumbled out of bed and pulled on a robe. She searched for her slippers but finally gave up and walked barefoot to the door.

"You're early," she accused as she opened the door to a grinning Tony and his very wide-awake father.

"See, Dad, I told you we should've called," Tony said.

From the expression in Nick's eyes, Dana could tell that he wasn't the least bit sorry he'd awakened her. In fact, he looked delighted to see her in her robe, with her hair disheveled and her bare toes curling against the cool floor. She belted the robe a little tighter and stood aside to let them in.

"I thought you said eight-thirty," she said, trying one more time for an explanation for the early arrival.

"I did, but it was such a beautiful day I thought we ought to get an early start." Nick nudged her in the direction of the bedroom. "Go, get dressed. I'll make some coffee. Do you want breakfast?"

"No, but if you want some, help yourselves."

"We've already eaten," Tony chimed in. "Dad fixed waffles. Sort of." He wrinkled his nose in disgust and Dana was immediately intrigued.

"Sort of?"

"Yeah. There's gunk all over the kitchen."

"Quiet," Nick ordered as Dana grinned. "Don't tell her all my bad traits. They tasted okay, didn't they?"

"Heck, yeah. I like charcoal," Tony retorted, ducking as his father took a playful swipe at him.

"Tony, if you want some cereal while you wait, it's in the cabinet by the stove," Dana offered, laughing.

"The waffles weren't that awful," Nick grumbled.

Impulsively, Dana patted him on the cheek. "I'm sure they weren't, but perhaps you should stick to building houses."

"Somebody in our house has to cook."

"I vote we eat here all the time," Tony said, his voice muffled as he poked his head into the cupboard. "Ms. Brantley's got lots of good stuff."

As Dana's eyes widened, Nick turned and grinned at her. "See, my dear, you have to be very careful what you say around him or he'll be moving in."

Before Dana could come up with a quick retort, Nick added in a seductive purr meant only for her ears, "And where my son goes, I go."

Dana's heart thudded crazily. "I'll keep that in mind," she said, hurrying from the kitchen.

She took her time dressing, trying to regain her composure. Nick always teased her when she least expected it and he had an astonishing ability to unnerve her. She knew he could do that only because she was beginning to lower her defenses. She might as well admit it; Nick was making her feel special. He also made her feel intelligent and desirable again. Their flirting was heady stuff, especially for a woman who'd felt none of those things in a very long time.

"Just don't let him get too close," she murmured as she slipped a pair of jeans on over her bathing suit.

As the day wore on, she found it was a warning that was getting exceptionally difficult to heed.

After riding along a winding road edged by towering pines and oaks they arrived at Westmoreland State Park. They spent the day swimming, walking along the trails, playing volleyball in the water and, finally, cooking hamburgers on a grill.

"Let Ms. Brantley do it, Dad."

"Oh, 'How sharper than a serpent's tooth it is to have a thankless child,'" Nick bemoaned dramatically.

"What?" Tony said.

"That's Shakespeare," Dana told him. "It's a line from *King Lear*."

"What's it mean?"

"It means, my boy," Nick said, "that a kid who is rotten to his old man may not get any birthday presents next week."

"That's a very loose translation," Dana noted dryly.

Tony grinned. "I get it, Dad. You want me to shape up or ship out. How about if I go swimming again?"

"Only if you stay where we can see you. No going out over your head, okay?"

"Promise," he said, taking off across the sand.

When he had gone, Dana and Nick were left alone, sitting side by side on a blanket.

"When is his birthday?" she asked, uncomfortably aware that Nick's bare chest and long, muscular, bare legs were just inches away from her.

"Wednesday."

"Are you doing something special?"

"His grandparents are throwing a party for him." Nick trailed a sandy finger along Dana's bare back, moving back to linger at a tiny ridged scar on her shoulder. She could feel the sensation clear down to her toes. "Want to come with me?"

Dana tried to stay very still so Nick wouldn't see how his touch and his offhand invitation were affecting her. Then she drew her knees protectively up to her chest and folded her arms across them, resting her chin on her hands. She thought about Nick's invitation. It was one more link in the chain to tie her to him.

"I don't think so," she said finally.

"Because you don't want to go?"

She glanced over at him and shook her head. "No, it's not that."

"What, then?"

"I don't think I belong there."

"Why not? The party is for Tony's friends, and as you must know, he thinks you're one of his very best friends." His hand came to rest on her shoulder. "Dana, look at me. Is it because you think Ginny's parents might resent you?"

"That's certainly one reason," she said, struck anew by his perceptiveness and sensitivity.

"They won't. They've been asking for some time when they were going to get to meet you. I thought this might be a good time because there will be a lot of other people there. There won't be so much pressure on you."

"You're sure that's how they feel?"

"Absolutely. But you said that was *one* reason. Are there more?" Before she could reply, he said, "Of course there are, and I'll bet I can guess what they are. You think people will start making assumptions about us if we're seen together on a family occasion."

"That's part of it," she admitted. She hesitated, then

took a deep breath. "It's more than that, though. To be honest, I'm also worried about what I'll feel."

"Trapped?"

She met his gaze and saw the guileless expression in his eyes. She nodded.

"You won't be. I'll never try to trap you into more than you're ready for, Dana. Never. This is just a birthday party for Tony."

She thought about what Nick was saying to her and realized that if she was ever to take another chance on letting a man get close to her, Nick was the right choice. She turned and smiled at him. "In that case, I'd love to come."

His gaze met hers and her breath caught in her throat. There was such a look of raw desire, of longing, in his eyes that it made her pulse dance wildly. His hand tangled in her wet hair and he drew her closer. Dana's heart thundered in anticipation, but before the longed-for kiss could happen, Tony's shout drove them apart. He was racing across the sand, tears in his eyes, holding his arm. Nick was on his feet in an instant, tension radiating from him.

"What is it, son?"

Tony looked disgusted. "Just a dumb jellyfish sting," he said, panting from his run across the sand.

"Are you okay?" Dana asked, noting the relief in Nick's eyes.

"Yeah, I'm used to 'em," Tony said bravely, surreptitiously swiping away the tears. "It just hurts a little."

Nick glanced at Dana with regret, then ruffled Tony's hair. "Come on, kiddo. We'd better go see the lifeguard and get something to put on that. Then we'd better think about getting home if you want to go to the early movie with your friends tonight."

When they got back to River Glen, Nick pulled up in front of Dana's house. "How about having dinner with me tonight? We'll go out for crabs."

"I'd like that."

Nick seemed startled by her quick acceptance. "Terrific. I thought I was going to have to twist your arm."

"Not for crabs. I've discovered an addiction to crabmeat since I moved here."

"Then we'll feed your habit tonight. I'll be by for you about seven."

Dana had butter dribbling down her chin and crab shells in her hair. Nick thought she'd never looked lovelier or more uninhibited. He reached across the table and wiped her chin with an edge of his napkin.

"You're really into this, aren't you?" he said with a grin. "If I'd had any idea cracking crabs was the way to your heart, I'd have brought you here days ago."

Dana didn't even look up. She was concentrating instead on shattering a crab shell so she could get to the sweet meat inside. Newspapers were spread across the table, shells everywhere. Only one of the dozen crabs they'd ordered remained untouched. Nick sipped his beer and watched her pounding away on the next-to-last crab. The shell on the claw finally cracked and she lifted a chunk of tender white crabmeat as triumphantly as if it were a trophy.

"For me?" Nick teased.

She scowled at him. "You get your own. This is hard work."

"And you do it so neatly. If Tony could see this table

now, he'd never again make sarcastic remarks about the messes I leave in the kitchen."

"I suppose you're any better at this."

"As a matter of fact, I am something of an expert," he retorted. "Which you would know if you'd been watching me, instead of smashing your food to bits."

He picked up the last crab and gently tapped it a couple of times. It yielded the crabmeat instantly. He picked up the biggest chunk on his fork, dipped it in butter and held it out for Dana. She hesitated.

"Don't you want it?"

"Oh, I want it. I'm just trying to decide if it's worth the price."

"What price?"

"You'll just sit around looking smug the rest of the night."

"No, I won't," he vowed. "Even though I'm certainly entitled to."

Dana wrapped her hand around his and held it steady while she took the crabmeat off the fork. As she bit down, her eyes clashed with his and held. Nick wondered if she could feel the tension that provocative look aroused. Every muscle in his body tightened.

"Dana," he murmured, his voice thick. She blinked and released his hand. "Dana, I want you."

She met his gaze, then glanced away, her expression revealing the agony of indecision. "I know." She sighed deeply and looked into his eyes again. "Nick, I can't get involved with you. I thought you understood that this afternoon."

"Why do you equate involvement with being trapped?"

"Experience."

"*Past* experience," he reminded her.

"It doesn't matter. I've made decisions about what I want for the rest of my life and involvement isn't included."

"How can you make a decision like that so easily?"

"It's not easy, believe me. Although I thought it would be before I met you."

She hesitated and Nick waited for the rest. "A part of me…a part of me wants what you want."

"But?"

"But I can't change the way I am. You have to accept me on my terms."

"Which are?"

"If you care about me, you'll accept that we'll never be any closer than this."

"I'll never accept that!" he exploded, feeling a fury fueled by frustration building inside him. He saw the flicker of fear in her eyes and tried to force himself to remain calm. "I'll give you space, Dana. I'll give you time, but I will never give up hope for us."

"You must." She touched his hand, then jerked away when he would have held hers.

"I can't," he said simply. "That would mean living a lie. I can't do that any more than you can."

"Nick, I don't want to talk about it anymore. My decision is final."

"Sweetheart, nothing in life is ever final," he said softly before calling for the check.

On the way home, Dana sat huddled close to the car door, as if afraid that by sitting any closer to Nick she would be tempting fate. When they got to her house, he walked her to the door, careful not to touch her.

"May I come in?"

Chapter 6

It was barely ten o'clock in the morning and the temperature in the library had to be over ninety degrees. Dana had clicked on the air-conditioning when she'd arrived at eight. It had promptly given a sickening shudder, huffed and puffed desperately, and died. She'd tried to open the windows, but most of them had long since become permanently stuck. She propped the front door open with a chair, then found an old floor fan in the closet, but it only stirred the humid air. With no cross ventilation, it didn't lower the temperature a single degree.

"Dana, what on earth's wrong in here?" Betsy Markham said, mopping her face with a lace-edged hankie as soon as she crossed the threshold. "It's hot as hades."

"The air conditioner broke this morning. Come on

over and sit in front of the fan. It's not great, but it's better than nothing."

Betsy sank down on a chair by Dana's desk and fanned her face with a book. "What did we ever do before the invention of air-conditioning?"

"We sweltered," Dana replied glumly. Then she brightened. "Wait a minute. Betsy, you must know. Do we have a contract for repairs?"

"Never needed one. Nick's always done that sort of thing."

Dana groaned. "I should have known."

"What's that supposed to mean? I thought you two were getting close. Looked that way when I saw you together last week."

"That's the problem. I can't go running to Nick for help again. He's already done way too much for me, especially around the house. I feel like I'm taking advantage of our friendship."

"Land sakes, child, it isn't as if this is some personal favor. This is town property and Nick's always been real obliging about having his crew work on whatever needs fixing. He only charges for parts." Betsy regarded her closely. "You sure that's all it is? You didn't have a fight or something, did you?"

"No. You were right. We've been getting along really well. It scares me sometimes. Nick seems too good to be true."

"He's a fine man."

"I know that's what you think. I think so, too, but can you ever really know a person well enough to be sure of what he's like underneath? What about all those women who wake up one day and discover they're living with a criminal? Or that their husband has three other wives in other cities?"

Betsy looked scandalized. "Goodness gracious, why on earth would you bring up a thing like that? Nick's never broken a law in his life, except maybe the speed limit."

"Do you really know that, though? You're not with him twenty-four hours a day."

Betsy seemed genuinely puzzled by Dana's reservations. "Honey, you're not making a bit of sense. With Nick, well, I've known him since he was just a little tyke. He's always been a little stubborn, maybe a wee bit too self-confident, but you'll never find a more decent, caring man."

The book's pages fluttered slowly, then stopped in midair as Betsy's thoughts wandered back. She shook her head sadly. "Why, the way that man suffered when Ginny was sick, it was pitiful to see. He couldn't do enough for her. Anybody with eyes could tell he was dying inside, but around Ginny he was as strong and brave as could be. He kept that house filled with laughter for her and Tony, and he made sure Ginny's friends felt like they could be there for her. Lots of times when someone's dying, folks don't want to be around 'cause they don't know what to say. Nick put everyone at ease for Ginny's sake. You can tell an awful lot about a man by the way he handles a rough time like that."

Dana felt that wistful, sad feeling steal over her again. "He obviously loved her very much."

Betsy seized on the remark. "Is that what's bothering you? Are you afraid he won't be able to love you as much?"

Dana sighed. "I wish it were that simple, Betsy."

"Then what is it, child? Something's sure worrying at you. Is it Nick who's got you so confused or something else?"

"I can't explain. It's something I have to work out on my own."

"An objective opinion might help."

"Maybe so, but I'm not ready to talk about it."

"Child, sometimes I think you and Nick were meant for each other," Betsy said in exasperation. "You're both just as stubborn as a pair of old mules and twice as independent."

"Betsy." There was a warning note in Dana's voice.

"Okay, I get the message. But if you ever feel the need to talk, just remember I'm willing to listen and I can keep my mouth shut." Betsy patted her friend's hand. "Now let me call Nick and get somebody over here to work on this air conditioner before you melt right in front of my eyes."

"Thanks, Betsy."

When Betsy had gone, Dana sat staring after her. Their talk had helped her to crystallize some of the uneasiness she'd been feeling lately. She and Nick really had become close. Sometimes it felt as if she'd known him all her life, as if he was a part of her. Occasionally, it seemed he knew what was going on in her mind before she did. That ability to communicate should have reassured her, but it didn't.

When she and Sam had met, they'd shared that same sort of intimacy. A glance was often enough to tell them what they needed to know about the other's thoughts. She had been awed by the closeness back then, but she'd learned from bitter experience not to trust it.

"What you really don't trust is your own judgment,"

she muttered, disgusted with herself. Nick had done nothing in the weeks she'd known him to betray her trust. People like Betsy, who'd known him since childhood, trusted him implicitly.

But everyone had trusted Sam, too, she reminded herself. He was a well-respected member of a highly prestigious law firm, a devoted son, a supportive brother, a sensitive and generous fiancé. He was all that, but he had been a terrible husband. For reasons she had never understood, he was incapable of dealing with his wife the way he dealt with the others in his life. She had learned that too late. The price for blinding herself to Sam's flaws had been a high one.

"Is the town paying you to sit here gathering wool?" Nick's hands rested on her unsuspecting shoulders. He leaned down to kiss her, but as his lips touched her cheek, Dana trembled.

Nick sat in the chair Betsy had vacated and studied her with troubled eyes. "Hey, I was just teasing. What's wrong?"

"Nothing a little cool air wouldn't cure."

"Coming up," he promised, getting to his feet. He hesitated. Hazel eyes swept over her as if by looking closely he could discover whatever it was she was hiding. "Is that all it is?"

"That's it. Mildew could grow on your brain in this humidity."

"A pleasant thought," he chided lightly as he went to the air-conditioning unit and began dismantling it. "I came over here thinking how lucky I was to get a chance to see my favorite lady in the middle of a workday and you want to discuss mildew."

"I don't want to discuss it. I want the damn air conditioner fixed!"

Nick spun around and stared at her in astonishment. The next minute, tears were streaming down her cheeks and he had her in his arms. "Dana, sweetheart, what is it?"

"I'm sorry," she mumbled against his shoulder.

"Don't be sorry. Just tell me what's wrong."

"Nothing. That's just it. There's nothing wrong."

"You're not making a lot of sense."

"Betsy said the same thing," she said, leaning back in his embrace and looking into his eyes. They were filled with concern and something more, a deeper emotion that she wanted desperately to respond to. She sighed and put her head back against his shoulder. His shirt was damp from her tears and the awful heat, but underneath his shoulder was solid, as if he could take on the weight of the world.

She wanted so badly to trust what she felt when he held her, but she wasn't sure she dared.

"Dana." He handed her a handkerchief.

"Thanks." She dried her tears and blew her nose. "I don't know what got into me."

"I think you do." Her eyes widened and she started to protest, but he put a finger against her lips. "I'm not going to try to make you tell me today, but someday you must."

She nodded. Maybe someday she would be able to tell him.

By the end of the day she was snapping at her own shadow. She was in no mood to be going to a birthday party at the home of Nick's former in-laws, but she knew a last-minute cancellation would puzzle Nick and hurt Tony.

Fortunately, Tony was so excited he kept up a constant stream of chatter most of the way to his grandparents' home outside of town. Nick kept casting worried looks in Dana's direction, but he maintained an awkward silence, speaking only when Tony asked him a direct question.

Finally, exasperated by the pall that had settled over the car, Tony sank back into his seat and grumbled, "You guys are acting really weird. Did you have a fight or something?"

"Of course not," they both said in a chorus, then looked at each other and grinned.

"Sorry," they said in unison, and chuckled.

Tony gazed from one to the other and shook his head. "Like I said…weird. I can hardly wait to get to Grandma's. Maybe there'll be some normal people there. You know, people who'll sing 'Happy Birthday' and stuff."

"You want 'Happy Birthday'?" Nick said, glancing at Dana. "We can give you 'Happy Birthday,' right, Dana?"

"Absolutely."

Nick's deep voice led off and Dana joined in. By the time they pulled into the Leahys' long, curving driveway, there was a crescendo of off-key singing and laughter. Nothing could have lightened Dana's mood more effectively. Whatever nervousness she'd been feeling about this meeting with Ginny's parents had diminished, if not vanished. Nick squeezed her hand reassuringly as she got out of the car, then draped his arm around her shoulders as they crossed the impeccably manicured lawn to meet the Leahys.

The older couple was waiting on the porch of an old farmhouse. Joshua Leahy's thick white hair framed a weathered face that seemed both wise and friendly. His ready smile deepened wrinkles that had been etched by sun and age. His work-roughened hands clasped Dana's firmly.

On the surface his wife's greeting was just as warm, but Dana sensed an undercurrent of tension.

"We're so glad you could come," Jessica Leahy said, her penetrating brown eyes scrutinizing Dana even as she welcomed her. Dana's own quick assessment told her that Mrs. Leahy had reservations about her but that she was holding them in check for the sake of her son-in-law and grandson.

"I'm glad you're here before the others," she said to Dana. "It'll give us some time to chat before they arrive. Nick, dear, why don't you and Tony help Joshua with the grill? He never can get the charcoal right. Dana, would you mind helping me in the kitchen?"

"Of course not," she said as Nick looked on and gave her a helpless shrug.

In the kitchen, Mrs. Leahy assigned tasks with the brisk efficiency of a drill sergeant. When she was satisfied that Dana was capable of following her directions to finish up the deviled eggs, she picked up a platter of ribs and began brushing them with barbecue sauce.

"So, Dana… Do you mind if I call you that?"

"Of course not."

"Well, then, Dana, why don't you tell me about yourself? Nick and Tony think the world of you, but I must admit they don't seem to know too much about your background."

"What exactly would you like to know, Mrs. Leahy?" Dana asked cautiously.

"Oh, where you're from, what your family is like. I find people absolutely fascinating, though sadly we don't get too many strangers settling around these parts."

She tried to make her questions seem innocuous, but Dana had a feeling they were anything but that. Mrs. Leahy had a sharp mind and she had every intention of using her wits to assure herself that her beloved family was not in any danger from the unknown.

"My background's no secret," Dana said as she spooned the egg mixture into the whites and sprinkled them with paprika for extra color. "I'm from New York. My family is still there. My father works for an international bank. My mother raises money for half a dozen charities. I have two sisters, both married and still living in Manhattan."

"You must miss them."

"I do."

"Why did you leave?"

"The pace of the city didn't suit me. I wanted a place to catch my breath, start over."

"Were you running away?"

Dana dropped the spoon with a clatter. "Sorry," she murmured as she bent to pick it up and clean up the egg that had splattered on the gleaming linoleum.

She stood up to find Mrs. Leahy staring at her astutely. "I'm sorry if my question upset you."

"Why should it upset me? I wasn't running away from anything." She met Mrs. Leahy's dubious gaze directly, challenging her. In the end, it was the older woman who backed down and just in time. Nick was opening the screen door and poking his head into the kitchen.

"Mind if I steal the lady for a minute, Jessica? There are some people here I want her to meet."

"Of course, dear. We're almost finished in here anyway." She gave Dana a measured glance. "It was nice talking to you. I'm sure we'll be getting to know each other better."

To Dana's ears, those words had an ominous ring, but then she told herself she was being foolish.

"Sorry about the inquisition," Nick murmured in her ear as they went into the yard. "Thwarting Jessica's plans is a little like trying to stop an army tank with a BB gun."

"No problem. She's bound to be curious about me."

"Did she unearth any deep, dark secrets I ought to know about?"

Dana frowned. "Why would you ask that?"

"I was only teasing." He studied her closely, an expression of concern in his eyes. "She must have been rough on you."

"Not really," she said, and put her hand on Nick's cheek. Suddenly she needed his strength, needed the reassurance of feeling his warm flesh under her touch. "Don't mind me. I'm just a very private person. It threw me a little to have someone I'd just met asking a lot of questions."

Nick wrapped his arms around her and linked his hands behind her waist. His chin rested on top of her head. Her body was locked against his, and the strength and heat she'd needed were there. Nick embodied vitality and caring, passion and sensitivity, and he was generously offering all of that to her.

With a final reassuring squeeze, Nick released her and took her hand. "Ready to face more people?"

"Do I have a choice?" she muttered. "Let's go."

The rest of the evening passed in a blur of children's laughing faces, introductions and reminiscences, all of which seemed to have Ginny prominently at the center. Dana felt slightly uncomfortable, but Nick appeared downright irritated by what seemed an obvious attempt to keep Dana firmly in place as an outsider.

After he'd dropped an exhausted Tony at home, he drove Dana to her house. "I'm really sorry for the way the evening turned out. I don't understand what got into Jessica tonight. She's not a petty woman."

"She's just trying to protect her family."

"From what?" he exploded. "You? That's absurd. The only thing you've done is bring happiness back into our lives."

"I'm sure that as she sees it, I'm taking her daughter's place."

Nick sighed and bent over the steering wheel, resting his forehead on hands that gripped the wheel so tightly his knuckles turned white. "Ginny is dead."

After a split-second hesitation, Dana reached over and put her hand on Nick's shoulder. "She knows that. That makes it even worse. Why should I be alive when her daughter isn't?"

"You're not to blame, for heaven's sakes."

"She knows that, too. I didn't say her feelings were rational. She may not even be aware of them. It just comes out subconsciously in her actions."

"I'm going to talk to her."

"No, Nick. Let it go. Give her time to adjust. This must be very hard for her. She doesn't understand that I'm not trying to replace her daughter."

Nick sat back and shook his head. "You're really something, you know that? How can you be so understanding after the rough time you've been through?"

"Don't go nominating me for sainthood," she cautioned with a grin. "There were a couple of times in the kitchen when I came very close to tossing a few deviled eggs at her."

Nick reached across and massaged Dana's neck. "I wish I didn't have to get home right now," he said softly, his eyes blazing with desire.

"But you do," she said, wishing in so many ways it were otherwise, while knowing at the same time that it was for the best. "There will be other nights."

When Dana made that vow, she meant it. She was sure she was prepared to risk taking the next step in her relationship with Nick. Like a wildflower that beat the odds to survive in a rocky crevice, love had bloomed in her heart. As impossible as it seemed, she was beginning to believe in a future with him.

Then the mail came on Thursday. In it was a letter from Sam's parents. When Dana saw the Omaha postmark and the familiar handwriting, her hands trembled so badly the letter fell to the floor. She stared disbelievingly at the envelope for what seemed an eternity before she dared to pick it up.

How in God's name had they found her? Surely her parents hadn't revealed her whereabouts.

What does it matter now? They know. They know.

It seemed like the beginning of the end of everything

she'd worked so hard to achieve. Serenity vanished in the blink of an eye, replaced by pain. Hope for the future was buried under the weight of the past.

Reluctantly, she opened the envelope, daring for just an instant to envision words that would forgive, rather than condemn. Instead, she found the all-too-familiar hatred. The single page was filled with unrelenting bitterness and accusations. All of Sam's parents' pain had been vented in that letter. They promised to see her in hell for what she had done to their son.

What they didn't understand was that she was already there.

Badly shaken, Dana closed the library early and walked home. The arrival of that letter had convinced her that while the Brantleys might not make good on their threats to expose her today or even tomorrow, sooner or later the truth about her past would come out. When it did, it would destroy the fragile relationship she was beginning to build with Nick. She would rather die than see the look of betrayal that was bound to be in his eyes when he learned the truth.

Sitting on her front porch, idly rocking through dusk and on into the night, she decided it would be better to distance herself from Nick. She stayed up all night, and by dawn her eyes were dry and painful from the lack of sleep and the endless tears. She had vowed to end their relationship the next time she saw him. And if Nick wouldn't let her go, she was prepared to leave River Glen.

The next time she saw Nick began with a kiss so sweet and tender it made her heart ache with longing. Nick's lips were hungry and urgent against hers and

Dana felt herself responding. Heat spread through her limbs until she was clinging to him. *The last time, the last time,* was like a refrain she couldn't get out of her head, even as her body trembled and begged for more.

At last she pushed him away. Turning her back on him so he wouldn't see the tears welling up in her eyes, she walked into the back room at the library and began unpacking the lunch she'd brought for the two of them.

"We have to talk," she announced.

Clearly puzzled, Nick studied her. "Why so serious?"

Dana took a deep breath and said, "We're spending too much time together."

He stared at her in astonishment. "Where did that come from?"

"It's something I've been thinking about since the other night."

"Since the birthday party."

She nodded.

"I see. Do I have anything to say about the decision or is it unilateral?"

"It's my decision and my mind is made up."

Nick watched her as he peeled a tart Granny Smith apple, then split it and gave her half. "The way I see it," he began slowly, never taking his eyes off her face, "we're not spending nearly enough time together. You and I are going to be together one day. It's as inevitable as the change in seasons. You know it, Dana."

She felt color rise in her cheeks, but she met his gaze straight on and made her tone cool. "I'm not denying the attraction, Nick. I'm just saying that's the end of it. Eventually you're going to want a wife. Tony needs a mother. We've talked about this before. I'm not about to be either of those."

She nearly choked on the words. The ache in her chest was something she would have to live with for the rest of her life.

"Why not?" Nick demanded. "You care for both of us." When she started to protest, he silenced her. "Don't deny it. I know you do and all that nonsense at the Leahys is just that: nonsense."

"That doesn't matter. How many times do we have to go through this? I've made choices for the rest of my life. You don't fit in. Leave it that way now, before we all get hurt."

"I can't do that, Dana. You're in my heart and there's no way to get you out. I said it the other night and I'll say it again and again until I make you understand: I'll give you time if that's what you need, but I won't leave you alone."

She grasped at straws. "People are already talking about us, Nick."

"Let them."

"That's easy for you. You've lived here your whole life. People respect you. They don't even know me. I don't like being the subject of gossip. It hurts."

"If you're worried about your reputation, there's an easy way to resolve that. Marry me."

Dana's heart pounded and blood roared in her ears, but she forced herself to say, "You're missing the point. Didn't you hear what I said? There will be no marriage, Nicholas. Not for me."

"Was your last marriage such a disaster? Is that it?"

Dana felt something freeze inside her as her thoughts tumbled back in time. Sheer will brought them back to the present.

"I won't discuss my marriage with you," she said, her lips tightly compressed. "Not now. Not ever."

Sound seemed to roar in her head until she could stand it no more. The hurt look in Nick's eyes was equally impossible to bear.

She clamped her own eyes shut and held her hands over her ears, but she could still see, still hear. "Go, Nick. Please."

"Dana, this doesn't make any sense."

"It does, Nick. It's the only thing that does."

Nick stared at her, his eyes pleading with her to relent, but there was no going back. This was what she had to do. For Nick and Tony. For herself.

But, dear God, how she hated it.

Chapter 7

It was impossible to grow up in a small town without harboring a desire for privacy. The same things that made a community like River Glen so appealing were the very things that could set your teeth on edge. Friendly support could just as easily become outright nosiness. As a result, Nick was a man who understood the need for secrets, and until he had fallen in love with Dana he had been perfectly willing to let each man—or woman—keep his own.

But he sensed there was something different about Dana's secrets, something deeper and more ominous than an understandable need for privacy. Her reluctance to discuss even the most basic things about her marriage, her effort to maintain a distance, the tension-laden silences that fell in the midst of conversation, were all calculated to drive a wedge between them, to prevent him from asking questions about a past she didn't care to reveal.

Though he hated it, for days Nick tried playing by Dana's latest rules. He resumed eating his lunches at Gracie's and spent his evenings at home. He didn't even drive past her house, though there were times when he longed to do just that in the hope of casually bumping into her.

Foolishly, he thought time would make her give in or at the very least make it easier for him. Instead she held firm and it was getting more and more difficult for him to keep his distance. He was lonelier than he'd been since the awful weeks after Ginny's death.

With so many empty hours in which to brood, he even found himself jealous of his own son, who continued to spend his afternoons at the library and came home filled with talk of Dana. Nick listened avidly for some hint that she was as miserable as he was, but Tony's reports were disgustingly superficial and Nick was too proud to probe for more.

It wasn't until the following week when he stopped by town hall that Nick got any real insight into Dana's mood. He walked into Betsy's office and sank down in the chair beside her desk. He removed the hard hat he'd put on at one of his building sites and turned it nervously around and around in his hands.

Betsy glanced up from her typing, her fingers poised over the keys. She frowned at him.

"Nicholas." There was a note of censure just in the way she said his name.

"Morning, Betsy."

She took off her glasses. "You look like a man who could use a cup of coffee," she said more kindly, and went to pour him one. Then she sat back down, folded her hands on her desk and waited.

Nick scowled at her. "You're not going to make this easy for me, are you?"

"Should I?"

"I'm not the one at fault, Betsy, so you can just stop your frowning."

"Is that right?"

He finally swallowed his pride. "Okay, dammit, I'll ask. How is she?" Betsy opened her mouth, but it was Nick who spoke. "And don't you dare ask me who."

She chuckled. "I think I know who you're interested in, Nicholas. I'm not blind."

"Well?"

"Oh, I'd say she looks just about the way you do. Every time I've tried to get her to tell me what happened, she snaps my head off. Maybe you'd like to explain what's going on."

He crossed his legs, propped the hat on one knee and raked his fingers through his hair. "I wish to hell I knew. One minute everything was fine and the next she didn't want to see me anymore. I tried my darnedest to get her to tell me what was wrong, but she kept giving me all this gibberish about needing space."

"Maybe you pushed her back to the wall."

"Is that what she said?"

"She hasn't said a thing. She looked downright peaked when I saw her on Monday, so I went back to the library again yesterday and she was still moping around. I tried to get her to open up, but she just shook her head and said it was something she had to work out on her own. I invited her over to have dinner with Harry and me and she turned me down."

Betsy pursed her lips. "I don't like it, Nick. Dana's hurting about something and it's not good that she's closing out the only folks around here she knows well. She has to talk to someone or she'll explode one of these days. Can't you try to get through to her? Looks to me as though she needs a friend real bad."

"A friend," Nick repeated with a touch of irony.

Betsy reached over and patted his hand. "You always were an impatient man. Being a friend isn't such a bad place to start, Nicholas. Try to remember that."

Nick sipped his coffee to give himself more time before answering. At last he nodded. "You're right, Betsy. I'll talk to her tonight, if she'll see me."

"Maybe this is one time you shouldn't take no for an answer."

"Maybe so." He bent down and dropped a grateful kiss on her cheek before he left.

All afternoon he tried to plan his strategy. He vowed to unearth the real cause of Dana's sudden retreats, of her obvious fear of commitment. A woman as gentle and generous as Dana would make a wonderful wife and an incredible mother, but each time he stepped over the boundaries she had set—both spoken and unspoken— something seemed to freeze inside her and the chill crept through him, as well.

Nick had the resources to check into Dana's past, but using them offended his innate sense of decency. Confrontation would only send her farther away. The only alternative was to push her gently, to create an atmosphere in which revelations would flow naturally. Nick wondered if he possessed the subtlety necessary for such a tricky task, especially when he felt like cracking bricks in two to vent his frustration.

It was dusk when he walked through town toward the library. As he strolled, he was oblivious to the friendly greetings called out by his neighbors, who stared after him in consternation. All his attention was focused on Dana and the intimidating realization that he was putting his happiness and Tony's at risk by forcing the issue. He tried to remember Betsy's caution that what Dana needed right now was a friend, not an impatient lover.

As he waited for Dana to close the library, he leaned against her car and listened to the calls of bobwhites and whippoorwills as night began to fall. Fireflies flickered and the first bright star appeared in the sky, followed by another and then another, until the blue-black horizon was dusted with them. The air was scented by the sweetness of honeysuckle and the tang of salt spray from the river. It was a perfect night for romance and his body throbbed with awareness.

"Nick!"

Dana's startled voice brought him out of his reverie. He looked up and grinned at her, hoping to get a smile in return. Instead, she wore a frown. She stayed away from him, her arms folded protectively across her chest. Her stance was every bit as defensive as it had been on the day they'd met, and the realization saddened him. How could two people spend so much time together and still be so distant?

"What are you doing here?" she asked warily.

"I thought we should do some more talking."

"Why didn't you come inside, instead of lingering out here in the shadows?"

"I wasn't sure I'd be welcome."

Her shoulders seemed to stiffen at the implied criticism. "The library is public property."

"That's hardly the point," he said gently. "The library is your domain and you made it very clear the other day that my coming there was a problem."

"I'm not sure I'm following your logic. You wouldn't come into the library because it might upset me, but it's okay to lurk around on the street."

"You didn't say anything about the street," he pointed out, hoping to earn even a brief grin from her. She didn't relent.

"It's not just your coming to the library, it's…oh, I don't know." She threw up her hands in frustration. "It wouldn't work for us. I was only trying to save both of us from being hurt somewhere down the line. Can't you see that?"

"I don't see how I could hurt much more than I do now. I've missed you."

For an instant he thought a similar cry might cross her trembling lips, but she only said, "Nick, it will pass. You'll meet someone new."

One brow arched skeptically. "In River Glen? I've known everyone here since I was born."

"You could drive to Richmond or Washington if you were all that interested in meeting new people."

He shook his head, dismayed by her cavalier attitude, her willingness to hand him over to some other woman. He felt an explosion building inside, but he fought to remain cool, controlled. "You just don't get it, do you? You're not some passing infatuation for me. I'm not chasing after you because you're the first attractive woman to move to town in years or the first one to tell me no. I…"

He stumbled over saying he loved her, afraid that such a declaration would be too intense for her to handle. Betsy had warned him of just that. "I care about you. You're a very special woman and I don't want to replace you."

"I have to have some space, Nick," she said at last, leaning up against the car beside him and staring into the darkness. "That's what I came here for."

"I've given you space."

Even in the shadows he could see her lips curve in a half smile. "No, you haven't. Until these last two weeks, you've been at the library every day for lunch. You've taken to dropping by my house whenever you like. Do you realize that in the two months I've known you, I haven't finished a single project around either the house or the library on my own?"

"We fixed the roof."

"You fixed the roof."

"What about the bedroom?"

"You did that, too."

"What about the garden? It's flourishing. When I helped you weed it…"

"You see? That's just my point. You're taking over. First the roof, then the bedroom, the garden. There's nothing left that I can point to with pride and say, 'That's mine.' I need that feeling of independence. I need to stand on my own two feet. I can't have you jumping in to do things before I even get a chance to try."

He tried not to show how much the comment hurt. "I thought I was helping."

"I know you did, and you were a help, Nick. There were a lot of things I couldn't possibly have done by myself, even if I'd wanted to, but you didn't even wait for me to ask."

"And that's a problem?"

"It is for me." She swallowed hard, then said quietly, "I don't want to begin to rely on you."

"I don't mind."

"I know you don't. You're a very generous man, but I feel pressured by that generosity."

"I don't mean to pressure you."

Dana sighed. "I know that. It's *me*. It's how I feel. I won't allow myself ever to be trapped by a man again. I won't be dependent on someone else for my happiness."

The revelation took him by surprise, but it made sense. Everything she'd done pointed to a woman crying out for freedom and independence, a woman determined not to repeat some past mistake.

"Tell me about it," he pleaded, desperate for something that would make him understand. "Why did you feel trapped? Was it because of your marriage?"

"Yes," she admitted with obvious reluctance. "And that's all I'm going to say on the subject."

He reached out to touch her, then withdrew. "It's not enough. I need answers, Dana. More than that, I think you need to give them. You have to deal with whatever it is, then let it go."

"That's what I'm trying to to."

He felt the frustration begin to build again. "By keeping it all inside? You have friends who want to help. Me. Betsy. Let us."

"Can't you just accept the fact that this is the way it has to be and let it go?"

"No." The cornered expression in her eyes had almost made him relent, but he was determined to have this out with her. His vow not to confront her faltered in the face of her resistance. Confrontation now seemed to be the only way to open up a real line of communication. If she still wanted him out of her life, so be it, but he was going to know the reason why. The real reason.

Up to now that reason had been hidden behind her carefully erected facade. All this talk about feeling pressured and needing independence was part of it, but he sensed, as Betsy had, that there was more. Something had triggered those responses in her and apparently it had to do with her marriage.

"Dana, I'm not just being stubborn," he said at last. "Any fool can see that something is eating away at you. Can't you understand how important it is to me to be here for you? I think you and I could have something really special together, but it won't happen if you keep shutting me out. Talk to me. I can be a good friend, Dana, if that's what you need now. I'm on your side."

"This isn't a game where people have to choose sides, Nick." She sighed again. "Oh, what's the use? I knew I couldn't make you understand."

"Say something that makes sense," he retorted. "Then I'll understand."

"Nick, please. I don't want to hurt you. You have been a wonderful friend, but that's all it can be between us."

Dana watched as Nick fought to control his irritation.

"Isn't that what I just said?" he demanded, his voice rising. Dana flinched and felt the muscles in her stomach tense. Then she relaxed as he hesitated, swallowed and said in a more level tone, "Have I ever asked you for anything more?"

"You know you have."

Nick jammed his hands in his pockets in a gesture that had become familiar to her. "If I have, I'm sorry. When we make love, I want it to be what you want, too. I would never knowingly rush you into doing something you weren't ready for. If you want nothing more than friendship now, I'll give you that."

"But you'll go on wanting more. It's there in your eyes every time you look at me."

"It's in your eyes, too, Dana," he said softly.

Only a tiny muscle twitching in her jaw indicated that she'd heard him. She didn't dare linger to examine his meaning too closely. She didn't dare admit that he might be right. She couldn't cope with that explanation for the unending restlessness, for the inability to sleep after an exhausting day.

Ignoring the obvious, she went on determinedly without even taking a breath, "I'm flattered that you feel that way, but it won't work. I can't handle an involvement in my life. Not now. Maybe not ever. You're a virile, exciting man. You deserve more than I can offer."

She reached up, wanting to caress his cheek. Nick's breath caught in his throat, but in the end she drew back. She heard Nick's soft sigh of regret.

"Oh, Nick, please try to understand. You have big plans for the rest of your life," she said. "You can't put those on hold while you wait for me to see if I can deal with a relationship."

"You're at the center of my plans. Do you want to know what I see when I look at the future? I see you and me together forty years from now. We're sitting on the porch of that house of mine, looking at the river, talking, sharing, while a dozen grandchildren play in the yard. I see two people with no regrets, only happy memories."

Tears glistened in her eyes as she listened to his dream, and her heart slammed against her ribs. She wanted that dream as much as he did. It cost her everything to resist the need to walk into his waiting arms, to kiss him until all of her doubts fled.

"It's a beautiful dream, Nick," she said gently. "I wish I could make it come true for you, but it's impossible."

"You keep saying that, but how can I accept it if you won't tell me why?"

"If you care about me as much as you say you do, couldn't you just accept it for my sake?"

Nick searched her eyes and Dana fought the desire to look away, to avoid the pain that shadowed those hazel depths. His shoulders slumped in defeat.

Finally, with obvious reluctance, he asked, "What do you want me to do?"

Hold me, her heart cried. *Fight me on this.*

Aloud all she could say was, "Let me go. Give me some space for now. We can still be friends. Stop by the library if you want, but no more, Nick."

"And Tony? Are you planning to cut him out of your life, too?"

"Of course not. I don't want to hurt him, Nick. I don't want to hurt anyone. This is the only way to do that. If we keep seeing each other, Tony will want more for the three of us, too."

He gave her a penetrating stare. "What are you afraid of, Dana? Aren't you really scared that you'll begin to feel as much for me as I do for you?"

She met his gaze evenly. "Maybe so," she admitted candidly.

She saw the brightening of his expression and was quick to add, "But that doesn't change anything."

Nick sighed heavily. "Okay, sweetheart, you win." He stood up and dropped a light kiss on her brow. "For now."

When he walked away, he didn't look back.

Dana watched him go, struck anew by his tenderness, by the gentleness that shone through even when he was frustrated and angry. If she'd ever doubted his love before, she did no longer. That love was strong enough to temper fury, resilient enough to withstand pain. It was a love some women never found, deep and true and lasting.

And because a love just as powerful was growing inside her, she had to let him go.

Once again, Nick tried giving Dana the space she claimed to need. In fact, just to prove a point, he gave her even more than she'd bargained for. It wasn't easy. His body tightened at the memory of her in his arms and he was filled with heated, restless yearnings. If the days were long without the excitement of those midday conversations at the library and the chance meetings around town, the nights were endless.

Irritated all the time, he'd just finished snapping at one of his employees when the private line in his office rang.

"Yes, hello," he barked.

"Nicholas, dear, I hate to bother you at work, but I need to see you," Jessica Leahy said, her voice taut. The tension in her greeting was enough to worry him and to temper his tone.

"Is there some problem, Jess? Is Joshua okay?"

"Joshua's fine, but we need to talk."

"It sounds urgent."

"I think it may be. Could you come by this afternoon?"

He didn't hesitate for an instant, despite his recent irritation with Jessica. He'd always loved his wife's family. They'd begun treating him like the son they'd never had long before he and Ginny had married. Since her death, they had remained close, growing even more so because of Tony. The only time he could ever remember growing impatient with Jessica was on the night of Tony's birthday party. Thanks to Dana's insights, he'd even come to understand her uncharacteristic behavior that night.

"I'll be there in a half hour."

When he arrived, his mother-in-law was sitting on the porch in her favorite rocker staring off into space, the rocker idle. Her figure as trim as a girl's, she was wearing jeans and a Western-style plaid cotton shirt. But despite the casual attire, every white hair was in place, her makeup flawless. There was a silver tray with a pitcher of iced tea with lemon and mint beside her. She was the picture of serenity, except for one jarring note—she was absentmindedly twisting a handkerchief into knots.

She watched him come up the walk with troubled eyes. When he'd perched on the porch railing beside her, she poured him a glass of tea and took her time adding the lemon and mint as if she wanted to postpone their talk as long as possible.

"I know how busy you are, Nicholas, so I'll get right to the point," she said finally. "How much do you know about this Brantley woman?"

Nick flinched at her phrasing. It implied that a judgment had been made, that Dana had been found wanting in some way. He took a slow, deliberate sip of the tea before he spoke. "All I need to know."

"I don't think so," she said, her tone curt to the point of rudeness. Her shrewd eyes assessed him. "Are you in love with her?"

"Yes."

As if his quick response pained her, she closed her eyes for an instant, then said softly, "I was afraid of that."

Nick exhaled sharply. So that was it. She was going to pursue this illogical campaign to discredit Dana in his eyes.

"She's a lovely young woman," he said gently. "I think if you gave her half a chance, you'd like her."

"I thought perhaps I could, too, but now I'm not so sure. There are some rumors going around." At his indignant expression, she held up her hand. "I know, Nicholas. I'm not one for gossip, either, but I think you'd better look into this. If it's true, then I think you should keep Tony away from her."

"What the devil are you talking about?" Nick said, getting to his feet and beginning to pace. The creaking boards under his feet only increased his agitation. He stared at Jessica incredulously. "There couldn't possibly be anything about Dana that would make me want to keep Tony away from her. She's absolutely wonderful with him. And he adores her."

"I'm very much aware of that. He talks about her all the time. That's why I'm so concerned. If she's to be a big influence on his life, I want to be sure she's a fit person. He's my only grandson, Nick. I want what's best for him."

"This is ridiculous. Of course she's fit. How can you even suggest something like that? Is it Ginny? Would you feel the same way about any woman?"

"Perhaps so, but I like to think not." Her expression softened and she caught his hand as he stood beside her. "Darling, I'm not just being jealous on my daughter's behalf. Honestly I'm not."

She waved aside his attempt to interrupt. "Wait a minute, please. I know that's the way it must have seemed the other night. Joshua read me the riot act over my behavior. I don't need you to do it, too. Ginny would be the first one to want you to be happy again. But if these things I've heard about Dana Brantley are true, I don't think this woman's the right one for you. If it were just you, perhaps I wouldn't be so concerned. You're a grown man. You can make your own choices, your own mistakes. But there's Tony to consider, too. He's just an impressionable boy. I should think that would be important to you, as well."

"Dammit, you're being cryptic, and it's not at all like you to make judgments about people without giving them a chance. If you think you know something about Dana, tell me."

"I don't *know* anything. All I've heard is the gossip."

"Gossip that's usually nothing but half truths."

"An interesting choice of words, Nicholas. *Half truths.* Don't you deserve to know if there's any truth at all to the rumors? Find out about Dana Brantley's past. That's all I'm asking you to do. If she has nothing to hide, she'll tell you and that will be the end of it."

Suddenly the secrets and silences came back to haunt

Nick. For the first time, he was genuinely afraid. If he probed too deeply, what would he find? Would it be the end for him and Dana?

Chapter 8

Thunder rumbled ominously as Nick drove away from his mother-in-law's house. Dark clouds rolled in, dumping a torrential rain in their wake. Troubled by his meeting with Jessica, Nick went to his favorite spot overlooking the river, parked under a giant weeping willow and sat staring at the water through the rain that lashed at the windshield. Usually the serenity of the Potomac soothed him, but today the storm-tossed water churned in a way that mirrored his emotions.

Why hadn't Jessica told him about the rumors and been done with it? But even as he asked himself the question, he knew the answer. She was not the type of woman to spread hurtful gossip. Whatever she'd heard about Dana must have been terribly convincing, and very damning, for her even to mention it. But for the life of him, he couldn't imagine Dana ever having done something for which she might be ashamed.

"We all make mistakes," he muttered aloud, thinking of Dana's silences. "We all do things we regret." As wonderful as he thought Dana was, she wouldn't be human if she hadn't made some mistakes in her life. Whatever hers might have been, he believed they could deal with them if they could only get them out in the open.

Dreading the task before him, Nick drove back to his office and called the library. It had been days since he and Dana had talked, and he had no idea what sort of reception she would give him. Dana answered on the fifth ring, her voice breathless and edgy.

Nick was immediately alert. "Hey, are you okay?" he asked. "Is something wrong?"

There was a long silence.

"Dana, what's going on over there?"

He heard her take a deep breath, as if she were drawing in the strength to speak.

"Nothing, Nick," she said finally. "I'm fine. I was up on a ladder in the back when the phone rang. It took me a minute to get here. That's all."

"I see."

This time he was the one who hesitated for so long that Dana eventually asked, "Did you want something, Nick?"

"Yes. Dana, could I see you tonight? There's something I think we should talk about."

More guarded silence greeted the suggestion. At last, she said wearily, "Nick, we've been through everything."

"Not this."

"No. It's not a good idea."

"Dana, please. It's important. We could go to a movie."

"I thought you wanted to talk."

"I do. We can stop for coffee afterward." What he didn't say was that he wanted to prolong their time together, that sitting beside her in a movie would at least give him the temporary illusion of the togetherness he'd missed so much. It would also put off a conversation that was likely to have a profound impact on their future.

"How bad could it be spending a few hours together?" he coaxed. "It's even that George Clooney movie you've been wanting to see. Remember we talked about going?"

There was a heavy sigh of resignation. "Is this going to be like bingo? Are you just going to badger me until I give in?"

"Probably."

He thought he'd detected a glimmer of amusement in her voice, but it was gone when she answered. "Okay," she agreed with such obvious reluctance that it hurt as much as an outright rejection.

"I'll pick you up at six-thirty," he said. "We'll go to the early movie."

"Couldn't I just meet you there?"

Nick closed his eyes. "Why, Dana? Are you that afraid to be alone with me?"

There was a sharp intake of breath and this time there was real emotion in her voice. "Oh, Nick, I'm sorry if that's what it sounded like. Of course I'm not afraid to be with you."

"Fine. I'll pick you up at six-thirty, then."

Nick held the receiver for a long time after Dana had hung up, irrationally unwilling to break the connection. From that moment until six-fifteen, when he left his house after showering and shaving and sending

Tony off with grandparents, he tortured himself over the questions he'd have to ask. He felt like a traitor for wanting to know about a past Dana clearly wanted to forget. He'd been expecting trust from her. Didn't he owe her as much?

When he arrived at her house, he was dismayed to see that the circles under her eyes were darker than ever. Her complexion had a gray cast to it despite the attempt to heighten her color with a touch of blusher. Her slacks hung loose, as if she'd lost weight just since he'd seen her last. Despite his worry, Nick's pulse raced with abandon. His body tightened and he had to resist the urge to draw her into a protective embrace.

As they drove through town, she said, "We could skip the movie and just get this over with."

He glanced at her, saw again the obvious signs of tension and exhaustion, then shook his head. "No. I think we both can use the relaxation."

She shrugged indifferently and settled back in the bucket seat. It took only a few minutes to reach the town's single theater, but the thick silence between them made it seem like hours. Tension seemed to have wrapped itself around Nick's neck, cutting off his voice. He was grateful they were a few minutes late and had no time to talk as they found seats in the already darkened theater.

The movie passed in a blur as his own reel played in his mind. He recalled Jessica's behavior on the night of Tony's party and again this afternoon. He had no doubt that her concern was genuine, but he was equally convinced it was unwarranted. Still, with Tony's welfare at stake, he had no choice but to explore her veiled charges about Dana.

He gazed at Dana, who sat stiffly next to him, and wondered how things had gone so terribly awry between them. Faced with the uncertainty of their situation, the tension inside him built. He felt as though he were out with a distant stranger, instead of the warm, giving woman with whom he'd fallen slowly but inevitably in love.

When the lights came up, Dana blinked and Nick realized she, too, had been lost in thought.

"Maybe we should stay for the next show," he suggested wryly. "I don't think either of us saw this one."

"I doubt it would help. I think we both have too much on our minds."

"Shall we go, then? Maybe we can unburden ourselves."

"Talking doesn't work miracles," she said with a note of regret.

"Maybe not, but it's a start."

He got to his feet and Dana followed. As they walked out into the deepening twilight, Nick saw two old friends. He'd known Ron Barlow and Hank Taylor since childhood, and though he had no desire to stop and chat with them now, he felt he couldn't ignore them.

"Do you mind, Dana?" he said, gesturing in their direction. "We should go over and say hello. Hank does a lot of subcontracting work for me. Ron is a vice president at the bank. The three of us used to bowl together with our wives when Ginny was alive."

"Maybe you should speak to them alone. I might make them uncomfortable."

"Don't be silly. Come on." He slid an arm around Dana's waist and steered her in their direction.

"Hey, Ron. Hank." He patted Ron on the back and shook hands with Hank. "Did you enjoy the show?"

"It wasn't bad," Ron mumbled awkwardly just as his wife, Lettie, came up and linked an arm through his. She didn't look at Nick at all, just whispered to Ron and hurried him away before Nick could even introduce Dana. Hank and his wife followed, though Hank shot a look of regret over his shoulder as they left.

"I don't understand," Nick apologized, staring after them in confusion. He gazed into Dana's eyes and saw the hurt she was trying so hard to cover. He searched for an explanation that made sense. "Maybe they're like Jessica. Maybe they're thinking about Ginny."

"Maybe so," Dana said tiredly.

The whole thing was a thoroughly disconcerting experience for a man who'd always made friends easily and usually commanded fierce loyalty from all who knew him. But tonight it was as though he and Dana were being intentionally shunned without knowing what they had done to deserve it.

No, he reminded himself. Dana might very well know why attitudes had changed so abruptly. Jessica certainly thought she did. That was what this evening was all about: putting an end to the secrets and evasions.

Even though she might know the cause, Dana seemed every bit as disturbed as he was by the whispers and covert examinations.

"Shall we stop by Gracie's for coffee and pie?" he suggested.

"No. We can talk just as well at my place," she said, staring after a woman who'd just ignored her greeting. It was evident to Nick that she didn't want to deal with another such rejection. By the time they got back to her house, she was badly shaken. He would have felt better if she'd simply been angry. Instead, she acted as though there was no fight left in her.

She poured them both a glass of iced tea, but her hand was trembling when she handed Nick his. Then she took up pacing around the kitchen. At last she asked, "Am I crazy or were people avoiding us tonight? Not just those two couples but everyone?"

"I'm sure it was just your imagination," he said, but his voice lacked conviction.

"What about your imagination? Was it getting the same impression?"

"There's probably some perfectly logical explanation. Maybe I just split the seat out of my pants and no one dared to tell me."

Dana glowered at him. "Don't try to make a joke out of this, Nick. Something's very wrong. Everyone's been very friendly to me since I arrived in town—until tonight. Have you heard any rumors going around?"

"What sort of rumors?" he hedged.

"I don't know. It seems around here buying a new dress is cause enough for gossip."

Nick's eyebrows arched at the sarcasm. "I've never heard you sound bitter before. Is it what happened tonight or is it something more? Have there been other incidents you haven't mentioned to me?"

Dana stopped her pacing to declare, "I'm just fed up with people digging around in my life. I came here to escape that. I should have known it would be worse than ever in a place like this." Angrily, she clenched her hands into tight fists. Nick reached out and caught one hand in his and rubbed his thumb across the knuckles until her grip relaxed.

"Come on," he urged. "Sit down. Let's talk this out. There has to be some reasonable explanation."

She yanked her hand away and began pacing again. "I can't sit down. Do you have any idea what it's like to feel people staring at you, making judgments about you, especially people you thought were your friends? It's awful," she said, her voice rising at first in outrage, then catching on a sob.

She stared at Nick and her mournful expression almost broke his heart. She sat down and put her head in her hands.

"I thought it was over," she said, her voice muffled. "I thought it couldn't follow me here, but it has."

Nick seized on the remark. "What has followed you? Dana, what are you talking about? What rumors could there be?"

She looked up and stared at him blankly, as if she'd been unaware of the full implications of what she'd said, then she shook her head. "Never mind."

"Dana, stop hiding things from me. I care about you. Please, can't you talk to me about what's worrying you? There's nothing you can't tell me. I promise you I won't make judgments."

Her lips quivered, but her voice held firm. "I can't, Nick."

"Why? Why can't you tell me, dammit? You know I'm not just being nosy."

Tears trickled down her cheeks and she bit her lips. "Dana?"

When she still didn't respond, he slammed his fist down on the table and Dana's eyes widened in fear. "For God's sakes, Dana, talk to me. Fight back."

She shuddered, then squared her shoulders deter-

She hesitated, then said, "Of course. Would you like some coffee or tea?"

"Tea."

She busied herself at the stove for a few minutes, her back to him. Nick tried to understand the stiff posture, the return of distance when they had seemed so close throughout the day. He knew Dana was afraid, but of what? He was certain it was more than commitment, but nothing he could think of explained her behavior.

"Would you like your tea in here or outside?"

"On the porch," he said, craving the darkness that might lower Dana's resistance, provide a cover for her wariness and make her open up to him.

They talked for hours, mostly about impersonal subjects, until Nick's nerves were stretched to the limit.

"It's getting late, Nick. Shouldn't you be getting home to Tony?"

"Tony's staying at his friend Bobby's tonight and I'm exactly where I want to be." He dared to reach across and clasp her hand. After an instant's hesitation, Dana folded her fingers around his. He heard her tiny sigh in the nighttime silence.

They sat that way until the pink streaks of dawn edged over the horizon, occasionally talking but more often quiet, absorbing the feel of each other. There was comfort just in being together, Nick thought, in seeing in the new day side by side.

And, despite Dana's protests to the contrary, there was hope.

minedly. "You can't help, Nick. I can't even help my-self." Her eyes were empty, her voice expressionless. "Go on home. I just want to go to bed."

"Dammit, I am not leaving you alone when you're this upset. You're shaking, for heaven's sakes." All thoughts of his planned confrontation vanished now as he responded to her pain. "Dana, please, let me help you."

"I'll be fine," she insisted. "Go home to Tony."

"Tony's with his grandparents tonight. You're the one who needs me. I'm staying right here."

Dana apparently saw the implacable look in his eyes, because she finally shrugged and gave in. "Okay, fine. Stay if you like. You can sleep in the guest room."

With that she whirled around and left him alone at the kitchen table wishing he had some idea how to com-fort her. But how could you offer comfort to a woman who refused to admit she needed it? Dana was all stiff-necked pride and angry determination. By hinting that he sensed a weakness, a vulnerability, he had forced a denial. She had virtually rejected him, as well.

He listened to the simple, routine sounds of Dana getting ready for bed: the water running, drawers open-ing and closing, then finally the rustle of sheets. Vivid images played across his mind, taunting him. When he could no longer see a light under the bedroom door, he tiptoed down the hall and stood outside her room, cer-tain he could hear the choked sound of her muffled sobs.

"Dana."

Only silence answered him.

Dana bit her lip to keep from responding to Nick's call. Hot, salty tears slid down her cheeks and damp-ened the pillow. They were tears for a past she couldn't forget and a present she couldn't prevent from whirling out of control. Her arms ached from the effort it had cost her to keep from throwing them around Nick's waist and holding on for dear life. His strength could get her through this, but she didn't dare begin to count on it. Far more than pride had held her back. She loved him. No matter how she had angered him, how deeply she had hurt him, he had given her gentleness and understanding. She couldn't give him more heartache in return.

A fresh batch of tears spilled down her cheeks. Dear God, how she needed him, but she had to be strong enough to let him go. Tonight after the movies, feeling the stares burning into her, she had seen more clearly than ever that it was the only way. She couldn't embroil Nick in her problems, not when those problems seemed to be mounting every minute. She'd only be an albatross to a man who might one day want to run for office. She and Nick had never discussed his political aspirations, but she'd heard about them. He deserved the chance to make a fine legislator.

She swallowed another sob and clung to her pillow, pretending it was Nick she held. She tried to imagine his strength seeping into her. With him by her side, she could face almost anything. Without him, it was going to be hell all over again.

She heard the creak of the ancient bedsprings in the guest room and it sent a shiver down her spine. *You could be with him,* she told herself. *All you have to is walk down the hall, go to him. He won't turn you away.*

But it wasn't nearly that simple and she knew it. In the morning she would find the strength to say goodbye again and convince Nick that this time she really meant it.

* * *

Nick woke before dawn, and after hesitating inde-
cisively in the hallway, he opened the bedroom door
and crept in to check on Dana. The dim light from the
hall cast the room into patches of golden brightness
and dim shadows.

Dana was in the middle of the bed in a tangle of
sheets, her nightgown of silk and lace twisted midway
up her thighs. She was sleeping soundly now, though
he had heard her restless tossing for most of the night.
He tiptoed closer and sat down carefully on the edge
of the bed.

She looked so peaceful and vulnerable lying there,
her hair flowing over her shoulders in rich brown waves,
her skin slightly damp and flushed from the summer
night's heat. He brushed the hair back from her face,
then lingered to caress her cheek. Even in sleep, a re-
sponsive smile tilted the corners of her mouth. Unable
to resist, he leaned down to press a kiss on her lips.
They were like cool satin beneath his touch, smooth
and resilient.

Dana sighed at the touch of his mouth on hers and
Nick deepened the kiss, lingering to savor the sensations it aroused, to delight in her sleepy responsiveness.
His hand drifted down to skim over her bare shoulder,
then slid the thin strap on her gown aside. His thumb
followed the curve of her jaw and his tongue tasted the
soft hollow of her throat. She stirred restlessly and he
tried to soothe her by gently stroking her arm.

Suddenly, as if trapped in the midst of a waking
nightmare, she sat straight up in bed. Her eyes snapped
open and stared around in unseeing terror. Her hands

were thrown protectively up in front of her. Her whole body shook violently.

"No, please. No."

The words were a desperate whimper that stunned Nick into silence as she frantically drew the sheet up like a protective shield, clutching it around her and huddling in a corner of the bed.

Finally, his thoughts whirling, he forced himself to speak. He had to break through this blind panic.

"Dana, love, it's me. Nick. It's okay. I'm not going to hurt you." His voice was low and soothing. He spoke steadily, despite the pounding of his heart and the fear unleashed inside him. "Shh, sweetheart, it's okay. Nobody's going to hurt you."

She blinked as his words began to register. "Nick." Her eyes seemed to focus. The fear seemed to slowly dissipate, but not the trembling.

"Darling, I didn't mean to frighten you. Can I hold you?" he asked softly, reluctant to make another move without her approval.

She sat rocking, wrapped in the sheet, her arms around her stomach, her gaze locked on some awful, distant memory.

"Dana?"

At last she nodded. "Please."

As Nick's arms went around her, one last shudder swept through her and she curved herself into his comforting warmth. Then her tears began. They flowed endlessly. She wept until he thought both their hearts would break.

Chapter 9

Dana clung to Nick, her whole body shuddering with deep, wrenching sobs brought on by the unexpected reawakening of old wounds. Nick's gentle kiss had plucked her from a lovely dream and cast her into a nightmare he couldn't possibly have anticipated. Yet despite the seemingly irrational violence of her reaction, he continued to soothe her, his hands gently massaging her back, brushing the hair from her face.

"It's okay, love. It's going to be okay," he promised, and because she needed to, she believed him.

His words soothed her like a balm until at last she was still, totally drained by the experience. She drew in a deep breath and tried to pull free, but Nick held her still. For once, she hadn't the strength to resist. She burrowed her face in the male-scented warmth of his shoulder, while his arms circled her, lending strength and comfort. His steady breathing and slow, constant heartbeat were like the rhythmic sounds of a train, lulling her.

For this brief moment in time Dana felt safe, as if no harm could ever come to her again. She knew all too well, though, how fragile and fleeting that feeling could be.

"Feel better?" he asked.

She nodded, unable to trust her voice. Deep inside lurked the fear that if she opened her mouth at all, it would be to scream with such agony that Nick would flee just when she was discovering she needed his steadiness and quiet calm the most. Already she'd shown him a side of her she'd hoped he would never encounter. She could only begin to imagine what he must think of her after her unintentional display of histrionics, yet he hadn't run.

"I'm sorry," she said finally.

"There's nothing to be sorry about," he said, giving her a reassuring squeeze. "I'm the one who should be apologizing. I obviously frightened you. I guess I wasn't thinking. You looked so peaceful while you slept, so beautiful, that I couldn't resist kissing you. When you kissed me back, I wanted more. I shouldn't have given in to the feeling. I should have realized you'd be startled."

Surprisingly, she felt her lips curve into a half smile. "I think that's a slight understatement. You must have thought I was demented."

"Hardly."

She felt his fingers thread through her hair. When he reached her nape he massaged her neck until the knots of tension there began to unwind, replaced by a slow-spreading warmth that settled finally in her abdomen. Desire, dormant for so long, flared at his touch. She felt alive again and, despite everything, hopeful. She relaxed into the sensations, allowing her enjoyment of Nick's seductive caresses to last far longer than was wise.

Just a few minutes, she said to herself. *Just let me have a few minutes of solace in the arms of a man I love. Let me feel again, just for a little while. Surely that's not asking too much.*

"Dana, talk to me about your marriage. What went wrong?"

The seemingly innocent request snapped her out of her quiet, drifting state. Her muscles tensed immediately and her heart thumped so loudly and so hard she was sure the sound must echo through the bedroom.

She shook her head. "I can't talk about it."

"You must. I finally realize that must be what has been standing between us from the beginning. It's the only thing it could be."

"Nick, please. Let the past stay buried."

"I wish that were possible, but it's obviously not. Just look at your reaction this morning."

She stiffened and her tone became defensive. "That's a pretty big leap in logic. What makes you think that has anything to do with my past? Any woman who normally lives alone would be startled to find herself being attacked while she's still half-asleep."

His brow lifted at her choice of words. "Is that what it was?" She heard the doubt in his tone, saw it in his eyes, and suddenly she couldn't bear to go on with the facade a minute longer. Nick truly cared about her, perhaps even loved her, though he'd never said the words aloud. She'd seen the emotion, coupled with desire, time and again in his eyes. At the very least he deserved the truth, no matter how difficult the telling of it might be for her.

Sighing in resignation, she met his gaze. "What do you want to know?"

"How did you meet your husband?"

"We were in college together. He was a few years older. He was already finishing law school just as I started undergraduate school. We met at a fraternity party."

"Did you marry right away?"

"No. We waited until he'd finished school and gone to work."

"Were you happy?"

"In the beginning, yes. We were very happy."

"But not always?"

"No."

"What happened? Did he start running around with other women? Spend too much time at work?"

"Why are you so sure that I'm not the one at fault?"

"Because it's very clear that commitment is not something you take lightly. You'd fight for your marriage."

"Yes," she said very softly. "I suppose, in a way, I did."

A thousand images from those five long years flashed through her mind. The mental album began with Sam as he'd looked on their wedding day, his gray eyes watching her with pride, shining with love. She recalled vividly the nights of glorious passion, when his slightest touch fired her blood. Then there were the pictures of Sam at an endless series of parties, her arm

tucked possessively through his, or Sam staring hard
at her every second they were separated in a room as if
in search of the slightest hint of betrayal. And then…
She shut her eyes against the images of what happened
next, but the visions stayed with her, burned indelibly
in her memory.

Nick's arms tightened around her. "Tell me, love.
Maybe talking it out will help." His breath whispered
across her bare shoulder.

Dana had also once thought that talking was an answer. She had tried to talk to her family, but they'd
turned a deaf ear. They'd been so impressed with her
perfect marriage to a man they admired that they hadn't
wanted to listen to the flaws. Her sisters had their own
problems just trying to make ends meet. They couldn't
understand how anyone with Sam's and Dana's financial resources could possibly be troubled.

The next time she'd dared to talk it had been to a
psychiatrist, and by then it had been too late for anything to help. There was no reason to believe that opening up to Nick would bring her anything but more pain.
She was so afraid of the expression she would see in his
eyes when she'd finished. Pity, doubt or condemnation
would be equally difficult to bear.

"Oh, Nick," she murmured in a tone that decried his
innocence. Would he ever fully understand how truly
fortunate he had been in his own marriage? How rare
the unselfish joy he had found with Ginny was?

"You want to know what went wrong in my marriage, as if it were possible to pick out a single moment
and say, 'Ah, yes, that's when it began falling apart.
That's what all the arguments were about.' It doesn't
work that way. The disintegration takes place in stages,

so slowly that you don't always recognize it when it be-
gins to happen and the cause may have very little to do
with the symptoms."

Nick shook his head in denial. "I can't accept that.
Maybe you can't see it at the time, but now, in retro-
spect, surely you can."

"Not really, and believe me, I've tried and tried. I
kept hoping I could pinpoint the start of it so I could
understand it myself. We had arguments at first, like
any newly married couple trying to adjust. They were
always over little things. I squeezed the toothpaste from
the bottom, Sam squeezed it from the top. I left my
pantyhose hanging in the shower. He dropped his socks
on the bedroom floor. Was that when it began? Did it
fall apart over toothpaste, pantyhose and socks?"

She looked to Nick for a comment, but he simply
waited. "Okay, maybe it was the first time he dumped
an entire meal on the dining room floor because I'd
fixed something for dinner he didn't like. Or maybe it
was the first time he accused me of paying too much
attention to one of his coworkers at an office party.
Maybe, though, it wasn't until the night he slapped me
for challenging his opinion in public."

Her tone took on an edge of belligerence. "Which
time do I pick, Nick? Which time was just your normal,
everyday marital squabble and which was the first sign
that my husband was sick, that he was unable to cope
with pressure and that I was likely to become the tar-
get for his anger?"

Nick swallowed hard as the implication of that sank
in, but his gaze was unblinking, compassionate and unrelenting. "Go on."

Dana shivered in his arms and closed her eyes

against the memories again, but as before, that only seemed to focus them more sharply.

She spoke in a voice barely above a whisper, fighting against the sickening tide of nausea that always accompanied her recollections.

"I remember the first time Sam hit me. I was so stunned." Even now her voice was laced with surprise. "I had known he was upset. His anger had been building for weeks. The pressures at work were getting worse and he was tense all the time. One night he just snapped. It was over what I'd considered a minor disagreement in public. When we got home, he started yelling at me about it. All of a sudden he was practically blind with rage. After he hit me, he cried. I sat on the bed with this red mark on my face and Sam kneeling on the floor beside me, crying, apologizing, promising it would never happen again, begging me to forgive him."

She looked up and saw tears shimmering in Nick's eyes. She had to turn away. His pity was unbearable.

"But it did happen again, didn't it?" he said softly.

She shrugged, trying to appear nonchalant. "That's the pattern, isn't it? The first time, the husband apologizes and the wife believes him and things do get better...for a while. Then it happens again." She pressed her hands to her face. "God, I was so ashamed. I kept thinking it must be my fault, that if only I were a better wife he wouldn't be doing this. I tried so hard not to do anything that might set him off, but it seemed as though the quieter and more amenable I became, the more outraged he was."

"Did he drink?"

"Sometimes. He knew he couldn't handle it, so usually he stayed away from liquor. It was always much worse when he'd been drinking. I used to turn down drinks, hoping that he wouldn't take one, either, but it didn't work. It just meant I was sober enough to watch while he got drunk, knowing that sooner or later he was going to take it out on me. Sometimes he would come home very late, after I had gone to bed, and he would wake me up...."

She choked back a sob and put her hands in front of her face. "He...he would wake me up and... Oh, God, Nick, I felt so violated. It was like being raped by some horrible stranger."

Nick's breath caught in his throat. "Oh, my God." The words seemed to be wrenched from somewhere deep in his soul. "It was like that this morning for you, wasn't it? No wonder..."

"No, Nick. It wasn't like this morning," she said, reaching up to tentatively caress his cheek. She couldn't let him equate his tenderness with Sam's ugly violence. "You were gentle, not like Sam. It's just that when I first woke up I was disoriented. For a minute..."

"For a minute you thought it was happening all over again."

Dana nodded. She felt Nick's hand on her shoulder, warm and comforting as it tried to counter the chill that swept through her.

"I am so sorry, Dana. So very sorry."

"So am I," she said, her voice laced with bitterness. "But do you realize how many women go through exactly what I did? Some sources say around thirty percent. One out of every three women will be abused at some time by a man in her life, a husband, a boyfriend. Not just me. I couldn't believe it when the psychiatrist told me. I had been so sure I was all alone."

Nick drew her more snugly into his arms and held her. She felt his tears run down his cheek and mingle with hers. He rocked her back and forth, murmuring softly. She was hardly aware of what he was saying, just the soothing sound of his voice washing over her, trying to ease the pain.

Finally he loosened his embrace and brushed away her tears. She remembered being frightened of those hands, terrified of their strength, but now she felt only their gentleness.

"I want you to listen to me for a minute," he said. "I know that what you experienced was awful. I can't even begin to imagine how horrible it must have been for you, but that was Sam. Not me. It's over now. I can understand how you would be wary of men. In fact, a lot of things make sense to me now: your fear of getting close to me, your defensiveness, your need for independence. But, Dana, you can't build a wall around yourself and live the rest of your life in isolation."

"You're wrong," she replied wearily. "It's the only way I can live."

"Dana, I'm not like Sam Brantley. Don't you know I would die rather than harm you? What we have is special and good. We owe it to ourselves to give it a chance."

"I know that's what you want and on one level it's what I want. Intellectually I can tell myself that you and Sam are very different men, but emotionally I can't convince myself of that. There are too many scars." Nick flinched and she reassured him. "Not physical scars, psychological ones. They're just as long-lasting. I don't know if I'll ever feel totally comfortable around men again."

"Even after all these weeks, can't you see you can trust me?"

Dana heard the hurt in Nick's voice, but once started, she had to tell him the truth. She touched his cheek with regret as she said, "No, I can't."

"But—"

"No, wait. This isn't something that's your fault, Nick. Without living through it, you can't possibly understand what abuse like that does to your ability to trust your own judgment," she countered.

She searched for words to make Nick understand the inexplicable. "My husband was attentive, kind and loving all during our courtship. He was an educated man with an excellent career. That's the man I fell in love with, but there was a dark side to him, a side I never saw before we were married. Maybe he hid it. Maybe I blinded myself to it. I'll never really know.

"You talk about the weeks we've shared. Remember, Sam and I had known each other for three years in college, and I still hadn't guessed that he was capable of violence. Sam would pick up an injured animal from the side of the road and take it to a vet. He was a soft touch for any sob story. How could a man like that possibly be abusive to another human being, especially his own wife?"

"I still don't understand why you didn't leave him once you did know, why you subjected yourself to more suffering."

"There are so many reasons a woman doesn't leave. For some it's the children."

"But you didn't have that problem."

"No, because I refused to get pregnant by a man with no control over his anger. We had some horrible fights over that. Sam wanted kids. We'd planned for them, but when the time came for me to stop using birth control, I couldn't go through with it. I even tried to use that as leverage to make him get help, but it was as if he had no idea why I thought he needed it."

"Then I'll ask you again. Why did you stay?"

Dana closed her eyes. "Oh, God, there were so many reasons. For a while I kept deluding myself that it would never happen again. There were good days, you know. Sometimes months passed, and then I could believe that Sam was still the wonderful man I'd married. I also didn't get much sympathy. The one time I tried talking to my parents, they sided with him. They were sure I must have deserved his anger or that I'd exaggerated it. After a while I began to believe that, too. Sometimes the psychological abuse is more devastating than the physical. Each day chips away at your self-confidence until no matter how bad it is, you're afraid to leave.

"Besides," she went on, "even if I had left, where would I have gone? I hadn't finished school. I had no marketable skills. I had no money of my own. Sam made sure I never forgot that. I halfheartedly tried hiding away some of the grocery money for a while, but he always found it. Finally I just stopped trying."

"There are shelters."

"I know that, but at the time I tried to convince myself I didn't need that. I wanted to believe that those shelters were for some other kind of woman, that if I tried hard enough I could handle Sam without anyone ever having to find out."

"What about your parents? Why didn't they listen to you?"

"They didn't want to hear. My parents were from

the old school. They believed a wife made the best of whatever happened. Whither thou goest and all that. They wouldn't have taken me in."

Nick appeared shocked. "Surely they couldn't have realized how dangerous it was for you."

"No, they probably didn't. Maybe if I'd persisted, it would have been different. That's what they say now, anyway." She shrugged. "At the time, I was too embarrassed to tell them how bad it really was. They thought we were just having little spats. They never saw the bruises on my arms and legs or the gashes where his wedding ring cut into my flesh when he hit me. Ironic, isn't it, that the ring I'd given him in marriage was used as a weapon against me?"

A shudder swept through her. "Do you know once I actually went out to get a job? I thought if only I could be economically independent, I could get out. The only thing I could find was a job as a checkout clerk in a neighborhood grocery store. I took it. When Sam found out about it he accused me of trying to undermine his position in the law firm. He claimed my working in a demeaning position like that would make it seem as though he couldn't provide for me."

Her memory replayed the scene they'd had, and she drew her knees up to her chest and wrapped her arms around them as if to ward off the pain. "It was awful. He threatened to rip up all my clothes so I could never leave the apartment, and then he…" She swallowed a sob. "Then he saw to it that I had enough bruises to keep me from showing my face in public for a while. When I think back on the humiliation, I wonder how I lived through it."

"You made it because you're a survivor. You're stronger than you realize, Dana. After all that happened, you got out and you've pulled your life together. I wondered why you'd waited until last year to finish your master's degree. Now it makes sense. And I can see now why you would choose a place like River Glen."

He tilted her chin up until she was looking into his eyes. "Don't you see how far you've come? That's what's important. You took that experience and turned it around."

"I'm not so sure about that. Did you ever wonder why I would choose to be a librarian? I chose it because I was afraid, Nick. I was afraid of real people, of real emotions. I still am. I came here looking for a quiet, safe life. No bumps. No highs or lows, just a steady, predictable existence."

"Dammit, Dana, you deserve more than a mere existence. Let me make it up to you for all the years of happiness you missed. You got out of one kind of jail. Don't shut yourself up in another one."

"I wish I could accept what you're offering. With all my heart I wish that I could be the kind of woman you deserve."

"You are exactly the kind of woman I need in my life, Dana. You are gentle and giving, despite everything you've been through. Perhaps even more so because of it. Tony sensed that instinctively and so did I. Don't let bitterness and fear rule you. If you do, Sam Brantley will have won as surely as if you'd stayed with him. Are you willing to give a contemptible man like that so much power over the rest of your life?"

"Nick, I want to do as you ask, but it's too soon. The scars haven't healed yet."

"Then let's heal them together. Don't go through this

alone when you don't have to. Let me in. Let Tony in. We love you. We can make it easier for you."

She heard more than Nick's words. She heard the pleading tone. His eyes were shining with love. He held out his hand.

"Please. Don't fight what you're feeling for me. Accept it, build on it."

Dana hesitated, tempted. She was filled with longing, but she was also tortured by fear. She gazed into Nick's eyes, then glanced at his outstretched hand. It was trembling as he waited for her decision. Her blood surged through her, hot and wild with the promise of a new chance.

"I'll try," she said at last, slipping her hand into his. "I can't promise any more than that, but I'll try."

Nick's fingers closed lightly around hers, enveloping her in warmth. Even the roughness of his skin felt right somehow, as if it was meant to show her that strength could still be tender.

"This is right, Dana," he said, as though he had read her thoughts. He drew her close until her back was resting against his chest, where she could hear the steady, reassuring thump of his heart. "I promise you."

And for now, with summer's brightest sunlight dappling the bed and Nick cradling her in his arms, she could almost believe in the future.

Chapter 10

The image of Dana's pale, silken flesh marred by bruises almost drove Nick insane. He swore if he ever ran into Sam Brantley, he'd make him pay dearly for what he'd done to Dana. The man—no, he was less than a man—deserved to suffer tenfold the same wretched humiliation his ex-wife had suffered.

For hours after Nick had left Dana's, he had seethed with both anger and a desire for retribution. Only the certainty that more violence would slow Dana's healing had kept him from traveling to Manhattan and going after Brantley.

Now Nick sat in his office, staring blankly at the walls. He vowed to concentrate on overcoming Dana's doubts. He would have to gentle her like a brand-new frightened filly and teach her that love could be tender and passionate, rather than filled with anger and pain.

Now that he'd discovered the way it had been for her before, he would have to find new ways to prove that their love would be blessed with joy. Convinced more than ever that their relationship could be truly special, he pushed aside his mother-in-law's warnings. Surely now he knew everything.

With his goal firmly established, Nick picked up his phone and dialed the library, then tilted his chair back on two legs as he waited for Dana to answer. When she did, her voice bore no trace of the emotional turmoil she'd been through just a few hours earlier. If anything she sounded as though a tremendous weight had been lifted from her shoulders.

"I had an idea," Nick announced.

"That's your trouble," she retorted lightly. "You're always getting ideas."

"Not that kind of idea," he said, thoroughly enjoying her upbeat mood and the suggestive tone of her teasing. Perhaps on some subconscious level their talk had released her from some of the past.

"I think it's time we have some fun," he said.

"I thought that's what we'd been doing."

"Okay, more fun. Now will you be quiet a minute and let me tell you what I have in mind?"

"Certainly."

"Dancing. I think we should go dancing."

"In River Glen? Does Gracie's have a jukebox?"

"Very funny. No. I thought we'd go to Colonial Beach. There's a place there that has a band on weekends. It's lacking in decor, but it does sit out over the water. What do you think?"

She hesitated and Nick had a hunch he knew exactly what she was thinking. "Dana, you have to face people sooner or later. We really don't even know *what* they've heard. Maybe it had nothing whatsoever to do with you or your past. Whatever it is, the gossip will die down as soon as something more interesting comes along."

"When did you start reading my mind?"

"It's not all that difficult under the circumstances." He paused thoughtfully, considering something that had been bothering him. "Dana, do you have any idea how those rumors would have gotten started in River Glen in the first place? Could Sam have planted them somehow? Does he know where you are?"

Dead silence greeted his questions.

"Dana?"

"No," she said finally with absolute conviction.

"You're sure? He sounds like the kind of man who'd go to any lengths to hurt you."

"It wasn't Sam. I can't explain how I know that, but I do."

There was an odd note in Dana's voice, but Nick couldn't doubt her certainty. "Okay," he said at last, resolving to ask his mother-in-law where she'd heard the gossip. Perhaps he could trace it that way.

"Now," he said, "what about tonight?"

"If you want to endure my two left feet, it's fine with me."

"Terrific. I also thought maybe you and Tony and I would have one of our backyard picnics tomorrow. I plan to challenge you to a championship-caliber badminton game afterward."

"In this steamy weather I think croquet is more my speed."

"Maybe it'll cool off by tomorrow. Anyway, are we on for all of it?"

"As long as I get to fix the food."

"Don't tell me you're casting aspersions on my cooking, too?"

"If the shoe fits, Mr. Verone," she teased, and her tone made him smile with delight.

"Oh, it fits," he retorted, "but it's damned uncomfortable. I'll pick you up at eight."

His pulse was racing and he was filled with anticipation as he hung up. He wasn't prepared to look up and find his mother-in-law in the doorway, a disapproving frown on her face.

"Jessica, what are you doing here?"

"I came to see you, obviously. Were you talking to that Brantley woman, Nicholas?"

His gaze hardened. He hated to be rude to her, but it was time she understood exactly where things stood. His relationship with Dana was not open for debate.

"Not that it's any of your business," he said curtly, "but yes."

"Then it's clear you haven't asked her about the rumors."

"Not directly, no, but I do have a question about them for you. Where did you hear the gossip?"

"It's not important."

"I think it is."

"Why? So you can rush out to her defense?"

"Dana doesn't need my defense. We've had a long talk and I think I have a pretty good idea what the rumors are about. I see no reason to hold Dana's past against her."

Jessica's eyes widened in shock. "You mean it *is* true! Then how can you say that?"

Nick lowered the front legs of his chair to the floor

and stood up. He walked around his desk and put his hands on her shoulders. "Jessica, I am only going to say this once, so please listen very closely. I don't want to hurt you. You've always been a very important part of my life, but my relationship with Dana is none of your concern."

"It is when it involves my grandson."

"No, it isn't. If you really want to do what's best for Tony, you'll get to know Dana and welcome her into the family, because I have every intention of marrying her when she's ready."

His mother-in-law's lips tightened into a forbidding line and she shrugged off his touch. "Never, Nick. Obviously this woman has taken advantage of your good nature to lure you in, but I won't allow her to do the same with Tony. I'll fight you, Nick. In court, if necessary."

"That's an idle threat, Jessica. You have no case. I'm warning you, though, don't say one word to Tony about any of this." Nick's voice softened. "Don't you see you'll lose, Jess? Don't risk it. Don't risk losing your grandson's love."

"You've given me no choice," she said, whirling away and stalking from the office.

Nick stared after her, puzzled by her unforgiving attitude. How on earth could she hold Dana accountable for what had happened to her during her marriage? She had been the victim. Despite Jessica's attitude, though, he didn't for a moment believe she would make good on her threat. If she didn't drop the idea on her own, Joshua would see to it that she did. He was a fair man. He had already stood up for Dana once against his wife's unreasonable behavior. Nick had no doubt he would do it again, but in the meantime Jessica could make things damned uncomfortable. The only thing he could do would be to reassure Dana that she was not alone. They would face down whatever talk there was together.

With that thought, he put Jessica from his mind and began counting the hours until he would pick up Dana.

"Hey, Ms. Brantley," Tony said, pressing his thin body against her side as Dana sat at her desk. His eyes were cast down and he was chewing on his lower lip. She'd never seen him looking quite so troubled. "Can I ask you something?"

"Anything."

"How come my grandma doesn't like you? Did you have a fight or something?"

Dana felt a little frisson of fear curl along her spine at Tony's guileless question. "Why would you think she doesn't like me?"

"She was acting real weird last night. Every time I said your name she'd change the subject and Grandpa kept making these funny faces at her. I think he was mad, 'cause after dinner they were arguing in the kitchen. Grandma broke one of her best plates, too. I heard it. And then she cried."

Dana felt like crying, too. How could Jessica put Tony in the middle this way? No matter what she thought of Dana, Tony's grandmother was wrong to let her feelings affect a ten-year-old who'd already suffered too much in his young life. "I'm very sorry about that, Tony. The last thing I'd ever want to do would be to come between you and your grandparents."

She took a deep breath and forced herself to say, "Maybe it would be better if you didn't spend quite so much time at the library for a little while, especially now that it's summer and school's out."

His eyes immediately clouded over and his shoulders stiffened at what he obviously considered a rejection. "Don't you want me here?"

She put a comforting arm around his waist and squeezed. "Oh, kiddo, don't ever think that. You're my best pal. But before I came to town, you used to go to your grandparents' place every day after school, didn't you? And I'll bet you'd been spending your summers out at the farm."

"Yeah, but I like it here better. There are other kids around and you're here. Dad says it's okay with him if I come here instead. I told him I was helping you."

"And you are a big help. But did you ever think that maybe your grandparents are missing you? Grandparents are pretty special people. I never had a chance to know mine. They lived far away and they died before we could go to see them. I certainly don't want to keep you away from yours all the time."

Tony chewed on his lip as he considered what she'd said. "Maybe I could go there some days," he said grudgingly. "And I'm staying there again tonight. Dad said so when he picked me up this morning. He said he was gonna take you out."

"Oh, he did, did he?" Obviously she was going to have to stay on her toes or Nick would be railroading her into a relationship before she was ready. She had promised him a chance. She hadn't planned to let him dominate her life. Tonight she'd make that very clear.

But that night, Nick seemed determined that there would be no serious talk. Each time she tried to broach anything important, he took her back onto the virtually empty postage-stamp-size dance floor and whirled her around until she was too breathless to say anything.

"I'm too old for this," she said, gasping as she tried to return to the table.

"You're younger than I am. Get back over here."

"I have to have something to drink."

"No problem," Nick said, sweeping her into his arms. Two artfully executed and dramatic tango steps later, they reached their table and he picked up her glass of soda and offered it to her with a flourish.

"One sip," he cautioned. "The tango is my favorite dance. I don't intend to miss a second of it."

"Why couldn't you like to waltz?" she moaned, collapsing dramatically in his arms, an action that drew smiles and applause from the people at neighboring tables.

"Waltzing requires no energy."

"Do you consider this a form of exercise? I always thought dancing was supposed to be romantic."

"The tango is romantic."

"Two hours ago the tango was romantic. Now it's an endurance test."

"On your feet, Brantley. I didn't put this badminton net up for the fun of it," Nick said the following afternoon.

"I still haven't recovered from dancing," Dana said, lying on the chaise lounge waving a magazine to stir a breeze. She felt a little like the way Ginger Rogers must have felt after a particularly tiring movie date with Fred Astaire.

"Stop complaining, get up and serve."

She dragged herself to her feet, picked up the racket and shuttlecock. She took a halfhearted swing. The bird barely lifted over the net before taking a nosedive to Nick's well-tended lawn. He was caught standing flat-footed about ten yards back.

"What was that?" he demanded indignantly.

"A winning serve," she retorted modestly.

"Tony, get out here. Your father needs help. This woman is cheating."

"No, she's not," Tony called from the swing on the porch. "I saw her, Dad. She won the point fair and square."

"Thank you," Dana said. She glowered at Nick and said huffily, "If you're going to be a sore loser, we could switch to croquet."

"Just serve."

Dana won the game handily and turned the racket over to Tony. "Be kind to your father," she said in a stage whisper. "He's not as nimble as he once was."

"What's nimble?"

"It means his bones are getting old and creaky."

"Thanks a lot," Nick grumbled.

Dana waved cheerfully as she went inside to check on the potatoes for the German potato salad she'd promised to fix for Tony. As she plucked the steaming potatoes from the water and peeled them, she watched the badminton game through the kitchen window. Suddenly she realized she was humming and there was a smile on her face. She couldn't remember the last time she had ever felt this lighthearted. Her life felt right for the first time in years. This was what marriage was supposed to be like, relaxed and joyous with an edge of sexual tension. Yes, indeed, all the elements were there.

Lost in her thoughts, she didn't notice that the game had ended or that Nick had come into the kitchen.

"Why the smile?" he said, coming up behind her and circling his arms around her waist. His breath whispered along her neck and sent shivers dancing down her spine.

"I was just thinking how good I feel. Complete, somehow. Does that make any sense?"

He turned her around in his arms and held her loosely. "I think it does, and you couldn't have said anything I would rather hear."

Nick's gaze caught hers and she swallowed hard at the look she saw in the hazel depths. "Nick…"

"Don't analyze it, Dana. Just feel." He hesitated. "Okay?"

Her heart raced, thundering in her chest. Never looking away from his eyes, she nodded and he slowly lowered his lips to hers. The quick brush of velvet was followed by the hungry claim of fire. Nick's hands rested lightly on her hips in a gesture meant to reassure her of her freedom to choose between the bright flame of passion and the gentle touch of caring.

She had thought the tenderness would be enough, that it would be all she could handle, but she found herself wanting more and she stepped toward the heat. Her arms slid around Nick's neck, lifting her breasts against his chest. The nipples hardened into sensitive buds. Her hands threaded through the coarse thickness of his hair. His tongue found hers and together they performed a mating dance as old as time.

She could feel the tension in the breadth of Nick's shoulders, could sense his struggle for restraint, and that, in the end, caused her to step away.

Nick watched her closely. "Are you okay?"

"It was just a kiss, Nick."

"It was more than a kiss and you know it. It was a beginning and we both know where it's going to lead."

Her pulse lurched unsteadily, but she couldn't tear her gaze away from Nick's intent examination. "I know," she finally said in a choked whisper.

"I won't rush you, Dana. It won't happen until you're ready."

"I'm not sure I'll know when that is."

"I will," he said, and his confidence made her blood sing with giddy anticipation.

"How could you possibly double with a bridge hand that looked like that?" Nick demanded of Dana a few nights later.

"I warned you I wasn't very good."

"But any idiot knows you don't double unless you have high points in your opponent's trump suit. Did you have a single diamond?"

"I had the two and five," Dana said meekly.

Nick's voice thundered through Betsy Markham's living room. "The two and five!" He came up out of his chair and leaned toward Dana. Instead of being frightened and backing away, she stood up, put her hands on the card table and glared right back at him. They stood there nose to nose, Nick glowering and Dana's eyes glinting with amusement.

"I warned you," she said again, relishing the new-found self-confidence that permitted her to bicker with Nick publicly without fear of repercussions.

Betsy chuckled. "Maybe I should get the peach pie now, before war erupts in my living room."

"Maybe you'd better," Nick agreed, still not taking his eyes away from Dana. When Betsy and Harry had made a discreet exit into the kitchen, Nick muttered, "Come here."

"Why should I get any closer if you're just going to yell at me?"

"I'm not going to yell."

"What are you going to do?"

"This." His mouth captured hers for a lingering kiss.

When he finally moved back, Dana caught her breath, then said, "I'll have to remember to foul up my bid in the next hand, too, if that's the punishment I'm going to get."

"That was no punishment. That was a warning. When you get to the library tomorrow, check out a book on bridge."

"Why don't you just play with Betsy as your partner? She knows what she's doing."

"Yeah, but she's not nearly as pretty." He punctuated his comment with another kiss. "Or as sexy." And another. "Or as much fun to tease."

The last kiss might have gone on forever, but Betsy and Harry came back with the pie and ice cream.

"We'll finish this lesson later," Nick promised, earning an embarrassed blush from Dana and a wide, approving smile from Betsy.

Dana found herself humming more and more frequently as the days sped by. She no longer froze up inside at Nick's caresses. She welcomed them. She even longed for them, when she was lying in her bed alone, an aching heaviness in her abdomen, the moisture of arousal forming unbidden at the apex of her thighs.

The need to have him fill the emptiness inside her was growing, overwhelming her senses.

One morning she was wandering around the library daydreaming, humming under her breath, when the aging postman came by.

"Morning, Ms. Brantley."

"Hi, Davey. I hope that's not another batch of bills."

"Don't think so. Seems like there's a couple of new books today and a couple of letters."

"Thanks. Just put the whole batch on the desk. Help yourself to something cool to drink in the back if you want to. It's a real scorcher out there again today. I'm already looking forward to fall and it's not even the Fourth of July."

"I know exactly what you mean. Back when I was a kid around here we'd go to the icehouse on a day like this and get a bag of shavings and have a snowball fight. Cooled things down pretty well. Now I'd just welcome a soda, if you have any."

"They're in the refrigerator."

When Davey had gone into the back, Dana picked up the stack of mail and idly flipped through it. As Davey had said, it was mostly flyers from the publishers. The corner of a white envelope caught her attention. Suddenly her heart slammed against her ribs, then seemed to come to a halt.

Dear God, no. Not another one.

She gingerly pulled the letter from the pile as if it were dynamite. In a very real way it was. It threatened to explode everything she held dear.

With shaking hands, she ripped it open and found another hate-filled note from Sam's parents. Her eyes brimmed with tears as she read the cruel barbs, the vicious threats. They had seemed such wonderful people when she'd met them, kind and gentle and delighted about the marriage. They had adored Sam, however, and refused to see his faults, even after all the evidence was a matter of public record.

"Dammit, no," she muttered, shredding the letter with hands that shook so badly she could hardly grasp the paper. "I won't let them do this to me. I won't let them make me go through it again."

"Are you okay, ma'am?"

Dana blinked hard and looked up to find Davey staring at her, his rheumy old eyes filled with concern.

"I'm fine."

"Wasn't bad news or something, was it?"

"No, Davey," she said, trying to put a note of dismissal in her voice.

Davey took the hint, and after one last worried glance in her direction he shuffled out. "See you tomorrow, ma'am."

Dana didn't respond. She just sank down in her chair and stared blindly at the shredded letter. Desperate to rid herself of the awful reminder, she jerked open the drawers of the desk one after another in search of matches. She knew she'd brought some in along with some candles, in case of a power outage during one of the frequent summer storms.

She finally found them in the back of the bottom drawer. She put the offensive letter in the trash can and set fire to an edge of one piece. She watched as the flame darkened the corner, then curled inward to consume the rest.

But even after the tiny fire had burned itself out, she

sat there shaken, wondering how long she could live with this torment before she shattered like a fragile glass figurine thrown against a brick wall.

Chapter 11

Nick could hear the creaking of Dana's rocking chair as soon as he turned onto her street. He'd noticed for some time that the speed of her rocking increased in direct proportion to her level of agitation.

"She must be fit to be tied about something tonight," he muttered as he slowed his pickup to a stop. He tried to glimpse her through the thick green branches of the lilac bush, but his view was blocked. She never had gotten around to pruning it back.

He approached the corner of the porch and held a paper sack up high where she could see it.

"Hot apple pie from Gracie's. Interested?"

The rocking came to an abrupt halt, but she didn't answer.

"Dana?"

"Hi, Nick." There was absolutely no enthusiasm in her voice, and a knot formed in his stomach.

He parted a couple of branches so he could get a better look at her. "Hey, what's the story? Can't you do any better than that? Whatever happened to 'How thoughtful of you, Nick,' or maybe, 'You're wonderful'?"

He saw a faint smile steal across her lips, but it vanished just as quickly as it had come. She began rocking again and that, as much as the woebegone look on her face, sobered him.

Releasing the branches, which sprang back into place, he walked slowly around the house and entered through the back. He left the pie on the kitchen counter and went straight out to the porch. He caught hold of the back of the rocker and halted its motion long enough to drop a kiss on Dana's brow. He gazed into her eyes and found the all-too-familiar sadness was back.

"What you need," he prescribed, "is a long drive in the country."

She shook her head. "I don't feel much like going out."

"Which is exactly why you should go. It's a nice night. There's a breeze stirring. We can ride along the river, maybe stop for ice cream. If you play your cards right, I'll show you my favorite place to stop and neck. We can watch the moon come up."

"I don't think so."

Nick sat down next to her and put his hand on the arm of the rocker to stop the motion again. He struggled to curb a brief surge of impatience. "What's wrong?"

When she started to respond, he held up his hand. "If you tell me I can't help, I'm going to pick you up, rocker and all, and dump you in the river."

She blinked at the lightly spoken threat, and this

time her smile was full-blown. Her eyes sparkled, albeit unwillingly.

"Oh, really?" she challenged. "You and whose army?"

"You don't think I can do it?" He got to his feet, put a hand on each armrest and lifted the chair. Dana crossed her legs and grinned at him.

"Now what?" she inquired demurely.

Nick tried to take a step, but the bulkiness of his burden made movement awkward, if not impossible.

"I thought so," she said. "All talk."

"Oh, yeah?" Nick lowered the chair, scooped Dana out of it and stalked across the porch and through the house.

"Nick Verone, put me down."

"And have you think I'm some hundred-and-seventy-pound weakling? Oh, no." The back door slammed open, rattling on its hinges.

"Nicholas, where are you taking me?" Her voice rose, but it was laced with laughter.

"I told you—to the river. It's a great night for a swim, don't you think?"

"Don't you dare."

"Who's going to stop me?"

"I am."

"Oh, really?"

"Yes, really," she murmured provocatively. Suddenly Dana's lips found the sensitive spot at the nape of his neck. Nick gasped as her tongue drew a little circle on his flesh.

"Dana!" It came out as a husky growl.

"Umm?" She nibbled on his earlobe.

Blood surged through him in heated waves. His

strength seemed to wane and he lowered her to her feet, letting her slide down his body as his mouth sought hers and captured it hungrily. Her arms slid around his neck and she pressed her body close to his until shudders swept through him. She smelled of lavender soap and feminine musk, and the scent drove his senses wild.

"Dana," he said softly, trying to tame the moment, but it was like trying to tame the wind.

"Hold me, Nick. Just hold me."

His arms tightened more securely around her waist and she fitted herself to the cradle of his hips, undaunted by the hard press of his arousal. Nick was caught between agony and ecstasy. Some unknown desperation had driven her into his embrace, but regret, he knew, would steal her away. He took a deep breath and stepped back.

Her eyes blinked open and she stared up at him in mute appeal. He ran a finger across her swollen lips. "Why, Dana?" he asked quietly. "Why tonight?"

A sigh whispered across her lips. "Why not?" she countered with a touch of defiance.

"Because when I walked onto your porch not ten minutes ago, you were barely speaking to me. Now you're ready to make love. It doesn't make sense."

She watched him, her expression turning grim. "Not much does these days." She regarded him wistfully. "Why couldn't you just feel, Nick? That's what you're always telling me to do."

"As long as it's honest. Can you tell me it would have been for you tonight? Or is there something you're trying to forget?"

"Maybe…maybe there's something I'm trying to remember." She gazed up at him, her eyes bright with unshed tears. "Can you remember what love felt like, Nick? I can't."

"Oh, babe." He swallowed hard and reached for her, but she shook her head sadly and held him off.

"No. You were right. It wouldn't have been honest. I'm not ready for a commitment and that's the only thing that would make it right."

Puzzled by her bleak expression, Nick brushed the hair back from her face and caressed her cheeks. "What happened today to put you in this mood?"

"Just a lot of old memories crowding in."

Nick held out his hand. "How about we go replace them with some new ones? That pie's still waiting."

She hesitated, but finally she took his hand and they walked slowly back to the house. They sat at the kitchen table, lingering over the pie and iced tea, talking about everything but what was really on Dana's mind.

By the time Nick left an hour later, her mood had lifted, but his was uneasy. He went home with an odd sense of dread in the pit of his stomach.

Over the next few days he saw that his fears were justified. Dana began to withdraw from him again. She could pull back without saying a word. She'd stare at him blankly and let him see the emptiness. There was a perpetual frown on her lips, and dark smudges returned under her eyes. No matter how hard he tried to learn the cause, he kept bumping into silence. After days of feeling that happiness was within their reach, it suddenly seemed farther away than ever. It hurt all the more because he had no idea why this was happening. Dana evaded his questions with the deftness of a seasoned diplomat.

A few days after his visit Nick was sitting in his

study supposedly going over the company books. Actually he was thinking more about Dana's odd mood. Tony crept in quietly and came to stand behind him, his elbows propped on the back of Nick's easy chair.

When Nick glanced around, Tony said, "Can we talk, Dad? You know, sort of man-of-man?"

Nick had to bite his lip to keep from smiling. Tony was far too serious to have his request taken lightly. He put down his pen and drew Tony to his side. "Sure, son. What did you want to talk about? Is there a problem at the day camp?"

"Nope. The camp's okay. I'm learning some neat stuff."

"That's terrific."

"It's okay." He shrugged dismissively. "But I wanted to ask you something about Ms. Brantley. Have you noticed how she's been acting kinda funny lately?"

Nick was instantly alert. If Tony had noticed, then the problem was even more serious than he'd thought. No matter how distraught she'd been, she had always managed to hide it from Tony.

"What do you mean?"

"Well, like today. I went to the library right after camp and she wasn't in front like she usually is. The door to the back was closed, but I went in anyway and she was crying. I know I probably should have knocked, but I just forgot and she was real mad at me. She never used to get mad at me, Dad."

"Maybe she was just having a bad day. We all do sometimes. Did she say why she was crying?"

Tony shook his head. "But it's not the first time. I think somebody's making her afraid."

A frown knit Nick's brow. Tony was an unusual child in that he wasn't prone to flights of fancy. He'd never had an imaginary friend or exaggerated his exploits. If he thought Dana was afraid, then she probably was, but of what?

"Why would you think that?" Nick asked. "Has she said anything about being worried or afraid?"

"Not exactly, but you remember that day I had off from camp last week? Well, I went to the library earlier that day and Davey had just been there with the mail. When I went in, she was tearing up some letter."

"Maybe it was just junk mail."

"I don't think so, Dad, 'cause she burned it."

Nick was startled and more than a little unnerved. "She burned it?"

"Yeah, in the trash can, like you see sometimes on TV. Do you think something's really wrong? I wouldn't want anybody to hurt Ms. Brantley."

Nick ruffled his son's hair, trying not to let him see the depth of his own concern. "We won't let that happen, Tony. I promise. Thanks for telling me."

Now more than ever Nick was determined to find out what was going on. That upsetting mail she was apparently getting would be a starting point. He wasn't about to give up on Dana without a fight. They'd come through too much already.

Nick made sure he was at the library day after day when the mail came. She usually left it in an untouched heap on her desk as they sat in her office sharing the sandwiches she once again automatically brought for them.

Fortunately, she didn't notice the way he surreptitiously sifted through the mail as he moved it aside, studying the return addresses, searching for something that might make an increasingly strong, always resilient woman cry. He had no doubt she'd be infuriated if she realized he was spying, no matter how well-intentioned his actions might be.

On the following Wednesday the stack was bigger than usual and Nick wasn't quite as quick. At first glance, it seemed as though there was nothing more than the familiar circulars for upcoming books, an assortment of magazines and end-of-the-month bills. Then he caught the panicked look in Dana's eyes as she spotted an envelope stuck between a farming journal and a women's magazine.

"I'll take all this," she said, grabbing for the mail. If it hadn't been for the edge of desperation in her voice, the offer might have seemed offhand and insignificant.

Nick let her take the stack, but he caught the edge of the letter and withdrew it.

"That, too," she said, reaching for it.

"What's so important about this?"

"Who said it was important? I just want to put it over here with the other stuff." Her feigned nonchalance was painfully transparent.

Nick held the letter away from her and studied the fearful look in her eyes. Tony was right. Whatever was in this envelope frightened her badly and she didn't want him to know about it.

"What is it about this letter that frightens you?"

"I'm not frightened."

"You are. I can see it in your eyes. You've had these letters before, haven't you?"

"Why would you say that?" The words were casual enough, but her tone was suddenly defensive. Nick knew he'd hit the mark.

"Because of the way you're acting. You're jumpy

and irritable. It's not like you to snap, but you've been doing a lot of it lately."

Her eyes flashed at him. "If I'm snapping, it's because you seem to be intent on reading something that's personal. That letter is none of your business."

Nick ignored her anger. "You still haven't answered my question: have you had these before?"

"Yes, dammit! Now hand it over."

"So you can burn it?"

The mail fell to the floor as Dana shot him a startled glance. The color drained from her cheeks and her hands trembled, but she squared her shoulders and faced him defiantly. "How do you know about that?"

"Tony told me. He watched you do it. He's also seen you crying and it worried him. He finally came to me about it a few nights ago. Frankly, I'm glad he did. What's going on, Dana? Is Sam bothering you? If that's it, I'll take care of it. I'll go see him. We can get a court order, if that's what it takes."

She sank down in her chair and covered her face with her hands. Nick felt some of her fear steal into him, tying his stomach into knots.

"Dana?"

"It's not Sam."

"Then who? Is it some jilted lover who won't let go? Dana," he said softly. "Is that what it is? I can understand if there's some unresolved relationship in your past."

"If only it were that simple," she said with a rueful sigh. She glanced up at him. "After my marriage do you actually think I'd ever get seriously involved again?"

"You have with me."

"This is different. We're friends." The look she cast

was pleading. It was clearly important to her that he accept that simplified definition of their increasingly complex relationship.

"Okay," he soothed. "If that's how you want to see it for the moment, I'll let it go. The important thing is these letters and what they're doing to you. Let me help. There's nothing we can't work out together."

"Not this," she said. "We can't solve this. Look what it's doing to us already. We're fighting about it."

"Sweetheart, I'm not fighting with you. I'm just trying to figure out why you're so afraid."

"Let it go."

"No. I've already done that too often. Let me see the letter."

She continued to hold it clutched tightly in her hand. Frustrated by her stubbornness and torn by her obvious distress, Nick risked infuriating her even more by snatching the letter away from her. To his surprise Dana accepted defeat stoically once he had it in his hands. Refusing to meet his gaze, she went to the window and stared out, her shoulders heaving with silent sobs.

Now that he had her tacit agreement, Nick held the cheap white envelope with its scrawled address and debated what to do. The honorable thing would be to give it back to Dana unopened, to let her deal with whatever crisis it represented in her own way. However, she wasn't dealing with it. Rather than asking for his help, she was allowing it to eat her alive. If the stress kept up much longer, she'd fall apart.

At the image of the deepening shadows under her eyes, he made his decision. He ripped open the envelope. At the sound of the paper tearing, he heard a muffled sob. It was almost his undoing, but in the end he knew he really had no choice if he was to help her.

"I'm sorry, Dana," he said finally, relentlessly taking the letter out of its envelope.

As he read the hastily penned lines, so filled with venom that they seemed to leap off the page, his complexion paled and his heart pounded slowly. He had no idea what he'd expected exactly, but it wasn't this. Dear God, in his wildest imaginings, he would never have considered something like this. He felt a surge of outrage on Dana's behalf even as bile rose in his throat.

At last, when he had won the fight for control over his churning emotions, his gaze lifted and met hers. Her eyes were filled with a heart-rending combination of anguish and dread.

"Is it true?" he asked, hating himself for even posing the question. His heart cried out that it had to be a lie. Yet on some instinctive level, he believed the words he'd read. They fit, like the last, crucial puzzle piece that made the picture complete.

"It's true," she said curtly.

Nick winced. He had to swallow hard to keep from barraging her with questions. She had to tell him the rest in her own time, but as he waited, he wondered if it was possible to go quietly mad in the space of a heartbeat.

He's so quiet, Dana thought miserably, watching Nick's struggle. *He must hate me now.* Then she wasn't thinking of Nick at all but of the horror of that night nearly eighteen months ago.

New Year's Eve, the beginning of a bright new year. What an incredible irony! Instead of bringing joy and anticipation, everything had ended on that night. There had been that split second of stunned disbelief, then a cold, jagged pain that tore at her insides and then, unbelievably, relief and a blessed emptiness. The guilt hadn't come until later. Much later.

And it had never gone away.

Now she looked directly into Nick's eyes and repeated quietly, "It is true. Every word of it."

She took a deep breath, then forced herself to say the words she'd never before spoken aloud.

"I killed my husband."

Chapter 12

The flat, unemotional declaration hung in the air between them. Dana had made her statement purposely harsh, wanting to shock Nick with the grim, unalterable truth. There was no point now in sparing him the ugliness.

As she had both feared and expected, his expression filled with stunned disbelief. He closed his eyes, and when he opened them it was as if he'd wrestled with some powerful, raging emotion. Finally, at immense cost, he brought it under control.

"How could you?" The words seemed to be torn from deep inside him.

Her lips twisted and she said bitterly, "Sometimes I only wonder how it took me so long."

Instinctively, he reached for her ice-cold hand and caressed it, warming it. Then he released it, got up and

walked away, prowling the room like an agitated tiger.
Dana's breath caught in her throat as she waited nervously, watching the stark play of emotions on his face,
praying for forgiveness or, at the very least, understanding.

When he finally turned back, to her amazement he
apologized.

"I'm sorry. I didn't mean that accusingly, Dana. I
meant that you're the gentlest person I've ever met.
You couldn't even cut back that overgrown lilac bush,
for heaven's sakes. I can't imagine you actually killing
someone. God knows, from everything you've told me
that husband of yours was sick and he probably deserved
to die, but you…" His eyes were filled with pain and a
tormented struggle for understanding.

Dana felt a new, raw anguish building up inside. She
believed she was watching love wither and die right in
front of her eyes. She deserved to lose his love. She'd
been naive to dare to hope that with Nick things might
be different, that eventually they could shape a future
together without his ever learning the complete truth
about her past. She'd wanted desperately to believe that
he would never look at her the way he was staring at her
now, his eyes filled with doubt and confusion and pain.

It had been a fool's dream. Secrets had a way of
catching up with you, no matter how far you ran.

Just let him understand, she thought, then wondered
if even that was asking too much. The real truth was
that Nick was a compassionate, reasonable man. He
saw honest, open dialogue as the solution to all problems. How could he possibly accept something as
cold-blooded and final as murder? Never mind that
the authorities had ruled it an accidental death. She

was responsible just the same. Nick would have found some other way out of a situation as horrible as hers had been, but at the time, God help her, she'd felt trapped and defenseless and more alone than she'd ever imagined possible. Her troubles with Sam had escalated far beyond the reach of mere talk.

"Tell me about it," Nick said at last. "Please. I need to understand."

Dana sighed. She didn't want to relive that night. The events that had passed still came to her all too often in her dreams, tearing into middle-of-the-night serenity to shatter her all over again. During the day she was able to keep her thoughts at bay with hard work and endless, mind-numbing chores. Now a man she loved more than anything wanted her to explain that one moment in time, that single moment in her life that had changed things forever, and had made her an eternal captive of the past.

When she didn't speak, Nick pressured her, his words ripping into the silence. "Did you shoot him, stab him, what? For God's sakes, Dana, tell me. Nothing could be worse than what I'm imagining."

The demand for answers was raw and urgent. She couldn't possibly ignore it. Why keep it from him now, anyway? He already knew the worst, and if he was ever to fully comprehend the tragedy, he had to know everything.

"No, I didn't take out a gun and shoot him," she said, feeling numb and empty. Passiveness stole over her, distancing her from everything. She tried to blank out the horrifying images in her mind and envision only the words she had to say. "God knows, there were times when I wanted to, but I didn't have the courage."

She dared a glance at Nick and found there were tears of empathy that tore her in two.

"I know this is horrible for you. I can only imagine how horrible, but I have to know it all," he said with incredible gentleness. "If I'm going to help you, if we're going to put a stop to these letters and the threat they represent, I have to know exactly what happened."

Startled, she examined his expression and saw that he meant what he said. This wasn't the curiosity or pity she'd feared. There was no condemnation in his eyes. He needed to know not for himself but for her. Only time would tell if his feelings for her had really changed as a result of what he learned, but for now he was thinking only of protecting her from any more pain. He was viewing her as the victim, not the perpetrator. It was far more than she'd dared to hope, and a wave of incredible relief washed through her.

She took a deep breath and began again. Eyes closed, she spoke in a whisper, slowly, each hesitation an instant in which she relived the devastating horror of that last night with Sam.

"You know the background. This time it all started at a party, I guess. Sam pulled me into the kitchen and accused me of flirting with some man. I don't really remember who, and it doesn't matter. It was always someone. His accusations were an excuse. When I denied everything, he pinned me against the wall and grabbed a butcher knife. He—"

She swallowed the lump in her throat. "He held it to my neck. I could feel the blade pressing against my skin."

She shuddered and clasped her arms around her middle. "Maybe it was because there were people nearby.

Maybe it was just that I'd finally had too much and didn't care anymore. I don't know. Maybe I'd finally found my last shred of self-respect. Whatever it was, I screamed. I said if he ever came near me again, I'd kill him."

"And some people heard you say that."

"*Everyone* heard. They'd run toward the kitchen when they first heard me scream. Sam let me go, tried to make a joke of it. It was an awkward moment and everyone was obviously very relieved it was over. They were glad to take him at his word. But I knew that wasn't the end. I knew things would be worse than ever when we got home."

"Then why did you go? Why didn't you stay with a friend? Go to your parents? Anything, except go home with him."

Dana laughed, the sound echoing bitterly. "Would you believe that after all he'd done to me, I was still embarrassed? I still didn't want anyone to know. Everyone loved Sam. He was a real charmer. They only accepted me for his sake. My old school friends... I guess I'd cut myself off from them after the wedding. I'd tried so hard to fit in with his crowd."

When Nick attempted to protest, she stopped him. "No. It was true. In his circles I was an outsider. Because of that, I was at first afraid they wouldn't believe me. And then, after it had gone on for a while, I was too damned embarrassed to admit to anyone that I hadn't left him before."

"But just that one night, Dana. People knew you'd had a fight. No one would have questioned it if you'd just asked for a place to stay until your tempers cooled. They wouldn't have had to know about the rest."

"It all makes perfect sense when you say it, but you have to understand the syndrome. After a while you begin to feel utterly defeated and alone. You can't understand the true meaning of despair, Nick, until you've lived with it day after day, month after month. Not only that, Sam had repeatedly warned me that if I told anyone, if I tried to leave him, he'd come after me and make whoever took me in pay. I couldn't put anyone else at risk like that. And always, in the back of my mind, was that slim hope that this time would be different, that the wonderful man I'd fallen in love with would return, that he would be gentle and caring the way he was when we met. Some tiny part of me still loved that man."

She caught Nick's incredulous gaze, then glanced away. "I read something an abused woman in Maryland said not long ago. She said her marriage, her love for her husband in spite of all he'd done to her, was like an addiction. I think she's right. Making the decision to get out is no easier than kicking a drug habit or quitting smoking. All the well-meaning advice in the world won't make you leave, until you can admit to yourself that there *is* a problem."

"After all you'd been through, you couldn't admit even that much?"

"Not until that night. Until then, I had seen it as *my* failure."

Nick listened to the words and she could see that he was still tormented by the struggle to accept the twisted emotion behind them. Perhaps no one who hadn't experienced something like her situation could ever understand. She had made the only choices she could at the time, but she had learned from her mistakes. She would never again allow herself to be a victim.

"So you left together," Nick said, his tone dispassionate. It was as if he'd fought for objectivity and now clung to it desperately. "Did you fight on the way home?"

"No, the silence in the car was almost eerie. But by the time we got to our apartment, I thought maybe the worst of it was over after all."

Her lips curved in a wry grin. "'Hope springs eternal....' Isn't that what they say? As it turned out, that ride was simply the calm before an even more violent storm."

"What happened?"

"I went upstairs to the loft and began to get ready for bed. Sam stayed in the living room and had another drink. By the time he stumbled up the stairs, he was muttering jealous accusations again.

"I heard him and knew what was going to happen. I ran for the bathroom, planning to lock myself in, but he caught me. He grabbed my arm and whirled me around." Unconsciously she rubbed her arm where the bruises had marred her delicate skin for days afterward. She closed her eyes and the images flooded back.

"Sam was a handsome man, but that night his face was twisted with fury. He was somebody I couldn't even recognize. It was a frightening transformation, as if he'd finally gone over the edge. He was beyond thinking, beyond reasoning.

"When he pulled back his fist to hit me, something finally snapped inside me for the second time that night. I woke up to the reality. I knew then that things would never change, that if I didn't get myself out I was condemning myself to an eternal hell. I was the only one who could decide how I was going to spend the rest of my life."

"And so you fought back."

"This time I fought back with more strength than I imagined I had. I hit him first. The blow wasn't much, but it was enough to throw him off balance, and I ran toward the stairs. He lunged after me."

Her eyes clamped more tightly shut as tears began to roll down her cheeks. Even with her eyes closed, the visions came back, as vivid as the night it had happened. She shuddered.

"God, it was awful. Sam was very drunk, clumsy. I shoved him back, moved out of the way."

Suddenly she was choking, sobbing as the memories flooded back. "He...he threw...threw himself at me again."

She covered her face with hands that were shaking violently. "Then—I can't remember how—then he was falling, head over heels, down the stairs. Maybe I even pushed him. I don't know. There are a few missing seconds in my mind, a complete blank. The psychiatrist says I'll remember when I'm ready."

"Oh, babe." Nick reached out to her, but she shivered and pulled away.

The words came faster now, as if by getting them all out, by telling the whole story, it would somehow cleanse her at last.

"When I came to, I was standing at the top of the steps, shaking, staring down at him, his body all crumpled, his leg stuck out at an odd angle. I thought I heard him moan, but I was terrified to go down there. I couldn't bear the thought of touching him. It must have been ten minutes or more before I finally called the rescue squad, but it was too late. He was dead."

She sighed heavily and opened her eyes. "I'd already guessed as much. The police came and they called Sam's parents in Omaha. His mother was hysterical. She had to be hospitalized. Later they made a lot out of the fact that I was so calm. The doctor said it was due to shock, but Sam's mother and father didn't see it that way. Then a few people came forward and told about the threat I'd made at the party. The whole thing blew up into a pretty nasty scandal."

"But, Dana, it wasn't murder. It was an accident. That's all, and it's over now."

She shook her head. "That's what the court said, but it will never be over. His parents can't let it go. They've convicted me."

Her voice was flat and she stared at Nick with eyes that were empty. "And don't you see? That's not what really matters anyway, because of the way I felt."

"I don't understand."

"I was glad he was dead." Her tear-filled eyes gazed at Nick and her chin lifted defiantly. "I didn't mean to do it, I didn't mean for it to go that far, but I was glad that it was finally over. What kind of person does that make me?"

"A desperate one. A woman who had been hurt time and time again by a man she loved."

Nick's own eyes were damp and his whole body seemed to be shaking, but he took her in his arms and held her until both their trembling abated. Dana clung to him, drawing on his strength.

"Oh, babe, it's going to be okay," he promised. "It may take some time, but it will be okay."

Dana wanted desperately to believe Nick, but she'd lived through too much to believe in miracles. "You can't dismiss it that easily, Nick. Sam Brantley is dead because of me, and his parents will see to it that the story follows me wherever I go."

"There must be a way to stop them. We can see a lawyer this afternoon."

"It's too late. People here already know. I don't know how they found out, but they've obviously heard something. You've seen how I've been shunned the last few weeks. The word is spreading. It's bound to blow up pretty soon. The Brantleys won't rest until it does."

"Then that's all the more reason for us to fight back."

"For *me* to fight back, not us, Nick. It's my battle, one I'd hoped to avoid, but I'm going to stay here and fight it. I like River Glen. I'm happy with my new life. I won't let them take it away from me. I won't be victimized again."

She touched his lips with trembling fingers. "It's different for you, though. If you stay with me now, it will kill whatever chances you might have for a state or national political office."

"How can you even think about something like that? To hell with a political office, if the cost includes giving you up. Being a politician has never been my dream."

"But Betsy told me—"

"She told you that people around here think I should run for the General Assembly. That doesn't mean I've wanted to. I like what I do. Being a contractor, a father to Tony and maybe someday a husband to you—that's all I want. I have a good life, Dana. A rich, full life. I don't need to be running off to Richmond or Washington."

"If you gave that up for me, though, I could never forgive myself. It's more than enough for me just to know you'd be willing to."

"I'm not giving up anything important. Maybe if we hadn't met, I would have run for office just because it would have filled the empty spaces in my life, given me something meaningful to do after Tony's grown. But there are no empty spaces now."

Dana watched in wonder as he opened his arms. She tried to read his expression, searching for doubts, but there were none. She found only unquestioning love that sent a wild thrill coursing through her.

"Are you sure?"

"Very sure."

After an endless hesitation, she nodded and stepped into his arms.

Chapter 13

The provocative sensation of Dana nestled in his arms, drawing comfort from his embrace, her body settled between his splayed legs, stirred far more than Nick's protective instincts. He wanted her with an untimely, unreasoning desire. For weeks now he had tempered his ardor, but he could no more. His blood roared through his veins, stirring a fierce, urgent passion. A low moan rumbled deep in his throat as he tightened his arms around her.

"I need you, Nick." The tentatively spoken appeal wrenched his heart.

"You have me, sweetheart. I'm not going anywhere."

Round eyes, shimmering with tears, stared back at him. "No. I mean I really need you. I need to be with you." Her voice broke. "Please. Make love to me, Nick. Help me prove to myself that I can still feel."

His heart hammered harder. He brushed her mussed hair back from her face and studied her expression. He was searching for a hint of the fear he'd seen so often in her eyes whenever he'd openly wanted her. He understood that fear now, knew its cause, and he wanted no part in resurrecting it. If he had to wait forever for Dana to feel right about the two of them as lovers, he would.

"Are you sure? You're very vulnerable right now. I don't want to take advantage of that."

"But you do want me, don't you?"

He drew in a ragged breath. "Oh, yes. Never doubt that, Dana. I want you so badly it frightens me. I've spent weeks lying awake at night wanting to hold you in my arms, wanting to explore every inch of your body with my kisses, wanting to bury myself in you. But now, Dana? Today? I don't know."

She bit her lower lip to still the trembling. "Because of what you found out about me? Does it bother you so much?"

He ached for her and cursed himself for raising new self-doubts in her. He should have realized instantly that this had been her greatest fear of all, that this was what had kept her silent.

"No, my love. It's not that. I swear it. I don't blame you for anything that happened in your past. I just don't want you to have regrets. If we make love now, with all that's gone on today, won't you wonder later why you did it?"

She shook her head, her brown eyes never leaving his face. They shone with surprising self-confidence.

"I know why, Nick. I love you. I was afraid to admit it before today. Even if you can't love me, I have to tell you how I feel."

She rubbed an unsteady finger across his lips and they burned in the wake of that fiery, gentle touch. "You've made me feel whole again. No matter what happens between us, you've given me that and no one will ever take that feeling from me again."

She said it solemnly, with absolute conviction, and Nick felt something tear loose inside him. Doubts fled and passion rampaged more violently than ever. He wouldn't make her ask again.

He nodded and took her hand. "Let's go home."

A sweet, sensual tension throbbed between them as Dana closed the library, turning off the lights in the back, making a sign for the door announcing that it would open again in the morning. It was nothing more than routine and yet there was nothing ordinary about it. The tasks took on a heightened significance. By the time she turned her key in the lock at last, Nick's nerves were stretched taut with anticipation.

"We'll take your car," he said, holding out his hand for the keys. She dropped them into his hand without comment.

During the brief drive to her house, he glanced at her often, still looking for some sign of reluctance, any indication that she was already regretting her impulsive declaration. He found none.

Dana met each glance with a faint smile that was almost shy in its pleasure. That look made Nick want to slay dragons for her. Perhaps, he thought once, perhaps that's what I'm doing.

When they reached the cottage, he turned off the ignition, then twisted around to read her expression again.

"Any second thoughts?"

"None," she said without hesitation. "This feels right for me, Nick."

"It feels right for me, too."

When she started to open the car door, he stopped her. "There's one more thing I want you to know now, before we go inside."

"What?"

"I love you, Dana. I don't ever want you thinking that we're here for any other reason." He touched her cheek and repeated quietly, "I love you."

A sigh shuddered through her. "Thank you for saying that. Thank you for everything."

The walk to the back door seemed endless. Nick's sharpened senses were overwhelmed by the heavy scent of an array of colorful blossoms, the summer sounds of birdsong and bees hovering over the flower beds and the subtly provocative sway of Dana's hips as she made her way through the ankle-high grass dotted with buttercups and dandelions.

On the way, Nick plucked a pale pink rose from a bush at the side of the house. He stripped it of its thorns and tucked it into Dana's dark hair, his fingers lingering to caress the sun-kissed warmth of her cheek.

"You are so beautiful," he murmured. "This setting suits you. There's a surprisingly earthy sensuality about you."

She smiled at him and reached up to touch the rose. "Why surprising?"

"Because for so long you only allowed me to see the cool indifference, the sophistication."

"I had no choice, Nick. I was too frightened to allow anyone to get too close, especially you."

"Why especially me?"

"Because I sensed from the beginning that this day would come. Even when I was fighting you the hardest, I trusted you and I wanted you. It terrified me, because the last time I felt that way about anyone—"

"I know. You were betrayed."

"No," she said sharply. "It was worse than a betrayal. It was a mockery of what love was supposed to be."

"That's all behind you now."

She shook her head. "No. It's still very much with me, but I can deal with it now. As long as I have you, I can face it."

"You have me," he whispered, his lips claiming hers in gentle confirmation of the promise.

From that moment on, things seemed to happen in slow motion, each sensation drawn out over time until it peaked at some impossible height of awareness. Dana moved through the house in a reversal of her routine at the library, opening windows, allowing the breeze to air the rooms. When she was finished she came back to the kitchen, where Nick was waiting, his heart in his throat.

"I couldn't find any champagne," he said, holding up two glasses of apple juice. "We'll have to toast with this."

Dana took a glass, her hand trembling. But when she met his eyes, her gaze was steady, sure.

"To beginnings," Nick whispered, touching his glass to hers.

"And to the endings that make them possible."

They sipped solemnly, their gazes clashing. It was Dana who took the glasses and set them aside. She reached for the buttons on his shirt, never taking her eyes from his. "Do you mind?"

"Be my guest."

His pulse raced as her fingers fumbled at their task. When his shirt was finally open, she touched the tips of her fingers to his heated flesh, at first tentatively and then with more confidence. Nick felt the wild pounding of his heart, the surge of his blood, and wondered just how much of the unbearable tension he could take. But it had to be this way. Dana had to be the aggressor. She had to see that with him she could be in control, not just of her own responses but of his. This first time had to have beauty and love and, perhaps most important of all, respect.

She ran her palms across his chest in a slow, sweeping gesture that set his skin on fire. When she left the matted hair on his chest and reached the curve of his shoulders, she caught the edges of his shirt and slipped it off, leaving him bare to the waist.

Her eyes lifted tentatively to meet his. "Okay?"

"Whatever you want," he said on a ragged sigh. "This is your show. You set the pace."

Her gaze swept over him lazily, and where it lingered, her touch followed so predictably that Nick could anticipate each one. The curve where neck met shoulder. The tensed muscles in his arms. The masculine nipples almost hidden beneath coarse, dark hair. The flat plane of his stomach.

But if Dana's touches were predictable, Nick's responses were another thing entirely. Never had he anticipated the sweet yearning that was building inside him. Never could he have predicted the urgent hunger, the demanding need that made his legs tremble and tightened his muscles until they ached for release. Never before had he known it was possible to feel so much at the simple brush of a finger, at the fleeting touch of lips. If Dana's thoughts were bold, her exploration was still shy and all the more exciting because of it.

She sighed softly. "I've wanted to do this for so long." She looked into his eyes. "Would you kiss me again?"

Nick touched one finger to her chin, tilted her face up and very slowly lowered his mouth to hers. The first kiss was sweet and gentle. The next was an urgent claiming. His body shook with the effort of restraint. When he would have pulled away, Dana slid her arms around his neck.

"No," she cried out softly, and this time it was her passion, her hunger, that showed him the way.

"Take me to bed, Nick," she said at last. "Make love to me."

Nick scooped her into his arms without comment, his mouth claiming hers again as he moved through the hall. Dana's shoes fell to the floor. Her arms circled his shoulders and she rained kisses on his cheeks, his nose, his neck and then, at last, his mouth, lingering there for a sensual dueling of tongues that left Nick gasping.

Before they even reached the bedroom, Nick had lowered her to her feet, allowing her to slide down his fully aroused body, wanting her to know in full measure what her touch had accomplished.

"I need you very badly," he said, tilting her hips hard against him. She held back for just an instant, then swayed toward him emitting a low whimper of pleasure. "Very badly."

Dana heard the urgency in his hoarse cry and felt at first a momentary fear, then a blessed sense of triumph.

This was love as it should be, demand tempered with caring, need gentled by tenderness. She caught Nick's hands and drew them to the buttons on her blouse.

"Your turn."

His fingers were much more certain than hers had been, but still she felt the trembling as they grazed her skin. She watched his eyes and in their hazel depths she saw what she had never thought to see again. She saw love. So much love that it made her ache inside. She saw her beauty reflected in his eyes, and in that awed appreciation she found contentment, a serenity that would carry her through all time.

Her blouse fell away and then the lacy wisp of her bra. Nick cupped the fullness of her breasts in his hands, rubbing the nipples with his thumb until the peaks were sensitive coral buds more than ready for the soothing moistness of his tongue. The flick of his tongue magnified the sensitivity, sending waves of pleasure rippling through her.

When he reached for the clasp on her skirt, she drew in her breath, holding it as the skirt drifted down to her ankles. She stepped out of the circle of material, then waited, breathless, as he hooked his fingers in the edge of her slip and panties together and slid them off.

When she was standing before him completely nude and open to his touch, a shudder swept through him.

"You are so beautiful," he breathed softly. "So very beautiful."

"Only with you, Nick. I feel beautiful with you."

He scooped her into his arms again and at last they finished the journey to the bedroom. When Nick low-

ered her to the bed at last, Dana felt as if she had finally
reached the edge of forever.

She watched through partially lowered lashes as Nick
removed the rest of his clothes, then stood before her in
unself-conscious splendor, his body as finely tuned and
well muscled as an athlete's, tanned and proud. Her lips
curved into a smile and she tilted her head thoughtfully.

"I think, perhaps, you're the one who's beautiful,"
she whispered huskily.

The mattress dipped as Nick stretched out beside
her. A smile played about his lips and laughter danced
in his eyes. "We could fight about which one of us is
more beautiful."

Dana shook her head. "No fighting. Not now and
certainly not about that. We have better things to do."

"We do?"

She rolled toward him, feeling the first thrilling
shock of having the full length of his body against
hers. "We most definitely do," she said as her mouth
found his.

Nick's hands claimed her with a gentleness that she
blessed at first, then came to curse. She wanted more
than the light, skimming, feathery touches and she
urged him on, gasping when he moved from the tender flesh of her thighs to the moist heat between her
legs. He hesitated until she put her hand on his and en-
couraged more.

An unbearable tension coiled inside her until she was
pleading for release, begging Nick to set her free. Un-
accountably, his fingers stilled as he insisted that she
drift back to earth and join him.

Her body glistened with perspiration, more sensitive
than ever to his gliding touch.

"Why are you waiting?" she asked, confused and let down.

"This is your trip, Dana. I want to be very sure we take it when you're ready."

Suddenly she understood what he was doing and she felt a swell of love in her chest. "You told me once you'd know when I was ready."

"Oh, I think you are, but it's your decision, your move."

She knelt on the bed beside him. "Now, Nick. I'm ready now."

A faint smile touched his lips as he grasped her and lifted her into position straddling him. Slowly, with the utmost care, he settled her in place. As he filled her, Dana knew a glorious instant of possession and then she was beyond thought. She was only feeling as she rode him, taking her pleasure from him. The spiral of tension wound tight again and then, like a top, she was spinning free, exultant, taking Nick with her in a burst of joy that set them both free from the past and sent them whirling on, into the future.

Much later Dana awoke in Nick's arms, feeling secure and unafraid in the circle of his strength. The bedroom was in the shadows of twilight, and in the dim, gray light, she watched him sleeping and thought again how incredibly handsome he was and how utterly right their love was.

She must have sighed because Nick's arms tightened just a little and he murmured, "What is it? Are you okay?"

"I am—" she searched for the perfect word "—complete."

His fingers ran through her hair, combing the tangles free. "You're not sore? I didn't hurt you?"

"You could never hurt me."

"I hope not, Dana."

She was troubled by his too-somber tone. She propped herself up on his chest and ran her hand along the curve of his jaw, peering intently into his eyes. "Why do you say it like that?"

He caught the tension in her at once. "Oh, sweetheart, don't look so serious. I didn't mean anything by it. It's just that it's impossible to predict whether we'll ever hurt someone. I'm sure in the beginning Sam didn't realize he would hurt you."

Dana flung herself away from him and in a voice icy with anger she said, "I don't want Sam Brantley in this bed with us, Nick. Not ever. There's no comparison between the two of you."

Nick sat up and put his arms around her shaking shoulders, soothing her until he finally heard her sigh.

"I'm sorry," she said. "I shouldn't have exploded like that. It's just that I don't want to ruin what we have."

"No. I'm the one who's sorry. I shouldn't have brought up Sam. Do you suppose we can get back to us?"

"What about us?"

"Well, for instance, are you interested in getting out of this bed and getting some dinner?"

"Dinner's an interesting option," she conceded. "But I have a better alternative."

"What's that?"

"I'll show you."

And she did. Again and again, Dana tried to show Nick just how much he had freed her from her worst memories. She replaced old nightmares with new dreams. She was fire in his arms and he was more than willing to be consumed by her flame. She took what he offered and tried to give it back tenfold, proving without a doubt the depth of her love.

Then, sated at last, they slept again.

Chapter 14

When Dana awoke, pale streaks of dawn lit the room and Nick was gone, his place in her bed already cool. For an instant she panicked, her heart thumping wildly. Why hadn't she noticed this sooner? How had she slept through his leaving?

Then she saw the note propped on her bedside table.

It's very late. You were sleeping so peacefully I didn't want to wake you. I had to borrow your car to pick up Tony. I'll come by for you in the morning.
Love, Nick.

"Love, Nick." She repeated the words aloud, just to hear how they sounded. They sounded wonderful. Terrific. Great. She pulled his pillow into her arms and inhaled deeply, enjoying the lingering traces of his rich masculine scent, recalling in sensuous detail his possessive branding of her body. Her flesh still burned at the memory of his wicked touch. She was Nick's now in every way that counted.

She discovered with a sense of astonishment she was at peace at last. Her thoughts were decidedly pleasant, her heart incredibly light. The past was still very much with her, but it was where it properly belonged: behind her. Nick was her present, and if good fortune remained with her, he would be her future, as well.

She bounded out of bed and scurried into the shower, filled with plans for the day, beginning with a huge, sinfully caloric breakfast to make up for the dinner they'd never found time for. She sang lustily as the water flowed over her, soothing the unfamiliar aching in her thighs. She washed her hair with her favorite herbal shampoo and then toweled herself dry until her skin glowed with a healthy blush and her hair fell to her shoulders in a damp, shining cloud that would have to wait for the taming of brush and dryer.

She straightened the tangled sheets on the bed with a smile of remembrance on her lips and moved through the house in search of stray clothing that had been tossed aside haphazardly in the night's urgency. When the last traces of their passion had been removed from everything except her memory, she began to prepare their meal—bacon, waffles, eggs, fresh-squeezed orange juice and raspberry jam. She found a vase for the rose that Nick had picked for her and set it in the middle of the table.

With an uncanny sense of timing, Nick pulled up out front just as the waffle iron hissed its readiness when she sprinkled a few drops of water on its heated surface. She threw open the back door and waited for him to turn the corner of the house. For just an instant his expression was unguarded and troubled, but when he saw her waiting there, his eyes lit up and he smiled one of his beguilingly crooked grins.

"I hope you're hungry," she announced.

"I am," he said, stealing a kiss that rocked her senses. "For you."

"In that case, you should have been here at dawn. Now you'll have to settle for breakfast."

He seemed to bristle at her comment. "You know why I had to leave, don't you?"

Puzzled by his sharp tone, she said, "Of course. You had to get home to Tony. I wasn't criticizing."

He raked his fingers through his hair. "Sorry. I suppose I'm just a little out of sorts."

Dana studied his expression more closely and saw the tiny tension lines around his set mouth, the shadows in his eyes.

"Not enough sleep?" she asked, guessing at the cause.

Nick drew in a deep breath. "Not exactly."

His mood frightened her. "What is it, Nick? What's really bothering you? Are you regretting last night?"

"No. Of course not," he said quickly, but for some reason it didn't reassure her.

"Then what?"

"Let's go in and sit down."

She dug in her heels and put her hands on her hips defiantly. "Just tell me."

He sighed heavily. "Have you seen today's paper?"

"No, I get it at the library. Why?"

But before he could respond, she knew. As surely as if she'd read each word, she knew.

"Oh, no," she breathed softly. "Is it the Brantleys?"

Nick nodded. "They sent in a letter to the editor."

He reached out to circle her shoulders and draw her close. Dana trembled violently in the embrace. "How bad is it?" she asked, her voice muffled against the warm solidity of his chest.

"It's all there. Everything." She looked up in time to see a rueful grin. "Or almost everything. I've already called a lawyer and explained the situation. He seems to think there's not much we can do. They've been very careful with their accusations. There's nothing really libelous in there. They've stuck pretty close to the court records."

"But the court declared me innocent."

"Yes, well, that's the one little fact the Brantleys didn't mention."

"You know Cyrus Mason. Will he let me tell my side of it in tomorrow's paper?"

Nick frowned. "Are you sure that's what you want to do? Do you really want to open up your past after you've tried so hard to forget it?"

"If I'm going to live in this town, I have to," she said with absolute certainty. "The Brantleys took the decision out of my hands."

"I see your point. But we'll go to the newspaper office together."

"No, Nick. I want to go alone. It's way past time I stood up for myself. Did you bring the paper?"

"It's in the car."

"Get it, Nick," she said. She felt her anger begin to

build, fortifying her for the battle ahead. "I might as well see what I'm up against."

It was even worse than she'd imagined. There were innuendoes from her in-laws, unsubstantiated by police records, that she'd been drinking heavily the night of the accident. There was mention of the party, made out to seem far wilder than it was. There were suggestions that she had a history of instability, that she'd been hospitalized often for undisclosed reasons.

Facts had been taken and twisted to make a sensational story. The point? To attack her fitness as a public employee. It was the damning work of two people who had promised revenge and gotten it.

She looked up from the paper, her eyes blazing.

"They won't get away with it," she vowed. "I will not let them cost me my job, my new life."

"No," Nick said softly, his eyes shining with pride. He lifted her clenched fist to his lips and brushed a kiss across her knuckles. "This time I don't think they will."

Anxious to get on with things, she asked, "Do you still want breakfast?"

"No. I don't think either of us has the stomach for it."

"Then let me clean this up and we'll go."

She left the dishes on the table, dumped the waffle batter down the drain and slid the eggs and bacon into the garbage. Pots and pans were left stacked in the sink. Her resolve grew with every minute.

"Wish me luck," she said a half hour later as she dropped Nick off by the library so he could pick up his truck.

He grinned at her. "For some reason, I don't think you'll need it. I'll stop by the library later to see how it went."

He had started away from the car when she called him back. She touched the hand that rested on the car and gazed up at him. "Thank you."

"For what?"

"For giving me back my strength, for reminding me of who I was before Sam Brantley came along."

"I didn't do that, Dana. You did."

He leaned down and brushed his lips across hers. The kiss was greedy, but it was meant to reassure and it did. She drove away with fire in her veins and determination in her eyes.

She stalked into the *River Glen Chronicle*'s office a few minutes later and demanded to see the editor. No one dared to ask if she had an appointment. They just pointed her in the direction of a tiny, cluttered office that was littered with old newspapers and half-empty Styrofoam coffee cups.

She waited on her feet for the return of Cyrus Mason, the man listed on the masthead as editor and publisher. She paced the well-worn floor, fueling her anger and readying her arguments. By the time he came in, his shirtsleeves rolled up, his tie askew, Dana was prepared.

Apparently he was already well aware of her seething anger, because he treated her gingerly.

"Mrs. Brantley, won't you sit down?"

"You can. I don't want to." She threw the morning paper on his desk. "How dare you?"

He had no need to ask what she meant. "It was a legitimate letter," he said defensively.

"Legitimate? You call that pack of innuendoes legitimate? How carefully did you check it out, Mr. Mason? How far did you go to verify the facts? Not very far, I suspect."

"We—"

Dana didn't take note of his interruption. She never even took a breath. "If you had, you would know that I was acquitted of all charges in my husband's death on the grounds of self-defense. You would have learned that for five long years that paragon of virtue they described abused me."

Cyrus Mason turned pale. He ran his tongue over too-dry lips as Dana rushed on.

"I learned how to hide my bruises. Like a fool, I tried to protect my dignity and Sam Brantley's by keeping silent, but it all came out in court. Those hospital records they mentioned will show that I was admitted time and again to recover from the beatings their precious son gave me. Now, Mr. Mason, are you prepared to print that, as well?"

She was leaning across his desk, staring into his wide eyes, watching the beads of perspiration form on his brow. "Well, Mr. Mason?"

He swallowed nervously. "I had no idea."

"No, you didn't, did you? Isn't that your responsibility, though, Mr. Mason? Or were you afraid that the truth would ruin a sensational little tidbit for today's paper?"

"Mrs. Brantley, please, I'm very sorry."

"Sorry won't do it, Mr. Mason. This is a small town and my reputation is at stake. I want a complete and accurate report in tomorrow's paper or I will personally see to it that your lawyer spends every cent of your money defending a libel suit."

Dana knew she was bluffing at the end, but the quaking Mr. Mason did not. Perhaps he even had some sense of justice buried in his soft folds of flesh.

"I'll do whatever you like."

Dana nodded in satisfaction. "Send a reporter in. I'll do the rest."

She spent the better part of the morning with the reporter, detailing step by step the agony she had survived in her marriage. The reporter, a young girl barely out of college, had tears in her eyes when they finished talking.

"Why are you doing this?" she asked. "How can you bear to tell everyone what you suffered?"

Dana thought about the question. Until that moment, she hadn't been quite sure what her motivation was. Revenge? The salvaging of her own reputation? Or something more?

"I think maybe this is something I should have done a long time ago. Maybe by telling what I went through, it will help some other woman to avoid the tragedy of a wasted life. If just one woman reads this and finds the strength to ask for help, maybe it will give some meaning to those five years I spent in hell."

A rueful smile touched her lips as she continued. "Or perhaps I just needed to get it out of my system for my own sake, so I can move on. Maybe there's nothing honorable about my intentions at all."

The girl was shaking her head. "I don't think you can dismiss what you're doing so lightly. I think you're very brave."

"I wish I had been five or six years ago," Dana said with genuine regret. "Then perhaps Sam Brantley would still be alive."

Dana drove to the library feeling as though a tremendous burden had been lifted from her shoulders. Whatever happened now, she could deal with it. She could move on with her life. If she had a life left.

By midday she had already heard there were efforts to see that she was removed as librarian. Betsy was the bearer of the bad news.

"Dana, they've been swarming all over town hall like bees. I tried to talk them out of it, but you know how quick some folks are to make judgments. They think you're going to corrupt the young people and turn the whole town into some sort of Peyton Place. You've never heard such ridiculous carrying on."

"I think I probably have," Dana retorted mildly. "Maybe when they see the whole story in the paper tomorrow, they'll stop and think about what they're doing."

"What if they don't? Tomorrow may be too late, anyway. Some folks don't give a hang about the truth. They'd just as soon run you out of town tonight."

"What about you, Betsy? You've already jumped to my defense and you don't even know what really happened."

"Good grief, girl, I don't have to ask. I know you about as well as I could ever know a daughter of my own. Whatever happened back then, you weren't to blame. Harry believes that, too."

Humbled by Betsy's trust, Dana had tears glistening in her eyes. "How can I ever thank you?"

"You just stick around here and fight back. Don't you go running anywhere."

"I'm not running this time, Betsy. I have something to stay and fight for."

"Nick?"

"Nick."

"Oh, child, I couldn't be happier."

"Neither could I."

But even that happiness was doomed to be short-lived. Betsy had no sooner left the ominously deserted library than Jessica Leahy came in. She circled Dana's desk like a wary fighter assessing his opponent.

"I saw the paper," she said at last.

"But you already knew, didn't you?"

Jessica nodded. "I had heard something about it. Mildred Tanner's son is a lawyer in New York. He told her, and she told me right after Tony's birthday party."

For a fraction of a second there was a look of regret in her eyes, then they were a cold, stormy gray again. "Despite what you think, I didn't want to believe it."

"I think perhaps you did."

"No, Dana. I asked Nick to talk to you. I wanted you to tell him it was all lies. I didn't want it to come to this. I didn't want to be forced into a showdown with Nick."

A twisting knot formed in Dana's stomach. "What kind of a showdown?"

"If Nick persists in this craziness of his, this idea of marrying you, then I'm going to court tomorrow to ask for custody of Tony. I think after he hears this, after he sees what kind of a woman Nick plans to bring into my grandson's life, I think the judge will grant my request."

"No!" The word echoed through the room. "You can't do that. It's so unfair."

"What you did was more than unfair. You took your husband's life."

"You're wrong, Jessica." Nick's voice was icy with rage. Neither of them had heard him enter and they turned to stare at him.

"We'll see who's wrong, Nicholas," Jessica said, undaunted by his fury and not waiting to hear more. "We'll see about that."

Then she turned and left, her back stiff, her chin held high.

In her wake, she left a terrible, gut-wrenching fear.

Chapter 15

Nick slammed his fist against the wall. "Damn her for this! I warned her to stay out of it."

"You knew she was considering this?" Dana said, horrified by what Jessica Leahy was threatening and equally astonished that Nick had apparently been aware of it. "You knew she was going to fight you for custody?"

"I thought she'd come to her senses."

"Nick, you have to go after her. You have to stop it."

Nick just stood there, obviously torn between offering support to her and going after his former mother-in-law.

"Go," Dana urged. "You can't let her go into court over this. You mustn't let Tony get caught in the middle because of me. Dear God, Nick, you could lose your son."

"It won't come to that," Nick said, his teeth clenched. "I won't allow it to come to that."

"The only way to stop it is to talk to her."

Troubled eyes surveyed her. "Will you be all right?"

"I'll be fine as soon as I know you've been able to resolve this with Jessica."

Nick nodded and left, leaving Dana's emotions whirling. What if he couldn't make Jessica back down? What if she insisted on going through with the custody battle?

Then she would have to leave River Glen after all. There would be no alternative. Dana wouldn't allow herself to come between Nick and his son.

It was one of the longest afternoons of Dana's life. Not one person came into the library. No one called. By six o'clock her nerves were stretched to the limit and her stomach was churning. On the short drive home, she almost ran her car off the road because she wasn't concentrating and missed a curve.

At home she was no better. She put the unused breakfast dishes away—in the refrigerator—and washed the pots and pans with laundry detergent. Then she scrubbed the kitchen floor, trying to work out her fears and anger with each swipe of the mop. She fixed a sandwich, then threw it in the trash after taking one bite.

When the phone rang, she knocked over her glass of tea in her haste to get to it, then skidded on the pool of liquid and nearly lost her balance.

"Yes. Hello," she said breathlessly.

"Dana, it's Betsy."

Disappointment flooded through her. "Oh."

"Were you expecting someone else?"

"I was hoping Nick would call."

Her comment was greeted with a silence that went on far too long. "Betsy, what is it? Is it about Nick?"

"Nick's at town hall. They called a special meeting to decide what to do about you and your job. It starts in a half hour."

Dana sank down in a kitchen chair and rubbed her hand across her eyes. The dull pounding in her head picked up in speed and intensity.

"Should I come down there?"

"Nick told me not to call. He said you'd already been through too much today, but I think perhaps you should be here. After all, it's your fate they're deciding. You should have a chance to speak up for yourself."

"Thanks, Betsy. I'll be there in a few minutes."

When Dana got to town hall, she could hardly find a place to park. She didn't consider it a good sign that most of the town had turned out for this impromptu meeting. It had all the characteristics of a lynch mob. The phone lines must have been buzzing all afternoon. She could hear the shouts through the building's opened windows.

Reluctantly she climbed the front steps and went down the hall to the auditorium, trying her best to ignore the occasional stares in her direction. The doors had been propped open to allow for the overflow of people who were milling around in the corridor before the meeting officially got under way. Most were so busy spreading their own versions of the gossip they took little note of Dana's arrival. She slipped inside the room and stood by the back wall.

Moments later the mayor gaveled the meeting to order. It took some time for everyone to calm down. Dana saw Nick and Betsy at the front, along with the council members. Jessica Leahy was only two rows from the front, her expression grim and very determined.

Suddenly Dana felt a tug on her arm and looked around to see Tony at her side, his eyes bright with unshed tears.

"Tony! What are you doing here?"

"I was supposed to be with Grandpa, but I snuck out. I heard they were going to try to get rid of you."

Dana was stumped over what to tell him other than the truth. "That's what some people would like to do."

"But why? You can't go away, Ms. Brantley. Dad and me need you." He wrapped his arms around her waist and buried his head against her side. She could feel the hot dampness of his tears through her blouse.

Dana tried to swallow the lump in her throat and blinked back her own tears. "Let's go outside."

"No," he said, clinging harder. "I want to stay."

"No. I think we'd better talk."

She took Tony's hand and led him outside. At the moment, as frightened as she was about her own future, nothing was more important than trying to explain to him what was happening.

"Let's sit over here," she said, drawing him toward the wide concrete railing alongside the steps. He sat as close to her as he could, his thin shoulders shaking. Dana put an arm around him and sighed. "How much do you know?"

"Only what Grandma said. She told Grandpa they were going to run you out of town on a rail."

"Did she say why?"

"I couldn't hear everything. Grandpa kept telling her to keep her voice down."

Dana took a deep breath. "Okay. Let me try to explain what's happening so you can understand it."

She paused, trying to figure out how on earth she was going to do that. How did you tell a ten-year-old boy that you were responsible for your husband's death? If adults found it inexplicable, what on earth would Tony think?

"You know that I was married before?" she began at last.

He nodded. "Dad told me. He said you weren't anymore, though."

"Well, that's true. When I was married, it wasn't like it was for your mother and father. They loved each other very much. Sam and I loved each other, but we weren't very happy. Sometimes we got really angry and we fought."

"Lots of grown-ups do that."

"That's right. One night Sam and I argued and he... he fell down some stairs."

"Was he hurt bad?"

"Yes, Tony. He was hurt very badly. He died."

Tony seemed more perplexed than ever. "And that's why they want you to go away? That doesn't make any sense."

"Some people don't understand what really happened that night. They think I made Sam fall on purpose. They don't think a person who did something like that should be around kids."

"But you didn't mean to do it."

Dana hugged him. A tear spilled over and ran down her cheek. "No. I didn't mean to do it."

"Then go tell them, so it'll be okay." He wrapped his arms tight around her. "I don't want you to leave."

"She won't have to, son."

Dana and Tony both looked up to find Nick towering over them. She tried to read his expression, afraid to hope that his words meant what she thought.

"It's over?" she whispered, suddenly very, very scared.

He sat down next to her and took her hand. "It's over."

"And?"

"They want you to stay on."

Relief and confusion warred for her emotions. "But how? What happened? Did you convince them of what really went on that last night with Sam?"

"I didn't have to. Cyrus Mason came and brought his reporter with him. She read the story she'd written for tomorrow's paper. It was an eloquent defense."

"And they believed me?"

"They believed you."

Nick's gaze caught hers and held, and time stood still for the two of them.

"Let's go home," he said at last, getting to his feet. He put an arm around each of them and steered them through the crowd.

When they reached Dana's car, Nick touched her cheek. "I have to take Tony home."

"I know."

"I'll see you in the morning. We have a lot to talk about."

Dana nodded and watched them walk away. They hadn't gone far when Tony turned around and ran back to throw his arms around her. "I'm glad you're staying, Ms. Brantley."

She smiled at him and ruffled his hair. "Me, too, kiddo."

It was only after he'd run back to his father that she

noticed Jessica Leahy watching them from the shadows. Suddenly those fleeting moments of relief and happiness were spoiled by the memory of what Jessica had sworn to do. Even after what she'd heard tonight, would Jessica still condemn her? She took a step toward the older woman, hoping to make peace or, at the very least, get some answers, but Jessica turned away.

Dana was awake all night thinking about the expression she'd seen on the older woman's face and about the threat she'd never retracted. Last night's revelations should have paved the way for her to have a future with Nick in River Glen, but now that future seemed in doubt. If, despite all the evidence, Jessica still condemned her and went on with her custody fight, then her own life here would mean very little. She wouldn't be able to bear seeing Nick and Tony parted. Nor would she be able to stay if she was forced to give up Nick so that he could keep his son.

There was only one thing to do. She had to be the one to see Jessica. She had to make at least one last attempt to make peace between the two of them.

As soon as she'd eaten breakfast the next morning, she drove out to the farm. She found Joshua on his way to the barn. He walked over to greet her, his expression every bit as warm as it had been the first time they met.

"Congratulations, Dana. I'm glad things worked out for you last night."

"Thank you." She regarded him closely. "I suppose you know why I'm here."

He nodded. "She's inside. I think you'll find her in the kitchen. She's making bread. It's what she always does when she's got some thinking to do."

Dana could feel Joshua's eyes on her as she slowly crossed the lawn to the back door. The feeling that she had his blessing gave her the strength to go on. She hesitated on the threshold, watching as Jessica kneaded the dough, pounding it with her fists. Her anger was evident with each blow.

At last, Dana took a deep breath and rapped sharply. Jessica looked up and the two women stared at each other, tension radiating between them.

"Come in," she said at last.

Dana moved to the kitchen table and sat down, linking her hands in front of her. Now that she was here, she was unsure how to begin.

"Joshua says you bake bread when you have some thinking to do," she said finally.

"I do." The lump of dough hit the counter with a crash and flour rose like a fine mist.

"I hope you're thinking about the custody suit."

"I am." *Slam* went the dough again.

"Have you decided anything?"

"Not yet."

"Would it help for me to tell you that I love Nick and Tony very much? They are very special, thanks in large measure to the gift of love your daughter gave them. I envy the time they shared. I…my marriage wasn't like that. I wish to God it had been."

When she looked up, there were tears shining in Jessica's eyes. "Oh, my dear, can you ever forgive me? All I wanted to do was protect my family."

Dana got up and went over to Jessica. She put her hand on hers, oblivious to the flour and dough that covered it. She could feel the trembling and knew something of Jessica's fear.

"Don't you think I know that?" she said gently. "I can see how much you care about them, how much they love you. I just want to be a part of that, not take it away from you."

The room crackled with silent tension.

"I won't fight you," Jessica said finally.

"Thank you. That's all I can ask."

Dana was hardly aware of how long she'd spent at the farm or how late it was as she drove back to town. When she arrived at the library both Nick and Betsy were pacing the front steps, Betsy's strides only half as long as Nick's.

Betsy saw her first. "There she is," she cried, running down the steps, Nick hard on her heels.

"Where have you been?" he demanded. "We've been half out of our heads worrying about you."

"Why?"

Nick cast an incredulous look at Betsy, who shrugged. "The woman wants to know why. Good heavens, lady, after all that's gone on around here, do you even have to ask?"

"But it's all resolved now," she said cheerfully, getting out of the car. "I took care of the last detail this morning."

Nick's shoulders tensed. "What detail?"

"I went to see Jessica."

"You what!" Nick demanded.

"I went to see Jessica."

"Why?" Betsy asked. "Why on earth would you go to see her first thing in the morning?"

Nick and Dana exchanged a knowing look. She reached out and put a reassuring hand on his arm, rubbing until she felt the knotted muscle relax.

"Everything is okay."

"Everything?" he repeated as if he couldn't quite dare to believe her.

"Will someone tell me what you're talking about?" Betsy demanded indignantly.

Nick put his hands on Dana's waist and scanned her face, his expression softening. "I think we're talking about getting married, aren't we?"

"If someone asks me, we could be."

Betsy's sharp intake of breath was the only sound for the longest time. Finally Dana chuckled.

"If you don't ask me pretty soon, Betsy's going to do it for you."

"Oh, no," Nick said. "This is my proposal. Betsy can go find someone else."

"Then get down on your knee," Betsy prodded.

"Are you planning to stick around to coach me through this?" Nick inquired.

"If it'll get you moving any faster, I am."

Nick finally shrugged and sank to one knee. He glanced to Betsy for her approval. She was beaming.

"Now?" she urged.

"Dana Brantley, would you do me the honor of becoming Mrs. Nicholas Verone?"

"Can't you do any better than that?" Betsy huffed. "What did I tell you, Dana? You young folks today have no sense of romance."

Dana's heart was pounding against her ribs, and her eyes were shining as she met Nick's heated gaze.

"I think we have a very good idea of romance," she retorted softly, taking Nick's outstretched hand. "Do you think anyone would mind if I left the library closed for the day?"

"I don't think anyone would mind at all," Nick said, getting to his feet and slipping an arm around her.

As they walked away, he glanced back over his shoulder. "This part is private, Betsy."

"As long as you invite me to the wedding."

"You can be the matron of honor," Dana told her.

But when she and Nick were alone at last, she touched his cheek with trembling fingers. Her self-confidence faltered. "Are you very sure about this?" she asked, searching his eyes for signs of doubt. "My past…it can't be an easy thing to accept."

"Dana, you've already been much harder on yourself than I could ever be. What happened was a terrible tragedy. Not just Sam's death, but all the years of pain that led up to it. It's time now to let it go."

"I want to, Nick. God only knows, I want to." She struggled against the relentless claim of the past. "I don't know if I can."

Nick's arms encircled her with warmth and strength and love. "We can do it," he promised. "Together."

His lips met hers, gently at first, the touch of sunshine, rather than fire. It was a kiss meant to reassure. Then hunger replaced tenderness and trust surmounted doubts.

"Forever," Dana murmured, eyes blazing with life and her heart filled with the hope she'd never dared to feel before.

"Forever."

* * * * *

Books by Patricia Davids

HQN Books

The Amish of Cedar Grove
The Wish

Love Inspired

North Country Amish

An Amish Wife for Christmas

The Amish Bachelors

An Amish Harvest
An Amish Noel
His Amish Teacher
Their Pretend Amish Courtship
Amish Christmas Twins
An Unexpected Amish Romance
His New Amish Family

Brides of Amish Country

Plain Admirer
Amish Christmas Joy
The Shepherd's Bride
The Amish Nanny
An Amish Family Christmas: A Plain Holiday
An Amish Christmas Journey
Amish Redemption

Visit the Author Profile page
at Harlequin.com for more titles.

MILITARY DADDY

Patricia Davids

And he said, Come. And when Peter was come
down out of the ship, he walked on the water, to
go to Jesus. But when he saw the wind boisterous,
he was afraid; and beginning to sink,
he cried, saying, Lord, save me.
—*Matthew* 14:29–30

*

This book is dedicated to Pam Hopkins.
If you don't know how much your belief in
my talent meant to me all those years ago,
let me tell you now.
It meant the world to me then and it still does.
Thank you from the bottom of my heart.
Oh, and please continue to baby me
when I whine about how hard this is.

Chapter 1

"Well? Are you going to tell him or not?"

Annie Delmar chose to ignore the question from her roommate, Crystal Mally. Instead she continued folding the freshly laundered clothes in the white plastic hamper on the foot of her twin bed. The smell of hot cotton vied with the dryer sheet's mountain-floral scent.

Hoping to change the subject, Annie asked, "Are you going out with Jake again tonight?"

"Jake and I broke up," Crystal said with an indifferent shrug as she continued to buff her bright red fingernail.

"I'm sorry to hear that."

Annie carried a stack of knit tops to the chest of drawers in the corner. She didn't want to talk about her current problem. It was too soon. It still didn't seem real. Why had God done this to her?

No, it isn't right to blame God. I did this to myself.

Crystal said, "Jake's a loser, like all the guys I date, and don't change the subject. Are you going to tell the guy?"

"I haven't decided." With a weary sigh, Annie closed the top drawer of the blue painted dresser and stood for a moment with her hands on the chipped and scratched surface.

Crystal plopped down on Annie's bed and leaned back against the headboard. Her short bleached-blond hair framed a face that was pale and too thin. The lacy black top she wore was too tight and, as usual, she had splashed on too much of her cheap perfume. "I don't think he needs to know. Besides, I thought you said he was being transferred overseas in a few months."

"That's what he told me."

"So if you don't tell him soon, how are you going to find him later?"

The door to the room swung inward as their house-mother came in with a second hamper of laundry. "That's a good question, Crystal. I'd like to hear your answer, Annie."

Moving back to her bed, Annie began folding her jeans. "If he moves away and I don't know where he went, then I can't tell him anything, can I?"

She glanced at the woman who had taken her in when she had been at the lowest point of her life. Marge Lilly stood with the laundry basket balanced against her hip. On the far side of fifty and slightly plump, Marge managed to look both motherly and formidable at the same time. Her eyes seemed to see right through Annie, but she didn't say anything. After a few seconds of awk-

ward silence, Annie felt compelled to answer the unspoken censure.

"My lack of action would be an excuse to pretend
the decision is out of my hands."

"Is that true?"

"No," she admitted with quiet resignation.

"So why not make a decision?" Marge asked gently.

Annie pressed a hand to her stomach to calm her
queasiness. "Because I'm afraid I'll make the wrong
one."

"And?" Marge prompted.

"And it's easier to do nothing."

"Doing nothing *is* a choice, Annie."

"But not a good one. I need to make *good* choices."
Annie had tried to add conviction to her voice, but she'd
failed miserably.

"You are in charge of your life, Annie. Just remember, God is always with you, and your friends are here
to help."

Annie nodded, but she still felt very much alone and
frightened of what the future held.

"Shane, the captain wants to see you on the double."

Corporal Shane Ross tapped the last nail into Jasper's
shoe before he dropped the horse's leg, then straightened
and looked over the animal's back at his friend and fel-
low soldier, Private Avery Barnes. "Did he say why?"

"No, but he had that tone in his voice that he usually
reserves for me."

Shane grinned. Mentally running over his duties list,
he couldn't think of anything he had done wrong or
missed. "I wonder what's up."

"It might have something to do with the pretty

woman who came in looking for you. If she's your sister, can I ask her out?"

"If I had a sister, I wouldn't let you within fifty miles of her."

"That's not nice."

"But it's the truth." Shane patted the horse's rump and moved to put his tools on the bench at the rear of the farrier shed. He pulled off the heavy leather apron he used to protect his clothing and hung it on a peg. Lifting his coat from the next hook, he slipped it on.

The fire in the forge popped and hissed, adding a smoky aroma to the cold air inside the small stone building. The calendar might say it was the middle of April, but the chilly, damp wind outside made it feel more like winter than spring.

Avery stepped up to stroke Jasper's forehead. "Now that your stint in this unit is almost over, will you be glad to get back to fixing helicopters instead of saddles and horseshoes?"

"I'll admit I'm looking forward to spending a year in Germany, but I'll miss the horses."

"And me?"

"No. You, I won't miss." He would miss Avery and all the men in the unit, but he was more comfortable trading friendly jibes than revealing his true sentiments.

Avery fell into step beside Shane as the two of them left the farrier building. They paused at the edge of the road as three green-and-tan camouflage jeeps sped past. The Army base at Fort Riley, Kansas, bustled with constant activity. When the way was clear, they crossed the street.

The Commanding General's Mounted Color Guard had its main office just south of the large, historic stone-

and-timber stable that housed the unit's horses and gear. At the door Avery smiled and said, "Your visitor is a real hottie. If you aren't interested, could you get her phone number for me?"

Shane gave his buddy a friendly shove toward the stable. "Make sure the wagon wheels get greased today. Our first exhibition is a week from Saturday, and you know the captain wants everything in tip-top shape."

Avery sketched a salute and sauntered away. Inside the tiny office building Shane pulled off his cap and tucked it under his arm, then knocked on the captain's door. When he heard Captain Watson bid him enter, he opened it and stepped inside.

Captain Jeffery Watson was seated behind his large gray desk. The walls of the room were painted the same drab Army-issue color. An assortment of photographs and commendations in plain gold frames added the only touch of color. A faint frown marred the captain's brow above his keen, dark eyes, and Shane wondered again what he had done wrong.

A woman sat in front of the captain's desk, but she had her back to Shane. He couldn't tell if she was pretty or not, but there was something familiar about her.

"Have a seat, Corporal Ross. I understand you know Miss Delmar." He indicated with a wave of his hand the woman sitting quietly before him.

The name didn't mean anything to Shane. She had her back to him, but he could see her dark hair was drawn into a tight braid that reached the center of her back. She was wearing a light gray jacket over a pair of faded jeans. Her shoulders were slightly hunched and she kept her head down.

Shane took a seat in the chair beside her. Glancing

over, he saw her hands were clenched together so tightly in her lap that her knuckles stood out white. He leaned forward to get a glimpse of her bowed face. Recognition hit him like a mule kick to the stomach.

She was the woman from the nightclub. He had spent weeks trying to find her, without success. His satisfaction at seeing her again was quickly tempered with curiosity.

Captain Watson cleared his throat. "I'll be in the stable. You are free to use my office for as long as you need, Miss Delmar. Corporal Ross will let me know when you are finished with this conversation."

"Thank you, Captain." Her soft voice held a definite edge of nervousness.

Captain Watson nodded, then left the room, closing the door behind him.

Shane unbuttoned his jacket. The room seemed hot and stuffy after the coolness of the farrier's shed. He took a moment to study the profile of the woman he had searched for fruitlessly. Now, after almost three months, she was here. Why?

Whatever she wanted, she seemed to be having trouble finding the courage to speak. He decided to get the ball rolling. "Delmar is it? I might have had an easier time finding you if I had known your last name."

Her head snapped up and she met his gaze. "Did you look for me?"

Her eyes were the same deep, luminous brown that he remembered. The same unhappiness he had seen before continued to lurk in their depths. He had the ridiculous urge to reach out and stroke her cheek.

"I went back to that club every night for two weeks hoping to find you again."

She unclenched her hands, folded her arms across her chest and leaned back in the chair. "Two whole weeks. Wow! I'm flattered."

Frowning at her sarcasm, he said, "You left first, remember?"

Her attitude of defiance faded. "I remember. Look, I made a mistake. A big, huge, gigantic mistake."

"You don't get to take all the blame. Nobody held a gun to my head."

"All right, *we* made a huge mistake."

Shane wasn't proud of his behavior that night. "Just so you know, I'm not in the habit of picking up women in bars and taking them to motel rooms."

A tiny smile curved her lips. "Corporal, I could tell. And just so you know, I used to pick up guys in bars all the time for the price of a drink and I've seen the inside of a cheap motel more than once."

Annie Delmar watched the soldier's eyes widen as the meaning of her words sank in. To his credit, he didn't make any smart remarks. She had heard plenty of them in her time, but she never got used to the hurt.

This was so much harder than she had imagined. She wanted to sink through the floor. Maybe she should just leave. That would be the easiest thing to do.

She needed a drink.

No, I don't. I want a sober life. I deserve a sober life. God, if You are listening, lend me Your strength. Help me do the right thing for once.

Drawing a deep breath, she launched into the speech she had worked on for the past week. There was a lot this man needed to understand. "I can tell by your expression that you get my drift. I used to live a very destructive lifestyle, but I'm in recovery now. I had been clean and sober for almost a year when I had a setback. That is no excuse. I made a choice to drink and to spend the night with you when I knew it was wrong."

"What kind of setback?"

His concern wasn't something that she'd expected. "You mean, what caused me to fall off the wagon? It doesn't really matter, does it?"

"It must have."

"Okay, maybe it did, but I've been sober since I left you at that motel. That's what's important. I'm getting the help I need and I'm getting my life back on track."

There was a joke if she'd ever uttered one. Her life was closer to being derailed than on track, but she didn't want this man to think she couldn't handle herself. She would handle this and she would do it the right way, with God's help and the help of others like herself in AA. Still, she found it hard to meet his frank gaze.

"That's good," he said at last. "I hope it wasn't something that I said or did."

She relaxed for the first time in days. "No. You and your buddies came along afterward. You were all so happy about something. You were all laughing."

He had a nice laugh. She remembered that about him even if other parts of that evening were fuzzy.

He pulled his hat out from beneath his arm. She watched him fold and unfold the red ball cap that matched the T-shirt he wore under his army jacket. She had no clue what he was thinking.

"Our unit had just returned from riding in the inaugural parade in Washington, D.C., and our sergeant had just gotten engaged. She'd be mad if she knew we went out drinking to celebrate. I don't mean to sound like a prude, but I don't normally drink."

"I could tell that, too."

It had been his cheerful smile and his happy laughter that had drawn Annie to him that night. She had craved being a part of that happiness as much as she had craved the liquor.

She cleared her mind of the memory. "Look, I need to make it plain that I don't want anything from you. I want you to know that. I don't want anything from you. Do you get that?"

He stopped scrunching his hat and looked at her. "You don't want anything from me. I get that, but I'm sort of hazy on all the rest. Amy, why are you here? How did you find me?"

"My name is Annie."

"Annie. I'm sorry."

She thought she was done feeling like this. Cheap and disposable. Crossing her arms again, she looked down at the floor. "Don't be. The music was loud. We were…"

Why does this have to be so hard? I'm trying to do the right thing, Lord. Please help me.

Shane looked down and began folding his hat again. "I never was good with names. I forget my own sometimes."

Annie saw his discomfort and took pity on him. The man was six feet tall and as good-looking as the day was long—if a woman liked the blue-eyed cowboy type with a Texas drawl that made every word in the English language sound as soft as a cotton ball. And he was embarrassed because he didn't remember her name.

"It's okay. It's not like we had any intention of becoming best friends."

Looking up, a slight grin pulled at the corner of his mouth. "My list of friends is pretty short. I'd be honored to add you."

Oh, yes, he was as sweet and kind as she remembered—and she was about to drop a bomb on his life.

"As for finding you," she continued, "that wasn't hard. It's a big Army base, but how many stables are there here?"

"One."

"Right. I called and spoke to your captain yesterday and he told me when you would be here today."

Annie glanced at her watch. She couldn't stay much longer. It was time to get it over with.

This is my step number nine: I need to make amends for the harm I caused. I need to admit the truth.

Was she doing the right thing? She wasn't sure she should burden this man with her news. Telling him wouldn't change anything, but Marge believed that he had a right to know, and Annie believed in Marge's wisdom. She had seen it in action time and time again.

Annie raised her head. She had come a long way in the last year even if she had slipped up one night. She could be proud of what she had accomplished since she'd turned her life over to God. Something good would come of this because it had to be part of His plan.

"Corporal Ross—"

"Call me Shane."

"Okay, Shane, I'll get to the point. I'm here because I'm pregnant."

Chapter 2

Shane blinked once, not certain he had heard Annie correctly. He opened his mouth but closed it quickly without posing the question that dangled on the tip of his tongue.

"Aren't you going to ask me if I'm sure it's yours?" she demanded.

The mixture of defiance and pain in her voice made him glad he hadn't spoken that thought aloud.

"I don't think you would have gone to the trouble of finding me if you weren't sure."

Her attitude softened slightly but not completely. "That's right."

She shot to her feet, clutching the strap of her scuffed black vinyl purse. "Okay, then, I guess we're done."

He stood in surprise. "Whoa! You can't just lay this on me and then scoot out the door."

"Why not? I told you I didn't want anything from you."

"You've just told me I'm going to be a father. I need more than a minute to process that information."

"Sorry, but one minute is all you get. Look, neither one of us wanted this. We were both looking for a good time, not for a family. My counselor convinced me that you deserve to know. Now you know. From here on out it is my problem and I'll handle it as I see fit."

"I'm not sure I agree with that. What are you going to do?"

"I'm going to leave here and get to my job before I'm late. Have a nice life."

She stepped around him and headed for the doorway. Was she kidding? She had hit him with this brick and now she was going to split? As she started to pull open the door, he reached over her head and pushed it shut with a bang. "Wait just a minute!"

The look she sent him was twice as sharp as the nails he had put in Jasper's shoe. "Take your hand off this door."

"I will as soon as we settle a few things."

She crossed her arms and glared at him. "Such as?"

"Do you plan to keep the baby?"

"None of your business."

"I hope you aren't considering an abortion."

"That is also none of your business."

"If it wasn't any of my business, you wouldn't be here. I'm not sure what I'm supposed to do or what I'm supposed to say, but this isn't just your problem."

She drew a deep breath. "I have to decide what is best for me. You don't get a say in that."

It was plain she didn't want his help or his interference. If she didn't want him involved, wasn't that her right? Past experience had certainly proven he wasn't father material. Why should this woman think differently? She barely knew him and yet she had already made that decision. He pulled his hand away from the door frame. "Okay, you need to do what is best for you. I guess I can understand that."

"Good."

Shane stuffed his hands in his pockets and stepped away from her. "I'm sorry this happened. If there is anything you need…anything…let me know."

"I won't need anything, and you don't need to worry that I'll show up again looking for support for this kid. For what it's worth, I'm sorry you had to find out like this. You seem like a nice guy."

He quickly crossed the room to the desk. Picking up a pen and business card, he scribbled his cell number. Returning to her side, he handed it to her. "This is my number. Could you at least let me know what you plan to do? I really want to know."

She hesitated, but took it from him. "I'll think about it."

Annie pulled open the door and walked out of the office with her heart pounding like a drum in her chest. Her hands felt ice-cold and her legs were barely able to hold her up. She prayed she could make it to her car without falling down. She was bad at confrontations.

Corporal Shane Ross had no idea how much it had cost her to maintain her mask of indifference. At least the dreaded meeting was over and she could stop worrying about it. Now it was time to look ahead and make a plan.

She managed to reach her car. A soldier stood on the other side of her beat-up peacock-blue hatchback, chatting through the rolled-down window with her roommate in the passenger seat. Crystal was laughing at something the man said. Annie glanced back. Shane stood just outside the building, watching her. His face wore a puzzled frown. Who could blame him?

The sudden *clop-clop* of hooves startled her as a soldier walked past, leading two brown horses with black manes and tails. She had heard a lot about Shane's unit from him during their one evening together. At first she had thought he had been teasing about being in the cavalry, but it had soon become apparent that he and his friends really did ride horses in a modern army.

Shane had spoken with quiet pride about his participation in the inaugural parade in Washington, D.C. She could still see his shy smile and the sparkle in his blue eyes when he spoke about it. He hadn't been the best-looking guy in the bar that night, but there had been something about him. In him she thought she had seen someone like herself. Someone without anyone.

Yeah, and look where that got me.

Opening the car door, she climbed in and slammed it shut. If only she could shut out her memories as easily.

Crystal leaned toward her. "How did it go?"

"I'll tell you later."

"Did you see those horses?"

"I saw them." Annie tried twice to get the key in the ignition before it finally slid into place. Her hands wouldn't stop shaking. *Please, please let it start.*

"Private Avery was just telling me that we can have a tour of the stable and even pet some of the horses."

"We don't have time. We're going to be late as it is."

"Come back someday when you can stay longer," Avery suggested. "I'd be happy to give you a private tour."

"I'd like that," Crystal gushed.

The car's temperamental engine turned over. Annie breathed a silent prayer of thanks, then backed out of the parking space.

"'Bye," Crystal called, waving as they drove off.

"Roll up the window," Annie snapped. "It's freezing in here and you know my heater doesn't work."

Crystal did as she was told. "You didn't have to be rude to Avery. He only wanted to let me see his horses."

"It was just another pickup line."

"It was not. Sometimes I think you don't like men."

"I don't dislike them. It's that I don't trust them—and neither should you." If Crystal couldn't see that, Annie wasn't going to waste her breath trying to convince her.

Shane turned away from the sight of Annie's car disappearing down the street. He knew he'd never hear from her again. She had already decided he had no business being a father.

Avery came over to stand beside him. "What did the lady want?"

"I thought I told you to grease the wagon wheels."

"Lee had already taken care of it. Obviously your friend didn't bring you good news."

"She told me I'm going to be a daddy and then she told me to get lost."

"What?"

"Do I have a sign over my head that says *Rotten Parent Material*? Do I have *Loser* written on my forehead?"

Shane began walking toward the farrier shed so quickly that Avery had to run to keep up.

"I don't think you really want me to answer that."

"You're right, I don't. Now, go away."

It seemed that Avery couldn't take a hint. He followed Shane inside the building and asked, "What are you going to do about your pregnant friend?"

Tossing his jacket aside, Shane slipped the strap of his leather apron over his head and tied it at his waist. "Annie Delmar wants nothing to do with me. In light of that fact, I'm going to respect her wishes."

Moving back to Jasper's side, Shane bent over and picked up the horse's hind leg. "This shoe needs to be replaced, too. Hand me the clinch cutter and the pull-offs."

Avery walked to the workbench at the back of the room and returned with the requested tools. Handing them to Shane, he said, "You can't drop your responsibilities like a hot rock."

"It's not my call."

"I beg to differ. It certainly is."

"Not according to Annie."

"You have the same rights that she does."

Shane tilted his head to see his friend better. "What do you mean?"

"The law is plain on this. A father has the same rights that a mother does. Well, almost the same. You do have to prove that the child is yours."

Jasper tried to pull his foot away and Shane let him put it down. Ordinarily the big gelding didn't mind having his hooves worked on, but he seemed to sense Shane's emotional turmoil. Patting the horse's side to reassure him, Shane drew a calming breath.

He knew what it was like to be the child waiting for a father that never showed up. "The law doesn't matter. I'm not going to fight Annie so I can force her to let me see my kid every other weekend—or less. That's not what a family is."

Avery said, "This doesn't sound like you. You've always been Mr. Responsible."

"I guess you don't know me as well as you think." Shane picked up Jasper's hoof again and began straightening the tips of the last few nails holding the worn shoe in place.

Maybe never knowing this child would be better than loving him and then having to watch some other man step in and take him away. Only…this was his child. How could he pretend it didn't matter? It might matter, but what choice did he have?

"When I start a family, I'll be married and I'll have a job that lets me come home every night. My kids are going to know who their daddy is."

Crossing his arms over his chest, Avery said, "Your plan is good except for one small detail. You've already started your family."

Struggling to keep his frustration and disappointment from showing, Shane said, "Look, I'm not even sure she's keeping the baby."

"If she plans to give it up for adoption, she'll need your consent or it won't be legal now that she's admitted it's your kid."

"I'll cross that bridge when I come to it." Picking up the long-handled tool that looked like an oversize pair of curved pliers, Shane positioned the tips under the heel of the horseshoe and began carefully rocking it back and forth to pry out the nails without damaging Jasper's hoof.

"I think you're making a mistake, but it's your life."

"Thanks for noticing. Be sure and shut the door on your way out."

He didn't want to talk about it anymore. If he didn't know how he felt about the situation, he sure couldn't explain it to someone else. He needed time alone to think about what he should do, if anything. When Avery didn't move and didn't reply, Shane tugged the horseshoe loose, let go of the horse's foot and straightened to face him.

"Even if I want to take some level of responsibility for this baby, Annie made it very plain that she doesn't want that. I don't even know where she lives or how to contact her to discuss it."

"I don't know where she lives, but I can tell you that she works at the Windward Hotel out on the interstate."

Shane scowled. "How do you know that?"

"Her roommate, Miss Crystal Mally, works there with her. If I'd had a few more minutes, I would have had a phone number and a home address to go with that information. Crystal is a talkative girl, even if she isn't exactly my type."

"I didn't know you had a type."

"I don't, really, but I do shy away from junkies."

"Annie said she is in recovery. She mentioned having a counselor."

"Annie may be clean, but I don't think Crystal is there yet. Believe me, I know the signs. I hung out with a fast crowd before the Army got a hold of me."

"Knowing where Annie works doesn't change anything." Shane walked over to the forge and thrust a metal bar into the coals.

"Maybe not, but at least you know how to find her when you've had a chance to think things over."

He didn't want to think things over. He wanted to rewind the morning and erase the part where a pretty woman with sad eyes had turned his life upside down.

Two days later, Shane rounded the corner of the snack-food aisle at the local Gas and Go and spied Annie paying for her purchase of a large soda. Confronted with the woman he hadn't been able to get off his mind, he simply stared.

She wore a pair of faded jeans with butterflies embroidered in pink-and-white thread at her ankles. An equally faded jean jacket with threadbare cuffs covered a dark pink blouse. Her long braid hung down to the center of her back and swayed softly when she moved. Her silhouette showed only the slightest fullness at her midriff. A casual observer wouldn't know she was pregnant, but he knew. She was carrying his child.

What he should do about it—if anything—had kept him awake most of the last couple nights.

She was searching in the depths of her purse for money to pay for her drink and she hadn't seen him. Should he stay out of sight until she was gone or walk up to the counter as though it didn't matter? It wasn't in him to take the coward's way out. He closed the distance between them in a few steps.

"I'll pay for the lady's drink," he said to the teenage boy manning the cash register.

Annie's eyes flew open wide as she stared at him in shock. Her surprised look vanished as a frown deepened the furrow between her brows. To Shane she looked tired, as well as mad.

Before she could speak, he said, "I didn't think cola was good for pregnant women."

"It's lemon-lime—not that it's any of your business what I drink. What are you doing here?" she demanded.

He felt a tug of admiration for the way she stood up to him. "Picking up a quart of oil for my car and getting a burrito. Not that it's any of your business. How much?" He directed his question to the clerk.

The boy rattled off the price and Shane pulled a ten from his wallet. Annie seemed to be having trouble finding a comeback. After a full five seconds of silence, she said, "I can pay for my own drink."

"Too late." Shane took his change, dropped the coins in the front pocket of his jeans and tucked the bills into his wallet.

Annie pulled herself up to her full height, which wasn't much over five feet. "I thought I made it plain that I didn't intend to see you anymore."

"You did, but Junction City isn't a big town. We may run into each other again." He nodded his thanks to the clerk and picked up the white plastic sack with his purchases.

"I was serious when I said I didn't want or need anything from you," she insisted.

"I know you were." He walked to the door and pushed it open. The bell overhead jangled and the sounds of the street traffic grew louder. "The trouble is, Annie, you forgot to ask *me* what I want to do about our little problem. I do have a say in this, no matter what you think."

"What is it you want to do?"

"I'm not sure yet, but I'll let you know when I reach

a decision." He walked out the door and let it swing shut behind him. He glanced back as he stepped into his car. Annie watched him from inside the doorway. She was biting her lower lip.

Shane felt the stirrings of sympathy for her. He didn't want to add to the worries she carried. He wasn't sure what he wanted to do, but he knew he couldn't let Annie Delmar just walk out of his life.

Early Monday morning Annie and Crystal sped into the Windward's parking lot. Pulling around to the area reserved for staff, they both bolted out of the car and rushed in the side door of the building. For once it wasn't Crystal and Annie's poor excuse for a car that had made them late. This time it had been Annie's fault. The sudden onset of morning sickness had stopped her cold just as they were leaving the house.

Inside the building, the women dashed to the locker room, where they quickly changed into gray pin-striped smocks and gray pants. Annie tossed her own clothes and purse into her locker and shut the door. Running a hand over her hair to tame the flyaways, she took a deep breath and followed Crystal into the windowless, drab room that served as a cafeteria and meeting room for the hotel staff. Four other housekeepers sat at one of the tables. Their supervisor was standing at the front of the room.

Mr. Decker looked at the clock on the wall. The hands pointed to two minutes after eight. "I'm glad you ladies could join us." His sour tone made Annie wince.

"I'm sorry, Mr. Decker," she said. "It won't happen again."

She needed to make sure of that because she really

needed this job. She would have a baby to take care of soon.

The thought hit her out of the blue: she was keeping this baby.

Sometime between tossing and turning half the night trying to make a decision and now, the answer had been found. This was her baby. She would love it and raise it and give thanks for the blessing every day for the rest of her life.

"All right, let's get started." Mr. Decker was short and as thin as a toothpick. His unnaturally black hair was combed carefully over his bald crown, but his gray pin-striped suit was meticulously pressed with a carefully folded white handkerchief peeking out of his breast pocket. He picked up a clipboard from the table and scanned it quickly.

"We have thirty-two guests checking out this morning. Crystal and Annie, you will take the ground floor of the west wing."

Annie relaxed as he finished giving the other maids their assignments in English or in fluent Spanish for the women who needed it. The west wing was longer and therefore had more rooms, but she knew Crystal would help her if she fell behind. After only a month on the job, Annie still wasn't as speedy as Crystal. Crystal had been a maid at this hotel for over a year.

After morning assignments were finished, Annie loaded her cart with fresh towels and linens and replenished her bottle of glass cleaner. At the first room on the west wing, she knocked briskly. There was no answer. She swiped her key card and pushed open the door as she announced herself. Stepping over the threshold, she stared in dismay at the mess awaiting her.

Trash overflowed from the wastebasket and dirty clothes were scattered around the room. The bedding was piled on the floor below the foot of the mattress. A large pizza box lay open on the table. It was empty, but one upside-down slice had made it to the floor, where the cheese and tomato sauce were still soaking into the carpet.

This wasn't going to be a quick turndown and wipe. She checked the dresser top. Of course the occupants hadn't bothered to leave a tip for the poor soul who had to clean up after them. With a sigh, she began picking up articles of clothing. Her day may have started out badly, but she wasn't going to let it get her down. She was having a baby!

It took her almost thirty minutes to finish the room, but when she'd pulled up the clean spread and tucked it beneath the freshly fluffed pillows, she straightened and looked around with pride. She wasn't the fastest maid, but she always did a good job. There was something satisfying about creating order out of disorder. If only it were as easy to straighten out her life.

By four o'clock she was exhausted and she had earned only a single five-dollar tip. It would be enough to put a few gallons of gas into her car, but she wouldn't be able to get her flat spare tire fixed or put any money aside. The list of things the baby would need almost made her cringe.

In the locker room she sat on the bench and rubbed her aching feet. Closing her eyes, she whispered softly, "The Lord will provide."

She was learning that faith was a tricky thing. Just when she thought she had a firm grasp on it, something happened that made her doubts come back. Things like a day with lousy tips.

Being a Christian isn't about material stuff.

Annie tried hard to keep that in mind. It was about eternal life and about His love. She couldn't know His plan for her, but was it wrong to hope that it might include enough money to get a new pair of shoes?

She glanced at the clock as she waited for Crystal to join her. When her roommate rushed in ten minutes later, her face was flushed and she looked as nervous as a cat in a dog pound. Opening her locker, she grabbed her purse, then tossed her coat and her clothes over her arm. Glancing over her shoulder, Crystal said, "Come on. Let's get out of here."

"Aren't you going to change? You know Mr. Decker doesn't like us taking our uniforms home."

"He's gone for the day. He'll never know. What are you waiting for?" Crystal pulled open the door to the hallway, checked both ways, then hurried to the exit.

Annie followed her, puzzled by her odd behavior. "Crystal, what's wrong with you?"

"Nothing, I want to get home, that's all. I'm meeting Willie in half an hour."

"Who is Willie?"

"I met him last night at Kelly's Diner and I think he's the one. He's so cool. I told him I could give him a lift home after his shift is over in the evenings. That is—" she paused and looked back "—if I can borrow your car? You don't mind, do you?"

"Oh, Crystal." Annie didn't try to hide her disappointment.

"What? This guy could be the one. You don't know him."

"And neither do you."

"Don't be that way. He makes me feel special." Crystal pushed open the outside door but stopped dead in her tracks with a sharp gasp. Just as quickly she relaxed and said, "Oh, it's you."

When Annie came out the door, she saw Shane standing beside her car. Her breath caught in her throat. Dressed in jeans and a dark blue sweater that accented the color of his eyes, he looked far too handsome and exactly like the man she had fallen for that night three months ago.

Calling on all her willpower, she hardened her heart against a sudden and frightening desire to step into his embrace and rest her head on his shoulder.

He nodded at Crystal but walked past her to stand in front of Annie. "We need to talk."

Chapter 3

Shane was prepared for a verbal battle, but to his surprise, Annie didn't tell him to take a hike. She edged away from him, toward her car. He had the distinct impression that she was afraid of him. That was the last thing he wanted.

She licked her lips quickly, then said, "We don't have anything to discuss. How did you find me?"

He smiled, trying to put her at ease. "Let me buy you a cup of coffee and I'll tell you."

"I don't drink coffee."

"Then make it a cup of tea or a lemon-lime soda—anything you want. Annie, I'm not going to go away until we've had a rational discussion about our baby."

He had come here intending to do just that, but now he found himself wanting something different. His motives had been hidden even from himself until he'd seen her face today. She looked tired, sad, vulnerable. That vulnerability was what he remembered most about her. It was why he had looked for her after their night together. It was why he couldn't get her out of his mind.

Now that he had found her again, he wanted to spend time with her. He wanted to get to know her better. He needed to find out if their one bittersweet meeting might have been the beginning of something special.

Crystal shifted from one foot to the other beside the car. "I need to get going. I told Willie I'd meet him after work."

Annie took another step toward the car. "I need to get home."

She was making it obvious that she had no desire, hidden or otherwise, to spend time with him. Shane took a step back and held up his hands. "All right, but I'll be here tomorrow…and the day after that and the day after that. Sooner or later, you're going to have to talk to me."

He watched her indecision play across her face. She chewed the corner of her bottom lip for a few seconds, then she turned to her friend and held out the car keys. "You go, Crystal. I'll be home later. Tell Marge that I went to get a cup of cocoa with Corporal Ross."

Crystal took the keys. "Are you sure you want to do that?"

Relieved by her change of heart, he said, "I'll see that she gets home."

Annie's smile looked strained, but she nodded. "I'm sure. You go on."

Shane worked to keep his elation in check. He didn't know where any of this was going, but at least he was doing something. She was willing to talk to him and he wasn't going to waste the opportunity.

As Crystal drove away, he faced Annie and asked, "Where would you like to go?"

"The hotel has a restaurant. We can go there."

"Fine by me. Lead the way."

It was too early in the evening for the Italian-themed bistro to be busy yet, but the aromas coming from the kitchen were tempting enough to make Shane hope he could convince Annie to have dinner with him. Once they were seated in a corner booth out of earshot of the other customers, he leaned back against the green plaid fabric and smiled to put her at ease. "Crystal told my friend where you and she work."

Annie frowned at him. He shrugged. "You asked how I found you."

"Oh." She rearranged the salt and pepper shakers and moved the green ceramic container of sugar and sweetener packets to the center of the table to form a straight line. She seemed to realize what she was doing and quickly clasped her hands together. The clink of tableware and muted voices from the other diners did little to fill the void of silence.

"So where do we start?" he asked as he studied her face. She was pretty in an exotic way with her long, dark hair and deep brown eyes. Dressed in a simple white blouse with short sleeves and a pair of black slacks, she seemed to want to blend in rather than stand out from the crowd. Her lips were full, and he remembered the way they had softened when he'd kissed her.

Was the sweetness he had tasted that night really there or had it been part of a dream? They were going to have a child together, but he realized he knew almost nothing about this woman. He wanted to know more. A lot more.

She met his gaze. "You tell me where to start. You're the one who insisted on this meeting. I still don't understand why. I thought I was letting you off easy."

"Easy? You call this easy? Every day of my life I'm going to wonder if I had a son or a daughter. You intend to go your merry way and I'll never know where he is. I'll never know if some other man is reading him the stories he likes or playing catch with him or taking him fishing."

Pressing his lips into a tight line, Shane looked down and struggled to keep the old pain in check. The waitress arrived to take their orders, and it gave him a moment to compose himself.

When she left, Annie said softly, "I'm sorry. I didn't mean to make light of the situation. There's something more going on here, isn't there?"

He was surprised by her perception. Shaking his head, he said, "It's a long story. I don't want to bore you with my ancient history."

"You wanted to talk. I'm trying to listen."

Touched by her compassion, Shane considered how much he should tell her. If he had any hope of convincing her to let him share in the decisions she had to make, he would need to gain a level of her trust. Wasn't that worth exposing a part of his past, even if it was a painful part?

Slowly he began telling his tale. "I was engaged about a year ago. Her name was Carla. She had a little boy named Jimmy. He was the cutest, smartest little kid you have ever met. At four he knew the entire alphabet."

He paused, remembering those happy times, remembering how proud he had been of Jimmy.

"He was your son?"

"No, but that didn't matter. It didn't matter to me, anyway. It was easy to love Jimmy and to think of him as my own. I believed that I was in love with Carla, but it was Jimmy who got me to thinking about making us one big happy family. For Carla it was a different story."

"How so?"

"Jimmy's father had split right after Jimmy was born. He never kept in touch, never paid support—you know the type."

The deep bitterness in his voice momentarily took her aback. "I've met a few guys like that in my time."

"One day he showed up again. Carla decided life would be better for Jimmy with his 'real' father. She broke it off with me, went back to him and they moved away."

"That must have been rough."

"It was. Jimmy didn't know his 'real' father from a hole in the ground. I was the only father figure he'd had in his life. Carla was an adult. She made her choice and I hope she is happy, but Jimmy didn't get a choice. I hope he's happy, but I'll never know for sure."

"So what do you want from me?"

He stared down at his hands clasped together on the tabletop, then looked up and met her eyes. "I keep asking myself that same question. I guess I want to know that you have all you need to make a good life for my son or daughter."

The waitress came back just then with their order. While Shane added a spoon of sugar to his coffee, Annie toyed with the marshmallows floating on her cup of hot chocolate. She hadn't expected him to reveal so much about himself. She hadn't expected to empathize with his feelings of loss or to find herself wanting to comfort him. What was it about him that broke through her defenses?

He had been a one-night stand. She had been with dozens of men in those years when addiction ruled her life and made getting another drink more important than food or shoes, more important than friends or family. The list of loved ones damaged by her sickness and her bitter refusals to get help was longer than her arm.

"Shane, I respect that you want to be involved, I do, I just don't see how I can promise you anything."

"I'm not looking for any promises. I just need to know that both of you are going to be okay."

"I'm okay without your help."

A lopsided grin made a dimple appear in his right cheek. Why did he have to be so cute and so genuine?

"I'm sure you are, but it seems that I'm not. Can't you see some way to…I don't know…to let me give you money to help with expenses?"

Annie's sympathy for Shane splintered like a cheap glass on a tile floor. Shards of it pricked her hard-won self-respect.

"I don't take money from men."

"Oh, man, that's not what I meant. Not at all. I'm sorry. I didn't even think—"

"Fine." She cut him off, wanting only to get home and curl up in her bed with her head under the covers. She started to get out of the booth, but he stopped her by laying a hand over hers on the table.

"Please don't go. I'm a total jerk. Ask anyone who knows me. I put my foot in my mouth fifty times a day."

The sincerity of his plea gave her pause, but it was the look in his eyes that made her stay. "That must make it hard to march in formation."

He relaxed, a ghost of a smile curving his lips. "I'm lucky—in my outfit the horses do all the legwork."

He drew his hand away slowly. Oddly she wished he hadn't. For a tiny fraction of time she had felt comforted by his touch.

It was ridiculous. She didn't need his help, his money or his comfort.

"Can you accept that I'm a well-meaning, if inept, person?" he asked.

"I guess I can accept that."

"Good. I honestly do want to help. Tell me how."

It would be so easy to give in to his pleading and let him shoulder the responsibility of providing the things she and the baby would need. Things like their own place to live, a crib, even clothes for the baby. But to do that would be like going backward in her recovery.

Once, she had used alcohol as her crutch to make life bearable. She wouldn't substitute that addiction for a dependence on this man, even if it seemed harmless on the surface. Her track record with relationships didn't include any that had been harmless.

"Thanks for the offer, but I think the best thing for both of us is to go our separate ways."

"I have rights as a parent." His tone carried a new determination.

So he wasn't harmless after all. "What are you saying?"

"Under the law, I have the same right to this baby that you do."

"Is that a threat? If you think you can take my baby away, you had better think again. I'm not afraid of you."

He held up both hands and shook his head. "It's not a threat. I'm not saying I would make the better parent." Leaning forward, he clasped his hands together. "I have no intention of trying to take this baby away from you. I'm only saying that I have an equal responsibility to take care of him or her."

She wasn't sure she believed him. Trusting men was as foreign to her as owning diamond earrings.

He sat back and wrapped his hands around his mug of coffee. "You should drink your cocoa before it gets cold."

Annie lifted the cup to her lips and took a sip of the rich, sweet chocolate. It helped steady her nerves and gave her a chance to think about what she needed to do next. Shane was making it evident that he wasn't about to go away.

Suspecting he was right about the law, she had no intention of making it a legal matter. Even with the testimony of Marge as her sponsor, Annie doubted that a judge would overlook her past in a custody battle. For the moment, Corporal Shane Ross had the upper hand.

Would he turn out to be a dog in the manger? Once he got what he wanted, would he lose interest? His story about the little boy he had lost to a deadbeat dad didn't mean that he wouldn't follow the same pattern. Perhaps instead of fighting him, she should wait and let time do the work for her. Not many of the men she'd known came through on their promises. Why should she think Shane would be any different?

She couldn't quite silence the small voice in the back of her mind that told her this man *was* different.

"Have you thought about adoption?" he asked after a few minutes.

"I've considered it, but I want to keep my baby."

She'd admitted the thought aloud for the first time and it felt right.

"That's good to know. Thank you for telling me."

Had she made a mistake? Confiding in him was easier than she'd expected. She quickly resolved not to give him any more information. "I should be going."

"But you haven't finished your drink."

"I want to leave now."

He looked ready to argue but finally nodded and said, "Sure."

He motioned to the waitress and paid the check. Annie picked up her purse and headed for the door.

Outside, he walked beside her to the staff parking spaces, stopping beside a low-slung red Mustang with a wide black stripe down the hood. The car was obviously not new, but it was in pristine condition. He unlocked and opened the door for her. As she got in, she took note of the difference between his vehicle and hers. His didn't have rips in the fabric of the front seat. His radio had buttons, while hers didn't even have the knobs it had come with. She was pretty sure his heater worked no matter how cold it got. Judging by this, he could afford to pay child support.

Temptation came in many forms. Only knowing that she would have to give up more than she would gain kept her from accepting his previous offer. She and her baby wouldn't have a lavish life, but they would have enough.

"Nice wheels," she said when he slid into the driver's seat.

"Thanks. This is a 1973 Mustang Mach One. This puppy is my pride and joy."

"You can afford a classic car like this on a corporal's salary?"

He laughed. "She wasn't much to look at when I first found her, but it still took two summers of roofing in the hot Texas sun to pay for her back when I was a teenager. Restoring her has been a kind of hobby of mine ever since. Besides, I live on base so I don't have many expenses. This car is my one luxury. Annie, is the fact that I'm in the Army part of the reason you don't want me involved with our baby?"

It was as good a reason as any. "To my mind, guns and babies don't to go together."

"There's a lot more to the Army than guns."

"I'm sure that's true, but how many years have you been in?"

"Six."

"And how many different places have you been stationed in in that time?"

"Including basic training? Four."

"That's not exactly a blueprint for maintaining close family ties."

"No, but it's not impossible if you're willing to work at it." She heard the resignation creeping into his voice, even if he wouldn't admit as much.

She drove home her point. "Tell me how we could make it work. Should we ship the kid back and forth between us every six months? Aren't you going to Germany soon?"

"We live in the same place now."

"But not for long. I might decide I want to move. Who knows where you'll be stationed after Germany. It's too complicated. I need to get on with my life and you need to get on with yours. I wish now that I hadn't told you."

"No, don't wish that."

A sadness to match his settled over her. "You probably wish you had never met me," she said softly.

He stared at his hands clasped around the top of the steering wheel for a long moment, then looked over and met her gaze. "No, I don't."

He started the engine and shifted into Reverse. She gave him her home address, then leaned back into the plush seat. He didn't speak during the ride and neither did she.

When he pulled up in front of her house, he shut off the engine and turned toward her. "I can't help thinking that one of the reasons you don't want me around the baby is because you don't know me well."

"I know you well enough."

"If you're referring to the night we met, I'll be the first to admit that we started off all wrong."

"So?"

He pressed his hand to his chest, his expression earnest and intense. "I'd like to change that. I'd like to get to know you and I'd like you to get to know me. Someday the kid is going to ask about me. I'd like you to be able to tell him something about what I do and what kind of person I am."

"What are you suggesting? That we start dating?" She didn't bother to hide her sarcasm.

"That's an excellent idea. What are you doing Saturday afternoon?"

Chapter 4

"Annie, you seem awfully quiet tonight. Is something bothering you?" Marge diced another carrot and added it to the large kettle of vegetable soup simmering on the back burner of her stove.

At the long pine table nearby, Annie closed the book she wasn't actually reading. Since she couldn't come to a decision about what to do by herself, perhaps Marge could help. "When Shane Ross brought me home yesterday... he asked me out."

"Like—on a date?" The astonished inquiry came from Marge's thirteen-year-old daughter, Olivia, as she breezed into the kitchen and pulled open the fridge door. With her sleek chin-length dark hair and dark eyes, she and Annie could have passed for sisters.

Marge turned and scowled at her only child. "Get out of the fridge. Supper will be ready in half an hour.

And what is so surprising about Annie being asked out on a date?"

Olivia rolled her eyes and took a container of flavored yogurt before she shut the door. "It's just that she never goes out."

While it was true, it was embarrassing to have a teenager point out her total lack of a social life.

Annie said, "He didn't exactly ask me for a date. He asked me to come and watch his unit perform on base Saturday afternoon. It's some kind of community appreciation day."

"Oh, oh, is he the one with the horses?" Olivia's eyes widened with interest.

"Yes, he's in the mounted color guard. How did you know that?"

"Crystal told me about him. Heather, one of my friends from school, saw them ride last year. She said they were *awesome.* She's going with her family. I heard that there's going to be a carnival and tons of stuff to see and do. I wish we could go. Could we, Mom? Please?"

Marge shook her head. "I'm sorry, sweetie, but I'm working at the clinic on Saturday."

Olivia's excited expression turned to disappointment. She plopped into a chair beside Annie. "You're always working at that clinic."

"Which is exactly why you have a roof over your head and food in the refrigerator, young lady."

"It's not much of a roof. It leaks like a faucet in the corner of my room when it rains."

Annie nudged the pouting girl with her elbow. "Your mom does important work at the mental-health clinic. If she hadn't been there for me, I wouldn't be here today. She saved my life."

"I know, but I'd really like to see the Army's horses."

Leaning forward, Annie winked at the girl. "Plus a few good-looking guys dressed in romantic cavalry uniforms sporting sabers and pistols."

Olivia's frown changed to a conspiratory grin shared between the two of them. "That, too."

After seasoning the pot with salt and pepper, Marge put the lid on and lowered the heat. Wiping her hands on a paper towel, she turned to Annie. "What did you say when Shane invited you?"

"I said I'd think about it."

"And have you?"

Far more than she cared to admit. With his deep-timbred voice and slow Texas drawl, his bright blue eyes and soft, enchanting smile, Shane was almost all she *had* thought about these past few days. Her plan to tell him about her pregnancy and then dismiss him from her life wasn't exactly working out. "I don't think I should go."

"Why not?"

Annie shrugged. "I don't know."

She didn't really have a reason, at least not one she wanted to talk about. She didn't want to go because she suspected that the more she saw of Corporal Ross the harder it would be to ignore his request to be included in her baby's life—*their* baby's life.

"Why don't you go and take Olivia with you? That way you won't have to go by yourself. Plus, Olivia won't have to spend the next two days giving me those deep sighs and pitiful looks that mean I'm the world's worst mother because I'm not letting her do something she wants."

Olivia's face brightened. "Yeah, that would be great! And I don't think you're the world's worst mom."

"That's not what you said when I wouldn't let you get your belly button pierced."

"Mom, that was weeks ago—and so not fair. Heather got hers pierced."

"Just because Heather does something doesn't mean you have to do it, too."

"She's not the only one in my class that has a belly-button ring."

"That still doesn't make it right. Besides, while you're—"

"I know, I know. While I'm living in this house I have to live by your rules."

"That's right, and I'm tough on you because…why?"

"Because you love me and you want me to grow up to be a responsible adult."

"Right!"

Listening to their exchange, Annie wondered if she would be as good a mother as Marge was. In spite of having lost her husband in a car accident when Olivia was a toddler, Marge's faith and courage never seemed to waiver. Making a home for herself and her child must have been hard enough, but somehow Marge found the strength to do more. She had reached out to other young women in need, opening her home to some of them and offering hope and compassion to everyone who came asking for help.

Olivia gave up arguing with her mother and turned to Annie. "Please, can I go with you to the base? I promise not to be a pain. We'll have fun and you can meet some of my friends."

Annie didn't have the heart to say no in the face of

Olivia's wide, pleading eyes and excited demeaner. Or maybe she really did want to see Shane again. "Sure, I'll take you."

"Sweet!" Olivia jumped up and threw her arms around Annie's neck. "Thanks. You won't regret it. I'm going to call Heather. We have to decide where to meet."

Scooping up her yogurt and pausing only long enough to pull a spoon out of one of the drawers, Olivia hurried toward the phone in the living room.

Marge drew out a chair and sat down beside Annie. "Maybe I shouldn't have suggested that you take her. Sometimes I let my own guilt about being a poor mother cloud my judgment where Olivia is concerned."

"You aren't a bad mother."

"Perhaps not, but I'm one that doesn't get to spend as much time with my child as I would like. If you decide you don't want to go, I'll make other arrangements for Olivia."

"I won't regret having Olivia's company, but I might regret going at all."

"Why is that?"

"I'm so confused about what I should be doing. When I found out I was pregnant, everything I hoped I could do with my life came to a grinding halt. I agreed to tell Shane about the baby because I honestly thought he wouldn't care. But he does care. At least I think he does. He says he does."

"Do you like Shane?"

Annie took a long time to form her answer. "Maybe, but what's the point?"

Marge tilted her head slightly. "What's the point of exploring your feelings for the father of your child? I think that's pretty obvious. The two of you have a lot to work out."

"Marge, I've never had a relationship with any man that wasn't based on alcohol, including the night I met Shane. By the time I was a junior in high school I was already keeping a bottle stashed under my bed so I had something to help get me started in the mornings. I don't remember half the dates I went on because I got smashed as often and as fast as I could. Once my parents kicked me out, I lived with one guy after another. Some of them, I barely remember their names, but if they were buying me booze…I thought I loved them."

"That isn't your life now."

"No. I've been sober for eighty-eight days, and in that time I haven't so much as looked at another guy. I have no idea how to judge Shane's sincerity or how to act around a man who doesn't have a drink in his hand."

"You told me that Shane wants you to keep the baby and he wants to be involved in the child's life. Do you have a reason to doubt that he's sincere?"

"No, but I can't see what he has to gain by it."

Shaking her head sadly, Marge said, "Not every man commits to a purpose because he has something to gain. Some men commit because it is the right thing to do."

"None of the ones I know."

"Then perhaps you should get to know Shane better. Find out if he is the kind of man you want your child to know."

Sighing, Annie picked up her book and opened it. "Maybe I'm making a bigger deal out of this than I need to. He only asked me to come watch his unit perform. It's not like he asked me to marry him or something."

Why that comment had popped out of her mouth,

Annie had no idea. She shot a startled glance at Marge in time to see her hide a smile behind her hand. Sitting up, Annie said, "That didn't mean that I've been thinking about him as husband material."

A quick grin curved Marge's lips, but she pressed them into a firm line. "No, of course it doesn't mean that."

"It doesn't!" Annie shot to her feet. "I'll be outside if you need me."

She stomped out the door, determined not to give Corporal Shane Ross another thought. Her determination lasted only as long as it took her to reach the backyard and look up into the cloudless blue sky.

Shane's eyes were bright blue. What color eyes would the baby have? Annie hoped they would be brown. Otherwise, she would be reminded every day that her child was his child, too.

Shane pulled his saddle cinch tight and checked the grandstands again. The colorful crowd was growing by the minute as the time for his detachment's demonstration neared. Twice he had seen women with long dark braids climbing the steps of the bleachers, but when they'd turned around to take their seats, neither of them had been the woman he was looking for. His faint hope that Annie would come today faded a little more.

"Do you see her?" Avery asked as he finished saddling his mount, Dakota.

Shane resumed checking Jasper's tack. "No, but I'm not surprised. I didn't really think she would show."

Adjusting his flat-topped trooper's hat, Avery said, "If she doesn't, there are plenty of other women out there waiting to be impressed. I'm ready to shock and awe those two blond beauties at this end of the bleachers."

Shaking his head, Shane said, "If you hit even one balloon with your sword, we'll all be shocked."

"Very funny. You know I'm better at sabers than you are."

"I don't know any such thing. You'll be breaking your neck trying to see if the pretty girls are watching, and I'll be cutting down targets. I think I'll hit four for every one that you get."

"Dream on!"

"We shall see."

Smoothing the coat of his dark blue wool 1854-style cavalry uniform, Shane stepped into the stirrup and swung into the saddle. "The crowd is a lot bigger than I was expecting. It's good to see so much support."

Avery spent another few seconds making sure his saddle and girth were secure, then he mounted Dakota. Prancing in eagerness, Dakota sidestepped into Jasper and then let out a loud whinny.

Sudden static filled the air as the loudspeakers on the reviewing stand came on. Avery tapped Shane on the shoulder and pointed to a woman with short auburn hair climbing the steps to the platform. "Hey, it's Sergeant Mandel."

Shane reached over to pat Dakota's neck. "You recognized her, didn't you, fella?"

"Lindsey's not a sergeant anymore," Shane reminded his friend. "She left the service and works in public affairs now."

"She'll always be Sergeant Mandel to me."

"Yeah, I miss her, too."

Until recently, Lindsey had been a member of the

Commanding General's Mounted Color Guard, and her brother had once owned Dakota. Lindsey's skills and her dedication to the unit and the Army were something rare. Even after leaving the service, she had found a way to promote public awareness of the many and varied jobs the Army performed.

Lindsey, dressed in a dark blue dress with a red-and-white scarf draped around her neck, leaned close to the microphone. "Ladies and gentlemen, welcome to Fort Riley's Community Appreciation Day. I hope you've been enjoying the festivities so far. I understand the obstacle tent where you get to wear night-vision goggles has been a big hit with the kids."

A dozen isolated shouts of agreement went up from the stands. She smiled in response. "If you were impressed with our latest gadgets, I'm sure you'll be even more impressed with the demonstration you're about to see here."

Music poured out of the loudspeakers around the field, and the muted but stirring strains of the Battle Hymn of the Republic filled the air.

"Long before we had tanks, planes and Black Hawk helicopters, the U.S. Army relied on another method of moving troops quickly into battle. I'm talking about the horse. While mechanization has made the use of the horse obsolete on the battlefield, we here at Fort Riley have not forgotten the contributions the horse soldier has made to our history. Once called the Cradle of the Cavalry, Fort Riley housed the Cavalry Training School until the cavalry was disbanded in 1943."

Captain Watson rode up beside the eight troopers waiting with their horses at one end of the parade ground. "Corporal, form up the detachment."

"Yes, sir." Saluting smartly, Shane called out the order and the men and horses moved into a column of two. Another soldier on the ground handed Shane the unit banner. When the colors were unfurled, he gripped the staff and awaited his orders.

"In 1992," Lindsey continued, "the Commanding General's Mounted Color Guard was reestablished to honor that long tradition. These men train from the same cavalry manual used to train soldiers during the Civil War. This unit serves as ambassadors for the Army, as well as a living history exhibition. It is arduous work, but the level of horsemanship these soldiers attain is nothing short of remarkable. Please give a round of applause to both the men and the horses of our own Commanding General's Mounted Color Guard."

Captain Watson gave the order, and the unit sprang into action.

The crowd cheered wildly as nine matching bay horses galloped across the grassy field with the flag snapping in the wind. For Shane, this was the best part of his job. The chance to reenact this special piece of America's past filled him with pride.

At the opposite end of the field, the column split in two. Both lines turning in unison, the men and their mounts continued at a gallop toward a row of low hurdles along the edges of the parade ground. A dozen red and white balloons decorated each end of the barriers, but by the end of the performance there would only be a few of them left.

When all the hurdles had been cleared, the riders merged into a double row again and came to a halt. Handing the banner to a man on the ground, Shane then drew his saber from its scabbard. He looked over at Avery and nodded. Together they rode back into the jumps. As his horse, Jasper, sailed into the air, Shane slashed the tops of two balloons. Jasper raced on, unfazed by the loud pops. At the second jump, Shane's sword caught two more of the helium-filled targets. From the corner of his eye he saw Avery take out three, and he chuckled to himself. Avery was good, but he often needed a little push to really excel.

When the entire group had completed their run, they reformed into two groups. At a command, they merged and began a mock battle designed to display both their swordsmanship and their mounts' abilities to maneuver at close quarters.

From the bottom row of the bleachers near the reviewing stand Annie listened to the clash of steel against steel as she watched the exhibition with Olivia at her side. A shiver of fear ran down her spine. It would be so easy for one of the men to be hurt. From the sound of it, the swords were heavy—but surely they weren't sharp.

She easily picked Shane out of the group of milling riders. He certainly seemed to be enjoying himself as he and another man traded what looked like serious blows.

On cue, the battling group parted and formed up for another gallop around the grounds. After one circuit, the riders headed into the hurdles again, this time with pistols drawn. The bark of gunfire and the smell of gun smoke filled the air as the men shot the remaining balloons while their mounts sailed through the jumps.

"I told you it would be exciting. Did you see the way their horses didn't even hesitate?" Olivia stood to get a better view.

"Very impressive," Annie admitted, watching Shane

complete the course with ease. He looked at home on horseback…and so very handsome in his uniform.

"There you are. I've been looking all over for you."

Annie leaned forward to see a young girl slide into a vacant space on the other side of Olivia. Dressed in a bright red tank top and short cutoff jeans, Olivia's friend appeared several years older than Annie had expected. On closer inspection, she realized the girl's heavy makeup helped disguise her youthful features. Olivia, wearing a blue T-shirt with smooching white puppies on the front, looked much younger and far more innocent.

"You said to meet you by the viewing stand. We've been here for half an hour," Olivia replied.

"Oh, right. Well, I'm here now. Come on, this is boring. Let's go over to the carnival rides."

Glancing between her friend and Annie, Olivia said, "Can I go with Heather?"

Torn between wanting to let Olivia go with her friends and not wanting her out of sight, Annie said, "I thought you wanted to watch the horses."

"I've seen enough."

With one last look at Shane, Annie pulled her purse strap up on her shoulder. "All right, I guess we can go take in a few rides. But you aren't going to get me on that Ferris wheel."

"You don't have to come," Heather said quickly.

"She's right, Annie. You can stay and watch the rest of this."

"We'll be back in thirty minutes, I promise." Heather's smile was disarming, but still, Annie hesitated.

"We shouldn't split up. This is a pretty big crowd."

"We'll ride a few rides and then come right back."

"If we hurry, we won't have to wait in line," Heather added. "Nearly everyone is here."

Annie glanced toward the midway and noticed that what Heather said was true. The spinning tilt-a-whirl and the Ferris wheel were only half full. Just the sight of the dizzying rides was enough to bring back her morning sickness. Getting on a ride was the last thing she wanted to do.

She studied Olivia's hopeful face. "Half an hour, right?"

Olivia's eyes brightened. "Right. Thanks, Annie. You're the best."

Watching the pair of them hurry away, Annie realized that she didn't feel like "the best." Instead she wondered if she had made a bad decision.

Her uncertainty kept her from enjoying the rest of the demonstration. Shane and his unit's feats of horsemanship barely held her interest. She glanced frequently toward the rides and checked her watch.

Forty minutes later, Shane's exhibition had ended and the stands began to empty. Annie's initial annoyance at being kept waiting rapidly turned to concern. By the time another twenty minutes had gone by only a handful of people remained, and most of them were working their way to the bottom of the bleachers or meeting in small groups at the edge of the field. Her growing concern turned to outright worry.

Where could they be? It wasn't like Olivia to break her word. A dozen unpleasant scenarios darted through Annie's mind, most of them fueled by distasteful memories of her own teenage years. Letting the girls go off alone had been a stupid decision.

As the few remaining onlookers cleared out, Annie

climbed to the top of the bleachers hoping to catch a glimpse of the girls coming her way. Searching the growing crowds on the midway proved to be fruitless. She was simply too far away. If she joined the throng and tried to find the girls, she could pass within a dozen yards and not see them.

Wait here or go out to look for them? She wasn't sure what to do.

Checking her watch again, she saw the girls were over an hour late now. She couldn't wait any longer.

Help me find them, Lord. I'm depending on You.

Hurrying back down the steps, Annie stopped short at the sight of Shane standing in a group in front of her. Several of the men in his company were gathered around the female announcer. A blond man leaning on a cane stood beside her. Smiling and joking with his friends, Shane looked like the answer to her prayers.

He happened to glance her way. His welcoming grin quickly faded as she closed the distance between them. He rushed toward her. "Annie, what's wrong? Are you okay?"

She hadn't realized she was reaching out to him until his hands closed over hers. The comfort of his grip helped slow her racing heart.

"Olivia—my friend's daughter—came with me today, and now I can't find her. She said she'd be back in thirty minutes, but that was more than an hour ago. Something's happened to her. I know it."

Chapter 5

Shane's fear dropped away and relief rushed in when he realized there wasn't anything wrong with Annie. Calming her became his next priority. She was seriously alarmed. That couldn't be good for either her or the baby.

"Take it easy. I'm sure nothing has happened to your friend's daughter. Where did you last see her?"

"She went with another girl to ride the carnival rides."

"Maybe she just forgot the time."

"Maybe, but this isn't like her. Olivia is only thirteen, but she is a responsible kid. She might be ten minutes late but not an hour and ten minutes."

"Okay, we'll help you search for her." He motioned to his friends and they gathered around.

Annie gave a brief description of both girls and what

they were wearing. Suddenly her eyes widened as she looked at Shane. "I don't know Heather's last name. I don't know how to contact her family. How could I be so careless?"

Captain Watson quickly took charge. "Avery, take five men and begin a search at the far end of the old post, working back to here. From horseback you should have an easier time searching the crowds. The rest of the base is closed off, so unless they left by car they'll still be here. I'll notify security to begin checking vehicles leaving the base. Have you called the girl's mother to see if she rode home with someone else?"

"No. Marge is at work. I don't know if I should call and alarm her or give the girls a little more time. I know Olivia wouldn't leave without telling me first. I should be out looking for her."

Shane realized that she was still holding his hand. Her tight grip and the tone of her voice told him how worried she was.

Lindsey stepped forward and said gently, "Why don't you and I wait here in case she comes back."

Shane nodded his thanks. "That's a good idea. Annie, this is Lindsey Mandel. She's a close friend of mine. And this is her fiancé, Dr. Brian Cutter. Lindsey can wait here with you while we go and look for her."

Annie turned to Shane. "I can't sit around any longer. I have to go look for her."

Somehow he knew not to argue with her. Maybe it was the determined look in her eyes or maybe it was knowing she didn't give in easily when she had made up her mind. "Okay, Lindsey and Brian will wait here in case she comes back. I'll come with you."

"Thank you." She drew a deep breath and gave his hand a squeeze before she released it.

"Let's start with the midway," he suggested.

She nodded in agreement and hurried away. He caught up to her in several strides. Side by side they made their way through the array of food vendors and military equipment. Shane searched the crowds for a glimpse of a girl in a blue shirt with kissing puppies on the front. Suddenly Annie darted away from his side toward a group of teenagers wearing Kevlar vests and helmets who were taking turns shooting paintballs from realistic-looking rifles.

Annie grabbed Olivia by the shoulder and spun her around, prepared to give the girl the scolding she deserved. In the next second she realized it wasn't Olivia but another girl with the same shirt who was staring at her in stunned surprise.

"I'm sorry," Annie mumbled. "I thought you were someone else."

Turning away, she surveyed the crowd again. Where could Olivia be? Pressing a hand to her forehead, she tried to imagine what she was going to tell Marge. Her friend had entrusted her with her daughter's safekeeping, and Annie had let her down.

If she couldn't keep an eye on one child for the afternoon, what on earth was she doing thinking about raising one of her own?

One of Shane's men came riding up. Stepping to his side, Shane asked, "Any luck?"

"Not yet. You?"

"Nothing. Where haven't we looked?"

"We've covered the midway, the Red Cross tent, the

shooting range and the grandstands. I don't know where else to look."

Annie bit her lower lip. "Has anyone checked the carnival workers' trailers?"

The rider shook his head. Shane said, "You start at the north end, we'll start over here."

With Shane close behind her, Annie headed between the red-striped tent of the snow-cone vendor and a small yellow trailer offering corn dogs and hamburgers for sale. The area immediately behind the midway was a jumble of stakes and ropes and electric cords running from loud, smelly diesel generators. Beside a long truck painted with the amusement company's logo and pictures of the different rides, Annie came to an abrupt halt.

Heather sat at a picnic table, laughing with two young men dressed in greasy white shirts and stained jeans. Olivia sat slumped at the table beside her. Empty beer bottles littered the ground around them.

Relief made Annie's knees weak. She drew a quick breath and said, "That's her."

With the next breath Annie's anger spiked and she stormed toward the errant pair. "Olivia Lilly, what do you think you are doing?"

Heather made a quick attempt to hide the bottle she held behind her back. "Ms. Delmar. I'm sorry, I guess we forgot about the time."

"I guess you did," Shane growled. "Annie has been out of her mind with worry. We've got half the base looking for you. Where are your parents?"

"They went home."

"They went home and left you here by yourself?"

"I told them I'd catch a ride with Olivia."

The young men with her took one look at Shane's scowl and suddenly found things to do elsewhere.

Olivia raised her head off the table and gave a vague smile. "Is it time to go?"

"It is way past time," Annie replied, pulling the girl to her feet.

Olivia swayed for a moment, then sat abruptly. "Oops."

"I can't believe this. After everything your mother has taught you about making good choices, this is what you do when her back is turned?"

"It's not her fault," Heather offered. "She just wanted to taste a beer."

Annie snatched the bottle from Heather's hand and tossed it in a nearby trash can. "I'm sure you can share the blame equally. As will the young men who were here. I want their names."

Knowing that her own life had spiraled out of control when she was only a few years older than Olivia made Annie's blood run cold. This never would have happened if she had taken her responsibilities more seriously. She was as much to blame as anyone.

Shane laid a hand on her shoulder. "I'll let the others know we've located her so they can call off the search. Wait here until I get back and I'll see that you get home."

Annie tried her best to smile. "Thank you for your help, Shane, but I can manage now."

"I'll be back anyway." He turned and jogged back the way they had come.

"I think I'm going to be sick." White-faced, Olivia pressed a hand to her mouth. A second later she was.

As Annie attended to her, she couldn't help but pray

that this would turn out to be a lesson Olivia wouldn't soon forget.

Later, as Shane helped Annie settle the teary-eyed girl in the backseat of her car, she tried again to thank him. He waved aside her expression of gratitude. "This isn't your fault."

"I don't see it that way—and I'm afraid Olivia's mother won't see it that way, either. She was very upset when I called her and told her what had happened. Did you locate Heather's family?"

"Yes. Her dad picked her up at the security booth a few minutes ago."

"Was he angry?"

"I think he was more upset by having to make a trip back here than he was about her drinking. He said, 'Kids experiment,' like that explained his underage daughter getting one of her friends drunk. He'd better rein her in now or he's really going to have a problem child on his hands."

A problem child. How many times had she heard that label from her family? Crossing her arms over her chest, she leaned against the car door and stared at the ground. "I was a problem child."

"Were you?"

She slanted a look at him, wanting to see his reaction. For some reason, it mattered. "Yes. When I wasn't much older than Olivia."

He settled one hip against the hood of the car beside her. "Why was that?"

"I wasn't a happy kid. I never felt like I fit in until I started drinking. I wish I could say I had a reason for my alcoholism, but the truth is I didn't. Unlike a lot of alcoholics, I wasn't abused or mistreated. Drinking was socially acceptable in my family, but I couldn't stop there. It became all I wanted, and I did anything I could to feed my habit. I lied, I cheated, I stole."

"What changed?"

"At first, nothing. My parents tried everything, but in the end they were forced to sever our relationship. I don't blame them. I wrecked their lives."

"I find that hard to believe."

"It took a long time for me to see the light. You have no idea of the harm I caused."

"No one leads a blameless life."

"True. We are all sinners. That's what makes God's love for us so very special."

"I don't know about that."

"Do you believe?"

"In God? Sure. Am I a churchgoer? No."

Annie turned and pulled open her car door. "I'm sorry to hear that. Of all the things our baby is going to need in his or her life, people who have strong faith tops the list."

As Shane watched Annie drive away, he allowed himself a small smile. She had said "our baby." It wasn't much, but it was a beginning. Now if he only had some idea how to make the next move. He needed help.

Leaving the makeshift parking lot that had been cordoned off on a grassy field for the festivities that day, he walked along the tree-lined streets of the old post. Large limestone buildings and Victorian-style houses sat back from the now-quiet streets. The white stone walls had mellowed over the decades to a pale yellow that gave this part of the post a special warmth and steeped it in nostalgia.

Clusters of lilacs in the yards beside the wraparound porches of several turn-of-the-century houses lent their sweet, coy fragrance to the late-afternoon air.

Following the twisting maze of roads and walkways, he eventually found himself outside the building that housed the post's public affairs department. He climbed a set of wooden steps and opened the door to a small reception room on the second story. It was empty. Down a short hallway he found an open office door. Lindsey Mandel sat at her desk, looking tired.

She glanced up at the sound of his knock on her doorjamb. "Shane, come in. I heard both missing girls have been found."

He nodded and took a seat in the chair in front of her desk. "All's well that ends well."

"Thank the good Lord for that. I'm certainly glad I didn't have to issue a press release about an Amber Alert. What can I do for you?"

"You met Annie Delmar today. What did you think of her?"

Lindsey leaned back in her chair. "I thought she seemed like an understandably worried woman at the time. Why do you ask?"

What he was about to tell Lindsey didn't reflect well on his own character, but he valued her insight into people—and besides, she was a woman. "Annie is pregnant with my baby."

Lindsey's eyebrows shot up. "Oh! That's a bit of a shock. I didn't know you were seeing anyone. The CGMCG is a small unit, and that kind of information generally travels fast."

She sat forward, propping her arms on the desk. "I guess congratulations are in order."

"Not really. Annie doesn't want me involved in any way, shape or form."

"I'm sorry your relationship with her didn't work out. That must be hard on both of you."

"That's kind of the thing. We never actually had a relationship. We had one night."

"I see." While her tone didn't convey outright disapproval, it came close.

"I'm telling you this because I need help."

Clearly puzzled, she asked, "Help with what?"

"I need to convince Annie that I deserve to be included in our child's life. I need to know how she thinks so I can come up with a way to sway her."

"In case you missed it, Shane, I don't have children. My wedding isn't until June. I have no idea what it takes to change a pregnant woman's mind."

"I understand that, but take pregnant out of the equation. You're a woman."

"Thank you for noticing."

"You know what I mean. You understand how a woman's mind works. How can I get Annie to trust me enough to include me? I need a plan."

"Spoken like a true military man. Shane, matters of the heart rarely, if ever, follow a plan. Do you love this woman?"

He squirmed in his seat as he tried to put his feelings for Annie into words. "I like her. A lot. There's… I don't know…something special about her. But I need to be involved with my son or daughter. I'm not willing to walk away from that."

"Then my advice would be to stop focusing on the kind of relationship you want with the child and start focusing on the kind of relationship you want with Annie.

Women will do almost anything to protect their children. If she sees you as a threat, you'll never earn her trust. Respect is the key."

"How do I make her understand that?"

Lindsey shook her head. "I'm not talking about her. I'm taking about you."

He scowled. "I respect women."

"You're thinking in general terms. Chivalry is fine, but true respect for another human being only comes from knowing them—and it comes from the heart."

Respect from the heart. He nodded. "I understand what you're telling me, but how do Annie and I get past the botched start we made?"

"Baby steps, Shane. Slow, careful baby steps."

Marge stood waiting for them on the front porch when they reached home. The look of disappointment in her eyes as she listened to her daughter's halting and slightly slurred confession was painful for Annie to see.

"Annie, will you excuse us?" Marge asked.

"Of course."

"Olivia, I want to speak to you in private."

Nodding, the girl walked with leaden feet through the doorway. Marge followed her daughter into the house and upstairs to the girl's bedroom.

Annie knew exactly how Olivia was feeling. She took a seat on the beige sofa covered with colorful throw pillows and waited with her gaze riveted to the staircase leading to the upper level. When Marge was done with Olivia, it would undoubtedly be Annie's turn to face the music. She didn't relish the idea.

Would Marge ask her to leave? The prospect was frightening. She didn't have enough money saved to get a place of her own. Without Marge's continued support and counsel, Annie couldn't help wondering if the urge to drink again would overwhelm her the way it had during her last setback.

After thirty long minutes the sound of a door opening and closing upstairs made Annie sit up straight. Only a few months ago she would have taken off rather than apologize and accept responsibility for her actions. Part of her wished she still could, but a deeper part of her was grateful that her newfound faith in God's love kept her from running away.

Marge entered the room and sank onto one of the green recliners flanking the large picture window. Pulling a green-and-gold throw pillow into her lap, Annie buried her fingers in the long fringe to keep her hands from shaking. "I'm so sorry, Marge. I should never have let her go off by herself. This was all my fault."

"Don't be so hard on yourself. Olivia knows right from wrong. I can't believe I didn't see this coming. How can I profess to counsel people for a living when my own daughter can pull a stunt like this?"

"Now who is being hard on themselves?"

Marge managed a weak smile. "You're right. I can only pray that she learned some kind of lesson from this. How many times can you tell a child that their actions can have serious consequences?"

"If you think it would help, I can talk to her about exactly what those consequences are."

"Thank you. For tonight, I think the headache and sick stomach is enough to stop her from trying this again anytime soon. I hope it is. Can I ask you a question?"

"Sure."

"How young were you when you started drinking?"

"Fifteen."

"How did you get alcohol at that age?"

Looking back, Annie couldn't believe how easy it had been. "My parents had it in the house all the time. They were 'social drinkers.'" She made quote marks with her fingers.

"I'm supposed to be the professional here, but the truth is I'm an angry, scared mother. What should I do?"

"Don't panic."

"That's easy to say." Marge raked a hand through her hair.

Annie sat forward. "Just keep talking to her. Pay attention to how she acts. Search her room if you suspect something. She'll hate you for it, but you can't let that stop you. Alcohol makes people great liars. If she says she's going to stay over at a friend's house, call and check up on her."

"In other words, don't trust my own daughter?"

"My mother trusted me. Maybe if she had been less trusting, things might have turned out differently. I'm not saying it was her fault—it wasn't. I'm saying I got away with it for a long time before anyone noticed. There is no easy answer. You're a good mother, Marge. You'll figure it out."

"I pray with all my heart that you're right." Marge pushed up out of her chair. "I wish my Ben was still here. Raising a child alone is no easy task."

As Marge left the room, Annie laid her head back against the sofa cushion and sighed. She knew raising a child alone wouldn't be easy. Olivia's stunt today had driven home that point and proven once again that Annie had trouble making good choices.

If someone as wise and full of faith as Marge struggles with being a single parent, what chance is there that I can do it by myself?

Yet raising her baby alone was her only option... wasn't it?

Chapter 6

The following Monday afternoon Annie finished cleaning her last room in the east wing of the hotel, happily pocketed a handsome tip and began pushing her cart toward the maids' closet. As she turned into the service corridor, she saw Crystal hurrying toward her. "Annie, you've got to come to the break room."

"In a minute. I need to get restocked first and empty my trash."

Crystal grabbed her arm. "Leave it. You've got to come see this."

"See what?"

"Come on. Quit stalling."

Apparently Crystal wasn't going to take no for an answer. Annie gave in and allowed her friend to pull her toward the break room. Yanking open the door, Crystal grinned and announced, "They're for you!"

Puzzled, Annie glanced from her friend to the group of maids lined up in front of a table. At the sight of Annie, they stepped aside. In the center of the table a large bouquet of sunflowers and green, lacy ferns filled a silver vase to overflowing.

Annie looked from her smiling coworkers to Crystal. "For me? There must be some mistake."

Crystal rushed past her. "There's no mistake. It's got your name on the card. I'm so jealous. Nobody has ever sent me flowers."

No one had ever sent Annie flowers, either. She crossed the room slowly. With hesitant fingers, she touched the velvetlike yellow petals. "Who would send me flowers?"

Marge was the only person Annie could think of who might do something like this, but it wasn't Annie's birthday or any special occasion that she could think of.

Crystal pushed her closer to the table. "Open the card and find out, silly."

Annie stuck her hands in the pockets of her uniform. What if it was some kind of mistake? If she opened the card and found out these weren't for her, she might actually cry. She looked at Crystal. "You open it."

Crystal pulled the card from its plastic holder and held it toward Annie. "I'm not going to read your love note."

Annie snatched it from her hand. "It isn't a love note."

"You don't know that."

After a half second of hesitation, Annie slipped her finger beneath the flap of the envelope. Ripping it open, she pulled out the card. Turning her back on Crystal's interested gaze, she read the brief note handwritten in bold, dark strokes.

I'm sorry you had such a fright on Saturday. I hope you and your friends are all doing okay. Shane

It certainly wasn't a love letter, but it did prove the flowers were for her. The thoughtfulness of his gesture touched her deeply. She *had* been frightened and worried out of her mind.

"Well, what does it say? Who are they from?" Crystal tried peering over Annie's shoulder.

Tucking the card in her pocket, Annie said, "They're from Shane."

"That is *so* sweet."

"Yes, it is."

"Are you sure you want to get rid of the guy?"

That very question had been buzzing around in the back of Annie's mind since Shane had so willingly offered his help to find Olivia. He wasn't behaving like most of the men she knew. Maybe she had been too quick to dismiss him as another in a long list of mistakes in her life.

She stared at the bouquet, noticing the tiny white flowers tucked in among the greenery. They were baby's breath. Had he asked for them or had it simply been the florist's choice? It was another question that would remain unanswered in the back of her head.

Excluding Shane wasn't an error in judgment. Even if she wanted her baby to know his father, Shane was shipping out to Europe in a few months. One stable, caring parent would be enough for this child. Yet even as the thought ran through Annie's mind, it was quickly followed by the one doubt that never quite faded.

What if she couldn't stay sober? What kind of mother would she be then?

* * *

When the doorbell rang the following evening, Annie wasn't surprised to see Shane standing on Marge's front porch. She had been expecting him ever since she had received the flowers. What did catch her unawares was the little skip her heart took at the sight of him. Surely it wasn't because she was happy to see him again. After spending so much time and energy trying to convince him to forget about her and the baby, she should have been angry that he kept showing up. Only…she wasn't.

Dressed in his formal military uniform, he looked even more handsome than he had in his cavalry outfit. For a moment she considered not opening the door, but she realized that was the coward's way out. She needed to show him that a bouquet of flowers, no matter how pretty, wouldn't change her mind about what was best for her baby. Taking a firm grasp on the knob and struggling to compose herself, she opened the door. "What do you want?"

Looking taken aback, he said, "Hello, to you, too."

Annoyed at her lack of composure, she struggled to hide the effect he had on her nerves with bluster. "I'm sorry. Hello, Shane. Now what do you want?"

"Is Olivia home?"

It was Annie's turn to feel taken aback. "Yes."

"May I speak with her?"

She couldn't think of a reason to deny his request. "I guess."

He waited a moment longer. "May I come in or would you rather I wait out here?"

Giving herself a mental shake, Annie stepped back. "Come in. I'll tell Olivia that you're here."

"Thank you."

As he walked in, she couldn't help but notice how large he seemed in their small entryway. The spicy scent of his cologne filled the foyer, and the close quarters left her feeling breathless. She gestured toward the living room through the archway to the right. "Have a seat and I'll tell Marge and Olivia that you're here."

He started into the room, then turned back to smile at her. "I see you got my flowers."

The arrangement sat in the middle of the coffee table in front of the sofa. For an instant Annie wished she had left them in her room, but the bright flowers were simply too pretty not to share with the other women in the house.

"Yes. Thank you. It was a kind thought."

"Don't mention it. How are you feeling, by the way?"

"Fine."

"No ill effects from your scare?"

"None."

"I'm glad. You certainly look well—and very pretty, I might add."

Annie rubbed her palms together and took a step toward the kitchen. "Marge and Olivia are in the backyard. Have a seat and I'll get them."

Turning, she hurried out of the room. The man made her as nervous as a cat in a room full of rocking chairs.

At the back stoop, she saw Olivia unenthusiastically raking grass clippings and depositing them in the trash can. While she hadn't outwardly complained about being grounded, it was plain that she would rather be elsewhere. Marge was pruning the shoulder-high hedge that separated their small yard from the property behind them.

The scent of freshly mown grass and cut cedar

mingled with the aroma of someone barbecuing up the block. The sun disappeared behind a mass of dark clouds off to the west, and a cool breeze sprang up to cool Annie's warm cheeks, but the sight of storm clouds piling up in the west only served to increase her nervous tension. Storms terrified her. She quickly crossed the lawn and stopped beside Marge.

"Shane Ross is here and he'd like to speak to you."

Pushing her hair out of her face with the back of one gloved hand, Marge frowned. "He wants to see me?"

"Yes. You and Olivia."

"Me?" Olivia's eyes widened in concern as she propped her rake against the red picnic table that sat in the shade of the yard's ancient maple tree.

Marge scowled at her daughter as she walked past the table and laid her clippers on the corner. "You keep working. I'll see what he wants."

Crossing her arms over her chest, Annie waited anxiously for Marge to return. Away from Shane's overpowering presence, Annie's mind started working again, and she tried to figure out why he had come. When she first saw him at the door, she had assumed he had come to see her—to take up where he had left off trying to convince her that he had as much right as she did to be involved in her baby's future. But he hadn't so much as mentioned the baby except in a roundabout way when he'd asked how she was feeling. So why had he asked to see Marge and Olivia? What was he up to?

She glanced toward the clouds as she rubbed her hands up and down her arms. Were they moving this way?

"I wonder what he wants. Do you think I'm in trouble with the Army?" Making only a halfhearted attempt to continue raking, Olivia's eyes were glued to the back door.

Annie shook her head. "I don't think so."

Olivia frowned at her. "How can you be so sure?"

"Because if you were, they would send someone with a higher rank than a corporal to talk to your mother."

"You mean, like a general?"

"I think a sergeant at the very least."

"I'd really hate to be thrown in the brig."

Annie kept the smile off her face with difficulty. "I might be wrong, but I think you actually have to be *in* the Army to spend time in the brig."

"Oh, well, that's a relief."

The back door opened and Marge emerged from the house with Shane close behind her. They crossed to where Annie and Olivia stood. Marge said, "Olivia, this is Corporal Ross."

"I remember you—sort of."

"You weren't feeling your best when we last met. With your mother's permission, I have a few questions I'd like to ask you." The gentleness of his smile made Annie wish he were looking at her.

Marge said, "We'll be in the house if you need us."

He nodded once. "Thank you, ma'am."

Taking Annie by the elbow, Marge steered her toward the back door. Once they were inside, Marge went to the kitchen sink. Annie joined her, pulling the blue-checkered curtain aside so that she had a view of the pair taking a seat at the picnic table. Marge began to wash her hands. The fragrance of lemon soap vied with smell of ham baking in the oven.

Annie couldn't contain her curiosity any longer. "What does he want?"

"He wants to ask Olivia about the boys who supplied the alcohol. The Army is looking into the incident. They recognize that underage drinking is a very serious problem in the community and they want to help. The military police are questioning Heather. Shane offered to come here because he felt Olivia might feel less threatened by a friend of yours."

"He's not exactly my friend."

Marge pulled a sheet of paper towel from the holder under the cabinet and dried her hands. Turning to face Annie, she said, "He wants to be."

Looking away, Annie chose to ignore the remark. "I hope she tells him what she knows."

"I hope so, too. She didn't want to tell me anything that would get Heather in more trouble, but perhaps she won't feel the same misguided loyalty toward those young men. Tell me—why don't you believe that Corporal Ross wants to be your friend?"

Startled, Annie frowned at her. "I didn't say that."

"Not in so many words, perhaps, but the look on your face plainly says you don't believe he does."

"Do you think he does?"

"I think it's worth taking the chance to find out."

Annie focused her attention out the window. Shane had risen to his feet. He offered his hand to Olivia. She stood and shook it, looking almost grown-up and shyly proud. Dropping the curtain so Shane wouldn't see her spying on him, Annie moved away from the window. When the pair came into the kitchen, she busied herself pulling a stack of plates from the cupboard. She chanced a peek at him. He grinned and winked at her, then spoke to Marge.

"Thank you for letting me speak with Olivia. She's been very helpful."

Marge smiled at her daughter. "I'm glad. Have you had dinner, Corporal?"

"Please call me Shane. No, I haven't eaten." He glanced at his watch. "I'll pick something up on the way back to the base."

"Why don't you join us? We have plenty."

Annie spoke up quickly. "I'm sure that the corporal has to get back to his duties."

"Actually, I'm done for the day. Whatever you're having smells good. If you're certain it won't be a problem, I'd be happy to stay."

"Wonderful. Pull up a chair and join us. It isn't fancy, but it's filling. Olivia, would you please tell Crystal that dinner is ready. Annie, could you set another place for Shane? I'll be back in a minute. I need to put my tools away. They're forecasting rain tonight."

Annie's apprehension about the approaching weather jumped a notch. "Are they calling for severe weather?"

Marge patted Annie's arm. "No, dear. Just a few showers. Are you okay?"

Nodding, Annie turned back to the cupboard. The sound of the back door closing told her Marge had left the room.

"Not scared of a little thunder, are you?" Shane asked, his amusement plain.

Annie bit her tongue to keep from making a rude reply. He probably wasn't scared of anything. It must be nice.

She didn't want him here, but this was Marge's home and Marge had invited him to dinner. Pulling a plate from the shelf, Annie spun around, determined to make the best of it.

"Can I do anything to help?" he offered.

"Leaving would be good."

"Besides disappearing forever through a crack in the floor, is there anything else I can do?"

"That's all I had in mind."

"Sorry. Army regulations strictly forbid military personnel from melting." The hint of humor in his tone had her struggling to hide a smile.

"The front door would work just as well."

"Ah, but then Marge would think that you ran me off."

He was right, but she hated to admit it. She moved past him, being careful not to touch him, and plunked the extra dish on the table.

"Annie, I will leave if my being here upsets you."

"I'm not upset," she countered quickly. *Lord, please forgive that little white lie.*

"Good, because I haven't had a home-cooked meal in ages. Mess hall food is…mess hall food, and something in this kitchen smells great."

"Marge is a good cook." Turning the subject of the conversation to her friend seemed like a safe move.

He leaned a hip against the counter. "She comes across as a very caring person. How long have you known her?"

"Almost two years." She pulled out the flatware they would need from the drawer at the end of the counter and carried the pieces to the table.

"How did you meet?"

"Marge was assigned as my caseworker when I was brought into the emergency room one night."

Annie didn't tell him that it had been the night she had tried to kill herself. Thankfully most of those terrible hours were nothing but a black hole in her memory.

The door to the kitchen opened and Crystal came in, followed by Olivia.

Shane could have growled aloud with frustration. He wanted time alone with Annie. Time to get to know her and for her to get to know him. While he sensed her reluctance to talk to him, as least she hadn't made an excuse to leave the room. It was a small victory but one he would have to be satisfied with for now.

The outside door opened and Marge came in. "I'll just wash up and then we can get started. Sit anywhere you like, Shane. We're not much for ceremony here."

Olivia sat and patted the seat next to her. "Sit here, Shane."

Smiling at her, he took the chair she indicated, but it was Annie he followed with his eyes as she moved around the kitchen, getting the food on the table and filling everyone's glasses with water. When it came to his glass, she leaned in to pick it up and her arm brushed against his shoulder. The sound of her quick indrawn breath sent a jolt of awareness straight through him. Her hands trembled ever so slightly and she sloshed some of the liquid onto the tabletop.

"I'm sorry." She had to lean in farther as she mopped up the spill with his paper napkin.

"I'll get it." He took the soggy mess from her and finished the task, half afraid she'd pour the rest of the ice water in his lap if he didn't let her escape.

Crystal made a beeline for the chair across from him. "Hi, there. I'm so glad you could join us, Corporal Ross.

I've just been dying to tell you how beautiful I thought your flowers were. I sure wish someone would send me something like that. I'd be forever grateful."

He took note of her come-hither glance. The realization that it didn't interest him as much as catching Annie's downcast gaze came as no surprise. Annie was special in a way he couldn't quite put his finger on. He wanted to spend time with Annie. He wanted to get to know her.

His pending reassignment overseas loomed like the approaching storm clouds outside that were fast blocking the afternoon sunlight. Faced with Annie's reluctance to admit him into her life and the limited amount of time he had to change her mind, he didn't see a way to accomplish that goal.

Marge, at the head of the table, held her hands out to Olivia and Annie seated on either side of her. "Let us give thanks and ask the Lord's blessing on this family and the company gathered here."

Shane met Annie's eyes as she glanced in his direction. The longing in her expression stunned him. Before he could be certain of what he'd seen, she looked away again.

Olivia took her mother's hand and then reached for Shane's. Feeling a bit awkward, he grasped it. Crystal's smile widened as she stretched her arm across the table toward him. He hesitated only a second before clasping her hand. She squeezed his fingers and cast a sidelong glance at Annie before bowing her head.

Marge closed her eyes and said, "We give You thanks, Lord Jesus, for the bounty You have bestowed upon us. Let us be ever mindful that our true strength comes through You. Bless the people gathered here and grant that through Your intercession we may come to grow in love, faith and wisdom. Amen."

"Amen," Shane added to chorus of voices around him. If he couldn't convince Annie of the wisdom of accepting his help, he certainly wasn't above asking God to give him a hand.

"How long have you been in the Army, Shane?" Marge asked as she passed the platter of meat to Olivia.

"Six years now."

"Are you making it your career?"

"Yes, ma'am. The pay isn't great, but it offers me the chance to serve my country, to travel and to learn new things. I can honestly say if it hadn't been for the Army, I never would have learned to shoe a horse."

"Your performance was so cool, wasn't it, Annie?" Olivia slid a thick slice of ham onto her plate and passed the dish to him.

"You mean, the part of it you actually saw?" Marge asked, giving her daughter a disapproving stare.

"Yeah. I wish I had stayed to see all of it," Olivia replied, clearly chastised.

"Maybe you'll get another chance to see us in action." He took a piece of meat and handed the platter to Marge.

Olivia gave him a half smile. "I kinda doubt it."

Marge's stern features relaxed. "I would be interested in seeing your unit in action someday."

Olivia's eyes brightened as she looked at her mother. "Like, after I'm not grounded anymore?"

"Yes, like then."

Crystal leaned toward Shane. "Do you give special tours of the stable?"

"Tours can be arranged through the Department of

Public Affairs. The captain assigns the personnel for each tour."

"So it might not be you?"

"Not usually. I have other duties." He forked a piece of meat into his mouth.

"Oh." Clearly disappointed, Crystal turned her attention back to her meal.

"This ham is great," he said. Hoping to draw Annie out, he asked, "Do you like to cook?"

Olivia and Crystal both burst out laughing. Annie stared at her plate.

"Annie can't boil water," Crystal said. "Never let her cook you a meal."

"Annie is learning," Marge said. "Cooking is a skill that takes practice, like everything else."

"She makes an okay tuna casserole," Olivia added as if trying to make up for her unkindness.

The sound of thunder suddenly rumbled through the house. Annie flinched and grew pale. "It's storming."

Marge laid a hand on her arm. "It's just a shower. It will be over soon."

"Please excuse me." Laying her napkin on the table, Annie hurried from the room.

Shane looked to Marge for an explanation. Smiling sadly, she said, "Annie is deathly afraid of storms."

He could have kicked himself for teasing her earlier, but how could he have known? Still, it must have made him look like a first-class jerk in her eyes.

"What made her scared of them?" he asked.

"I'm not even sure she knows."

Olivia tossed her napkin on the table. "May I be excused also?"

"Are you scared of thunder, too?" he asked, glancing at the others in the room.

"No, but when it rains, the roof leaks in my room. I need to put a pail under the spot before my floor gets wet again."

"Of course, dear. Would you check on Annie before you come back?"

"Not a problem."

"Thanks, honey. The pail is under the sink in the bathroom."

Crystal rose, too. "I noticed a spot on the ceiling in the laundry room after the last storm. Maybe I should get a pail, too, just in case."

Shane frowned at Marge. "If your roof is leaking that badly, you should see about getting it fixed before you have serious damage."

"I know. Getting the roof repaired is on my to-do list. While the shingles themselves may actually fit into my budget, the cost of a roofing contractor won't. They're expensive."

"I worked as a roofer when I was a teenager. My foster father was a contractor and he taught me a lot about the business. I'd be happy to take a look and see exactly what you need."

"I couldn't ask you to do that."

"You didn't ask. I offered. It could be that you only have a few shingles missing and you don't need a whole new roof."

"Wouldn't that be wonderful? If you're sure, please take a look. I'll get you a ladder."

"After the rain stops."

Grinning, she nodded. "Of course. After the rain. In the meantime, would you like some dessert? I picked up a sinfully delicious lemon pound cake from the bakery today."

As Marge served him a generous slice of cake, Olivia and Crystal rejoined them, but Annie remained absent. Outside, the summer storm produced a brief, generous downpour as it passed overhead, but it soon moved off into the distance and the sound of thunder faded away.

He glanced frequently toward the door to the other room, but Annie didn't return. Perhaps she had found a way to avoid him after all.

Chapter 7

Annie chanced a peek out the door of her room when she heard the front door open and close downstairs. A few seconds later she heard the sound of someone climbing the stairs. When Olivia came into sight, Annie opened the door wider. "Is he gone?"

"You are such a chicken."

"I can't help it that storms petrify me."

"I wasn't talking about the weather."

"I know, but is he gone?"

"I think so. He and Mom walked out together."

Annie wanted to be relieved, but instead she realized what she felt was disappointment. How silly was that?

A loud thunk sounded against the outside of the house. She and Olivia stared at each other for a moment. Wide-eyed, Olivia whispered, "What was that?"

"I don't know."

They both hurried to the window in Annie's room. The top rungs of a ladder protruded above the roof of the back porch. As they stared, Shane's head appeared above the edge.

Annie did a double take. "What is he doing?"

"Beats me. Hey, are you two eloping? That is so romantic. It's just like Romeo and Juliet."

"Don't be an idiot. I have no intention of eloping with the man."

"Then why is he on a ladder outside your bedroom window?"

"How should I know?" Annie jerked up the sash. "Shane, what do you think you're doing?"

He had taken off his jacket and tie and discarded them before his climb. The sleeves of his white shirt were rolled up and displayed brown, muscular forearms. Stepping gingerly off the ladder, he looked up and located her in the window.

"Are you okay? When you didn't come back to finish dinner, I was worried about you."

"So you climbed onto the roof to look for me?"

"Marge asked me to take a look at the shingles and see how much work needs to be done. Just from here I can see that she is going to need a whole new roof on this porch. Excuse me."

He walked up to the low edge of the eaves beside her window and hoisted himself up and out of sight. Leaning out the window, she twisted around to stare at the spot where he had vanished. The sound of scrambling feet overhead made her call out, "Be careful up there."

His face reappeared above her. "Worried about me?" He sounded almost hopeful.

"No."

His smile widened into a cocky grin. "Yes, you are. Admit it."

"I am not." Pulling her head back in, she slammed down the window hard enough to rattle the glass, but it didn't completely block the sound of his hearty laughter.

"I have no idea what I thought I saw in him."

Olivia leaned against the dresser. Crossing her arms over her chest, she regarded Annie with one eyebrow raised. "Are you kidding? He's a hunk."

"A lot of men are cute. That doesn't mean anything."

"He's a hunk and he's really nice. I was scared silly when he asked to speak to me earlier. I thought I was in for another scolding. But he talked to me like I was a grown-up. I didn't want to rat on Heather and the boys who got us the beer, but Shane made me see that I wasn't helping them by keeping quiet."

"He did?"

"Yeah. Why are you so dead set against liking him?"

Why was she? He'd shown nothing but kindness and concern for her since the day she told him about the baby. If she hadn't known that men were users, she might have been tempted to accept his offer of assistance. Shaking her head, she said, "It's complicated."

Rolling her eyes, Olivia uncrossed her arms and headed for the door. "Adults always say that when they don't know the answer to the question."

Out of the mouths of babes, Annie thought as Olivia closed the door behind her. She didn't know why she couldn't accept Shane's offer of friendship. Distrust was an old habit that was hard to break.

Like drinking.

Footsteps overhead made her look up. Giving her life over to God had been her salvation from alcohol.

What if God had brought Shane into her life for a reason? But for *what* reason? To show her how weak she still was? If meeting Shane had been some kind of test, Annie knew she had failed miserably.

The sounds of scraping and scrambling gave way to the sound of a heavy object sliding down the roof, then the muffled thud of something hitting the ground. Annie dashed to the window and jerked it open with her heart lodged in her throat.

"Shane, are you okay?"

Had he fallen? The front side of the house didn't have a porch like the one below her window. It was a straight two-story drop to the concrete drive. Could he survive it? She closed her eyes and prayed.

Please, God, don't let anything bad happen to him.

"Sorry if I scared you." She opened her eyes to see a pair of black boots dangling from the eaves overhead. A second later he jumped down and landed in front of her. His wide grin turned her fear to annoyance.

"What was that?" she demanded.

"Just a limb that had blown down in the storm. It was wedged against the chimney. After I fix this roof, I'll cut those trees back a little. A limb that size could break a shingle or two, and Marge would be right back where she started with the rain pouring in."

"We don't need you to fix the roof."

"Someone needs to do it and I don't mind this kind of work. A few hours each evening and I can have it done in a couple of weeks." He walked over to the ladder.

"You have a job," she called.

Stepping onto the ladder, he gave her a short salute. "The Army is more than a job. It's an adventure."

He vanished from sight before she could think of a

comeback. She sat on the windowsill in disbelief. Shane would be here! He would be working where she lived. Possibly for several weeks! The only way she would be able to avoid him would be to lock herself in her room or stop coming home. Why on earth would Marge agree to such a thing? She had to know what an uncomfortable position it put her in.

The answer was obvious: Marge liked Shane. While Annie's instincts might be biased against men, Marge had no such problem. Marge liked everyone. She believed in the goodness of people until they proved her wrong. It was one part of her new faith that Annie hadn't fully come to accept.

A short time later there was a knock at her door. What if it was him? If he had the nerve to invade her room, she would give him an earful. "Who is it?"

"It's Marge. Are you okay, Annie?"

"Come in."

Marge eased open the door. "I know you must be upset with me."

"I can't believe you invited him back. You know I don't want to see him."

"That's what you say, but that isn't the whole truth, is it?"

"I don't know what you mean."

"Honey, I've seen the way you look at him and I've also seen the way he looks at you."

"How is that?"

"Like he's found something rare and precious."

"You can't be serious." Did he look at her that way?

"It's the same way my husband looked at me when we first met."

"It's not me he's seeing. It's the baby."

Tilting her head to one side, Marge studied Annie's face. "No, I don't think he sees the baby when he looks at you. He sees the same woman I do. Someone who is incredibly strong but who doesn't yet believe in herself."

"I believe in God. That's enough."

"It's a wonderful start, but that isn't all it takes to live a Christian life."

"I'm trying, Marge."

"I know you are, sweetheart."

Looking down, Marge said, "This is going to sound very materialistic on my part, but I really do need this roof fixed before it falls in on us. He's willing to do it in exchange for a meal each evening he's here. And he's even going to get the shingles on base for me—at a discount that I couldn't turn down."

"So you're telling me that he is a caring and practical man and that I'm a fool to try and keep him out of my baby's life."

"I would never say that you were a fool. Annie, you're entitled to your feelings. I'm just asking you to take a closer look at them. Your past has made you distrustful of men, and with good reason, but you've turned your life around. You aren't the same woman who let men take advantage of you."

Annie managed a wry smile. "I'm not that woman anymore, but sometimes…I'm afraid she'll come back."

"She won't if you don't allow it. You have found God. He is your strength now. He will guide you in the right direction."

"Would that be toward or away from a certain corporal?"

Marge chuckled. "I don't know the answer to that,

but I'm hoping the good Lord lets me get my roof fixed while you and he work it out."

The following evening Shane borrowed the unit's pickup with the captain's permission and purchased the needed supplies at the Post Exchange. With the help of Lee and Avery, he soon had several large loads of new asphalt shingle bundles delivered and stacked at the back of Marge's house.

Crystal and Olivia watched the activity from the picnic table nearby. When the men finished unloading the last of the materials, Olivia jumped up. "Would you like something to drink?"

Shane wiped the sweat from his brow with the back of his sleeve. "That would be great."

"We have soda, iced tea or water. What would you like?"

"Iced tea for me," he answered.

Olivia took everyone's orders and hurried into the house. In a few minutes she returned with a large glass of tea and two sodas. Lee and Avery had already made themselves comfortable on either side of Crystal at the picnic table. After giving the men their drinks, Olivia brought Shane his glass.

Leaning against the lowered tailgate of the truck, he took a long swallow of the icy drink and sighed with pleasure, then glanced up at Annie's window. He had half hoped to catch her spying on him.

Olivia hopped onto the tailgate beside him. "Annie's in the living room, studying."

"Studying what?"

"Stuff about becoming a counselor like my mom."

"Annie's going to school?"

"She goes to classes on the weekend. She says she can't afford to go to school full-time. Her job doesn't pay well and her tips aren't always good."

"I think it's great that she wants to get an education." He wasn't sure if it was right to encourage Olivia to talk about Annie, but he was hungry for any information he could get about her.

"That's what Mom says. Why is Annie pretending that she doesn't like you?"

He looked at his little confidante in surprise. "What makes you say that?"

"Because she must have peeked out the kitchen window fifty times while you were working back here earlier. For someone who's says she doesn't want you around, she sure checks on you a lot."

"That's interesting." So Annie wasn't indifferent. That was good news. He took another sip of his tea. Maybe it was time he stopped pursuing her. Maybe it was time to see if she would make the next move. He finished his drink and handed the glass back.

Olivia took it and rolled the amber tumbler between her palms. Slanting him a quizzical look, she asked, "Do you like Annie?"

"I do."

"Why don't you two go out on a date or something?"

"It's not as easy as it sounds."

"Why not?"

"It's…complicated."

She held up one hand. "Pleease! If one more person tells me that, I'm going to scream."

Over the next several days Annie spent her hours at work torn between her dread of going home because

Shane would be there and an equally irrational eagerness to see him again. The first two evenings he had worked on the roof, she had stayed shut up in her room, claiming she needed to study—as if anyone could concentrate with the nail gun going off almost constantly.

Each night when darkness fell, he put up his tools and the ladder and left without making any attempt to see her. He even declined the meals Marge offered. Knowing he was doing the work he had promised without any compensation—because of her—began to gnaw at Annie's conscience.

On the third evening she sat at the table with Marge, Olivia and Crystal and listened to his footsteps overhead. The smell of broiled hamburgers, dill pickles and potato salad reminded Annie of the picnics her parents had taken her on when she was a kid. Suddenly she couldn't stand it any longer.

Loading a second plate with a generous helping of food, she excused herself and carried it outside. Walking to the ladder, she looked up and called, "Shane, I brought you something to eat."

The silence lasted about five seconds.

"Thanks, but I'm fine."

"You've been working for hours. It won't kill you to take a break and eat a bite."

"The longer I work, the sooner I'll have this done."

Boom, boom, boom.

Balancing the plate with care, she began to climb the ladder one-handed. She reached the top and was setting his plate on the sloping roof when his startled voice rang out. "What do you think you're doing?"

"I'm bringing you supper."

He grabbed the ladder with both hands to steady

it. His face was only inches from hers. "Are you nuts? You shouldn't be climbing up here in your condition."

"I'm pregnant, not acrophobic."

"Not what?" His eyes were wide and he had a death grip on the ladder beams.

"Acrophobia is a fear of heights."

"Okay, let's just say I get that when I see a pregnant woman fifteen feet above the ground. Please get down."

"Will you eat?"

"I'm trying to get this finished before it rains again."

"There's no rain in the forecast for the next thirty minutes, so you have time for dinner. I'm not going down until you eat."

"I can't eat. My hands are busy holding this ladder so you don't fall."

"The ladder is perfectly sound. You've been going up and down it for days." She tried to pry one of his hands loose but only managed to get his pointer finger undone. His strength surprised her.

"Okay, you win." The sudden change in the timbre of his voice sent waves of tingles racing across her nerve endings. He let go of the ladder and closed his grip over her hand.

"Good." Oh, that had sounded breathless even to her ears. The rough texture of his skin against hers only served to make her more aware of her femininity. The size of his hand made her feel small and protected, not frightened.

He sank back cross-legged onto the roof, letting her hand slip out of his in a slow caress. "I eat and you get down. Do we have a deal?"

Clearing her throat, she nodded. "We do."

Picking up the burger, he stuffed it in his mouth in two bites. Pointing downward, he mumbled, "Go."

"Are you trying to choke yourself?"

Chewing momentarily silenced him, but his eyes spoke volumes as he glared at her. Swallowing at last, he said, "Get your feet on the ground. That's an order!"

She opened her mouth to object to his manner, but he shot to his knees and gripped the ladder again. "I know how to do a fireman's carry. Don't make me prove it."

A dignified retreat seemed like her best choice. "I'm going."

Backing down the ladder with care, she stepped off the last rung and moved to the side. A moment later he slid down without using his feet and landed beside her.

Impressed, she asked, "Where did you learn to do that?"

"My foster father ran a roofing business. When I was old enough, I worked with him."

"What happened to your birth parents?"

"My mom died of cancer when I was eleven."

"I'm sorry."

He shrugged. "It was a long time ago."

She couldn't help but notice that he didn't mention his father.

"What about you?" he asked, walking toward the picnic table. Unbuckling his tool belt, he tossed it onto the wooden surface.

"My parents live on Long Island. We don't keep in touch."

"Why not? I'm sorry—that's none of my business."

It wasn't something she normally talked about. But then, her relationship with Shane could be called anything but normal. Without knowing exactly why, she wanted him to understand who she had been.

"My addiction made me a very destructive person. I hurt my parents in a lot of ways. I can't tell you how many times they got me out of jail or picked me up at some hospital. I took money from them every chance I got. When they stopped keeping cash in the house, I stole their credit cards. I ruined them. My mom lost her job. Eventually they even lost their house. In the end, they had to cut me out of their lives. I have a younger brother. I know they did it for his sake. I don't blame them now, but I did for a very long time."

"Do they know you're sober now?"

"I wrote them a letter last year to tell them how sorry I was and that I had found God, but they didn't write back. I still hope someday that they will find it in their hearts to forgive me."

"So what happened the day we met, Annie? What made you go into that bar?"

Chapter 8

Annie crossed her arms over her chest as she faced Shane. Sharing her experiences with other recovering addicts was one thing. They understood. How much of what she had been through could Shane understand? Would telling him make him doubt her ability to be a good mother? No matter what he might think, she knew that this baby was God's way of helping her overcome her disease. For her child's sake, she would never drink again.

"Why did I get smashed the night we met? I wish I had a plausible explanation. I wish I had a good reason, but the fact is, I don't. I'm an alcoholic, Shane. I don't need an excuse to drink."

He settled his hip onto the table edge. "Something must have happened. You said that you had been sober for almost a year before then."

"The day we met I had just been fired from my job. It wasn't a great job, but I needed it. I really felt like I was making some progress turning my life around and then—*pow!*—I'm unemployed."

"Why were you fired?"

"The little company I was doing secretarial work for needed to make cutbacks. Last hired, first fired. It was as simple as that. Life wasn't being fair. God had failed me. I didn't know what to do. So I returned to the one thing I knew would make me feel better."

"Only it didn't help."

It was tempting to share her painful journey to sobriety with this man, but she held back. She wasn't ready to expose her innermost fears and doubts to him. Her failure was between herself and God.

"No, it didn't help. It made things worse. Just look at me now."

"I think you look fine. In fact, I think you look amazing."

His compliment caught her off guard. "Are you sure you're putting those shingles on right? Because I don't think you see so well."

"I see a young woman in a difficult situation who is making a positive change in her life. That is an amazing thing. My son or daughter could do a lot worse in the mother department."

He sounded so sincere. Her usual flippant comeback didn't materialize. Instead she murmured, "Thank you."

He straightened and reached for his tool belt. "I'd better get back to work. The roof won't replace itself."

"But you didn't finish your dinner." Her desire to stay and talk with him surprised her as much as his compliment had. For some reason, being near him didn't make her as uncomfortable as she had expected. Instead his nearness left her feeling happy and a little giddy, if she were being honest.

Shane rubbed one hand over his jaw. "Truthfully, I ate before I came over tonight. But thanks for the hamburger. It was good."

"Did you even taste it?"

"I was too afraid you'd fall."

He cared about her and about the baby. The knowledge wrapped itself like a warm blanket around her heart.

"Tomorrow evening you'll join us at the table, and that is an order, Corporal. I know you agreed to do this work in exchange for some home-cooked meals. If you don't start eating them, Marge is going to feel compelled to pay you."

He sketched a quick salute. "Yes, ma'am. I'll be here tomorrow and I promise to bring my appetite."

"Good. You'll be expected to clean your plate."

"I will."

Picking up his tool belt, he slung it around his waist but paused in the act of buckling it to look at her. "Unless you're having okra or goat. I can't promise to eat those."

"You're kidding, right?"

"I'm deadly serious. I never joke about okra."

"Who eats goat?"

"Lots of people," he said with a straight face.

"Eew!"

"My thoughts exactly. I guess it's safe to assume those two things won't be on the menu tomorrow?"

"You're pretty safe with that assumption, but just in case, I'll let Marge know that you don't eat goat."

"Or okra."

She nodded slowly. "Or okra. I'll go cross it off the shopping list right now."

"Thanks." He finished buckling on his tools and headed for the ladder.

The following day Shane arrived at Marge's house in high spirits. His conversation with Annie had given him a new measure of hope. She wasn't averse to spending time with him. He would even go so far as to say that she had enjoyed their talk. He certainly had enjoyed his time with her—once she was safely off the ladder.

Now, if he could only sway her to his way of thinking. A child needed a mother *and* a father. There had to be some way for them to work out their differences.

Opening the trunk of his car, he pulled out a roll of nails for the nail gun he had rented for the project. Any work was easier if a man had the right tools for the job. If only he could figure out what tools he needed to convince Annie he was father material. Spending time with her was the key. This roofing project would only take a few more evenings. Somehow he had to get her to agree to see him after it was done. So far, he knew that independence, education, helping others and her faith were things Annie valued deeply. He valued the same things—all but faith. Why was it so important to her?

Annie drove up just as he closed his trunk lid. Parking behind him, she turned off the engine, but it chugged several times before it finally died. Crystal jumped out of the passenger side and hurried into the house with only the briefest of waves in his direction. He walked toward Annie.

"You should get this vehicle looked at," he suggested when she stepped out of the car.

"I will. It just has to keep running until payday." Closing her eyes, she put her hands on her hips. A grimace crossed her face as she leaned backward.

"You're home late. Tough day?" he asked, walking to stand beside her.

"I've had worse."

"Turn around."

"What for?"

"Just do it."

After giving him a long, suspicious stare, she finally did as he'd asked. Placing his hands on her shoulders, he began to massage her tense muscles.

She stiffened for a second, but then she gradually relaxed. After a few more moments her head lolled forward. "Mmm, I'll give you until next Tuesday to stop that. Do you do feet?"

"If you need horseshoes, I'm your man."

She giggled. "The last thing I need is iron shoes. My feet hurt enough as it is."

Shane couldn't believe how much it pleased him to hear her laugh. After a minute she stepped away from his massage, and he let his empty hands fall to his sides. The urge to pull her into his arms and hold her close was almost painful in its intensity. It took all his willpower not to act on the impulse. This wasn't the time or the place. Instinctively he knew he would lose what little trust he had gained. "Okay, no new shoes from my forge."

The rush of color in her cheeks told him she wasn't indifferent to his touch.

"How's the roof coming?" she asked quickly.

"I should be able to finish next week. The gables and the steep pitch make for slow going." That and the fact that he wasn't in any hurry to complete the project.

"You are staying for supper tonight, aren't you?"

"I'm looking forward to it."

"If I get a move on, it will be ready in about an hour."

"You aren't cooking tonight after working so late, are you? You look exhausted."

"Food won't fix itself because the cook is tired. We take turns with the chores and tonight is my night to make supper. I'll manage."

He clearly remembered Olivia and Crystal laughing at the idea of Annie cooking. "Maybe we should call out for pizza or something."

She scowled at him. "Are you afraid I can't cook a decent meal because I'm a little tired?"

He found himself on the defensive and tried to back-pedal. "That's not what I was saying. I just thought that you should be taking it easy. You are pregnant, after all."

She smacked her palm against her forehead. "Wow, I completely forgot that. Thank you for reminding me. How did I get this way? Oh, that's right—you helped." Stepping toward him, she poked her finger into his chest. "For your information, being pregnant doesn't affect the way I cook, either."

He held up both hands. "Whoa, I'm not sure how I got here. Can we go back to the point where I didn't have my foot in my mouth and you were happy to see me?"

Glaring, she crossed her arms over her chest. "Was I ever happy to see you?"

"I thought so—but I've been wrong before."

She arched one eyebrow. "I'm sure you have."

"Yes, a lot. Well, maybe not a lot but often. Sometimes."

He gestured toward the house. "Okay, I'm going to climb up on the roof with my hammer now and try to pry my foot loose."

"You do that."

"I'll just go do that," he muttered as he picked up the roll of nails and headed for the backyard.

A little over an hour later Annie placed her tuna casserole in front of Shane and took her place opposite him at the table.

"It sure smells good," he said for the third time since he'd come in.

How a man his size managed to look like a repentant first-grader was beyond her understanding. She took pity on him and gave him a small smile. "I hope you enjoy it."

Nodding, he grinned in return. "I'm sure I will."

From the head of the table Marge asked, "Where is Crystal?"

Annie glanced at the clock. "She said she had a few errands to run and not to wait for her."

A small crease appeared between Marge's brows. "She's been gone a lot lately. Did she borrow your car again?"

"Yes, but I don't mind. She puts gas in it. Don't worry—she knows she has to be back before the meeting tonight."

The smile Marge tried for looked forced. "Still, I

think I should talk to her. I have the feeling that something isn't right."

Smiling at her, Annie said, "You worry too much."

"Maybe you're right." Marge looked at Shane. "Would you like to lead us in prayer tonight?"

"Me?" His voice didn't quite squeak, but his apprehension was painfully clear.

Olivia giggled but quickly subdued her mirth at her mother's quelling stare.

Looking sheepish, he said, "I'm afraid I don't know many blessings for eating except the one that goes 'Good food, good meat'…and I don't think that's what you had in mind."

It was Annie's turn to choke back a laugh. Marge scowled at her, then turned her attention to Shane. "There aren't any rules. Just tell God what you have to be thankful for."

"Okay." Taking a deep breath, he bowed his head and closed his eyes. "God, Thank You for the food on this table."

Annie felt his gaze. When she opened her eyes, she found him staring at her.

"Thanks, too, for giving me the chance to know these special people," he said quietly.

Hoping their interplay and her blush would go unnoticed, Annie glanced toward Marge. Mercifully Marge's perceptive eyes were still closed and her head was bowed in prayer.

"And thanks for not letting me fall off the roof today. Amen," he added in a rush.

"Amen," Marge echoed, but not before Annie saw the tiniest twitch at the corner of her mouth.

"We still can't thank you enough for fixing our roof," Marge said as everyone began filling their plates.

"It's my pleasure. It's been kind of fun doing something besides taking care of horses and riding."

"I'd never get tired of taking care of a horse if I had one," Olivia asserted, passing a bowl of peas and pearl onions to her mother.

"Don't be too sure of that," Shane said. "They take a lot more looking after than you might imagine. Especially horses that work as hard as ours do."

"Annie tells me that you'll be leaving soon." Marge spooned a portion of vegetables onto her plate and handed the bowl to Annie.

"My tour with the Commanding General's Mounted Color Guard will be finished the end of July. After that I'll be returning to my regular unit."

"Will you, like, be driving tanks and things?" Olivia asked.

"Mostly I'll be fixing helicopters. It's what I do."

"That's cool." Olivia forked a bit of casserole into her mouth.

"Shane is being transferred to a base in Germany," Annie added. That, among other things, was part of the reason she resisted his requests to be involved with the baby. He wouldn't even be in the country, so how could she include him? She couldn't—even if she wanted to— which she didn't.

Olivia turned her attention to Annie. "Are you going to find out if you're having a boy or a girl tomorrow?"

Glancing toward Shane, Annie caught the sudden interest in his eyes. Looking down at her plate, she separated a small piece of carrot from the noodles with her fork. "I see my doctor tomorrow, but the sonogram isn't until next week. I haven't decided if I want to know or not."

"Why not?" Shane asked.

"I'm not sure. It seems a little like peeking at my Christmas presents three months early. I think I'd rather wait until the big day."

"What about you, Shane?" Olivia asked. "Do you want a girl or a boy?"

"I'd like to know that everything is okay. Whether it's a boy or a girl really doesn't matter."

"I hope it's a girl," Olivia said. "But a boy would be nice, too."

Annie looked up to see Shane hiding a smile. He winked and said, "I'm sure it will be one or the other."

Olivia rolled her eyes at him. "Well, duh! Have you picked out names yet, Annie?"

Watching Shane's face, Annie said, "I've always liked the name Joshua for a boy. I haven't decided on a girl's name yet."

Shane met her gaze. "Joshua. Josh. It's a good name."

"What about you, Shane?" Marge asked. "Have you given any thought to names for the baby?"

Shaking his head, he looked down. "I haven't. I think that should be Annie's decision, but I do have one request. If it's a girl, please don't name her Pat or Jane."

Perplexed, Annie asked, "And why not?"

"Something tells me that any daughter of yours will already have a predisposition to stubbornness without being named after the mules in the Commanding General's Mounted Color Guard." The humor in his voice made Annie grin in return.

"Very well, I'll take Pat and Jane off my list of girl's names."

"Thanks, that's all I ask."

Annie's smile faded. If only that were true. But it wasn't. He was asking for so much more—more than she could give. Yet every day she found herself questioning that conviction.

What would sharing the burdens and the joys of raising a child with Shane be like? More and more she found herself imagining them all together. It was foolish, but deep in the corners of her heart she wished it could be real.

When the meal was finished, Marge pushed back her chair. "I'm sorry to eat and run, but I'm manning the phones at the crisis center tonight. Olivia, I expect you to mind Annie at the meeting tonight."

"Aw, Mom, do I still have to go? You know I'm not going to pull a stunt like that again."

"I never expected you to pull a 'stunt' like that in the first place. So, yes, you still have to go. I want you to see exactly what kind of harm alcohol can do to people's lives."

"I already know!"

"I don't think you do. You're going with Annie tonight and that's final. Maybe after this you'll think twice about following someone else's lead when you know it's wrong."

"I already said I was sorry. It's been a week. I can't understand why I'm still grounded from seeing my friends or why I have to go to some gross AA meeting with people I don't even know."

"That's enough, Olivia."

Looking as if she wanted to protest further, Olivia opened her mouth, but Marge forestalled her. "Not another word."

"Fine. I'll be in my room. Call me when you're ready to go, Annie."

Olivia stomped out of the kitchen without a backward glance. Rising, Annie picked up her plate and stacked it on top of Marge's. The clacking of stoneware on stoneware sounded unusually loud in the sudden tense silence.

Marge sent both Shane and Annie apologetic looks. "I'm sorry about that. Annie, I should be the one taking her. I shouldn't pawn off the task on you."

"You aren't pawning anything off on me. I'm glad to do it. Besides, it might feel less like punishment to her if you aren't there."

"That's what I'm hoping. If I went with you, she'd only spend her time sighing and glaring at me. I don't know why she's so angry. I'm the one who should be mad."

Annie set the dishes down to give her friend a quick hug. "From personal experience I can tell you Olivia's anger is more about being disappointed in her own behavior than about being mad at you. She'll get over it."

"I hope so. Shane, I'm sorry that you had to witness my daughter's surly behavior."

"That's okay, Mrs. Lilly. I wish my dad had cared enough to ground me when I was Olivia's age. If you ladies will excuse me, I'm going to get back to work while I have some daylight left."

Annie nodded and watched him leave by the back door. As she began to gather up the rest of the plates,

Marge stopped her with a hand on her arm. "He seems like a good man, Annie. Are you sure you're doing the right thing by excluding him from your baby's life?"

Annie glanced toward the door to make sure he was gone. "It's the right thing. He'll forget all about us in a few months."

"I don't think so."

"I'd like to believe that, but I just can't. I need to do this myself. I have to be strong for this child. I can't risk depending on someone who'll let me down when I need him."

"I know you've been in bad relationships before."

"Yes, I have, and every time I thought they were men I could depend on, but they weren't. When things got rocky, they all took off, and I spiraled deeper into depression and drinking because of it. I got sober with God's help. I'll stay sober with God's help and because this baby needs me."

"I'm sure you will, Annie. You've come so far already. But don't count out the support of your friends."

"I don't. I know that you and Crystal and the people at group will always be here for me. That's enough."

Marge glanced at the clock. "I wish we had more time to talk about this, but I have to get going."

"Marge, I'm fine. Stop worrying. I don't want to make you late."

"Are you sure that you're all right with taking Olivia?"

"Of course I am. Now, get going. There's no telling when God will send some other needy soul in your direction."

Smiling, Marge nodded and headed for the living room. At the doorway she paused and looked back.

"I'm really glad He sent you to me. You're a special person, Annie."

"You're nowhere near as glad as I am."

"I wish you would consider the fact that God may have sent Shane into your life for a reason."

"I don't need him."

"That may be true, but what if *he* needs *you*?"

Chapter 9

It was beginning to get dark by the time Shane finished the section of the roof he had been working on. After climbing down, he removed the ladder and carried it to the garden shed at the back of the yard. He then brought his tools around to his car parked at the side of the house. Since Marge's coupe was gone, he assumed that she had already left for the evening. Annie's car was gone, too.

He couldn't help but wonder if Olivia was giving Annie the same attitude about attending the AA meeting that she had given her mother earlier. He hoped not. Annie deserved praise for her efforts, not criticism.

After opening his trunk, he threw his gear in and closed the lid. He heard the sound of Marge's front door opening and glanced toward the house. To his surprise, he saw Annie standing in the open doorway.

"I'm done for the night," he called, and gave her a brief wave.

Advancing down the steps, she paused on the walk. "I thought I heard a car door. I was hoping it was Crystal. She promised to be home before we had to leave for the meeting."

He took a step closer. "She isn't back yet?"

"No." She crossed her arms over her chest and stared down the street.

He walked toward her. "Maybe she had car trouble. Do you want me to wait?"

"Thanks, but I'm sure she'll be here any minute. She knows that I'm leading the group discussion tonight and that Olivia is coming with us. I've tried her cell phone, but she has it turned off. If she had car trouble, I'm sure she would have called."

"Maybe she just forgot the time."

"Maybe."

"Why don't I give you and Olivia a lift?"

"It's out of your way, but thank you."

He narrowed the distance between them until he was close enough to see the worry in her eyes. "Junction City isn't a big town, so I'm sure your meeting isn't *that* far out of my way."

She glanced back toward the door of the house. "I hate to impose."

The evening breeze carried the scent of her perfume to him. The sweet fragrance stirred a recollection from his early childhood. He leaned closer. She didn't pull away. Closing his eyes, he inhaled deeply and tried to capture the elusive memory.

"White flowers." He didn't realize he had spoken aloud until he heard her soft indrawn breath.

He opened his eyes and met her uncertain gaze. Large and luminous in the growing dusk, her eyes were filled with bewilderment and another emotion that sent his pulse racing.

"You smell like the white flowers my mother grew in hanging baskets on our front porch. I don't remember what they were called."

"Jasmine," she whispered softly.

He reached out and stroked her cheek with his fingertips. "Jasmine—that's right. I remember breathing in their fragrance and trying to so hard not to breathe out."

With sudden clarity Shane knew that this moment would become a treasured memory for him. He longed to capture and keep everything exactly as it was now. The way her long braid hung over her shoulder, begging him to run his hand down its soft length. The way the wind teased a few strands of her hair loose to flutter beside her small, delicate ears. The way her lips curved with the hint of a smile.

Oh, yes, the smells of a summer evening and jasmine would forever remind him of her.

If she only knew how much he wanted to stay near her, to help her, to make her smile. The astonishing thing was that none of the feelings running through him had anything to do with the fact that she was carrying his baby.

Annie struggled to calm her pounding heart. The touch of his hand on her cheek crystallized her jumbled feelings. In spite of her best efforts to remain indifferent, she was falling in love with this man. Head over heels in love. She longed to follow the flow of her emotions and step into his arms, but some small part of her brain recognized doing that was a recipe for disaster.

The streetlight on the corner flickered on. He let his hand fall to his side. "It's a good memory."

She stood there, looking up at him with a strange sort of wonder. Finally she said, "Good memories are something to cherish."

He drew a deep breath and smiled as he shoved his hands in his pockets. "So can I give you and Olivia a ride?"

His nonchalance helped steady her shaky nerves and forced her to think about the matter at hand. She didn't want to accept his offer. She needed time away from him. Thinking was hard to do when he stood so close. She glanced at her watch and then down the still-empty street.

It didn't seem that she had a choice, not if she was going to keep her commitment to her AA group and to Marge. Hoping she sounded as unaffected as he did, she said, "If you're sure you don't mind?"

"I don't mind at all."

"Let me leave a note for Crystal, then Olivia and I will be right out."

She turned away and hurried up the steps, but at the doorway she paused and looked back. "You don't have to do this. You don't owe me anything."

"Annie, you might feel that way, but I don't."

"How can I make you see that isn't true?"

"You can't. Go get Olivia and come on, or you will be late. Didn't you say you were the speaker?"

"If I weren't, I wouldn't be accepting your offer."

"How'd you get to be so stubborn?"

"Practice. How did you get that way?"

"It comes naturally—just like my charm."

Grinning, she turned away and entered the house. Olivia was waiting on the sofa. Pulling a piece of paper and a pen from the small pine desk by the window, Annie said, "Crystal isn't back yet."

Olivia sat up hopefully. "Does that mean we aren't going?"

"No, Shane has offered to drive us."

Sinking back into the cushions, she mumbled, "Great."

"It won't be bad, I promise." Annie finished her note and posted it on the message board the family used in the hallway.

When she came back into the living room, Olivia rose from the couch and headed to the door. "I guess if there's no way out of it, I might as well get it over with."

"That's the spirit." Annie patted her shoulder as she walked past.

Shane waited beside the car. He opened the door, pulled the seat forward and waved them in. "Ladies, your chariot awaits."

"I'll ride in back," Olivia said before squeezing herself into the sports car's rear seat. Annie was happy to let her. Getting into and out of tight places was harder now that her jeans were getting snug. Soon she'd need to invest in some maternity clothes.

After Shane shut the door, Annie laid a hand on her slightly rounded tummy. The idea of outgrowing her limited wardrobe had once made her frown, but tonight the thought brought only a glow of happiness. This baby was changing everything.

Shane opened his door and slid behind the wheel.

He glanced toward her, his eyes settling on her hand. "Are we ready?"

"I'm getting there," she answered, and smiled at him.

"That's a good thing," he said softly, meeting her gaze with a smile of his own. Knowing that he understood boosted her happiness a notch higher.

From the backseat Olivia muttered, "I'm as ready as I'll ever be."

Exchanging amused looks with Shane, Annie turned and pulled her seat belt out and fastened it with a click.

Following Annie's directions, it took Shane less than ten minutes to reach their destination. As he pulled into the parking lot of a small, modern brick church, he noted with surprise that there were several dozen cars already parked close to the building.

Annie opened her door. "Thank you for bringing us, Shane."

"I don't see your car in this bunch. It looks like Crystal hasn't made it yet. Why don't I stick around in case you need a ride home?"

"That won't be necessary."

Olivia spoke up for the first time since they'd left the house. "I'd feel better if he stayed."

Shane smiled at her. "Okay, maybe I'll stick around and see what AA is all about."

"That would be awesome. Thank you."

He could see that Annie was torn, but in the end she nodded. "This is an open meeting. Not all AA groups operate that way, but we do. You're welcome to stay."

Inside the building, Annie led the way to a small meeting room. Gray metal folding chairs were set in rows facing a table with a small podium in the center.

About half the chairs were already filled. A second table along the wall held a few plates of cookies, a coffee urn and several stacks of foam cups.

Shane scanned the faces of the people already assembled in the room. There were two young women chatting in the front row. One, a blonde in her early thirties wearing white sandals, crisp khaki pants and a pale blue sweater, looked as if she had just dropped her kids off at soccer practice. The woman beside her wore a short black skirt and a black tank top and sported maroon streaks in her black hair. Behind them sat a man in a business suit who looked to be in his fifties. Three rows back, a woman with gray hair and a brightly flowered red dress looked as if she should be baking cookies for her grandchildren.

"You can sit anywhere," Annie said, gesturing toward the chairs.

Olivia grabbed Shane's arm. "Let's sit in the back."

"I think we should sit up front and offer Annie a little moral support, don't you?"

"I don't want to sit up there where people will be looking at me and wondering if I'm the youngest alcoholic on record. Please—let's sit in back."

Annie nodded to the two of them. "Thank you for your offer of support, Shane, but let Olivia sit wherever she is comfortable."

"That would be at home on the sofa," the teen muttered. She sent an uneasy glance around the room and took a step closer to Annie.

Placing a finger under Olivia's jaw, Annie turned the girl's face back to her own. "Our actions have consequences. Your mother wants you to see that."

"I do. Honest."

"I know you believe that, but I think you'll see it much more clearly after tonight."

"Annie!" An elderly man wearing a short-sleeved black shirt and black slacks waved from across the room. Leaving the refreshment table, he came toward them.

Casting Annie a pleading look, Olivia begged in a whisper, "Don't tell Pastor Hill why I'm here."

"Of course I won't. That's entirely up to you."

Engulfing Annie in a bear hug, the man beamed. "My dear, it's good to see you." He reared back. "And I see you've brought Olivia with you. Welcome, child. Have you come to see firsthand the good work that God has led us to do?"

"Sort of, Pastor Hill."

"Excellent. And who is this?" He extended his hand toward Shane.

Taking the beefy hand, Shane noted the strength in the man's grip, as well as the friendliness in his eyes. "I'm Shane Ross, sir, a friend of Annie's."

"Any friend of Annie's is a friend of mine. She is a true pearl, isn't she?"

"I have to agree."

Sneaking a peek at the object of their conversation, he noted a blush adding color to her cheeks. Taking pity on her, he said, "If you'll excuse us, sir, we were just about to find a seat."

"Of course. Oh, there's Manny. I'm so glad he's here. This is his tenth straight meeting. I must go and see how he's doing."

Shane took Olivia's hand and tugged her toward the back of the room. "Come on, kiddo, let's sit down before all the good seats are taken."

Choosing the last chair on the center aisle, he settled himself on the hard metal seat, while Olivia slumped in the chair next to him.

A few moments later Pastor Hill stepped up to the podium and rapped on it with his knuckles. The hubbub of voices died away. "It's time we got started. I'd like to welcome all of you here tonight. My name is Gerry and I'm an alcoholic."

A chorus of voices called out, "Hello, Gerry."

Olivia straightened in her chair. She exchanged a startled look with Shane, then turned her attention to the front of the room.

Pastor Hill nodded and leaned forward, bracing his hands on the wooden stand. "Thank you. Tonight I'm going to turn the meeting over to Annie, who will lead our discussion. If you have questions, please raise your hand. Annie?"

"Thank you, Pastor Hill."

She waited until he took a seat in the front row, then she looked out over the crowd. "My name is Annie and I'm an alcoholic."

After the tide of greetings died away, she continued. "I see several new faces here and it gladdens my heart. While you may be here because of a court order or because a family member forced you to come, I want to tell you all that you have made an important first step. What you are going through, I have been through. I know that, as a newcomer, I was ashamed to be seen at an AA meeting despite knowing that nearly everyone present was also an alcoholic.

"Why? Because I didn't think I needed help. I knew that my drinking had messed up my life, but I hadn't yet admitted that I couldn't control it. Admitting that we are helpless against alcohol is painful, but it is the only way we can gain control over the disease that is destroying us and those we love."

As she spoke about her addiction and the suffering she had endured because of it, Shane found his respect for her growing by leaps and bounds. While he freely admitted that he found her attractive on a physical level, he faced the fact that he hadn't begun to see the true depth and inner beauty of this remarkable woman.

At her direction, members of the assembly stood and introduced themselves and began to talk about their personal journeys. The grandmother's name was Barbara and she had been drinking since she was twenty. She talked about how her husband left her and took their children and how she hadn't spoken to any of them in over ten years.

The woman with maroon streaks said her name was Nadia. She started drinking at the age of eleven. The day she turned twenty-six, she plowed her car into an empty school bus. The thought that it could have been full of children finally made her seek help.

The man in the suit hadn't been so fortunate. His name was Bill and his wife and daughter died in an accident that happened when he was driving drunk. Even then, he admitted, it took him another fifteen years to hit bottom and seek help.

Not everyone spoke. A few people passed without sharing. Two young men came in late. One of them waited only five minutes before hurrying out the door again.

As Shane listened to the stories and struggles of those around him, one clear thing took shape: all of these people had turned to God when everything else in life had failed them. Like Annie, they gave God credit for their healing and their strength. This was God presented not as some being above the clouds but as a vital presence. In his heart he knew he had been missing out on something important and he decided he wanted to know more.

When the time was up, Pastor Hill stood and faced the group. "Before we close, I'd like us to bow our heads and ask the Lord guidance for all of us here this evening."

Shane bowed his head with the others as Pastor Hill began to pray. "God, I offer my heart and my soul to You. I am but clay, waiting for the master's hand to mold me into a vessel of Your purpose. Help me to do Your will. Only through You can I achieve victory over my addiction. Let me bear witness to Your loving power. If I stumble, do not forsake me. Guide me to help others in need the way I have been helped. May I do Your will always. Amen."

Deeply moved by the words, Shane knew that he had to learn more about the faith shared by these people.

Annie helped herself to a glass of punch at the refreshment table and chided herself for being a coward. Shane had spent a long time talking to Pastor Hill at the back of the room, but he and Olivia were back in their seats with cups in one hand and cookies in the other. By visiting with several of her friends, Annie had managed to avoid making eye contact with him until now.

What had he thought of her story? Was he disappointed that she had wasted the education her parents had worked so hard to provide and drunk her way through college instead? Had he been repulsed by the knowledge that she had lived with several different men? Would he think she was an unfit mother now that he knew she had taken an overdose of painkillers and tried to end her life before she found God?

She drew a deep breath. *Wallowing in guilt and self-blame doesn't help. I have learned to live in the solution and not dwell in the problem.*

Gathering her courage, she crossed the room and sat down by Olivia. "Well, what did you think?"

Olivia looked up, her eyes as wide a saucers. "Did you hear that woman say she started drinking when she was eleven? I couldn't believe it."

"That's part of the reason your mother wanted you to come tonight. She wanted you to understand how dangerous a drug alcohol can be."

"I almost cried when Bill talked about drinking to make it through his daughter's funeral." Olivia looked around and lowered her voice. "And Pastor Hill—why would a minister need to drink?"

"Pastors are human, too. They have the same problems and burdens as—perhaps even more than—the rest of us. Alcohol seems to make those problems go away, but in reality it doesn't help. It only hurts. Part of our dependence is psychological, but a large part of it is physical. Our bodies process it differently. We truly can't stop after one drink."

"But you stopped," Shane chimed in at last.

"Yes, I did."

Tilting his head to the side, he studied her for a long moment, then asked, "Is there a risk that your son or daughter will have the same disease?"

Chapter 10

Annie tried to read Shane's face. "Are you asking if our baby will inherit my alcoholism?"

"That's a possibility, isn't it?"

"It is, but it's not the only possibility. Not every child of an alcoholic becomes an alcoholic."

"How do you plan to deal with that risk?"

At his question, her heart sank. He wasn't asking how they could face such difficulty together, he'd asked how *she* planned to deal with it. In one sentence the child had become *hers* again. The pain of his withdrawal cut surprisingly deep, although she had known all along that something like this would happen. She wasn't perfect, so her baby might not be perfect.

If only he hadn't made her dream of more. Without even realizing it, she had begun to lean on him. Now she stumbled to regain her emotional balance. Biting her bottom lip until she could speak without crying, she laced her fingers together over the roundness of her belly.

"Annie, are you okay?" Olivia asked.

Swallowing hard, Annie nodded. "I'm fine." She would be. With God's help, she would be.

She raised her eyes and met Shane's without flinching. "I'll face that risk by being honest. By raising my child inside a firm foundation of faith. And by making sure that the lines of communication always stay open."

He nodded, but she had to wonder if he even understood. He wasn't a man of faith.

Olivia spoke up again. "If you don't mind, I'm going to grab a couple of cookies before we head home."

Annie smiled at her. "Grab one for me, too."

The door to the meeting room opened. Annie looked over and saw Crystal step inside. One look at her friend's apprehensive face told Annie that something was wrong. She shot out of her chair and hurried to her. "Crystal, we were so worried about you. Is everything okay?"

Shoving her hands in the pockets of her cutoff jeans, Crystal avoided making eye contact. "I'm fine."

Concern for the younger woman prompted Annie to place a comforting arm around her shoulders. "What is it? What's wrong?"

"You're going to be so mad at me."

Puzzled, Annie tipped her head to the side. "Why would I be mad at you? Because you missed the meeting?"

"No."

"What then?"

"I kind of...loaned your car to Willie."

"You did what?" She stared at Crystal in astonishment.

"Willie needed a car to get to this job interview tomorrow," she said in a rush.

"You loaned my car to someone without asking me? Crystal, what were you thinking?"

"It's our day off. We don't have to go to work, so I didn't see the harm in letting him take the car for a day. You aren't mad at me, are you?"

"Yes, I am. You should have checked with me first. I have a doctor's appointment tomorrow. You knew that."

"Oh, man, I forgot about your appointment. I'm sorry, Annie. You and Marge are always talking about helping others in need. Willie needed my help. At the time it seemed like the right thing to do."

Sighing in defeat, Annie said, "I know you meant well, but you're going to have to call Willie and tell him you're sorry but I need my car tomorrow."

"That's kind of the thing—I can't. His job interview is out of town. He left right after he dropped me off here."

"Left for where?" Annie couldn't believe what she was hearing.

Crystal cringed as she said, "Kansas City."

"Kansas City!" The thought that she might never see her car again made Annie's knees weak. The old Ford wasn't much, but it was her most valuable possession. *Please, Lord, don't load anything else on my shoulders. I can't take it.* She sank onto the closest chair.

Shane came across the room to stand beside her. "Is everything all right?"

She pressed a hand to her forehead. "No, it's not. But I can handle it."

Crystal brightened. "Hey, maybe Shane could take you to the doctor tomorrow."

"Did your poor excuse for a car give up the ghost?" he asked with a grin.

Scowling at Crystal, Annie spoke sharply. "Not exactly, but it seems that it is temporarily unavailable. Shane has his duties on base, Crystal. It was nice of him to bring us here tonight because you didn't get home on time and didn't bother to call, but I'm not asking him to do more."

"Yeah, I'm sorry about that. The time just sort of got away from me. Maybe Marge can take you—or one of the gals from work. Gina might do it. She's off tomorrow, too."

"Do you know Gina's phone number?"

"Well, no."

"Neither do I. And Marge has to work." Annie tried to calculate the cost of taking a cab out to the free clinic but realized she didn't have a clue how much it would cost.

Crystal asked, "Can't you reschedule?"

"It takes weeks to get an appointment." She hated to do it, but what choice did she have?

"I guess that leaves me," Shane interjected, sounding excessively happy.

"I'll manage something. Can we go home now?"

Looking disappointed, he nodded. "Sure."

She rose to say goodbye to Pastor Hill. A few minutes later she joined Shane outside. He stood waiting to open the car door for her. Crystal and Olivia were already in the backseat.

Stopping beside him, Annie tried to ignore the way her nerve endings came to life when he was near.

"Annie, I'm coming over to finish the roof tomorrow anyway. I might as well give you a ride to your appointment." The husky tone of his voice sent her pulse racing.

Frowning, Annie couldn't help wondering why he was being so insistent. Had she jumped to the wrong conclusion earlier? Giving him the benefit of the doubt was hard. "Why are you going out of your way to help me?"

His eyebrows shot up. "Prenatal care is important. For your health, as well as for our baby. Why wouldn't I want to help?" Folding his arms over his chest, he said, "I don't get it. You accept help and support from people like Pastor Hill and from Marge, yet you act like my help is a bomb that will blow up in your face. Why is that?"

"Because that's the way my relationships with men have all ended in the past. They disintegrated when I needed them the most."

He leaned toward her so abruptly that Annie took a step back, but all he did was pull open the door. "I'm not one of those men, Annie. I'm not going anywhere."

Gazing into his eyes, she finally understood that what he said was true. He wasn't going to abandon her. She had been unfair to him from the start. She slid into the front seat of the car as the defensive wall she had built around her emotions crumbled, leaving her feeling weak and uncertain. He closed the door before she could think of what to say to him.

On the drive back to Marge's house Shane worked to rein in his anger. Teaching one of the unit's horses to fly would be easier than getting Annie to trust him. He had tried taking small steps to build a rapport with her, but each time he thought he was making progress, she retreated back into her shell like a startled turtle.

In spite of his words to the contrary, he had to wonder if he possessed the fortitude to stick with it. She didn't want him involved with their baby. Having parents at odds with each other had to be hard on a child. Would he only make life harder for his son or daughter by insisting Annie include him?

Crystal and Olivia were unusually quiet. Annie sat beside him staring straight ahead. He would have given a month's pay to know what she was thinking. Pulling up at a red light, he took the opportunity to glance over at her. She met his eyes and gave him a shy smile. Softly she said, "You're right and I'm sorry."

His annoyance dissipated, to be quickly replaced by remorse. "No, I'm the one who should be sorry. I need to stop forcing you into situations that make you uncomfortable."

"True, but you do have a way of getting a girl's attention."

"Is that good or bad?"

"Good, I think."

From the backseat Crystal said, "If the light gets any greener, you'll have to mow it."

Sending Annie a sheepish look, he shifted into gear and stepped on the gas. It took only a few more minutes to reach the house. As Olivia and Crystal went in, Annie hung back. When the others were out of earshot, she said, "Can I talk to you for a few minutes?"

Suddenly nervous, he shoved his hands in the front pockets of his jeans. "Sure."

"Shane, if you truly want to be involved with this baby, I'm not going to object any longer."

"Really? Thank you, Annie."

Nodding, she folded her arms across her middle. "I understand that you'll be overseas when I'm due to deliver, but I'll make sure that your name goes on the birth certificate."

"I'll put in for leave. There's a chance that they may let me come back then."

"That would be nice. I guess we can work out more of the details after he or she arrives."

"Details?"

"Visitation, holidays, summers when he's old enough. Details like that."

"Right." Hearing it put into words made it all sound so cold. Yet it was exactly what he had been fighting for. Now that he had it, where was the satisfaction?

"You don't sound happy."

"Of course I'm happy. I'm grateful, too. We'll make it work, I promise. This baby is going to know that he has two parents who love him."

"Or her."

"Or her," he agreed with a smile.

"So I'll see you tomorrow?"

"Bright and early. I want to get the roof done before I have to leave for our ride in Maddox the day after tomorrow."

"How long will you be gone?"

"Four days this time, but we've got a lot of appearances booked for the summer. It's our heavy travel season."

"Don't show up too early tomorrow. It's my day off and I intend to sleep in."

"How does ten sound?"

"About right."

"What time is your appointment?"

"Two o'clock at the free clinic over on Maple."

"I'll get you there. If what's-his-face doesn't get your car back to you tomorrow night, I'll leave you mine."

"No, I can't—"

He silenced her by placing a finger on her lips. "I'm not good at taking no for an answer. You need to get back and forth to work, and I'll be on horseback for three days. You might as well use my car."

She pulled his finger aside. "I started to say that I can't drive a stick shift."

"Oh. Well, we aren't taking the mules and the wagon with us. Maybe I could talk the captain into letting you use them."

"Ha-ha! Your offer is deeply appreciated, but I'm sure I'll have my car back."

"And if you don't, I'm leaving mine with you. You need transportation. I'll teach you how to drive a stick."

"I think I'd rather send Olivia to collect the mules."

"That works, too."

"Thanks for everything, Shane. I mean that."

"It was my pleasure, and I mean that. The meeting tonight opened my eyes to a lot of things. I admire you—and all the people there—for your bravery and your faith. The courage you displayed talking about your addiction showed uncommon valor."

He cupped her cheek with his hand. "You are something special, Annie Delmar, and I mean that, too."

Leaning in slowly, he waited for her to draw away or turn aside. When she didn't, he gently kissed her.

Chapter 11

"I saw you kiss him last night."

Startled, Annie looked up from her book to see Olivia leaning against the doorjamb of her bedroom. Dressed in blue cutoff jean shorts and a red sleeveless shirt, she managed to look both smugly teen and child-like at the same time. Raising one finger, she pointed to the ceiling. The sporadic *rat-tat-tat* of the nail gun could be heard everywhere in the house.

Annie knew she was blushing, but she hoped Olivia wouldn't notice. "It isn't nice to spy on people."

Straightening, Olivia advanced into the room and plopped down on the foot of Annie's bed. "I wasn't spying. I just happened to look out the window and see you two locking lips. You like him, don't you?"

The sweet memory of Shane's gentle kiss stole over Annie. Closing her eyes, she slipped back into the moment. The manly scent that was so uniquely his own, the way his lips had closed over hers with such tenderness, the feel of her heart beating like a drum inside her chest, the sound of his tiny sigh of regret when he pulled away.

"Yeah, I like him," she admitted.

"Is he a good kisser?"

"That's none of your business."

"Are you going to marry him?"

Shocked, Annie looked at Olivia in surprise. "What makes you ask that?"

"You're having his baby. It just seems like it would be a good idea to marry him."

"It would be a very bad idea."

"Why?" Raising her palm, she said, "No, don't tell me, let me guess. It's complicated."

"Yes, it is. Marriage isn't something to be taken lightly. Two people vow before God to spend the rest of their lives together. It's about acknowledging a profound love and respect for each other."

"So you don't love him?"

Not knowing exactly how to answer, she took her time and formed her words carefully. "I care about Shane, but two wrongs don't make a right. We barely know each other. If I were to marry him only for the sake of the baby, it's likely that we would both end up feeling trapped and unhappy. It might seem like the right thing to do, but in the long run it could be the worst thing for the two of us and especially for the baby. Do you understand?"

"Sort of. I guess it is complicated."

"Yes, it is, but since you're here, I meant to ask you what you thought about the meeting last night."

Olivia shrugged and picked at the frayed edge of her cutoffs. "I don't know."

"Was I too boring for words?"

Shaking her head, Olivia managed a half smile, "No, it wasn't that."

"Then what was it?"

"It was…sad. All those people had such terrible lives—even you and Pastor Hill. It doesn't seem fair. You're a nice person. Why did God do that to you?"

Reaching out, Annie tucked a lock of Olivia's dark hair behind her ear. "I did it to myself. I made bad choices over and over again. It took God and your mother to help me see that."

"Mom really does help people, doesn't she?"

"Yes, she really does."

Olivia looked down and tugged loose another string. "When you were in high school and drinking, did any of your friends care? I mean—could someone have helped you then?"

"Maybe, but no one tried."

"Wouldn't you have been mad if they told on you or something?"

"Probably, but I wish someone had."

Peering out from under her bangs, Olivia looked uncertain. "You do?"

"Of course I do. It would have meant that they really cared about me."

After a long pause, Olivia sighed. "I'm worried about my friend Heather."

"Why?"

"She's always talking about how cool it is that she gets drunk and her folks don't know."

"They know now. Shane told me that he spoke to her father that day at the base."

"She convinced them that it was her first time, only it wasn't, and she's been drinking since then."

"Have you been drinking, too?"

"Me? No way! Mom would ground me until I was a hundred if I ever did that again."

Smiling, Annie agreed. "At least that long. What do you think you should do about Heather?"

"I was hoping that you could talk to her. Only then she would know I squealed on her and she'd be mad at me."

"She might be mad, but if no one stops her, she's heading into a life of terrible pain. Have you talked to your mother about this?"

"No."

"Why not?"

"She's always so busy. Besides, she has enough to worry about."

"Olivia, your mother is never too busy to listen to you. She's a professional. She'll know what to do. I think it's very brave of you to try and help your friend."

"You do?"

"Absolutely."

Rising, Olivia started to leave but paused at the doorway and looked back. "Thanks, Annie."

"For what?"

"Just for stuff."

"You're welcome, kiddo."

"Hey, don't you have an appointment today?"

Startled, Annie glanced at the clock and jumped to her feet.

* * *

Shane entered the house just in time to see Annie come flying down the stairs.

"I'm ready," she said breathlessly. "I hope I haven't kept you waiting."

He stood speechless as she rushed past him to grab her purse from the coffee table. It was the first time he had seen her with her hair unbound. It spilled to her hips in a shiny, smooth cape that swayed as she walked.

"Thanks again for giving me a ride," she said.

"My pleasure," he muttered. He loved the way her hair seemed to capture and hold the light. The urge to reach out and touch it was overwhelming. It would be as soft and smooth as the finest silk.

Slinging her bag over her shoulder, she came and stood in front of him. Raising one eyebrow, she stared at him. "Well?"

He swallowed hard. "Well what?"

"Are you ready to go?"

"Sure." His feet felt rooted to the floor.

Pulling open her handbag, she withdrew a piece of colorful elastic fabric. Drawing her thick mane back with both hands, she deftly secured it at the nape of her neck. "Don't we have to actually leave the house?"

"For what?" He wished she would leave it loose.

"To go to the doctor's office," she said slowly and distinctly.

The word *doctor* brought him back to earth with a thump. "Oh, right. Sure."

He stepped back, allowing her to pass, and followed her out the door.

I'm a moron. How can I be mooning over her hair when she's pregnant with my baby?

The answer struck him as he watched her walk ahead of him to his car: he was falling in love with her.

She was a beautiful woman, but it was her inner beauty that was capturing his heart. If she cut off her hair and dyed it orange, he would still find her beautiful. He loved her strength and her determination. He loved the way she put her faith at the forefront of her life—even the way she stumbled and fell and got back up to face her mistakes. How could he ever be worthy of such a woman?

At his car, she tugged open the door and looked over her shoulder. "Is something wrong?"

Realizing that he was standing like a statue on the steps, he started toward her. "Nothing's wrong. I was distracted, that's all."

Did he dare tell her? He was sure that she liked him, but uncertainty held back the words. A year ago he had imagined himself in love with someone else. Someone who'd found it easy to leave him for another man.

Loath to risk that kind of pain again, he kept silent. Annie had made it plain from the start that she had her own life to live. Granting him the opportunity to stay involved with their child was a far cry from asking for a romantic relationship.

As he drove through the busy streets toward the clinic, he knew that he wouldn't say anything yet. Not until he was certain that Annie returned his feelings. If only his time with her wasn't so short.

Anything could happen while he was stationed in Germany. Annie could meet someone else.

"You need to turn right at the next corner," she said, pointing ahead.

"Thanks." He slowed the car.

"Shane, are you okay?"

He looked at her sharply. "Why do you ask?"

"You've been awfully quiet today."

"I'll try to talk it up on the way home."

"Are you nervous about coming to the doctor with me?"

"Now that you mention it—what if they don't have any good magazines in the waiting room?"

"They have a nice assortment. I'm sure you'll find something to interest you."

"Are you nervous?"

"No. I just hope I haven't gained too much weight. I hate getting on his scale. It weighs at least five pounds heavier than the one at home. Talk about depressing."

"You're no bigger than a minute. Why would you worry about your weight?"

"Okay, that was spoken like a man."

Pulling up beside the small redbrick structure with a blue-and-white medical symbol painted on the large plate-glass window, he parked the car. "Guys worry about important things."

"Like what?"

"Like is my hair getting thin? Or do these jeans make me look fat?"

"Ha-ha."

Annie pushed open her door and stepped out of the car. How was it that Shane could make her smile so easily? His company lightened her spirits and made her feel strangely happy. Could she trust the emotions he evoked? Were they real or only a matter of wishful thinking?

He joined her as she waited by the parking meter. She looked him up and down. His jeans were slightly dusty from his work on the roof and his blue T-shirt had seen better days, but to her eyes he looked tall, handsome and self-assured.

"They don't make you look fat at all, sweetie."

He half turned to look down at his hips. "You don't think so? Whew, that's a relief."

"I imagine your horse thinks the same thing when you dismount." She headed toward the building.

"Hey, that's not nice." He hurried to open the door for her.

"Ah, but is it true?" she threw over her shoulder as she walked past him.

Inside the building, the sounds of pop music came from a small television in the far corner of a long, narrow waiting room. The pale blue walls sported numerous posters with health information above the white plastic chairs that lined the perimeter. An elderly woman with a bandage on her hand glanced up as they came in, as did the two teenage girls in front of the TV. A harried mother holding a crying baby to her shoulder while a toddler tugged at the hem of her skirt paid them no attention at all.

Glancing at Shane, Annie said, "Why don't you have a seat?"

He nodded and made his way to an empty chair.

Annie crossed to the glass-fronted reception desk and spoke to the gray-haired woman seated behind it. "Hi, I'm Annie Delmar and I'm here for an OB appointment with Dr. Merrick."

"Have you been seen here before?"

"Yes, back in March."

"I'll need you to fill out this paperwork and then have a seat."

"Can you tell me how long it will be?"

The woman pushed a clipboard toward her. "It'll take as long as it takes."

Accepting the paperwork and a pen, Annie made her way to a chair beside Shane. He leaned toward her and motioned toward the toddler, who had begun screaming at the top of his lungs. "Are you sure you want one of those?"

Annie stared at him in openmouthed astonishment. "Shame on you."

Looking contrite, he held up his hands. "Kidding. Just kidding."

"I hope so."

A nurse came into the room with a manila folder in her hands. "Belinda Kemp?"

"That's me." The woman with the baby herded the toddler in front of her as she followed the nurse down the hall.

Annie glared at Shane once more, then began filling out the forms the receptionist had given her. A short while later the same nurse came to the doorway and called her name.

The doctor, a man in his late fifties with a worn and haggard face, sat waiting for her. He didn't bother to look up when Annie was shown into the exam room. "Hello, Miss Delmar. How have you been feeling?"

"Good. The morning sickness is gone, and except for feeling tired and a little swelling in my ankles, I'm doing okay."

"It looks like you're in your nineteenth week of pregnancy, is that right?"

"Yes."

"All right then, let's get started."

The exam itself didn't take long. After answering a barrage of questions, most of which she had already answered on paper, Annie was allowed to dress and waited as the doctor finished writing on the chart. She waited nervously for him to speak. Finally she asked, "Is everything okay?"

"As far as I can tell, it is, but I'd still like to get that sonogram just to make sure. Be sure to make that appointment next week and come in for a follow-up."

A stab of anxiety shot through Annie. "But I thought I wouldn't need to see you again for another month."

"I'd like to get the baseline sonogram and do some more lab work. Swelling in your feet this early concerns me a little, but your blood pressure is normal, so I'm not going to get excited about it. Limit your salt intake and put your feet up whenever you get the chance. I'm sure there's nothing to worry about. I'll see you in two weeks."

The doctor left the room and Annie stepped down from her seat on the exam table. Pressing a hand to her tummy, she tried to calm her apprehension. Dr. Merrick was taking precautions—that was all. The baby was fine. The sonogram would only confirm that.

She wished Shane were beside her instead of in the other room. She needed his arms around her and his voice telling her everything would be okay. In the next second, she decided not to tell him. She could worry enough for both of them.

Closing her eyes, Annie breathed a heartfelt prayer. *Please, Lord, don't let anything be wrong with my baby.*

Chapter 12

Thirty miles outside of Maddox, Kansas, Shane gazed forward between his mount's ears down the empty two-lane highway stretching away in the distance. The late-morning sun beat down on his shoulders, but he barely noticed. His mind was miles away—with Annie. He couldn't stop thinking about her.

It had only been two days, but it felt like weeks. If he missed her smile and her tart tongue this much after only forty-eight hours, what would it be like to be away from her for two years? The thought was depressing.

The creak of saddle leather, the sighing of the wind past his ears and the *clip-clop* of the horses' hooves were the only sounds. Until Avery opened his mouth again.

"I can't believe it. I can't believe you loaned your car to a woman. Are you nuts? What if she wrecks it?

I don't know why you won't sell it to me. I've offered you more than it's worth several times."

Glancing over at his buddy riding beside him, Shane said, "Can we talk about something else?"

"Like what? The weather? It's hot." Avery pushed his cap back on his head. "It was hot an hour ago and it's still hot." Raising a hand to shade his eyes, Avery scanned the countryside. "Maybe you want to talk about the scenery. I see flat. It was flat an hour ago and it's still flat. If you look to your right, you will see miles of grass, but if you look quickly to your left, you will see—yes, that's right—miles of grass. How long is this ride going to be again?"

"One hundred miles."

"I was hoping I dreamed that part. One hundred miles divided by twenty-five miles a day. Are we really going to spend four days in the saddle?"

"It's not like we haven't been preparing for this." In fact, during the past month the unit had been riding all over the post and surrounding areas for up to six hours each day, conditioning both the men and the horses for this Memorial Day weekend event.

Eight men and their mounts moved along the verge of the road under a cloudless blue sky. Orange reflective vests worn for safety and the support vehicle following behind them were the only concessions the unit made to modern times. All the rest of the equipment was what any cavalry detachment in the 1860s would have carried.

Hoping to distract Avery from his sour mood, Shane asked, "Are you going to Lindsey and Brian's wedding next weekend?"

"I guess. What about you?"

"Yup, I told her I'd be there."

"Are you taking anyone?"

Frowning, Shane said, "I hadn't thought about it. Are you?"

"Certainly."

"Who?"

"There is a long line of women who would be delighted to spend the day with me. I just have to pick one."

Shaking his head, Shane said, "I don't think I've ever met someone who is so conceited with so little reason to be that way."

"Are you kidding? I'm a matrimonial prize of the first magnitude. All I have to do is mention that my grandfather is worth a fortune and women flock to me. They just don't need to know that I'm opposed to wedlock on a very visceral level."

The same wasn't true for Shane. Not since he'd met Annie. She had changed everything. The idea of spending his life with her had a deep appeal that settled into his chest and wouldn't be dislodged.

"What?" Avery demanded.

Drawn back to the conversation at hand, Shane said, "It doesn't seem right to string them along that way."

"I'm as sincere in my affection as they are—which is to say, only as deep as their pocketbooks."

Shane shook his head in disbelief at his friend's attitude. "You take the cake."

"Speaking of cake, I'm hungry."

"You'll get fed at the next town."

Rising in his stirrups, Avery shaded his eyes to look down the road. "There's nothing in sight yet."

"It gives a guy pause, doesn't it? Knowing that men

like us rode this route as much as twice a week, escorting settlers westward, only a hundred and fifty years ago."

"The amazing part is that anyone stopped to settle in this place. They must have had a tree phobia."

A hundred yards ahead a white pickup rolled up to the highway and stopped beside a lone mailbox decorated with red, white and blue steamers. An elderly woman in a light blue skirt and a blue-and-white-flowered blouse got out of the truck and walked to the edge of the road. A man in a tan cowboy hat, red Western shirt and faded jeans joined her. She handed him a small American flag, then raised the one she held and waved it in the air.

Avery pulled his cap into place. Shane sat forward. All along the column riders straightened in their saddles. Even the horses lifted their heads and stepped higher.

"God bless you boys," she called out. "You make us proud."

At the front of the line Captain Watson turned aside and reined in. He touched the brim of his hat. "Thank you, ma'am."

Grinning, she stepped closer. "Our grandson is serving in the Middle East. He was so excited when I told him you'd be riding past our place. Would you mind if I took a picture?"

"I'd be delighted." Looking over his shoulder, he gave the order to halt. She pulled a camera from her white handbag and quickly snapped a half dozen shots.

Walking up, her husband took her arm. "That's enough, Lucy. They've got a long way to go."

She gave him an embarrassed smile. "Of course. Thank you for indulging a silly old woman, Captain."

"It was my honor."

"My husband's grandfather came west with the cavalry in 1857 and settled here afterward. I think it's so special that the Army is recreating this part of our history after a century and a half."

Her husband nodded in agreement. "It's been the talk of the town for weeks now. Even some of the high school kids have been asking questions about what it was like in the old days."

"He's been telling and retelling his granddad's yarns to anyone who will listen."

"They're true stories, woman. Folks enjoy 'em."

"Almost as much as you enjoy yammering on. Captain, you and your men hurry along into Windom," Lucy said. "The ladies from our church are fixing lunch for all of you. You'll find fried chicken and homemade peach, cherry and pecan pies."

As the column began moving again, Avery leaned toward Shane. "This ride may have some highlights after all."

"Yeah, talking to people like that makes me proud of what we're doing." Would Annie be proud of him if she could see him now?

"I was thinking more about the food. I love pecan pie. And speaking of nuts—I can't believe you loaned your car to some woman. You must be in love."

Annie pulled the living room curtain aside and checked the street for the umpteenth time. Shane was due back today. It was ridiculous the way excitement zipped through her veins at the thought.

"This is silly." Dropping the folds of fabric, she crossed the room and picked up the remote. Aiming it at the television, she turned the set on. Forty channels later, she snapped it off again. Nothing held her interest. She glanced at the window and willed herself not to walk back there.

He had only been gone four days, but it seemed so much longer. Surely he would come by this evening to collect his car. Laying the remote down, she walked to the front door but stopped with one hand on the knob.

"This is absurd. Why am I a basket case?"

"Beats me," Crystal said, coming up behind her.

Feeling sheepish at being discovered talking to herself, Annie moved aside as Crystal pulled open the door. A tan sedan with gray primer on the right front fender pulled up to the curb behind Annie's blue hatchback. Shane's Mustang still sat in the driveway. Willie, dressed in a grimy white T-shirt with the sleeves cut out and baggy black pants, got out of the passenger side but stood at the curb without approaching the house.

Annie looked at Crystal in concern. "Are you going out again?"

"For a little while. Are you my mother now?"

Hurt by Crystal's sarcasm, Annie said, "I didn't mean to sound disapproving."

"You're just mad because Willie kept your car two days longer than he said he would. He explained that— he had to stay an extra day for a second job interview."

"He could have called to let us know. He's lucky I didn't report the car as stolen."

"Whatever. I'll see you later."

Annie reached out and took hold of her friend's arm,

stopping her from leaving. "Crystal, I'm worried about you. You've been going out every night. You missed the last two AA meetings."

"So what? Do you think I'm drinking again? I'm not, so take a chill pill."

"I only want to help," Annie said softly.

Crystal's defiant attitude deflated. "I know. Don't worry. Willie is taking good care of me. He loves me. He's just going through a rough patch right now. His friend is driving us out to the lake for a couple of hours. Where's the harm in that? Trust me, okay?"

"I do. I just know how easy it is to get into a bad situation. Look at me. I'm the poster child for mistakes."

At the street, a military jeep pulled in behind the sedan. Shane stepped out of the passenger side. Bending down, he gave a brief wave to the driver. As the jeep pulled away, he straightened and began walking toward the house. Wearing jeans and the CGMCG's regulation red T-shirt that emphasized his muscular chest and flat abdomen, he looked wonderfully handsome. Annie's heart bounded into double-time.

As Shane walked past Willie, it was hard not to compare the two men. Shane's clean-cut, all-American physique contrasted sharply with Willie's slovenly dress and attitude.

Crystal's chin came up. "Your problem, Annie, is you can't stand to see people happy. You don't believe in love so you don't think anyone else should. Open your eyes. Grab a little joy before life passes you by. Happiness takes courage, too, you know."

Jerking her arm away, Crystal dashed down the walk and into Willie's embrace. After kissing him, she glanced back at Annie, then got in the car.

Pressing a hand to her throat, Annie watched them drive off. Something wasn't right with Crystal. As Shane came up to the bottom of the steps, his warm smile chased her worry about her friend from her mind. She said, "Welcome back."

"Thanks. Did you miss me?"

Oh, she had, but she wasn't about to admit it. "I certainly didn't miss the sound of your hammer on the roof."

"Will you miss the rain dripping in?"

"No, I won't miss that."

"Did you have any trouble with my car?"

"No. After Marge's quick refresher course on driving a manual transmission, I was able to manage."

"I'm glad."

"Thanks for letting me borrow your pride and joy. I know it must have been hard to leave it with me."

"You needed it more than I did."

She gestured toward the house. "Do you have time to come in? I just made a pitcher of lemonade, and Marge made some sugar cookies yesterday."

"That sounds great." The eagerness of his acceptance made her smile.

Happiness had been a rare thing in her life. She almost didn't recognize the emotion as it welled up inside her. Crystal was wrong. Annie wanted others to be happy—only she didn't expect it for herself. She hadn't done anything to deserve it. Feeling it now scared her witless.

Take a deep breath. Get a grip. It was good advice but hard to put into practice with Shane standing so close beside her. She took a step back. "How was your trip?"

"It was good. We met some wonderful people and I think we did some good PR for the Army."

He followed her into the house and into the kitchen. He took a seat at the table, still talking about the reception the unit had received at various towns along their route. Annie pulled the lemonade pitcher from the refrigerator and filled two tall tumblers, glad of the chance it gave her to compose herself. By the time she placed one glass in front of Shane and set the platter of golden cookies sprinkled with red, white and blue sugar crystals on the table, she had herself well in hand.

"How have you been feeling?" Shane asked, then took a sip of his drink.

"A little tired and fat but otherwise good."

"You don't look fat at all. In fact, you look glowing."

"Thank you. Nice comeback. Who's been instructing you on how to talk to a pregnant woman?"

He managed to look sheepish and sweet at the same time. "I've been doing some reading."

Pleased beyond words that he cared enough to learn about the changes she was going through, Annie grinned and let the happiness seep back into her heart. He was a good man. She was doing the right thing by allowing him to be involved with the baby.

He set his glass down and ran his finger slowly around the rim. Sensing a change in his mood, she waited for him to speak. Had he changed his mind? Was he getting ready to give her and their child the brush-off?

Clearing his throat, he looked up and met her gaze with uncertainty in his eyes. "I know this is kind of short notice, but I was wondering if I could ask you for a favor?"

Puzzled, she said, "If I can. You've certainly done more than enough for me."

"Okay, that isn't exactly where I wanted to go with this. You don't owe me anything, so feel free to decline."

Waiting a full ten seconds for a further explanation, she finally said, "Spit it out."

"Do you remember Lindsey Mandel?"

"I'm not sure. Should I?"

"She gave the introduction for the Commanding General's Mounted Color Guard at the Community Appreciation Day."

"I think I remember her. She was a pretty woman with short, curly red hair?"

"That's her. She was a sergeant in my unit until she left the service back in April. Anyway, she's getting married this weekend and I was kind of wondering if you'd like to go with me to the wedding."

Annie blinked hard. "You want me to come to the wedding with you?"

"It won't be a big affair, but there is a reception after the ceremony. I'd like you to meet some of my friends." He looked braced for her refusal.

She opened her mouth to do just that but found herself remembering Crystal's words. *Grab a little joy before life passes you by. Happiness takes courage, too, you know.*

Had she been letting the joy of life pass her by? Did she have the courage to risk seeking a little happiness with Shane? He would be gone soon and she would be alone again. Knowing how badly she had dealt with such disappointments in the past made her afraid to risk it. She already cared for him far too much.

What do I do, Lord? Should I send him away and protect what's left of my heart? Or do I say yes and gather a few more precious memories to treasure?

Either way, Annie knew heartache loomed in her future.

Chapter 13

The chapel parking lot was nearly full when Shane pulled in the following Saturday afternoon at a quarter till three. Looking up, he saw the steeple over the bell tower of the old stone building silhouetted against the fluffy white clouds drifting past. Stepping out of his vehicle, he paused to button the jacket of his dress uniform, then nervously tugged it down and smoothed the front of the dark green material. He wanted to look his best today.

The sound of organ music reached him coming through the open panels of stained glass at the bottom of the arched windows of the building. He walked around his newly washed car and pulled open the passenger door. The vision that took his hand and stepped out into the bright June sunlight stole his breath.

Annie wore a simple pink dress with wide sleeves

that ended just above her elbows. Her long hair was held back from her face by a band of matching material. Gathered gently at a high waist, the drape of the supple fabric below the vee neckline did little to hide her rounded tummy. *Beautiful,* he decided, didn't do justice to her. His heart swelled with protectiveness and pride.

Taking her hand, he steered her toward the chapel doors.

Inside the cool interior, organ music played softly while they were escorted to the bride's side of the aisle. The scent of candles and carnations filled the air, and white bows adorned the ends of each row of wooden pews. After taking his seat beside Annie, Shane ran a finger under his collar to loosen his tie. Looking around, he recognized a dozen former and current members of the CGMCG. A few of them had wives or girlfriends beside them, but the majority of the young men had come alone, including Captain Watson, Avery and Lee.

Shane almost laughed when he caught Avery's eye. So much for the playboy's assumption that he could get a date at a moment's notice.

A few minutes later the organist fell silent. The minister, followed by Brian and two groomsmen, headed to their places in front of the altar. Brian leaned heavily on a cane, but when he looked toward the back of the church, his face lit up with happiness. Suddenly the first strains of the "Wedding March" rang out. All heads turned toward the end of the aisle.

Lindsey, dressed in a simple sleeveless ivory gown, stood with her hand resting on her father's sleeve. Standing with obvious military erectness, the gray-haired man's face beamed with a mixture of pride and sadness. As Lindsey started down the aisle, a shy smile curved her lips and love shone from her eyes as she gazed at the man waiting to make her his wife.

Shane looked down at the woman beside him. Lindsey made a radiant bride, but to his eyes she didn't hold a candle to Annie. Was he crazy to hope that Annie might someday look at him with the same kind of love in her eyes?

As the bride walked by, Annie watched with a touch of envy in her heart. Having given up the idea of a fairy-tale wedding a long time ago, it surprised her how much of that dream she still carried. To have her father walk her down the aisle, to stand in front of a church full of family and friends and pledge her heart to a very special man…what girl didn't want that?

Looking down, she brushed a hand over her bulging midriff. She had given up the right to that dream and so much more. It would be easy to blame the drinking, but the simple truth was that she had thrown away her dreams and destroyed whatever dreams her parents had held for her for a quick buzz. Having seen exactly how much a child could hurt a parent, Annie sent a quick prayer heavenward.

Please, gracious God, don't let my baby make the same mistakes I have made. I think I could face anything except watching her destroy herself.

As the music died away and the minister began to address the couple, Annie glanced at Shane and found him watching her with a look of such tenderness on his face that her heart melted. He made her want to believe in dreams again.

Had God forgiven her sins? Wasn't she asking for too much by even thinking about a life with a man as kind and loving as Shane? In spite of all the Lord had done for her, she still found it hard to accept the goodness in life. So many times she had been sure she'd found someone to make her happy, only to discover that so-called love was nothing more than an alcohol-induced illusion. Trusting her own judgment was sometimes hard. Trusting these new emotions was even harder. Was it love?

As if answering her unspoken question, the minister's words penetrated her mind. "Lindsey and Brian, I know that as a couple you are both in love with one another, but as wonderful as this feels, it is not a perfect love. With God's blessing, you will grow in loving and grow in spirit by loving one another.

"Love is patient. Love is kind. It is never jealous. Love does not brag. It is not arrogant. Love takes hard work. Sometimes love means you will have to suffer. But it is only through suffering that we discover our true strength. I pray that your relationship grows stronger, deeper and more beautiful as you face life's hardships and joys together until you find at last the true 'perfect love' with our Father in heaven."

Annie felt Shane take her hand. Meeting his gaze, she basked in the warmth of his smile. Love was patient. Love was kind. *Patient* and *kind* were exactly the words she would use to describe Shane, along with handsome and funny and more than a little determined. If she put her heart in his hands, he would treat it with tenderness and care. Brave or not, foolish or not, she would give herself one last chance at happiness.

When the ceremony came to an end, Annie and Shane followed the newlyweds and the crowd to the reception in a nearby hall. Surrounded by people she didn't know and unable to hide her condition, Annie had expected to feel awkward and out of place, but she soon discovered that Shane's friends were open and accepting. Keeping her hand tucked firmly against his side, Shane moved from group to group introducing her, regaling her with stories about the men he served with and making her feel at ease.

When the bride and groom approached, Shane pulled Annie close and slipped his arm around her waist.

Nestled against his waist, Annie struggled to contain the joy leaping like a fountain in her chest. She smiled at the bride. "The ceremony was beautiful and you look lovely."

"Thank you. I'm so glad you could come today, Annie. Shane has told us so much about you."

"Has he?" Slanting a glance up at him, Annie thought she detected a faint blush creeping up his cheeks.

"I might have mentioned you a time or two," he admitted. "It was all good."

"I doubt that."

"Okay, it was mostly good. I can't help it that you're stubborn and contrary, as well as gorgeous."

"The gorgeous part was a good touch. Keep that up and I'll have to start liking you."

"So flattery is all it takes to get on your good side? I wish I had known that sooner."

"What makes you think you're on my good side?"

Lindsey laughed. "I see you are a woman after my own heart. Keep him in line, dear. Please excuse us. I believe it's time for us to cut the cake. Come on, Brian, your surgical skill with a knife will come in handy with this."

As they walked away, Shane grinned at Annie. "Are you having a good time?"

Happier than she could remember being in a long time, she smiled at him and nodded. "I am. Thank you for bringing me."

Shane battled the urge to kiss Annie there in front of everyone. He knew it would embarrass her, but the sight of her sweet lips parted in a smile just for him was almost too much to bear. Suddenly her eyes widened and she pressed a hand to her stomach.

"What is it? What's wrong?" he asked in concern.

"Nothing's wrong. Someone is just kicking me."

"Really? May I feel it?"

"You can try. It's very faint." Taking his hand, she pressed it against her belly.

Shane thought he detected the tiniest tap beneath his palm, but he couldn't be sure.

"Wow, did you feel that?" Annie asked.

His son or daughter had kicked his hand! There was a real baby, his baby, nestled under the heart of this beautiful and brave woman.

A sense of profound wonder and delight poured into his heart, followed quickly by gut-wrenching panic. With painful certainty, Shane realized he had absolutely no idea how to be a father.

God, I know You and I are just getting acquainted, but You've got to help me. Please don't let me mess this up.

"Yeah, I felt it," he admitted weakly.

She frowned. "Are you okay?"

He met her worried eyes. "I've been talking about having a son or a daughter for weeks, but until this minute it wasn't real."

Another faint thump-thump fluttered against his

fingers, causing a slow grin to spread across his face. "That's some kid we've got there. Does he do this all the time?"

"*She* does it a few dozen times a day."

"It feels so weird."

"You're telling me. You should feel it from the inside."

"It must be a boy. With that kind of kick, he's sure to be a soccer forward."

"Girls play soccer, too."

"My little girl is going to play house with her dolls and have tea parties. She isn't going to be a jock."

"I know your detachment reenacts things from a bygone era, but you are going to have to come back to the present, buddy. Girls can play house *and* soccer."

"All kidding aside, Annie, it doesn't make a bit of difference to me if it's a boy or a girl. I just want the two of you to be healthy."

"We are. Don't worry."

Reaching out, he brushed back a strand of her hair and let his hand cup her cheek. "That's the funny part— I can't help but worry. You have become very important to me, Annie."

She covered his hand with her own. "I feel the same way about you."

"You do?"

Grinning, she said, "Don't sound so surprised."

"I'm not—I mean, I'd hoped, but I wasn't sure."

"I wasn't sure myself until today."

"I hope you know how special you are and how happy I am whenever we're together. You've changed my life in so many ways. I want to spend every minute I can with you, Annie. I think we have something good going on."

"Really?" The shy uncertainty in her tone touched his heart.

"Really."

Looking down, she said, "Because of the baby."

With one finger beneath her chin, he lifted her face until she met his eyes. "Not because of the baby."

His transfer back to the First Infantry Division and his deployment to Germany loomed like a dark cloud over his delight in knowing Annie returned his feelings. There was so little time left for them to be together.

"Look, the color guard is leaving again early Tuesday morning, and we'll be gone another week. Maybe we could spend the day together tomorrow?"

Her smile faded. "I'd love to, but I have to work."

"Okay, what about Monday? I could get away for a few hours in the afternoon, but I'd have to be back at four. It's my turn to have the duty."

"I work until one. After that, I have a doctor's visit scheduled at two o'clock."

He tried not to sound disappointed. "Then we'll make time after I get back from our tour in Missouri."

Annie bit her bottom lip, then raised her chin. "If you want, you could come with me to my doctor's appointment and maybe stay for the sonogram. That way we could both see our soccer player's first photos."

"Do you mean it? Of course I'll come with you."

"You will?"

"Wild horses couldn't keep me away." Shane knew he was grinning like a fool, but he couldn't help it.

"I'll have to take your word for that since you're the horse-and-mule expert."

Someday he would tell her how much he adored the twinkle in her eyes when she teased him. He needed a distraction—fast—or he was going to have to kiss her.

As if she were reading his thoughts, she took a step to his side. "I think they've finished cutting the cake."

"Are you hungry?"

"I'm five months pregnant. I'm always hungry."

"Then I'll go get some for both of us."

"Don't forget the mints," she called after him.

Shane headed toward the linen-draped side table where several women were dishing up slices of white wedding cake onto clear plastic dishes. After requesting an extra-large slice and extra mints for one of his plates, Shane turned around to see Annie engaged in animated conversation with another young woman who was also obviously pregnant.

He stood for a moment, drinking in the sight of her. He loved the way she touched the roundness of her stomach with such tenderness. He loved the way she smiled at him from across the room. God had given him Annie and a child. He couldn't imagine feeling happier.

Two days after the wedding, Annie lay on the hard exam table at the clinic with only her bulging tummy exposed for her first sonogram. She was more excited than worried. After all, the baby was moving all the time now and Dr. Merrick had assured Annie that this was merely a precaution. The speckled ceiling tiles overhead were decorated with several colorful posters of babies sleeping in giant flowers. They were cute, but Annie was much more interested in the small black-and-white image wavering on the sonogram screen.

Shane, looking nervous, sat by Annie's side and held her hand.

The sonogram technician, dressed in pink scrubs with blue baby footprints scattered across her top, chatted constantly as she readied her equipment. "My name is Becky and I'm going to be doing your sono. Is this your first child?"

"Yes," Shane answered before Annie could, then sent her a sheepish grin. It was clear he was excited about the prospect of seeing his son or daughter on the machine's small screen.

"It's my first pregnancy, too," Annie replied, giving his hand a squeeze.

"All right, I'm going to put some gel on your stomach and it's going to be cold," Becky warned.

Cold and icky, Annie would have said. Static crackled as the wand made contact with Annie's skin.

"How far along are you?" Becky asked, typing on the keyboard of the machine.

"I'll be exactly twenty-one weeks tomorrow."

Becky arched an eyebrow as she looked at Annie. "You sound positive about that."

"We are," Annie and Shane said simultaneously, then grinned at each other.

"What are we looking at?" Shane asked.

"The lunar landing?" Annie suggested, turning her head slightly. She certainly couldn't make a baby out of the streaky image. Suddenly a rapid, faint knocking sound came out of the speakers.

"Is that her heartbeat?" The awe in Shane's tone made Annie's heart turn over. His grip on her hand tightened.

"Yes, it is," Becky said.

"Why is it so fast?" he asked.

"Babies normally have a heart rate of one-twenty to one-sixty beats a minute. Girls run slightly higher than boys. Your little one has a pulse of about one-eighty. That's a little fast, but maybe he or she is just excited to be on TV."

Annie lifted her head to see the screen better. "Does that mean it's a girl?"

"We'll get to that question in a few minutes if you want to find out, but first I have a few measurements to check. Ah, I see a foot." Becky pointed to the center of the screen, where the wavering gray image took shape.

"I see it." Shane moved closer, his voice brimming with pride and exhilaration.

Her baby's foot. Annie couldn't find the words to describe the feeling coursing through her. A second later it hit her. This was love—overwhelming in its intensity—and it took her breath away. She met Shane's gaze and saw the same raw emotion on his face.

Their child—conceived with utter carelessness—brought a joy more powerful than anything Annie had known in her life.

As Becky moved the wand over Annie's stomach, she kept up a running conversation about what she was doing and pointed out various parts of the baby's anatomy. Annie listened with only half an ear. The rest of her was tuned in to the sound of her baby's heartbeat.

Closing her eyes, she thanked God for the blessing He had given her. It was one she didn't deserve. It took several long minutes before Annie noticed that Becky had fallen silent.

Glancing at the young woman's face, Annie felt her

heart freeze, then begin to pound with painful intensity. "What's wrong?"

Pressing the wand more firmly into Annie's stomach, Becky avoided looking at her. "I just need to get a few more pictures of something here."

"Everything is okay, isn't it?" Shane asked.

Becky chewed her lower lip, then said, "I'm having a little trouble getting the measurements I need. I'm going to have Dr. Merrick give it a try. He's better at this than I am."

Annie didn't believe her. Looking at Shane, she saw he didn't, either. And she saw something else. She saw fear in his eyes. Her heart sank as panic welled up like bile in her throat and threatened to choke her.

Chapter 14

"It's going to be okay," Shane said quietly.

Sitting in a chair beside him in Dr. Merrick's office, Annie desperately wanted to believe Shane, but she couldn't. Trying to think about anything but what could be wrong, she glanced around the room. The small office contained only a desk with a computer and two gray filing cabinets sitting side by side against the wall. Over them hung several framed documents detailing Dr. Merrick's credentials. On the other wall hung several photographs of a little boy and a little girl.

Annie rubbed her hands up and down her arms. "What's taking him so long?"

"I wish I knew." Shane's knuckles stood out white as he gripped the arms of the chair. Annie's hands were ice-cold. She struggled to keep her composure. This couldn't be happening. Her baby was going to be fine.

God, why are You doing this to me? I'm sorry for all the things I've done wrong, You know that. Please let my baby be okay.

The office door opened and Dr. Merrick came in at last. "I'm sorry to keep you waiting, but I wanted to get a second opinion on what your sonogram was showing us and do a little research."

He sat down at his desk and faced them. "I've sent a digital copy of your sonogram to a colleague at Children's Mercy in Kansas City, and unfortunately he concurs with my diagnosis."

"What's wrong?" Annie asked the question, but she knew in her heart she didn't want to hear the answer.

Dr. Merrick folded his hands together. "There isn't an easy way to say this. Your child has a rare condition called congenital cystic adenomatoid malformation. We call it C-CAM for short. It is a birth defect that occurs when one or more lobes of the lungs develop into fluid-filled cysts instead of normal tissue. The result is that your baby has a large tumor inside her chest, and it's growing."

"It's a girl?" The thrill of knowing she carried a daughter couldn't offset the dread filling her mind.

"This tumor is treatable, isn't it?" Shane asked.

Hearing the desperation in his voice, Annie bowed her head and fought to keep from screaming. This couldn't be happening. She wanted to wake up from this horrible nightmare.

Please, God, let me wake up!

"Treatment depends on the size of the tumor. Many small ones don't require intervention, but in this case we can already see that the baby's heart is being compressed to the point that it isn't pumping blood adequately. With a tumor this size, the child can't survive."

"No!" The cry tore out of Annie throat. "Don't say that! There's some mistake!"

Shane reached over to take her hand, but she jerked away from him.

The doctor said, "I wish that were true. I'm very sorry. This isn't an inherited condition. You don't need to worry about it reoccurring with your next pregnancy."

"But I want *this* baby," Annie whispered. "Can't you help us?"

The man's silence spoke louder than any words. Annie's throat closed up, and tears poured unchecked down her face as the terrible truth sank in.

Shane's heart ached for Annie's pain. She seemed to shrink into a ball of agony before his eyes. He wanted to comfort her, but he didn't know how. The knowledge that their daughter was going to die numbed his mind.

None of his military training had taught him how to deal with such grief. He looked back at the doctor. "Is there any chance at all that the baby can survive?"

"I don't want to give you false hope. In a very few cases the cysts stop growing and the baby can survive until it is mature enough to be born and undergo surgery to remove the tumor. It isn't likely in this case because we can already see signs of heart failure in the fetus."

"But there is a chance?" Shane snatched onto that thread of hope with grim determination.

"I'll recheck a sonogram in a few days. That will tell us for sure if the tumor is still growing. The only other option would be fetal surgery. You'd have to go to a specialized center for that. I think the closest one would be Houston, but the baby may already be too sick."

Shane glanced at Annie. She sat silent in her chair, her head bowed in defeat. "This fetal surgery—it's been done in cases like this?"

"A very few, and not all have been successful."

"And we can have it done in Houston?"

"Among other places. But, Mr. Ross, there are other things to consider. Fetal surgery is risky for the mother. Many times the babies die anyway. Even if it is successful, Annie would need to stay in the hospital for weeks to be monitored for premature labor. She has no insurance, she has a minimum-wage job. You yourself are being deployed overseas in a few weeks and won't be there to support her."

"You don't know how strong Annie is," Shane said.

"I'm afraid I can't recommend fetal surgery as a course of treatment. I see from your records that this wasn't a planned pregnancy and that you two aren't married. An unwanted pregnancy places a terrible strain on a couple at the best of times. I see men and women trying to cope and failing all the time. They suffer and their children suffer. Doing nothing and letting nature take its course may be the best thing for both of you."

Annie's voice quivered as she asked, "Did I cause this? We were drinking the night I conceived. Is that the reason this happened?"

Shaking his head, Dr. Merrick said, "We don't know why these things happen. I'm sorry, Annie. This may sound cruel, but given your history of alcoholism, this may be a blessing in disguise. In time, you can continue to make a better life for yourself without the added burden of an unplanned pregnancy."

On a practical level what the physician said made sense, but Shane's heart wouldn't allow him to stand by and lose the very reason his life had taken on a new meaning. Annie and the baby were everything to him. God had given him a gift unlike anything he had ever expected or deserved. He couldn't—wouldn't—give up without a fight.

"We want you to find a specialist in Houston to see us," he insisted.

"Don't you think Annie is the one who should make that decision?"

Annie smoothed her hands over her stomach. "How will it happen? I mean, what can I expect? How will I know when the baby is…"

Dr. Merrick sat back in his chair. "Sometime soon, the baby will stop moving. Once that happens, labor should begin in a few days. If it doesn't, we can induce labor with drugs and deliver the fetus that way."

Annie sprang to her feet. "I can't… I'm sorry." With one hand pressed to her lips, she hurried out of the room.

Rising, Shane started to follow her, but Dr. Merrick stopped him by saying, "Give her a little time alone. I know this has been a shock to both of you."

Shock didn't begin to cover the emotions he was going through. It had to be so much worse for Annie. If he hadn't been so self-centered and thoughtless the night he met her, none of this would be happening. There had to be a way to save his child. "I want you to find a doctor in Houston that we can see."

"Very well, I'll see about a referral, but I think you're only looking at more heartache if you get your hopes up."

"Maybe, but I need to know I've done everything I can."

"Leave your phone number with my receptionist and I'll give you a call as soon as I hear something."

"Thank you."

After leaving the small office, Shane gave his number to the woman at the desk and went looking for Annie. He found her leaning against the hood of his car, looking lost and forlorn as she wiped away her tears with the back of her hand.

He enveloped her in a hug, holding her close and trying to offer some comfort. She stiffened in his embrace and turned her face away. "Take me home, please."

Shane pulled back but kept his hands on her shoulders. Lowering his face to try and meet her eyes, he said, "Dr. Merrick is going to find a surgeon in Houston for us."

She wouldn't look at him. "Just take me home."

"Annie, please. Don't give up."

"God is punishing us. We sinned and He is taking my baby away because of it."

"You don't believe that."

She looked at him then. Her eyes were dull and devoid of hope. "Yes, I do. I've led a terrible life. I should never have expected to get off scot-free. I'm sorry now that I told you about the baby. I should have kept my mouth shut. If I had, you wouldn't be suffering, too. I can't get it right. No matter how hard I try, I can't make good decisions."

"Don't blame yourself for this."

"Take me home." Her words were barely audible.

"I'm angry at God, too. You don't deserve this. Our baby doesn't deserve this, but I don't believe God would punish an innocent child for our indiscretions."

"Why couldn't God take me instead?" Her voice was little more than a whisper. "Why? Why let me love this baby and then steal it back? Our baby is going to die, Shane. Nothing else matters. Nothing."

He could feel Annie retreating further and further away from him, and he didn't know how to counter it. Sick with grief and rising fear, he shook her shoulders. "Listen to me, Annie. We're not going to give up without a fight."

"I can't fight. Not anymore. Not this, too. Let go of me. I'll walk home."

She tried to pull away from him, but he held on. "No, I'll drive you."

Perhaps talking to Marge would help Annie regain her perspective. He opened the car door. Annie hesitated but then got in. Moving around to the driver's side, Shane got in, as well. Starting the Mustang, he managed to make the drive to Annie's home, although when he pulled up at the curb he wasn't certain exactly how he had gotten there.

After pulling his key from the ignition, he paused with his hands on the wheel. Annie started to get out, but he stopped her by taking hold of her arm. "I know you're hurting, Annie. I'm hurting, too, so don't shut me out. I love you. We'll get through this together."

Annie recognized the numbness enclosing her. In some tiny corner of her mind she knew that when it wore off, the pain would be unbearable. There was only one way to keep the pain at bay. She had lived in an emotionless fog for years. Drinking would keep her numb.

Who would blame her? God had betrayed her. What could He do that was worse than what He had already done?

He could take Shane away, too.

All her hopes and daydreams of a life with Shane turned to ashes on her tongue. The baby would die soon. Just thinking the words shredded her soul.

Shane would leave for Germany in a few weeks. Without the baby to hold him, there would be no reason for him to come back. She'd be alone again with no one to care if she lived or died. No one to love and be loved by.

It's not fair!

She wanted to scream it to the heavens. It was bad enough that God was making her wait and watch as her child perished. She couldn't stand the thought of waiting and watching Shane's love wither, too. A clean break would be less painful for both of them.

"We aren't together, Shane. You wanted to be included in your baby's life. Now there isn't going to be a baby, so you can stop pretending I matter."

He reached out and turned her face toward his. "Of course you matter to me. I haven't been pretending. I love you, Annie."

"Then I guess I've been the one pretending." Her voice broke, but she didn't care as she pulled out of his grasp.

"Don't do this," he begged. "Don't push me away."

"I'll let you know…when…when it's over. Until then,

please leave me alone." Pushing open the door, she got out and hurried into the house as a new round of tears began to fall.

Chapter 15

Shane paced the small space in front of Pastor Hill's untidy desk. "Annie won't see me. I've been back to the house twice today. Marge says she has locked herself in her room and she won't come out. I'm really worried about her."

"Hearing such terrible news must have been very difficult for both of you."

"She blames God."

"That's not the least bit surprising. God's shoulders are broad. He understands grief. He watched His own son die a cruel death on the cross."

"I know. I'm trying to accept this. I'm trying to understand that it's His will, but part of me can't. I want to do something. Anything."

"That would be the human part of you, Shane. Do what you can and trust that God's love is there to comfort you no matter what the outcome."

"It's hard."

"For a man so new to this faith, I'd say you're doing remarkably well."

"Annie showed me the way. I don't think I would have gone looking for God if it hadn't been for her."

The sudden ringing of his cell phone startled Shane. He yanked it from his pocket, only to lose his grip on it. He juggled it in midair a few times before he regained his hold and snapped it open. "Ross here."

"Corporal Ross, this is Dr. Merrick."

"Yes, Doctor."

"I've managed to contact a surgeon in Houston who is willing to see Annie and evaluate her for surgery."

"That's great."

"You'll need to get her there as soon a possible. I would strongly advise against driving that distance. An air ambulance would be the safest and fastest way to get her there. I have the number of a service in Kansas City if you are interested. I'm afraid the cost will be about five thousand dollars up front, as Annie has no insurance. Will that be a problem?"

Shane's heart sank. Coming up with five thousand dollars quickly wouldn't be easy. He was certain Annie didn't have that kind of cash lying around, and neither did he. Even if he could manage the financial part, would Annie accept his help?

"Thanks for all you've done, Dr. Merrick."

"You're welcome. I wish you the best."

After writing down the air-transport service's number and the contact information of the doctor waiting for them in Houston, Shane snapped his phone shut and dialed Marge's number.

Olivia picked up on the second ring. "Hello."

"Olivia, this is Shane. Can I speak to Annie?"

"I'm not sure she'll talk to you, but I'll try."

"Good girl." He waited impatiently as Olivia laid down the phone. After several long minutes she came back on the line.

"She won't talk to me, but she let Crystal in the room."

"That's good. At least she's talking to someone. Is your mother home?"

"She had to go back to work for a little bit, to get someone to cover for her. She said she'd be back as soon as she could."

"All right, give Annie this message even if you have to yell it through the door. Tell her that I'm taking her to Houston tonight."

"How are you going to do that?"

"I'm not sure, but I'll pick up a crowbar on the way in case I have to break into her room."

"Mom isn't going to like that."

He had to chuckle. *Please, God, give me the chance to raise a daughter as adorable as Marge's.*

"I'm kidding, Olivia. I'll be there as soon as I take care of a couple of things."

He hung up the phone and turned to Pastor Hill. "Keep us in your prayers, Pastor."

"That goes without saying. Annie is a dear friend. She has suffered so much in her young life. Don't blame her for retreating from you. Experience has taught her to expect the worst from life. But did I hear you say you were going with her? Can you get emergency leave from the Army by tonight?"

"I'll do what I have to do. My daughter is going to get her chance at life even if I get court-martialed for doing it."

* * *

Annie lay curled on her side in her bed. Her pillow was damp from the tears she had shed. Tears that brought no relief from the pain in her heart. Through puffy eyes, Annie gazed out the window. The glass framed the top of the maple in the backyard and the dark clouds moving in from the west. The occasional flash of lightning in the distance warned of the storm's approach. Annie shivered and rolled over.

Crystal sat on the twin bed next to her. For the past half hour she had listened to Annie's story without saying much.

"I wanted this baby, Crystal. Maybe not at first, but later I did. I wanted someone to need me and love me."

Crystal stroked Annie's hair away from her face. "I'm really sorry, Annie. Life ain't fair."

"Why is God doing this to me?"

"If you ask me, God doesn't much care about the likes of us."

"I thought He did. I thought He loved me. Pastor Hill and Marge both talk about God's unconditional love, and I believed them. I don't know what to think now. I want this whole thing to be some terrible mistake."

"I wish I could help."

"No one can help. I haven't felt her move since I left the doctor's office today. That was hours ago. What if she's already...dead? How do I know? I can't bear to think about waiting for it to happen."

"I'm sorry, but the doctor may have been right about one thing—you don't need a kid messing up your life. I tried to tell you that, but you wouldn't listen."

"I want to forget everything. I want to forget that I

loved my baby and that I loved Shane. I don't want to go through this. Please, someone help me."

"If you really want to forget things, I can help with that." Crystal rose from the bed and dropped to her hands and knees. From beneath her mattress she pulled out a bottle of vodka. Standing once more, she held it out to Annie. "You need this more than I do."

"You started drinking again? Oh, Crystal, I knew Willie was bad news for you."

"I have things I want to forget, too, Annie. A lot of things. Willie understands that. He doesn't think it's wrong. He doesn't judge me the way others do. He loves me. Besides, don't tell me you don't want a drink right this minute. I know the signs. What's it going to hurt? Not your baby anymore."

Crystal tossed the bottle onto the bed beside Annie. As fascinating and as deadly as any viper, Annie couldn't take her eyes off it. It would be so easy to take one sip and then another and another. Soon she would forget everything as it numbed the terrible pain gnawing in her chest. It would be so easy.

Except it would harm the baby. If she were still alive. Was she suffering? Would alcohol numb her little one's pain the way it numbed hers?

Don't think like that. But once the idea had planted itself in her brain, it wouldn't leave.

"I don't want it," Annie said, pushing the bottle away. Oh, but she did. Anything to take away the pain in her heart and blot out this terrible day.

"Sure you do. I know I need one for the road." Crystal turned, moved to the closet and pulled out a worn black suitcase. She swung it up onto her twin bed and unzipped it.

Annie tore her gaze away from the bottle. "What are you doing?"

"I'm moving in with Willie." After scooping an armful of clothes from the dresser in the corner, Crystal dumped them in the bag, then turned back to the closet.

"Crystal, don't. Think about what you're doing."

Tossing dresses, hangers and all, onto her bed, she held up one final piece, a red tank top with a blue beaded flower on the front. "Is this one yours or mine? I forget."

"It's yours."

"Good." Tossing it toward the suitcase, Crystal then picked up three pairs of shoes from the closet floor. After stuffing them into the back corner of the bag, she closed the lid and leaned on it to zip it shut.

"Crystal, don't go. How can I go through this without you?"

Hefting the case, Crystal walked to the door. Annie rose and grabbed her arm. "Don't make me lose my best friend and my baby on the same day."

"I'm no good in a crisis, Annie. I never was. I'm really sorry about the baby, but there's nothing I can do to help. I'll be in touch. Keep the bottle. Willie will buy me another one."

Crystal unlocked the door, pulled it open and stepped out into the hall. Annie followed her. At the top of the stairs Crystal turned back and said, "Shane is downstairs. Do you want to see him?"

Clutching her head with her hands, Annie tried to think. She couldn't face Shane. She couldn't face anyone. "No. Tell him to go away."

Annie stepped back into her room and slammed the door shut. Turning the button on the knob, she made sure it was locked, then she leaned her head against the wood panel and hoped that Shane would go away.

Shane stepped aside as Crystal came down the stairs. She said, "Annie doesn't want to see you. This is your fault, you know."

"Where are you going?" Olivia asked from the sofa.

Crystal touched her eyebrows with her index finger. "I've had it up to here with God and AA. I'm leaving. Tell your mom thanks for everything."

Olivia shot to her feet. "But you can't go. Annie needs us. Tell her, Shane."

Crystal looked down and wouldn't meet his eyes.

He said, "If she wants to leave, we can't stop her. Someday she'll realize what a mistake she is making."

Turning his back on her, he walked up the stairs. Annie was the important one. At the top, he heard the front door closing, but he didn't pause. He approached Annie's door and took a deep breath. Raising his fist, he knocked softly. "Annie, it's Shane. Please let me in."

Silence was the only reply.

He tried a more forceful tone. "Annie, open this door."

"Go away! Go away! Why won't you leave me alone?"

"Because I love you. Please let me in." He tried the knob, but it was locked. The door and the jamb looked like solid oak. He wasn't sure he could break it down. Even if he tried, Annie might be standing on the other side. He couldn't risk hurting her by barreling through the door.

"Okay, Annie, you win for now." Again only silence answered him. He turned and hurried down the stairs. At the bottom, he turned into the kitchen. Olivia was close behind him.

"Where are you going? Is Annie okay?"

Recognizing the worry in Olivia's voice, he stopped and took her by the shoulders. "Annie will be fine."

"There's a storm coming. She's afraid of storms."

"I'm going to take care of her."

"Is it true the baby is dead?"

"We don't know that for sure. I'm taking Annie to see a doctor who can help save the baby." He pulled a card from his pocket. "I need you to give this to your mother when she gets back if we are gone by then. You're being really brave, Olivia."

"You are *so* wrong. I'm scared out of my mind!"

He pulled her close in a quick hug. "I'm sorry, kid."

"That's okay. Just go save the day. That's what the cavalry does, isn't it?"

He leaned back to grin at her. "That's the plan."

"What can I do?"

"I want you to run out and tell the taxi driver to keep waiting. I don't care how much it costs. Then I want you to go up and keep talking to Annie. Let her know she isn't alone."

"She tried to kill herself a long time ago. Do you think she might do something like that again?"

He drew Olivia close in a tight hug as he glanced at the ceiling. "Annie is so much stronger than she realizes. We just need to make her see that. Now, go on and don't stop talking until her door opens."

Olivia nodded and hurried to the front door. Shane went out the back.

Annie heard Shane leave, but instead of relief, all she felt was betrayal. God, Crystal and now Shane. They had all deserted her.

A cold anger replaced her grief. She had been foolish and naive to count on any of them. Turning back to her bed, she saw the bottle lying among the folds of her pink-and-white-patchwork quilt. There was one thing she knew she could count on.

Walking to the foot of her bed, she picked it up and held the cool glass to her chest. Was there enough to dull the pain? Enough to send her into oblivion? Slowly she unscrewed the cap.

The sound of Olivia's voice outside her door made her look up, and she caught sight of herself in the mirror over the dresser. Blinking hard, she took a good, long look. She saw a pathetic woman clutching a bottle of booze like a treasure above her pregnant stomach.

Shane had told Dr. Merrick that she was a strong woman. Shane didn't know the woman she had been. He didn't know the woman in the mirror.

Suddenly her anger came roaring to the forefront. "What do you want from me, God? Tell me what You want and I'll do it," she yelled. "I'll do anything except go back to what I was. I won't do that!" She threw the bottle at the mirror and they both broke into pieces.

A strange calm filled her mind, then a tiny flutter stirred under her heart. Relief made her knees weak. Her daughter still lived.

She took a step back and sat on the edge of the bed. Closing her eyes, she breathed a prayer of thanks.

She would treasure each moment, each quivering movement until the very end. If this was all the time she had left with her baby, she was going to spend it with the utmost care.

Sounds made her look up and she saw Shane stepping into her room through the window. The oddity of it didn't even strike her as strange. Smiling at him, she said, "The baby moved. She isn't gone."

He crossed the room and dropped to his knees beside her. "Thank God."

"I'm sorry I tried to keep you away. She's your child, too. I see how wrong I was."

"Are you okay?"

"I almost took a drink. I wanted to so badly."

"But you didn't."

She reached out and cupped his cheek. "No. Thank you for believing in me."

Covering her hand with his own, he turned his face to kiss her palm. "I believe in us." Rising to his feet, he said, "I have an air ambulance on its way to the airfield. There is a surgeon in Houston who will meet us at the hospital and tell us if he can help the baby."

"Oh, Shane, I don't know if I can do it. What if we get our hopes up only to hear that she can't be saved. Right now she is with us, surrounded by the people who love her."

"Annie, you're right, we both love her. No matter what happens, that love won't change. She is in God's hands. She always has been. If He takes her from us, it will be to carry her to a place of perfect peace."

"I know, but I want her here with me."

"So do I. I don't know what God has planned for us, but if there is even a remote chance that our baby might live, we have to try. We will do everything humanly possible and leave the rest up to God. Do you remember when I told you my father wasn't involved when I grew up?"

"Yes. I remember thinking how sad you looked when you said it."

"That wasn't the whole truth. My father lived in the same town as my mother and I did. He had a nice house and a successful business, while we lived in a run-down rented trailer. He also had a wife and three kids. Not once in my life did he acknowledge me."

"Oh, Shane." Her heart ached for the little boy he had been and the pain he had endured.

"When my mother died, he came to the funeral. I was so scared and worried about what would happen to me. I saw him, I thought he had come to take me home with him. I didn't have anyone else. But he left without even speaking to me. Do you know how unwanted, how unloved that made me feel?"

"I'm so sorry he hurt you."

"I vowed that day that I would never be anything like him."

"You aren't."

"That's why I can't stand by and do nothing. My baby has to know that I will turn the world upside down for her."

"I understand, but I'm afraid…afraid to start hoping again."

"I'll be with you, Annie. Together we can face the worst, because we have faith that it isn't the end."

She stared into his eyes, their bright blue depths full of pleading. Finally she nodded. "All right. I'll go."

He pulled her to her feet and into his arms. "That's my brave Annie. Come on, we have a plane to catch."

Sniffling, Annie wiped her eyes. "If I'm going to be staying in Houston until she's born, I'll need a few things."

"Okay, but hurry. I've got a taxi waiting outside."

He opened the bedroom door. Olivia sat on the floor

outside. Rising to her feet, she frowned at him and said, "How did you get in?"

"I used the ladder from the garden shed to get up on the roof and then I came in through the window."

"Cool. You Army guys rock."

Annie hurried to the closet but paused with her hand on the doorknob. Looking over her shoulder at Shane, she said, "Crystal left. She's drinking again."

"I know."

"I was too wrapped up in my own problems to see that she needed help."

"It's not your fault."

"I know that. She will have to find her own way back. I pray she does. Olivia, will you help me pack?"

In a few minutes Annie had the necessities gathered and stuffed into her threadbare green duffel bag. Shane picked it up and held open the bedroom door to let Annie and Olivia precede him. Annie was halfway down the stairs when a loud clap of thunder shook the house.

Irrational panic stole her breath. She collapsed onto the steps and covered her ears with her hands.

Chapter 16

"Annie, what is it?" Shane dropped the duffel bag on the steps and made his way to her side. She didn't answer him.

At the bottom of the stairs Olivia turned around. "It's the storm. She's petrified of them."

Shane pulled Annie's hands away from her face. "Annie, listen to me. We need to go. It's just a storm."

"I can't," she whispered.

He slipped an arm around her shoulders. "You can. I've got you."

Leaning into his embrace, she shuddered as the next roll of thunder cracked outside. It was quickly followed by the sound of the rising wind. He racked his mind for a way to comfort her. "Annie, remember the story in the Bible about Jesus walking across the water to the boat with His disciples in it?"

"Yes." Her voice was so small he almost couldn't hear it.

"When He asked Peter to come across the water to Him, what happened?"

"I don't remember."

"Yes, you do. Peter began walking on the water, but then he noticed the storm and he began to sink."

"Yes."

"Tell me what happened next. I know that you know."

"Jesus held out His hand and took hold of Peter."

"That's right. And what did He say to Peter?"

"Oh, ye of little faith. Why do you doubt me?"

"You aren't a woman of little faith, Annie."

She burrowed closer as the thunder rumbled again. "Sometimes I am."

"Okay, sometimes we all doubt, but not now. Say it. Say I'm a woman of strong faith."

"I'm a woman…of strong faith."

"Good. Now I'm going to pick you up and I'm going to carry you to the car outside."

"No."

"You'll get wet, that's all that will happen. I'm going to take care of you. Do you believe that? Open your eyes and look at me. Do you believe I'll keep you safe?"

She drew away from him enough to meet his gaze. "Yes."

"All right, then. Here we go." He stood and scooped her up in his arms. She wrapped her arms around his neck in a death grip.

He said, "Olivia, get the door. Here we go, Annie. I've got you."

She buried her face in his neck and whispered, "I'm a woman of strong faith."

"That's right. Just keep saying it."

"I'm a woman of strong faith. Oh, hurry."

He did just that, rushing down the steps to the waiting taxi, with Olivia carrying Annie's bag behind him. From the corner of his eye he saw Marge pull into the drive. At least now he didn't have to worry about leaving Olivia alone in the storm.

He placed Annie in the backseat and took her bag from Olivia. Marge came running up to stand beside him. Quickly he explained what they were doing and told Marge he would call when they got to Houston. After a quick hug from both mother and daughter, he climbed in beside Annie. She burrowed into his side as he gave the cabbie directions.

Twenty minutes later they were at the small commercial airstrip outside of town, where a twin-engine Cessna sat on the runway. The storm had moved on, leaving the tarmac gleaming with pockets of silver puddles glistening in the runway lights and the night air smelling freshly washed.

A crew of three met them at the door of the plane. A young man in a blue jumpsuit introduced himself as their flight nurse. After a few brief instructions, he settled Annie on the gurney and hooked her up to a small monitor. The steady bleep of her heart rate was all but drowned out by the engine noise as the pilot prepared for takeoff. After the nurse had Annie strapped in, he instructed Shane to take a nearby jump seat and then gave the all-clear to the pilot. Moments later the plane was airborne.

Once they stopped climbing, the nurse loosened Annie's straps and had her turn on her left side. She reached out, and Shane took her hand.

* * *

Shane's strong grip gave Annie a measure of peace as he squeezed her fingers in a gesture of reassurance. His determination gave her the strength she needed to nourish a small spark of hope.

"Thank you," she said, knowing the words were inadequate to express her gratitude for all he had done.

"You're welcome," he said with a soft smile full of love and understanding. "We'll be there in a couple of hours. Try and get some rest."

Annie closed her eyes, but she knew she wouldn't sleep. She kept one hand on her tummy, waiting for and rejoicing in each movement the baby made. When the baby slept for long periods without moving, Annie prayed.

Please, God, don't let it be too late. Please let this be the right decision.

Finally she felt the plane begin its descent. The young man in charge of her care made sure she was secure and then took his seat beside Shane. The plane touched down with a few hard bumps, then taxied along the runway to where an ambulance sat waiting.

Within minutes she found herself transferred into the waiting vehicle. Shane wasn't allowed to ride in back with her but had to sit with the driver. She missed the comfort his presence brought, but she knew she could make the rest of the journey alone if she had to. He believed she was strong. She would be for his sake. The pilot and her nurse wished her well as the door was being closed.

Annie realized that she didn't even know their names. It was humbling to know so many strangers were willing to help her and her child. The world might be full of pain and sorrow, but it was full of good people, too.

The ride to the medical center was uneventful. When the ambulance doors opened again, the bright lights and bustle of a busy emergency room surrounded her. As she was wheeled in through the hospital doors, she glanced back, trying to find Shane.

"We're taking you straight up to the obstetrical unit," the man pushing her bed told her as they passed out of the emergency room and into a long corridor.

"Where is Shane? The man who came with me."

"He's been shown to the admissions office. He'll be up when he gets finished with the paperwork and after they have you settled in your room on OB."

Annie nodded and tried to relax. Soon they would know if all of this effort had been for nothing. She wanted Shane beside her when she heard the doctor's report.

A flurry of activity greeted Annie when she reached her room. Nurses checked her vital signs and soon had her hooked up to a fetal monitor. The rapid beep-beep of her daughter's heartbeat was music to Annie's ears, but she caught the worried glance shared between two of the nurses.

"What is it?" Annie demanded.

"The baby's heart rate is a little too fast. We're calling for a stat echo. Dr. Wong will be here shortly."

There was nothing Annie could do but wait, worry and pray as the minutes dragged on.

Shane arrived just as the sonogram machine was being moved into the room. Intense relief at seeing him flooded her body and brought tears to her eyes. She blinked them back. It wasn't time for tears. Not yet.

Making his way around the people in the room, Shane reached her side and took hold of her hand. She brought it to her face and held it close. With his free hand he smoothed the hair back from her forehead and planted a kiss on her brow. Wordlessly they waited.

The sonogram technician had just started when a small Asian man in rumpled green scrubs came into the room, followed by a tall man with thick black-rimmed glasses. "What do we have?" the first one asked, taking the wand from the tech's hand and studying the image on the screen intently.

The nurse wrapping a blood-pressure cuff around Annie's arm said, "This is Dr. Wong and Dr Wilmeth."

"Hello, hello," Dr. Wong said, never taking his eyes from the screen. "I want to meet your baby first and then I'll talk to you. Ah, yes, it is a big mass. Even bigger than Dr. Merrick reported."

Dr. Wilmeth leaned over his shoulder. "This is not good."

"Can you save her?" Annie asked, squeezing Shane's hand tightly.

Dr. Wong looked up at his partner. "She's in trouble, but I think she has a chance if we go to surgery right away."

Pushing his glasses higher on his nose, Dr. Wilmeth said, "We can try. Do they know the risks?"

Dr. Wong handed the wand back to the technician waiting patiently at his side. "I've seen all I need. Get the rest of the measurements for me, please."

He pulled off his gloves with a snap and tossed them into the trash can against the wall. "I want you to know that this is a very risky and delicate procedure. Many things can go wrong. It has only been done a handful of times. I can't guarantee anything."

"We understand that," Shane assured him.

"It will be major surgery for both of you," Dr. Wilmeth added. "The baby isn't mature enough to survive outside the womb. Even if the surgery is a success, there is a chance you will deliver prematurely and she will die anyway or suffer major repercussions such as blindness, cerebral palsy, deafness or seizures. Miss Delmar, the risks to you include bleeding, infection and the possibility that you won't be able to have other children. You must be prepared to spend weeks here being monitored around the clock and given drugs to halt any labor."

Annie looked at Shane. He would have to go back to Fort Riley and on to Germany in a few weeks. She would be in a strange city alone, without anyone to support her if the worst happened. How could she do it?

Shane pressed his lips together, then said, "It's your decision, Annie."

When had she ever made a good decision? Her life had been filled with mistakes and bad judgment. Now Shane was asking her to make the most important decision of all. "You think I can do this?"

"I know you can. Hey, you went out in a thunderstorm, didn't you?"

She managed a half smile. "That's right. What was I thinking? I'm practically Super Annie."

"Honey, you're the closest thing to a superhero I have ever met—and I've met some tough people."

"Okay." She called on every ounce of faith she possessed and prayed she was doing the right thing for her baby and herself. Turning her gaze back to Dr. Wong, she said, "I'm ready when you are. I will do whatever it takes."

"Are you sure you don't have any questions?"

"None," Shane said. "But I do need you to do me a favor. I need a paternity test done. The Army requires proof that this is my baby before she can be considered a dependent since Annie and I aren't married. And I'm told we need to speak to a social worker about getting Annie a medical card."

"Very well. Nurse, if you will get the consents signed and take care of notifying social work, I will notify the operating room. Oh, and get my usual labs stat and notify the blood bank that I want three units of packed cells on hold for this."

As the doctors and nurses filed out of the room, Annie found herself alone with Shane. He pulled a chair close to her bedside and sat down with a sigh.

"Are you tired?" She had been so concerned about herself that she hadn't given any thought to what he had been going through.

He wrinkled his nose. "A little."

"I'll trade you places and you can go get some sleep in surgery."

"On second thought, I'm not tired at all." He glanced at his watch. "It's only four-forty in the morning. In twenty minutes I will have been up for twenty-four hours."

A sudden thought struck Annie. "Shane, how did you get emergency leave so quickly? I'm not even your dependent."

"I'm not exactly on leave."

"You're AWOL? Shane!" She rose on her elbows to stare at him in shocked disbelief.

"I will be in twenty more minutes. Don't worry. Captain Watson is a stand-up guy. He'll understand and he'll do what he can for me."

"You'll be thrown in the brig. You'll be busted in rank. You won't get the promotion you've been working for."

"No, but I got to hold your hand for seven hundred miles. I think that's worth a night in the brig."

"Be serious. You could be in big trouble."

"Relax. I'm not going to be in big trouble. I promise. A little trouble, yes, but nothing I can't handle. They'll tell me to get back as soon as possible and I'll do that."

She sank back onto the bed. "You didn't have to come. I would have come alone if I had known you were risking a court-martial to be here."

He reached out and cupped her cheek. "I didn't *have* to be here, Annie. I *want* to be here. With you."

Covering his hand with her own, she closed her eyes and drew a quick breath. "I'm so glad you are. I'm so scared."

"Me, too, but we'll get through this together. You, me, the baby and God."

The door to the room opened again and two women in blue surgical garb pushed a narrow cart into the room. "We're here to take you to surgery, Miss Delmar. I have some papers for you to sign, but first I need to see your identification bracelet."

Shane stepped out of the way as Annie answered questions and signed the necessary papers. Another woman came in, pushing a cart loaded with lab tubes and needles, and announced that she had come to draw blood. She gave Shane a pointed look and asked him to step outside. As he pulled open the door, another nurse came in pushing an IV pump and carrying a tray. Knowing he was only in the way, he stepped out into the hallway.

He checked his watch as he waited, and when it hit five o'clock straight up, he pulled his cell phone from his pocket and dialed Captain Watson's number. When his captain picked up, Shane took a deep breath and said, "Sir, this is Corporal Ross. I'd like to report myself AWOL."

For a long second there was dead silence on the line. "I see. This is a very serious matter, Corporal."

"I understand that, but Annie and the baby need emergency care that is only available to them here in Houston. I want you to know I did attempt to contact you last night, but I was told you were unavailable."

"Yes, I spent a very boring evening with General Adams and his wife. However, that's no excuse, soldier."

"I wouldn't have done it if I felt there was any other choice. The baby will die unless they can do surgery on her tonight. She might die anyway, but we had to try."

"Of course. You'll have to report back by tomorrow at the latest, but I can't do anything for you if you're gone more than forty-eight hours. You do realize this is going on your record. I'll try to see that you get ten days emergency leave, but I'm not going to promise you anything."

"I understand, sir."

"All right. Let me know how the surgery turns out and when to expect you back."

The door to Annie's room opened and she was wheeled out into the hall.

"I will, sir. I have to go now."

"I'll be keeping you in my prayers, son."

"Thank you, sir. We need all we can get."

Shane snapped his phone shut and stepped up to the cart. One of the nurses had placed a blue surgical cap on Annie's head. She looked like a very frightened young woman trying to look brave for his benefit. It almost broke his heart.

Bending down, he placed a gentle kiss on her lips, then whispered, "See you soon."

She laid a hand on his cheek. "I love you, Corporal Shane Ross."

How he could love someone so much was a mystery to him. That she loved him in return was a blessing he would give thanks for all his life. "I love you, too."

One of the nurses said, "We have to go now. You can wait here in the room. Dr. Wong will find you when the surgery is over. If you leave, just let someone at the nurses' station know where you'll be. Try not to worry. We'll take good care of her."

As they pushed the cart down the hall, Shane watched until they rounded the corner and were lost from sight. Suddenly the energy drained out of his body, leaving him weak and vulnerable.

Pushing open the door to Annie's room, he walked in and sat down in the chair by her now-empty bed. A lump pushed up in his throat, making it hard to breathe. He leaned forward and braced his elbows on his knees, but he couldn't draw a full breath. He pressed his fingers against his stinging eyes, but it was no use.

A single sob escaped his tightly clenched lips, followed by another and then another. Defeated, he dropped his head into his hands and wept.

Many long hours later there was a knock at the door and Dr. Wong walked in.

Chapter 17

Annie tried to open her eyes, but they wouldn't cooperate. She could hear voices near her, but she chose to ignore them. Sleep was a wonderful invention.

"Annie, open your eyes," someone insisted once more.

On the second try, Annie's lids fluttered up for a brief second before dropping closed again. Wasn't that good enough? Couldn't they just go away and let her sleep?

"Annie, wake up!" Recognizing the insistence in Shane's tone, she gave up the idea of ignoring him and opened her eyes. This time they stayed open and his face swam into view.

Annie smiled. He was so handsome and she loved him to pieces.

"That's a girl."

Little by little, the events of the past days fell into

place. She had to try twice before she managed to croak out, "How is she?"

"She came through the surgery okay. They removed the tumor without complications."

Thank God. Joy filled her heart.

"Things look good," Shane said. The tension in his voice caused her to frown.

"But?"

"But I have to leave now. I have to catch the first flight back to Kansas City and get back to the base by tonight."

"Already? But we just got here." She wanted to make him smile. He looked so tired and worn.

"Yes, but I'll be back as soon as I can."

"When?" Annie cleared her throat and wished she could get a sip of water. It seemed like too much trouble to ask for it.

"I'm not sure."

"Do you get to make phone calls from the brig?" Her eyes drifted closed.

"I don't think so."

"Okay," she managed to say. "I'm going to go back to sleep now."

"That's a good thing. Sleep and get well—both of you."

She felt the butterfly-soft kiss he placed on her cheek and she drifted back to sleep, knowing she had made the right decision after all. Her baby was okay and Shane loved her. She managed to pry her eyes open one more time. Her strong man stood by her bed with tears running down his face.

"Don't cry."

"I'm sorry. I just don't want to leave you like this."

"We'll be here when you come back. Have faith. I do."

If he heard her barely whispered words, she didn't know it because sleep had claimed her once more.

Sitting up in her hospital bed, Annie surfed through the TV channels for the fifth time, and there still wasn't anything she wanted to watch. Soap operas, talk shows and action movies couldn't hold her interest the way the sound of her daughter's heartbeat did as it emanated softly from the monitor overhead. A tiny, fast, repetitive bleep proved all was well. It was a blessed sound.

Another contraction tightened Annie's stomach, and she winced at the pain, then took deep breaths to ride through the discomfort. She glanced at the nurse adjusting the IV drug on the pump beside her. "I don't think that one was quite as strong."

"Good, then the terbutaline is doing its job. I'll keep an eye on your strip from the desk. Let me know if they become more frequent or intense. Can I get you anything else?"

"No, thanks. You have all been so wonderful."

"We're just doing our job. But I have to admit it's exciting to be taking part in such a rare medical procedure. Your case has been discussed at length in our staff meetings. Everyone is praying that we can get your baby close to term."

"I'll be forty weeks the first of October. You will all be tired of me by then." Today was only the twenty-third of June.

"Once we get these contractions to stop and stay stopped, you'll be able to move off the floor into something more homey."

"Yes, the social worker has made arrangement with the Ronald McDonald House for me to stay there."

"I've heard it's really nice." The beeper in the nurse's pocket went off, and she excused herself as she walked out of the room.

Annie glanced out the window. Her room had a wonderful view of the brick wall of the building next door. The only amusement it afforded was the pigeons that strutted across the window ledges. Sighing, she picked up the remote again, but before she could turn it on, her door opened again.

"May I come in?"

"Shane!" she shrieked. Joy rocketed through her body. She sat up quick enough to make her incision hurt and had to grab her tummy with both hands.

"She sounds glad to see you." Olivia pushed past him and came bouncing into the room. "Surprise."

Wrapping her arms around the child, Annie gave her a heartfelt hug. "Olivia, oh, it's so good to see you. Where is your mother?"

"I'm right here," Marge said, smiling from the doorway beside Shane. She came forward, holding a large bouquet of yellow roses, and hugged Annie as Olivia plopped into the chair beside the bed.

With tears of happiness blurring her vision, Annie held out her hands to Shane. It was all the invitation he needed. He strode in and sat on the opposite side of her bed. For a long second he simply held her hands, then he leaned in and kissed her with fierce longing.

Blushing, but happier than she could imagine, Annie pulled away and cupped his face in her hands to drink in the sight of her beloved. "I missed you."

"I missed you, too. So much. How is our soccer

player doing?" He laid his hand carefully on Annie's stomach.

"She's kicking one goal after another."

"Good for her."

"Can't you give the poor thing a name?" Olivia asked.

Annie and Shane exchanged sheepish looks. "We haven't discussed names," Annie said, squeezing his hands. Just touching him made her feel safe and loved. What a gift he was.

Olivia rolled her eyes. "Whatever you do, don't name her after me."

"What's wrong with your name?" Marge asked with a frown.

"She'll hate it when they call her Ollie for short. I do."

"We'll take that under advisement," Shane said.

Annie smiled at him. "I can't believe you brought them all this way. Thank you."

"Not!" Olivia said quickly. "We brought him. I didn't think Mom's clunker would make it this far, but it did."

Giving Shane a quizzical look, Annie said, "Why didn't you drive your own car?"

"I don't actually own a car anymore."

"What happened to your Mustang?"

"I sold it."

"Why? You love that car. Hey, *I* even love that car."

Shrugging, he said, "It was time for something different."

"I thought you sold it to pay for the air ambulance," Olivia interjected.

"Olivia Renee Lilly!" Marge said sternly.

"What did I do?"

Annie looked at Shane in disbelief. "You sold your

car to get me here? Are you nuts? That car is going to be worth a fortune someday."

"What does a man need with a fortune someday when he has a pearl of great price sitting beside him?"

"Ooh, that was smooth, Shane." Olivia clapped her hands.

Marge stepped forward and laid a hand on her daughter's shoulder. "Excuse us, we're going to step out into the hall and give you two some privacy."

"But why?"

Glaring down at Olivia, Marge said, "Do you remember what used to happen when I had to take you out of church when you were little and misbehaving?"

Olivia's eye widened. "You wouldn't."

"Don't tempt me."

Olivia rose quickly and headed for the door. Marge looked at Annie. "We'll be back in a little while."

Olivia leaned back in from the door frame. "Yeah, he has something he wants to ask you."

Shane tilted his head to the side and glared at her. She waved and then popped out of sight.

Marge glanced toward the ceiling. "I'm trying, Lord. I know she is a test of patience, as well as a joy for my soul, but can You do something about her attitude before I decide to do a major readjustment?"

Annie had to laugh. "Marge, you know that kid is just like you."

Clutching her chest with one hand, Marge grimaced. "You wound me to the quick. But it's true. We'll be back in half an hour." Setting the vase of roses on the nightstand, she followed her daughter out of the room.

Happy to be alone with Shane, Annie reached up to stroke his cheek, then laced her fingers together at the nape of his neck. "I'm so glad you're here. I'm so glad we made this choice—no matter how it turns out."

"I am, too."

"What did you want to ask me?"

He looked down for a second and she sensed his unease. His eyes, when he looked at her again, were serious. A small frown creased his brow. "I have some news. My transfer has been bumped up. I'm leaving for Germany a week from today."

She bit her lip. "I thought we would have more time together."

"We'll have five whole days—and we'll make the most of them."

Don't cry. Be strong for him. "Okay. I can deal with that. Five days."

"I'm pretty sure I can get more leave once the baby is born. The paternity test proved that she is mine, and as my dependent, all her care will be covered by my military insurance."

"That's good. One less worry, right?"

"Right." He looked down again.

"Is there something else?"

"Yes. I was wondering if—if we could name her Clara, after my mother."

"Clara. Clara. That's a nice name. I like it."

"Thanks." He relaxed, but something in his attitude puzzled her.

"Dear, what's wrong?"

Shane drew a deep breath and pulled the small black box from his pants pocket. He held it tightly in his palm. *Please, God, I know that I've put this woman through immeasurable pain and suffering, but I love her. Please let her say yes.*

Meeting Annie's gaze, he found the courage to offer it to her. "This isn't the time or the place I would have chosen, but I can't leave the country without knowing that we have a future together that is based on more than our child."

She opened the box. A silver band with a small diamond lay in the rich folds of satin. She pressed a hand to her lips. "Oh, Shane."

"I want you to be my wife. Annie Delmar, I love you with all my heart and soul. Will you marry me?"

For the longest moment she didn't say or do anything. Her eyes were wide with shock as she stared at him. Slowly her stunned expression gave way to the most beautiful smile he had ever beheld.

"Yes. Yes. Yes, yes, yes!" She threw her arms around his neck, then moaned and drew back and gripped her stomach in pain. "Oh, I forget I can't move that fast yet."

"Are you all right?"

She nodded as she grimaced. "I've never been happier in my life."

"Oh, Annie. I'm going to spend the rest of my life making this up to you."

"Good." She tried to laugh but couldn't. "I'll hold you to that."

Now that she had said yes, happiness fizzed through his mind, making him giddy with relief and joy. "When can we get married? I want to do it before I have to leave you."

"You want me to plan a wedding in less than five days?"

"You can't do it?"

She leaned back in the bed. "You're talking to Super Annie. Of course I can do it. How soon can you get Pastor Hill here?"

"My friend Avery has this great souped-up Mustang Mach One. I think he can have the pastor here in about eight hours."

"Saturday will be soon enough. You'll need to get a marriage license. Find Marge and send her in. She's going to have to find me a wedding dress. I refuse to get married in a hospital gown."

She pressed both hands to her cheeks. "Oh, my stars. Is this real?"

"As real as this." He leaned in and kissed her soundly.

On Saturday afternoon Annie, dressed in a simple white taffeta dress with a rounded neck and capped sleeves, sat in a wheelchair at the back of the hospital's small chapel and smoothed the pink sash that rested just above her bulging tummy. She couldn't tell if it was just nervous butterflies or if her little soccer player had taken up gymnastics. She looked down at her feet. The rhinestone-covered sandals had been borrowed from Olivia at the girl's insistence. After all, no one could get married in hospital slippers.

Shane and Avery, in their dress uniforms, stood beside Pastor Hill at the front of the chapel. The few rows of pews were filled with OB nurses, surgical staff and even Dr. Wilmeth and Dr. Wong.

"Are you ready?" Marge, dressed in a powder-blue suit, waited at Annie's side.

"I was just wishing that my parents could be here. I wish my dad were walking me down the aisle."

"You should have called them."

"There wasn't time, and I'm not sure they would have come anyway. No, I'm okay. We don't dwell on past mistakes. We dwell in the present and go forward from here."

She smiled at Marge as she stood up and stepped away from her wheelchair. "I'm ready. My future is standing there waiting for me, and I love him more than life itself. God has been good to me."

Epilogue

Annie gazed with love at the small bundle in her arms. Sitting up in bed the day after her C-section, she still couldn't get over how beautiful her daughter was. Her thick black hair stood on end and refused to lie down no matter how much the nurses tried combing it or how much lotion they applied.

Clara's little bow mouth was busy making sucking motions as she dreamed of her next meal. Even though her eyes were closed, Annie knew they were the same bright blue as her father's.

Annie glanced at the clock on the wall. According to the Red Cross volunteer who had called earlier, Shane should be arriving about five o'clock. It was a quarter to five now. Shane would be here any minute. She could barely contain her excitement. The long months of waiting were finally over. Clara Olivia Ross had entered the world three weeks early but in perfect health, at five pounds three ounces and with a squall that would wake anyone within half a mile.

A new nurse came in and stopped at the bedside. "I'm here to take your vital signs, Mrs. Ross. How are you feeling?"

"Wonderful." She ran her fingers through Clara's downy hair and smiled.

"Good. I'm going to give you a bath demonstration in a little while, but I'd like your husband to be here for that."

"He's on his way. His flight should have landed an hour ago."

"Oh, he hasn't seen the baby yet?"

"No, she showed up early and spoiled our plans for him to be here. She's had a way of messing with our lives from the get-go."

"What does your husband do?"

Clara stirred and thrust one hand in the air. Annie caught it and thrilled to the strength of her baby's grip. She bent and placed a kiss on the tiny fingers curled around her own. "You have a military daddy, don't you, Clara?" she cooed.

The door opened and Shane rushed in. His uniform was rumpled, and he looked as tired as a man who had been on a plane or in airports for the last twenty hours. He dropped his duffel bag off his shoulder and walked with unsteady steps toward Annie.

Smiling through tears of joy, Annie said, "Daddy, someone wants to welcome you home." She held the baby out to him.

The look of love and wonder on his face as he took

his daughter and held her close was something that Annie knew she would always remember and treasure.

"She's so beautiful." He raised his eyes to Annie. "She looks like her mother."

"But she has her father's charm."

Shane leaned in to kiss Annie—for a moment everything faded except for the feel of his lips on hers.

He pulled back and reached out to touch her face. "How are you?"

"I'm fine. Welcome home."

"I can't believe she is finally here. She's perfect, Annie, just perfect."

"Yes, she's a pure and simple gift from God."

"Oh, I almost forgot." He grinned at Annie and gave the baby back to her. "I brought you both something. Marge and Pastor Hill had been doing a little detective work for me. I had a four-hour layover in New York, so I took the ferry out to Long Island. Look what I found there."

He pulled open the door and motioned to someone in the hall. "Come in. Come and meet your granddaughter."

Stunned into speechlessness, Annie watched as her mother and father walked cautiously into the hospital room.

They were so much older than she remembered. Had she aged them that much?

Her mother spoke first. "Hello, Annie." She pressed a hand to her lips. "Oh, my, she is a pretty baby."

Walking up to stand beside his wife, her father thrust his hands in his pockets. "She looks a lot like you did the day you were born, Annie." His voice cracked with emotion and he wiped at his eyes.

Annie laid her daughter down carefully on the bed in front of her. "I can't believe you are here."

Her mother sniffed and nodded. "Shane has told us about all you've been through. I'm so grateful that you've been able to turn your life around. I've prayed for this day."

"And I'm so sorry for all that I put you through. Can you ever forgive me?" She held out her arms and found herself enveloped in her mother's embrace. A second later her father threw his arms around both of them. The tears they shed as they clung to one another washed years of bitterness and sorrow away.

From his place at the foot of the bed Shane looked on through tears of his own. His wife and his daughter were safe and he was with them. God was good.

* * * * *

We hope you enjoyed reading

Edge of Forever
by *New York Times* bestselling author
Sherryl Woods
and
Military Daddy
by *USA TODAY* bestselling author
Patricia Davids

Both were originally Harlequin® series stories!

From passionate, suspenseful and dramatic
love stories to inspirational or historical,
Harlequin offers different lines to
satisfy every romance reader.

New books in each line
are available every month.

HARLEQUIN®

Harlequin.com

BACHALO0619

"There won't be another bus going that way until the day after tomorrow."

"Are you sure?" Gemma Lapp stared at the agent behind the counter in stunned disbelief.

"Of course I'm sure. I work for the bus company."

She clasped her hands together tightly, praying the tears that pricked the backs of her eyes wouldn't start flowing. She couldn't afford a motel room for two nights.

She wheeled her suitcase over to the bench. Sitting down with a sigh, she moved her suitcase in front of her so she could prop up her swollen feet. After two solid days on a bus she was ready to lie down. Anywhere.

She bit her lower lip to stop it from quivering. She could place a call to the phone shack her parents shared with their Amish neighbors to let them know she was returning and ask her father to send a car for her, but she would have to leave a message.

Any message she left would be overheard. If she gave the real reason, even Jesse Crump would know before she reached home. She couldn't bear that, although she didn't understand why his opinion mattered so much. His stoic face wouldn't reveal his thoughts, but he was sure to gloat when he learned he'd been right about her reckless ways. He had said she was looking for trouble and that she would find it sooner or later. Well, she had found it, all right.

No, she wouldn't call. What she had to say was better said face-to-face. She was cowardly enough to delay as long as possible.

She didn't know how she was going to find the courage to tell her mother and father that she was six months pregnant, and Robert Troyer, the man who'd promised to marry her, was long gone.

Don't miss
Shelter from the Storm *by Patricia Davids,*
available September 2019 wherever
Love Inspired® *books and ebooks are sold.*

www.Harlequin.com

Uplifting romances of faith, forgiveness and hope.

Save **$1.00**

on the purchase of ANY

Love Inspired® book.

Available wherever books are sold,
including most bookstores, supermarkets,
drugstores and discount stores.

Save **$1.00**

on the purchase of any Love Inspired® book.

Coupon valid until September 30, 2019.
Redeemable at participating outlets in the U.S. and Canada only.
Not redeemable at Barnes & Noble stores. Limit one coupon per customer.

52616408

Canadian Retailers: Harlequin Enterprises Limited will pay the face value of this coupon plus 10.25¢ if submitted by customer for this product only. Any other use constitutes fraud. Coupon is nonassignable. Void if taxed, prohibited or restricted by law. Consumer must pay any government taxes. Void if copied. Inmar Promotional Services ("IPS") customers submit coupons and proof of sales to Harlequin Enterprises Limited, P.O. Box 31000, Scarborough, ON M1R 0E7, Canada. Non-IPS retailer—for reimbursement submit coupons and proof of sales directly to Harlequin Enterprises Limited, Retail Marketing Department, Bay Adelaide Centre, East Tower, 22 Adelaide Street West, 40th Floor, Toronto, Ontario M5H 4E3, Canada.

U.S. Retailers: Harlequin Enterprises Limited will pay the face value of this coupon plus 8¢ if submitted by customer for this product only. Any other use constitutes fraud. Coupon is nonassignable. Void if taxed, prohibited or restricted by law. Consumer must pay any government taxes. Void if copied. For reimbursement submit coupons and proof of sales directly to Harlequin Enterprises, Ltd 482, NCH Marketing Services, P.O. Box 880001, El Paso, TX 88588-0001, U.S.A. Cash value 1/100 cents.

5 65373 00076 2 (8100)0 12424

® and ™ are trademarks owned and used by the trademark owner and/or its licensee.

© 2019 Harlequin Enterprises Limited

BACCOUP92934

SPECIAL EXCERPT FROM

Paralyzed veteran Eve Vincent is happy with the life she's built for herself at Mercy Ranch—until her ex-fiancé shows up with a baby. Their best friends died and named Eve and Ethan Forester as guardians. But can they put their differences aside and build a future together?

Read on for a sneak preview of
Her Oklahoma Rancher *by Brenda Minton,*
available June 2019 from Love Inspired!

"I'm sorry, Eve, but I had to do something to make you see how important this is. We can't just walk away from her. It might not be what we signed on for and I feel like I'm the last person who should be raising this little girl, but James and Hanna trusted us."

"But there is no *us*," she said with a lift of her chin, but he could see pain reflected in her dark eyes.

The pain he saw didn't bother him as much as what he didn't see in her eyes, in her expression. He didn't see the person he used to know, the woman he'd planned to marry.

He had noticed the same yesterday, and he guessed that was why he'd left Tori with her. He'd been sitting there looking at a woman he used to think he knew better than he knew himself, and he hadn't recognized her.

"There is no *us*, but we still exist, you and me, and Tori needs us." He said it softly because the little girl in his arms seemed to be drifting off, even with the occasional sob.

"There has to be another option. I obviously can't do this. Last night was proof."

"Last night meant nothing. You've always managed, Eve. You're strong and capable."

"Before, Ethan. I was that person before. This is me now, and I can't."

"I guess you have changed. I've never heard you say you can't do anything."

He sat down on a nearby chair. Isaac had left. The woman named Sierra had also disappeared. They were alone. When had they last been alone? The night he proposed? It had been the night she left for Afghanistan. He'd taken her to dinner in San Antonio and they'd walked along the riverfront surrounded by people, music and twinkling lights.

He'd dropped to one knee there in front of strangers passing by, seeing the sights. Dozens had stopped to watch as she cried and said yes. Later they'd made the drive to the airport, his ring glistening on her finger, planning a wedding that would never happen.

"Ethan?" Her voice was soft, quiet, questioning.

He glanced down at the little girl in his arms.

"What other option is there, Eve? Should we turn her over to the state, let her take her chances with whoever they choose? Should we find some distant relative? What do you recommend?"

He leaned back in the chair and studied her face, her expression. She was everything familiar. His childhood friend. The person he'd loved. *Had* loved. Past tense. The woman he'd wanted to spend his life with had been someone else, someone who never backed down. She looked as tough, as stubborn as ever, but there was something fragile in her expression.

Something in her expression made him recheck his feelings. He'd been bucked off horses, trampled by a bull, broken his arm jumping dirt bikes. She'd been his only broken heart. He didn't want another one.

Don't miss
Her Oklahoma Rancher *by Brenda Minton,*
available June 2019 wherever
Love Inspired® *books and ebooks are sold.*

www.LoveInspired.com

Reward the book lover in you!

Earn points on your purchase of new Harlequin books from participating retailers.

Turn your points into **FREE BOOKS** of your choice!

Join for FREE today at
www.HarlequinMyRewards.com.

Harlequin My Rewards is a free program (no fees) without any commitments or obligations.

MYR18